THE AURORA MANDATE

A Science Fiction Conspiracy Thriller

By Sam Nash

To Mum, Dad and Ade, without your inquisitive minds to guide me, I would not have indulged my imagination to this extent - thank you.

This is a work of fiction. Names, characters, organisations, places, events, and incidents are either products of the author's imagination or are used fictitiously.

Cover art supplied by Carantoc Publishing Ltd
First edition, 2018
ISBN 978-1-9999960-2-4
Carantoc Publishing Ltd.
www.carantocpublishing.com

Please note that this product was created by a British author. Except for slang and dialogue, spelling and grammar is corrected to **British English**. There are also scenes which may offend more sensitive readers. It is not deemed suitable for children.

Reykjavik, Iceland - 2001

The cab interior was adequate, but stifling. Bench seats filled with fur-lined tourists ran along either side of the truck. Two tiny windows shut out the night beyond. The driver turned a dial on the dashboard, rocketing the temperature to that of a sweat lodge. Her hair stuck to her neck in wet cords beneath the hood of her ski jacket. She pulled off her mittens and stretched her fingers, luxuriating in the unconfined space.

"Keep those on when we get out, darling. It's minus thirty degrees out there."

She rested her head on her father's shoulder. Sleep, a fickle creature of enormous strength and agility. Its tentacles penetrating the conscious mind, constricting all rational thought, teasing the senses till exhaustion holds it in a half-lidded dream.

The over-sized wheels bit into a rut, forged in the banks of drifts by the convoy of wagons north bound. The force threw her head back, thumping it against a riveted panel behind her. She winced and sat upright. The air was heavy with body odours and circulated too many times to be of use to her lungs. A wispy green halo surrounded her grandfather's head as he sat opposite her, framed by a window. Blinking her daze away, she smiled.

"I can see it, we are almost there!"

The three trucks of passengers, one of scientific equipment, unloaded outside a wooden construction housing little more than a cloakroom for paying guests. The last stage of the journey was a short hike up above the treeline for an unobscured view. Her borrowed boots chaffed her ankles and hammered her toes as she clambered up the final leg of the trail. She monitored her beloved grandfather as he puffed through his ascent.

Their four hours of discomfort was finally rewarded by a spectacular scene, iridescent hues of jade and pink light, wafting across the sky in shimmering curtains of falling photons.

"Shakespeare…" Her grandfather said, resting his hands on his hips and inhaling through tired muscles.

"All the world's a stage…" She replied, keeping pace with his thoughts.

"Except the stars are the players."

Her father, missing the magic, said; "the particles get buffeted high up in the atmosphere and the colours are the result of energy exchange. We are fortunate to catch it when it is so vibrant. There must have been some sort of astronomical event."

"A truly *awesome* sight, eh kiddo?" Her grandfather waited for an answer, something facile regarding the teenage over-use of the word awesome. He gave her the perfect set up but there was no response. He nudged her arm - nothing. Bending low, he looked into the narrow aperture of the zipped-up hood.

She stood stock still, her body rigid, and eyes glassy. Her knees buckled and she slid to the ground. Convulsing in huge tremulous shakes, her head smashed repeatedly against the compacted snow, bloodying her nose and bruising her forehead. Her grandfather rushed to her aid, cushioning her face with his hand and tilting her shoulder away from the ground. The jerking motions grew fainter in his arms, till her consciousness returned for a moment. There was just a flutter of recognition for the anxious state of her kin before the seizure took hold once more.

"Somebody call for help!" Her father wailed, dashing down the trail in search of trip organisers. Tourists fumbled with mobile phones in gloved hands, but no reception was available. Scientists attempting to help, tuned and re-tuned two-way radio sets, but received no more than crackles and a deafening whine. Their scientific instruments read off the scales with an abundance of data. He grabbed the ski jacket of a man by the trucks. "Is there a landline I can use in the hut?"

He spotted a line of wooden poles delivering a strained length of cable over the mountainside and into the shelter and ran towards the door. A mild buzzing grew louder. Then, sparks sprang from the ceramic contact points till a flash of light ignited the cable and blew out the line. "No, please no!" He rushed into the office and picked up the receiver. The line was dead. He sprinted back up the hillside to his daughter, still shuddering in his father's arms.

"What do we do now?"

"Pray."

Chapter One

East Midlands, UK. Present Day.

"It's all over the Internet, there's been another one. Quick, Mary, switch the screen over to the news."

Grabbing the remote, Mary tuned the ceiling mounted monitor to the BBC Special Broadcast. With intense solemnity, the newscaster announced;

"Kumamoto City, in the Kyushu Region of Japan, has suffered a massive aftershock registering seven on the Richter scale. This devastating blow comes to them just sixteen hours after the first earthquake, at six point two, yesterday. We take you there now, live at the scene, with our reporter. Some viewers may find the following scenes distressing."

Aerial footage tracked along the expansive rift that gouged out the spine of the island, creating great canyons of fresh rock and cliff. Scenes of landlocked ships, dry docked on the bowing rooves of buildings long past repair; the sea having receded as fast as it had surged. Arable fields cleaved in two and shunted metres apart by ravines that engulfed lives and machines in equal measure. Broken grandmothers, weary of distress, carried to safety and a reckoning of lives lost. Occupied body bags, covered with a fresh coating of debris from the vicious aftershock.

Telegraph poles splintered as matchsticks, totems of the destructive force surrounding them. And people - tall, short, old, young, rich and the poor, all targeted by the quakes force. The reporter followed an aid worker through a makeshift hospital. Patients hugged their knees to create floor space for those who were nearing their end to lie outstretched in their final moments. Blankets, water, bandages and resilience meted out in doses along with a moment of relief that the two remaining nuclear power stations on either side of the island, remained intact.

The scene cut to a fractured street. The cameraman tightened the focus and zoomed in on the wreckage of mangled rubble. Men in coordinating jumpsuits and hardhats, dangled a colleague by his legs through a narrow gap in the shattered tarmac and hauled out a little boy by his spindly arm. Tear trails glistened against the matt grey powder coating his blackened and bruised face. His shin bone erupted in jagged spikes through his skin and twisted his foot at an awkward angle, making his extraction all the more painful.

Mary stood with her co-workers in the lab, aghast at the images unfurling before them. Tuts, gasps, then quiet murmurs of sorrow chorused from the technicians and research fellows alike. One or two of the gentler souls caught their grief in tissues pressed to their cheeks. Mary was mute. Her pain was tangible and instant – dry choking on the dust collecting in her windpipe and a sudden wrenching in her arm socket. The throbbing ache across her face and the sharp incessant stabbing, firing every pain receptor in her lower leg. Disorientated, she stumbled backwards, steadying herself against a workbench and clasping her head between her palms. The pounding in her face centralised inside her skull into a leaden ball of pressure that found release via a cathartic but garbled scream.

Every fluorescent light tube overhead arced and flickered, with an ominous high pitched squeal. In perfect synchronisation, the News Channel turned into a hissing screen of pointillism and a heat lamp on the bench closest to Mary blew with such ferocity that scorch marks fanned in a semi-circular array surrounding the now useless device. Finally, the electronic orchestra halted when the main laboratory trip switch snapped its lever, cutting the power and reducing the workforce to a stunned silence.

Slumping to the floor shaking, Mary felt the pain dissipate. She rolled her trouser leg up to the knee and where she expected to find splintered bone and blood, there was smooth, unmarked skin. Examining her forehead and chin, she found no sore bruises nor wounds. Peering up at the crowd of shocked onlookers, she blushed a red so profound that it heated her entire torso.

Mary's boss, Professor Cyril Plender, dispersed the congregation and addressed his senior lab technician;

"Mary. I might have known. What the hell have you done now?" He rested a fist on his hip, puffing out his chest and inclining his small frame over her head.

"I don't know what happened, it just blew. I'll pay for the damage, Cyril, I'm so sorry." She embraced her knees, hoping she could shrink into the industrial linoleum and disappear.

"Have you hurt yourself? I think you should see the campus doctor to be on the safe side. I don't want to be accused of being *uncaring*." He gestured the quotation marks, mid-air and pulled a face.

"No, it's alright, I can get my husband to check me over. I am very sorry."

"I wouldn't mind, Mary, but this is the third piece of electronic equipment you have broken this month. Really, it has to stop…" He paused his rant after noticing the salt water gathering in the lids of her eyes. "I'll call your husband, he can take you home. No one can say that I don't look after my staff."

He dug in his pocket for his phone and thumbed the address book while offering his other hand to help Mary up from her tangled mess on the floor. She looked at his fat, sweaty fingers and levered herself up, distancing herself as she rose. "Arora? Plender here. Can you get over to Biochem, pronto? Mary has had an accident… Good man." Cyril hung up and turned on his heels to greet a visitor who had been standing in the doorway, captivated by the spectacle. "Ah welcome. My office is just through here. If you'd like to follow me?" The man shook Cyril's hand with vigour, but his focus remained on Mary. He had curious green eyes, almost feline. Smiling, he turned away and sauntered back through the door.

Parth Arora arrived, panting and leaning on each bench in turn as he made his way over to his wife. No longer able to contain herself, she let the tears flow, hiding her face in his chest and holding him with a vice-like grip.

"Are you hurt? Plender said there was an accident?" He dipped his chin to the top of her head, resting his mouth against her hair.

"It happened again." The sobs were more urgent now, her shoulders heaving in time with her staccato breaths. "What is wrong with me?"

"Nothing, absolutely nothing. Come on, let's go home. It's a good job I brought the car today." He slipped a guiding hand down to the small of her back and limped with her towards the lockers.

"You've hurt your leg, there's blood on your trousers."

"Just a scratch. I tripped over some students' bikes running over here. I thought you were seriously injured."

Taking her bag from a locker, she turned and caressed his stubble covered jawline. "What would I do without you?"

"I hope you'll never have to find out."

***

Parth tucked Mary into their king-sized divan with a side tray of tea, dry biscuits and a bag of salted crisps and sat by her side until she had taken her medication. The short drive home and the recounting of events had been enough stimulation to bring on the warning signs of a migraine. Aristotle jumped on the bed and demanded attention, raising his tail and displaying his rear end too close to Mary's face for comfort.

"You must keep well hydrated to fend off migraine attacks."

"There is a limit to how much I can drink, Parth. I spend half my life in the bathroom as it is."

"And you really shouldn't have so much tea. Caffeine is a known trigger."

"I gave up booze for these bloody headaches. Tea is all I have left. I know you mean well, but please don't fuss so much."

"At least consider swapping to decaf. I'll be downstairs catching up on some calls and emails, love. Shout if you need anything." He drew the bedroom curtains on his way out and pulled the door to, leaving the customary gap for the miniature Bengal tiger to come and go as he pleased. She relaxed into her pillows with a long sigh and begged her mind to halt the loop of replayed images in her head. *Concentrate on the inside of my forehead,* she told herself. *Empty the mind and visualise the soothing of nerves and the pain receding.* Repeating the mantra twice through, she willed herself better, all the time the feeling of nausea swam inside her. Reaching across for her tea, she took a little sip and then rummaged in her cabinet for a sleep mask.

Downstairs, Parth had settled in his study. Mary heard the familiar jingle as his laptop booted into life and ran its systems check-up. He was talking quietly on the phone. She couldn't make out distinct sentences but the deep, masculine undulation of his speech was unmistakable. It was one of the things that had most attracted her to him. That and the precise way he enunciated his words, as if he was taking extra care with his adopted language. Donning her mask, she burrowed back beneath the covers with another sigh. Then, small footfalls pinched the sheets across her thighs. She waited until the predictable paws landed on her abdomen and braced herself while the four points of pressure became a curled mass of fur balancing on her roiling stomach.

"Oh Totty, must you? Why can't you sit on my feet instead? They feel like ice blocks." To her astonishment, the cat rose, stretched and repositioned his body across her feet. “No way.” She sat up, removing the mask. “Now go and pester Parth downstairs.” Aristotle barely lifted his head, narrowed his sleepy eyes at her and then covered his face with a leg. “Thought so. Like anyone could tell you what to do even if you did understand me.”

On Parth’s bedside table, his iPad pinged a notification, displaying the message across the top of the screen. Having cursed and fiddled for some time, he had managed to sync his phone and tablet to each other, enabling both devices to send and receive messages using a Wi-Fi connection. Mary leaned over and read the communication,

Excellent news. 10am tomorrow. Still malleable? Y

She frowned, contemplating who ‘Y’ was and the meaning of the text when Parth’s response pinged back.

Docile as a kitten.

***

Mary pretended to be asleep when Parth finally came to bed. She heard him complete his night time ritual of switching off table lamps and locking the doors, then ascend the stairs in his socks to avoid disturbing her. He cleaned his teeth in silence before slipping under the quilt and moving with caution to find a comfortable position. Listening for the rhythmic breathing of slumber, she removed her mask and opened her eyes to the silhouetted furniture shapes, and ruminated on the day. There were two options for who ‘Y’ could be; Yosef, the receptionist for the Neurosciences Building or Yelena Plender, Chief Finance Officer for the University and Mary's friend. She also happened to be bound in a miserable marriage to Mary's boss, but that seemed insignificant in light of the text to Parth. *How could a meeting about finance involve someone being malleable?* The question encircled her subconscious, a bat-like omen that would roost in the hippocampus of her brain and take flight each night before sleep.

When sleep overpowered her, she found her dreams had kept pace with the anxieties of the day, sending her crashing about science labs and offices. Tripping over equipment and breaking glassware, cowering in preparation rooms with lecturers hurling instructions and berating her for mistakes. Each time she saw a doctor or a student, she would ask; 'What is happening to me?' and 'Am I the docile one?' before reaching the top of a flight of concrete stairs and falling, falling…

Mary woke up and tried to move, but her limbs were rigid and lifeless, her spine fixed and paralysed. Her pulse quickened, sending a rush of adrenalin to her organs, fuelling the dread that there could be something wrong with her. She gasped her breaths in terror, fearing that they might be her last. *Am I dying? Is this what people mean when they say 'final death throes'?* Trapped inside her petrified body, she garnered all her strength and willed herself to rise. And then she did, but the feeling of weightlessness was unsettling. She could feel nothing substantial around her. Unable to move, speak or touch, only her vision seemed functional. It was as though her eyes were plucked from her skull, shrouded in a swirling cloud of energy and transported towards the ceiling. Her sight adjusted to the new vantage point, looking down at her serene body, motionless and alone in the night. *Is this it then? I am to die all alone? Where has Parth gone?* A peculiar resignation took hold of her thought processes. *I shall see my parents again, that is no small consolation, but I would like to see Parth once more before I leave...*

A moment's thought became a command. The ball of energy carrying her vision squeezed through the gap in the doorway and out onto the landing. She passed the top of the staircase and noticed, with almost idle regard, that the light fittings could do with a good clean. She flew past the banister and girded herself for the plunge down the staircase. Her body released more adrenalin into her brain, sharpening her focus on the sepia tones of the hallway, bathed in streetlight from the leaded glass in the window. The shards of radiance crossed the flagstone floor and illuminated Aristotle, who scratched unabated at Parth's closed study door. *Poor Totty, I shall miss you too. Did he just look up at me? Don't be stupid – I'm dead, how could he see me? If I am dead, I should be able to pass through the door like a ghost.* Her sight blended with the grain of the oak door, weaving between the striations as though they were directing her, making her pathway clear. Her mass of energy reassembled inside Parth's room. He was sitting in his underwear at his desk, immersed in typing on his laptop. The ridge of lines above his nose conveyed the intense concentration required for his task.

A wave of sadness rippled through her thoughts in realisation that she would never again feel those lithe mocha limbs entwined in hers, that cute little mole that looked for all the world like a third nipple and those taut stomach muscles pressed against her belly. She moved closer. He was wearing those turquoise boxer shorts with the pink pigs printed all over them that she had bought for a joke. *Bless him, he'd rather come down here and work than disturb me in bed. I wonder why he didn't tell me about the insomnia.*

Aristotle was making himself heard on the opposite side of the door once more. Parth tutted, then stood up and depressed the handle, allowing the cat to bound in and wrap himself around his owner's legs. Mary watched her husband push their pet away with a flick of an ankle and return to his frantic report writing. *What could be so important that it needs documenting at four O'clock in the morning?* She edged forwards again, trying to catch a glimpse of the screen when Aristotle jumped up onto the desk, padding across a leather folio of papers. An angry swipe sent the cat flying, scattering the documents across the floor. *That was unnecessarily harsh of you Parth. I thought you had more patience.* As he crouched down and began gathering the strewn sheets together, one partially covered phrase caught her attention. An unfamiliar crest was visible on the top right hand corner. In bold letters it read - *Less Lethal Weapons.*

Immediate distress activated a chemical cocktail in her brain so potent, the sudden shock jolted her presence, sucking her consciousness through the door, up the stairs and into the bedroom. In a thrilling rush of urgency, her amorphous mass reintegrated with a sickening thud back into her physical body. With one giant gasp of breath, she opened her eyes. Mary lay on her side of the bed, suffused in the dawn light that streaked through the gap in the curtains, trembling. *I am not dead and that was no dream.*

Chapter Two

There was no way that Mary could go back to sleep. She lay still, listening to the birds welcome in the new day and waited for the alarm clock to sound. Parth had not returned to the marital bed. Mary knew that he would appear at seven O'clock, carrying a cup of tea, pretending he had woken early. She contemplated telling him about her bodiless amble into his study. Given the revelations discovered in Parth's leather folio, she thought that he would attribute it to a vivid hallucination. Well acquainted with Parth's ridicule, she had no intention of affording him further opportunities to use it. She would have to verify the facts before confronting him. Asking straight out would prompt his usual response to anything he didn't want to answer; 'you know that some of my projects are classified, honey,' his get-out clause for everything. Perhaps Yelena would be more forthcoming about her messages to her husband. One thing was clear – Parth was hiding more than a couple of secret Neuroscience studies.

By the time the clock shrieked its warning, Mary had made the momentous decision to be selective with information. It would be a steep learning curve for her, to conceal rather than reveal, fighting against her natural inclination to be open and honest with everyone.

"Morning, darling. Did you sleep well? How is your head today?"

How does he act so sprightly all the time? She widened her eyes, fingering the sleep crystals encrusting her tear ducts, playing along with the ruse. "Better today, thanks." Mary pressed her knuckles into the mattress, pulling her bottom up close to the pillow and into a sitting position.

He twisted the mug around so that the handle was facing her. She took it from him, mouthing her gratitude. His attention focused and alert, he monitored her every move and gesture.

"I have booked time in the MRI suite for you this morning and sent Plender a text telling him you aren't fit for work. We'll do a round of tests and fast track them through the department, just as a precaution." He sat on the edge of the bed, attempting to analyse her pupils for any signs of inequality without her noticing. Mary did notice. He hovered too close, his motions strained and methodical, the detached medical practitioner displacing her husband's quiet care.

"Do you think I have a brain tumour?" Articulating the words suddenly made the possibility real. She swallowed hard.

"No, I'm sure you are fine. Just do this for me, please? Put our minds at ease?" He pulled a cutesy face, knowing how it would provoke her. Mary responded with a dazed amorous smile. *Damn him. He is so difficult to mistrust.*

"I thought you had a meeting with Yelena this morning?"

"How did you…?"

Mary pointed to his iPad, still sitting on Parth's bed side table. His blithe façade slipped a fraction, exposing an unexpected fear. He recovered it quickly.

"Oh yes, of course. Yelena and I have been working on a promising new investor for Neuro."

Trying to read his expression, Mary peered a moment too long into the resolute darkness of his eyes. Turning away first, she rebuked herself. *Stupid of me. There was bound to be a simple explanation.*

"Come on, honey. Get up, get showered and dressed. I'll drive us in and if you feel up to it, you can collect your bike and ride home. Leave it any longer on campus and someone will take the bolt cutters to your lock." He was rambling, distracting her train of thought.

Maybe I have got a brain tumour. That would make me hallucinate – probably. Maybe I really did nearly die last night, although it wouldn't account for all the weird experiences with electronics I've had lately.

***

Driving the few streets to the University, they left the Volkswagen in the staff car park and walked through the quads and clusters of buildings towards Neurosciences.

"You go and grab yourself a bite to eat and I'll text you when Yelena and I are done." He fumbled with his car keys, trying to slide them through an opening in his leather case.

"I didn't bring my phone." She grabbed the bottom corner of the dangling document wallet to assist his struggle.

"Why on Earth not?" Keys safely stowed, she let go of the case, allowing him to grasp its handle and let it swing to his side.

"Didn't think I'd need it." She shrugged. "Anyway, I can't face food right now. I'll come and sit in your department. I don't mind waiting." She watched his face switch from annoyance to evasion.

"No, it'll be noisy and smelly in there. They'll be cleaning the animal house out today. Give me an hour, then meet me at the front entrance." He leaned on her shoulder, pecked her forehead with a dry kiss and turned away, striding with purpose.

Mary watched him walk to the corner of the block and disappear before she headed for the Union Building. Pondering her options, she climbed a set of concrete steps to the first concourse and viewed the shop windows. The pharmacy was advertising a two for one offer on contraception and a student union member's discount on flu vaccinations. Wooden stalls gathered together in the rough shape of a market, had similar deals on glossy A1 posters. Beads, hemp bags and imported smoking bongs hung from racks and rails, surrounded by a massing crowd of unwashed youths, striving for adulthood. She nodded her amusement at the stall owner and entered the campus bookshop.

A sanctuary of calm, Mary browsed the titles in the Neurology section, then dismissed them for their complex titles. *Maybe the theology shelves will help to explain all the weird occurrences*. None of the cover blurbs struck her as being useful except for a tiny paperback, written by the Dalai Lama. Opening the pages at random, the sentences seem to speak to her in her hour of turmoil.

The wise sage spoke of a comparison between the mind and an honest and pure monarch or Prime Minister. He likened our thoughts and feelings, within the analogy, to cabinet ministers. Some of whom, provide good advice and care for the well-being of others, while some are only concerned for their own interests.

The passage continued to filter through her thoughts as she paid for the book, left the shop and queued for a drink in the canteen. The boards above the kiosk had a cartoon man holding his chin with a thought cloud painted above his head. In swirled green lettering his thoughts read "I think I'll eat healthy foods today." *I bet his mind doesn't go zooming around the house, spying on his partner in the middle of the night. I bet he hasn't got a brain tumour squeezing out all his logic and reason.*

"It's Mary, isn't it?"

I bet he hasn't got a partner who thinks you need wet-nursing and all your decisions taken out of your hands.

"Hello? Mary?" The tall man stepped from behind her in the queue to gain her attention. She snapped out of her self-pitying reflections and engaged.

"Dan! Oh, how lovely to see you." They did a little mistimed dance of shaking hands and air kissing.

"You remembered my name." He beamed, his eyebrows arched in surprise.

"Of course, I did. You are the only interesting person in the study group. Soon grow tired of all the students who are more interested in claiming their expenses than taking Parth's experiments seriously." They edged forwards in the queue.

"Parth?"

"Dr Parth Arora. He's my husband." A student tried to by-pass them carrying a tray stacked high with an assortment of sweet snacks. Mary shot him a *just-try-it-sonny* glare. The student resumed his place behind Dan.

"Good God, really? So, you're… Dr Mary Aurora? As in the Northern Lights?"

"Ha! No. Just plain old Mary Arora, spelled without the 'U'. Parth is of Indian descent. Arora is quite common, apparently." She drew level with the counter where a large lady wearing a smock was resting on her elbows.

"Here, allow me." With a chivalry seldom seen deep in the student territories, Dan paid for their drinks and carried the tray to a table of her choosing, folding his long legs beneath the cramped space in the American style booth. She thanked him.

"You have to admit, we made a pretty good team in that card pairing exercise." Dan said, keen to preserve the conversation's momentum.

"Yes, that's true, but those early activities were to select a group of what Parth calls his *Sensitives*." She removed the lid from the metal teapot and stirred the bag around with a plastic spoon.

"His what, now?" Dan licked the cappuccino froth from his top lip.

"People with a significantly above average guess rate in the card tests. He uses traditionally accepted psychology experiments to find his group of Sensitives, each study getting progressively more complex and involved." She paused to flick some errant crumbs from her teacup. "As he whittles the candidates down, he retains a smaller test group for neurological study and then passes the remainder over to the psychology department." She scrunched her nose up at the paltry amount of fresh milk the smock lady had poured into her tiny jug.

"What does he do with his target candidates?" A wry smile formed on his lips, watching her perform what was clearly a ritual pouring of her tea.

"They have a series of medical tests done to see if they are physically fit, then Parth decides which test group to place them in."

"Ah, that was why his staff took an armful of blood this morning." He showed her the tiny circular plaster nestled in the crook of his arm. "I don't really know what I thought the study would entail when I signed up. The advert seemed so intriguing, like we were going to discover the science behind all paranormal phenomenon." They giggled.

"Maybe we will. You are a sceptic then?" Mary took a sip. The tea was still scalding hot, but she bore the millisecond of pain like an old pro.

"I'm fascinated by it. I want to believe but I cannot find any evidence to support it. I have so many books back in the shop about it, I'm in danger of becoming a specialist supplier." Dan offered her a napkin to mop up the dribbles collected in the saucer from the leaky pot.

"You own a bookshop?" She scanned his apparel. The corduroy jacket should have been enough of a hint.

"Yes, the one just off West Walk, near De Montford Street." Dan saw her perplexed frown and added; "It's called Wildman's Books… blue canopy over the shop front."

"Oh yes, I know it. Never been in, sadly. I shall make a point of venturing over that way." Her expression was too eager.

He grinned. "That's what they all say."

Her ephemeral smile shone, then faded, replaced by something that resembled concern. "I don't suppose you have anything on weird experiences, do you?"

"Tonnes. Define weird." Taking the cue from her serious tone, he sat upright and moved in closer.

"Like leaving your body and spying on relatives weird. And I don't mean dreaming." Concern matured into full blown worry.

"Out of Body Experiences. They call it Extra Corporeal Travel, these days. Has that happened to you then?"

Mary nodded, the bridge of her nose wrinkling up the skin in her forehead. "Last night, but please don't tell Parth. He's making me have a brain scan this morning. If I tell him about it, he'll say it was a hallucination, probably from a massive tumour that'll kill me any minute." There was a catch in her voice, the note of panic straining her vocal chords.

Dan shook his head slowly. "I won't tell him, but perhaps you should. He sounds like a worrier. Must be nice to have someone care that much about you."

"Suffocating, sometimes. I mustn't grumble. He is very good to me." Keen to change tack before the wobble in her throat became a torrent of tears. "Do you have someone special?"

Dan blew out a forced puff of air. "That's debateable."

Mary lowered one eyebrow and held it there. He took the prompt and continued. "Connie. Constance –

she's French, but over here working as a freelance journalist."

"And the debateable bit?"

Dan took a deep breath. "Some months she practically moves in. Life is exciting – parties, soirees, theatre trips, mini-breaks, then the next month she'll vanish, completely. No warnings, no note, texts, phone calls, nothing." He pushed his cup handle from side to side. It made a grating noise against the Formica table. "The first time she disappeared, I was out of my mind with worry. I did the usual - called round to a couple of her friends' places, no luck. She wouldn't answer my calls, messages, I was frantic. Then I contacted the Police and registered her as a missing person." Dan's mouth dried. He took a gulp of coffee. "Within twenty-four hours, they'd tracked her phone and card transactions back to Paris and then cautioned me for wasting police time."

Mary sat captivated by his tale, supping her tea, feeling his desperation. She urged him to carry on.

"I thought she had split up with me but six weeks later, she lets herself into the flat above my shop as if nothing had happened."

"And you forgave her?" Mary poured her second cup, trying to maintain eye contact and watch the liquid slopping up to the brim.

"I tried to discuss it with her, get my side across, but she just shrugged and said that she was following a story. And, well, she can be maddeningly…"

"Charming."

Dan nodded.

"She sounds a lot like Parth." They raised their cups in silent meditation, contemplating their respective partners.

"She's dragging me to some posh ball around here next week. I have to go and book a rented dinner jacket this afternoon." He rolled his eyes.

"It's not the Investment Group bash, is it? At the Gilbert Murray Hall, near to the Botanical Gardens?" The sparkle reignited in her irises. It seemed to have a reciprocal effect in lightening Dan's mood.

"Yes, I think so. Are you going?"

"I was going to try and wriggle out of it. Those Investors Balls are deadly." She shifted backwards on the vinyl bench seats.

"Aww, please say you'll go. Connie will run off and grab any dignitary she can corner and I'll be stuck by the buffet holding a shrimp in one hand and an orange juice in the other, waiting to chauffeur m'lady home." He pawed at the table, affecting a pathetic air.

"Only if you will promise to rescue me from the Director of Biomedical Sciences. He's a lecherous old sod, with the personal hygiene of an elderly walrus and he always seems to find me no matter where I hide." Her bubbly warmth was infectious.

"Done. But wont Parth be your gallant knight?"

"Not when there are departmental funds up for grabs. He'd pimp his granny out if there was a promise of new equipment in it." They drained their drinks and Mary wrapped the strap of her satchel diagonally across her body ready to leave. "See you at the next study session on…"

"Tomorrow. Yes." They squeezed themselves out from the booth seats.

"Gosh, yes, tomorrow. Thanks for the tea, Dan." Mary double tapped his arm.

"Good to see you, Mary."

As she made her way to the door, she glanced back to see her new friend taking his long strides towards an exit at the far end of the room. Turning again, she bumped into a stocky man in suit trousers and formal shirt, who shoved past her and scuttled off in Dan's general direction.

"Don't mind me!" Mary shouted after him. He waved, but didn't stop to offer an apology. *Hmm, rude man. He's got a little finger missing, like Terry Nutkin. I wonder if he got it bitten off by an otter too.* She studied the wall clock. *Might have been sensible to have made a note of the time when I left Parth earlier. Has it been an hour yet?*

Resolving to wait on the Neurosciences front steps in the sun, Mary quickened her pace and lengthened her gait. She had always felt a sense of comfort on campus, like the buildings were cradling her, protecting her from the harsh outside world. Today she felt them watching her with ominous intent. Their friendly faces turned sour and sterile. Rounding a corner, she caught sight of her boss, Professor Cyril Plender, carrying a bulging document wallet into the Biochemistry building. Halting abruptly, she back-tracked and shuffled behind a wall, peeking out every few seconds to see if he had cleared the entrance. *I can't face Cyril today. He jars my nerves on regular days let alone brain scan days. His ranting could make my tumour pop in my head and kill me.* Between him entering the building, walking up two flights of steps and unlocking his office door, she estimated a thirty second opportunity to dash past before he would look out of his window and see her.

Holding her satchel to her chest, she made a run for it, her hips swinging at full tilt until she was out of sight and heading for Neurosciences. Heart racing and calf muscles twinging, she sat on the front entrance steps, out of puff and clutching her ribs. The sweet pain of lactic acid build-up receded from the cramping muscles. Mary took the little Dalai Lama book out once more and contemplated the first few pages. *I bet he has had an Out of Body Experience. I suppose he would call it religious enlightenment. I don't feel enlightened and it could still be the result of a tumour, slowly destroying my sanity. Perhaps I should go to Dan's bookshop and read up about it, or maybe not. He might think I am stalking him. I'll look it up on Parth's iPad later.*

Delving into her bag for a tissue and a handful of Tictacs, she wiped her brow and neck and dragged her long, dark curls back into a ponytail. Holding her bunched locks with one hand, she rifled through the smaller pockets of the satchel for a hair band. A woman tapped her shoulder as she descended the steps, slender and elegant in her grey silk suit and killer heels. Mary looked up at her, dropping her hair and crunching the sweets in preparation for her greeting.

"Hello, Mary. You look a little distraught. Are you well?" The accent was mild, but conspicuous, natural but undiluted. This was a woman proud of her St. Petersburg roots.

"Yelena, Hi. I'm fine, thanks. Are you? Well, I mean?"

"I am very well, thank you. Why are you sitting on the steps?"

"Waiting for your meeting with Parth to finish." She squinted at her friend, angling the little book over her forehead to shield her from the sun.

"Oh. He told you about that, did he? Yes, we had to discuss a new piece of equipment he ordered recently." Only the languid sweep of her eyelids across her impassive gaze, signified her as a living, breathing human being. Her mastery over emotion was second to none.

Mary locked her expression. She half expected the lie, but hoped for a different response. It saddened her that both her husband and friend could fabricate the truth so easily. She couldn't look up at Yelena's sculpted face, those almond eyes would detect Mary's disappointment. Yelena continued, "I will be wearing a sage green full length gown for the ball. I trust you will be in your usual black?"

"What? Oh, yes. Black." Mary began packing the mints and book back into her bag.

"You are… out of sorts today?" Yelena stepped sideways, blocking the glare of the sun and casting Mary in shadow.

"No, no, everything is fine. Well, no, everything is not fine, to tell the truth." She fastened and re-fastened the buckles on her satchel.

"You would like for us to talk about your problem?" Yelena tilted her head, listening intently.

Oh, you moron, Mary. Filter your feelings before you open your big mouth. Quick, think of something to say other than, why are you and my husband texting about being docile?

"Your husband is very cross with me. I think he's going to issue me with another formal reprimand. One more, and I swear he'll give me the boot." Mary tried to look suitably troubled.

"The boot?"

"Sorry. Sack me. He is holding me responsible for some damaged electrical equipment. Yelena, I really like my job, I don't want to lose it." It shocked her just how much she meant it.

"I will speak with Cyril, leave him to me. No one will be losing their job. I suggest you get up from steps and dry your eyes. Grandmother would say sitting on cold concrete give you haemorrhoids." Yelena sashayed down the remaining stairs, her rich auburn bob flaring at her ears with each step.

Chapter Three

Parth hung from the handgrip of the glass door. "Mary, come on love, I'll take you through." The reception desk was Yosef's domain, a burly chap who always wore a genuine smile.

"Hello again, Mrs Arora. I wasn't expecting to see you today. We have you booked in for tomorrow evening." He scrolled through the calendar on his screen, then activated the scanning peripherals.

"I know, I know. He's making me have more tests." She stuck a thumb out towards Parth. Yosef grinned at her. He liked to see Mary teasing his boss.

"I'll sign you in, if you could just swipe you ID badge across the scanner for me, please." Yosef tapped away at some commands on his computer and a small printer spat out her access card. It had *Zone One & Two* in big red letters beneath her photograph and a bar code to the side. He clipped a lanyard to the card and handed it to Mary.

"Cheers, Yosef." Parth said, then swiped his own ID through the access point, opened the door and allowed Mary to pass through under his outstretched arm.

They passed quickly through Zone One – conference rooms and education suites, a lecture hall and a couple of ground floor student labs. Zone Two, was where the medical equipment and examination rooms were.

"We need to take some blood samples, honey. Do you want me to do it or the nurse?" Parth hurried her along, grasping her arm and dictating their speed. Mary scurried to keep up.

"Please, can you do it? You know how much I hate needles." She leaned in and whispered "Plus, I don't think Nurse Ratchet over there likes me very much."

The nurse pretended not to hear, placed the tray of sealed sterilised tubes and syringes down on a table and left the examination room. Parth was out of practice. He hadn't drawn blood since his medical school days, but he refused to let his nerves show.

Mary exposed her arm and helped him to adjust the strapping on the tourniquet. "Look away now, honey. Sharp scratch." Parth having found a vein first time, secured the needle in place with surgical tape, clicked a labelled glass phial into the open syringe and released the strapping on her arm. Blood flowed rapidly into the tube. Unclipping and securing the lid, he removed the needle and pressed a ball of cotton wool to the injection site. "All done. It's like riding a bike." He recorded the date, initialled the label on the phial and then gave Mary the paperwork to sign for the scan. She began reading it as they shuffled down the corridor to the waiting room next to the MRI suite.

The radiology nurse glanced at the wall clock and then back at Mary, who sat scraping the toes of her canvas shoes against the floor tiles beneath her plastic chair.

"Won't be long, Mrs Arora, we're running a bit late. If you could start taking off jewellery, watches and anything metallic, and I'll come and collect you in a few minutes." She pitched Mary a one-smile-fits-all, generic expression and disappeared behind the heavy swing door.

"I think you are over reacting, Parth. I don't think I even need this scan. I've always had migraines. If it was anything sinister, I'd be dead by now. My dad had them, bless him, and old Grampy still gets them, occasionally, although that might be his fondness for Ruby Port. Don't let me forget to send his card. Let's get him one of those lovely hampers this year. I swear he neglects himself."

Parth opened his mouth to reply, stealing himself in case her anxious prattle continued unabated, then when it failed to materialise he ventured a tentative, "Yes, dear," and patted her knee.

"Why is your department always so hot? It's positively tropical. Reminds me of our trip to the Amazon, do you remember?" She toyed with a stubborn curl of hair that refused to stay tucked behind her ear.

"Yes, dear."

The nurse reappeared. "We're ready for you now, Mrs Arora."

"Right, yes. Thank you. Parth, will you take my handbag with you into the computer suite?" Mary bundled her leather satchel into her husband's arms and followed the nurse into the MRI unit.

"If you could just go behind the screen, Mrs Arora, and put this gown on. No need to remove your trousers, it's only your head we're interested in," another stiff smile.

Mary complied, taking a few deep breaths to compose herself before unbuttoning her blouse. "What about my bra?"

"Does it have an underwire?" The nurse stood at the edge of the screen, keeping her sight fixed on her clipboard.

"Yes, it does."

"Then you had better take that off too. We don't want it slipping up and throttling you, do we?" The nurse trotted out her standardised quip, followed by a forced chuckle, which prompted a polite, "No, quite" from her patient.

"Just to confirm your answers to our questionnaire on the release form then, Mrs Arora, you have no pacemaker, metal implants, stents or shunts, loose oral bridgework and no metal fragments in your eyes?"

"Yes. I mean No." The nurse peered over her spectacles waiting for a definitive answer. "I mean, yes, that's correct. I have none of those things."

"And you have removed all objects from visible and um, less than visible piercings?"

Mary frowned. The nurse pointed to her own, ample bosoms and repeated herself, "less visible piercings?"

"Oh God no. There are no less visible piercings." She shook her head with vigour.

"And you have read the pamphlet about the procedure?" The nurse followed the list of questions down the board with her biro.

"Yes, twice." Mary stood in her hospital gown with her arms limp by her sides, swallowing back the resurgence of unprocessed tea in her gullet. The dark circles from her restless night accentuated her high cheekbones. A little orphaned waif.

"Good. Hop up onto the platform for me, please."

Mary looked over her shoulder at the machine behind her. It loomed large, like a gigantic mechanical monstrosity hiding its menace beneath a veneer of beige enamel. Its circular face dominated by a tubular mouth and a long, tongue-like bed, protruding rudely. *I am voluntarily feeding myself to this computerised leviathan.* She half expected to see saliva trickling down the edges of the platform as she sat, gingerly at first, then swung her legs up and settled centrally on the hygienic paper sheet covering the narrow bed.

"If you could place the back of your head onto this block, Mrs Arora…that's right, then this cage clips across your face, like so."

What the hell? Now I'm placing my head between its molars. Are they sacrificing me to their Gods, Watson and Crick? Her stomach cried mournfully, twisting and writhing in sympathy for her motionless limbs.

"Did we forget breakfast this morning, Mrs Arora? Not to worry, it'll all be over in an hour or so."

"An hour?"

"Yes. Now then, when I adjust the mirror in your halo, you tell me when you can see Dr Arora, sorry, your husband, in the booth at the rear of the room. That's right, give him a little wave. Now you must not move a muscle or we will have to start all over again. The panic button is next to your index finger – here." Manually manoeuvring Mary's hand, the nurse helped her to locate the smooth, cold button standing proud from a plastic shape. Instinct told her it would be bright red if she could see it.

"But like I said" the nurse continued, "if you move or press it, we would have to start all over again. It'll be very noisy, so these headphones will play some music and the doctor can talk to you through them, from the booth." It was a time-worn speech, delivered day in, day out in a monotone drawl, the pace dictated by the proximity to lunchtime. "In you pop then." Pressing a combination of switches on the control panel, Mary moved in jerky thrusts into the yawning maw of the beast.

A throbbing blood rush coursed behind her ears. Her breath oscillated in her chest. The bitter tang of bile passed her tonsils. She tamed the secretion with a controlled swathe of spittle. The last quota of moisture her mouth could supply. *Focus on Parth in that little window – he's smiling, everything is fine. I can do this.* She told herself, willing her body to cooperate with her demands. Her entire physique was now cocooned in a cylinder, inches from her face.

"Just raising the platform now, Mrs Arora." Her voice was indistinct.

Is she mocking me? Surely there can be no room to…I was wrong. If she raises me another centimetre, this torture contraption around my face will shatter. Her pulse hammered through her spine, making her breaths shallow and ragged.

"I'm feeling dizzy, Parth. I don't like this."

He clicked the intercom and his tinny voice seeped from the crackling headphones, "A touch of claustrophobia, darling. Give it a minute and you'll acclimatise. I'll put Mahler's 5th on, you like that."

Soothing viola strings washed over her mind like an anaesthetic for her soul. She closed her eyes. *I can do this. I can do this. Stay still. I can...do this.*

"Just cranking the machine up now, Mary."

"You mean it isn't even switched on yet?" She tensed her leg and stomach muscles, stilling the tremor that threatened to engulf her.

A deep, all-encompassing hum, emanated from the electronic creature and Mary could feel an odd pulling sensation in all directions at once.

"First scan is a relatively quick one, sagittal plane through the cranium, that's head to toe direction, honey. Hold still."

A loud clunking superseded the humming noise as heavy magnets moved into position and locked into place. *I can do this, keep still. Don't embarrass Parth in front of his colleague. Slow, deep breaths.*

It began. Mahler faded into the background as the pendulum of judder-clunk, judder-clunk found its noisy rhythm around her. The pulling sensation grew. Her temples shrank into her skull and a sharp pain branched in a spider's web of parallel pathways throughout her brain.

"Parth, I think I'm going to throw up." She swallowed hard, trying not to move her face.

The intercom connection clicked on. "Bear with it, darling. You'll be okay."

"I'm serious, Parth. It hurts. Can you stop it, please?"

"You have probably wound yourself up to the start of a migraine. Stay still, the first one is almost over."

It was Beethoven now, his piano concerto number twenty-one, interrupted by her echoing husband.

"Next one takes a little longer, Mary, axial plane." He didn't wait for her to respond. She could see him in her cage mirror, chatting and laughing with the nurse. More whirring and thumping as the magnets repositioned, and then a deafening buzz that Beethoven could not compete with. As soon as the machine started, a searing pain shot across her head, gnawing at her brain before volleying back again. She squinted into the gloom. *Is the cylinder tightening around me? Is this the final digestive constriction as the creature devours me? Now I know how Captain Ahab felt.* She was close to passing out, then she remembered the panic button. She pressed down hard. A lamp started to blink in the booth and an alarm sounded. Parth clicked the intercom, "Almost there, Mary. You're doing very well."

"Get me out! It hurts. It hurts a lot!" She panted, the noise of the machine drowning out her thumping heartbeats.

"It's electromagnetism, silly. It's painless. You're over halfway through." Mary could see him in the halo mirror. He was still smiling at the nurse.

"GET ME OUT, NOW!" There was a low rumbling sound. The platform shook beneath her, as the magnets fell from their choreographed positions and clanged together in submission to gravity's pull at the base of the machine. An over powering smell of molten plastic caught in her throat, as the electronic panel cooked the circuit board inside. A wisp of smoke curled like tendrils towards the ceiling. The magnetic behemoth was finally dead. Her pain subsided but the panic remained. In the confined space, she grappled with the cage that still imprisoned her head, trying frantically to locate the securing clip, but only succeeding in dislodging the mirror. The lack of visibility, unnerved her all the more. She dug her heels into the thin platform cushion and tried to drag herself free but her knees grazed the top of the cylinder. Her feet slipped on the paper sheet. She heard the booth door open.

"What did you do? Have you any idea how much this machine cost?" Parth ran around to the control panel. A brown, foul stinking slurry dripped from the switches onto the floor. The nurse freed Mary from the jaws of the carcass.

"I'm just fine, thanks for asking." She sat on the edge of the platform tugging at her gown.

"Oh yes, sorry. Are you alright?" He strode back towards her, scooping her up in his arms.

Mary allowed him to embrace her, pat her back ineffectually and murmur his usual kind words. Her arms hung loose by her sides. She could sense his gaze fixating on the control panel of the machine and his heart quicken in his chest.

"We got one decent scan done before it, um… come, have a look." Parth ushered his wife into the booth. The nurse followed, until Mary threw her a venomous glare that induced an involuntary shudder. Blinking rapidly, the nurse said; "I'll just um…" and then she left via the heavy swing door.

They sat in front of the triple spread monitors. Parth wittered on for a while, pointing at various segments of the brain sections on the screen. "Remarkable. Look, darling. See how the pineal gland in this mid sagittal section is enlarged?"

"No."

"This bit here…" Parth pointed with a pen nib to a small pea-like structure in the very centre of the picture. “It’s quite large relative to your brain size. We also spotted from this image,” His biro wagged at the next screen, “that strangely, like Albert Einstein, you have a similar truncated Sylvian Fissure.” He offered her a goofy grin, turning his face to watch hers.

“Meaning what exactly?” Mary kept her focus on the screen, determined not to cave in to his antics.

“Well, that’s the million-dollar question, honey, and the start of some very exciting studies.”

Mary tipped her shoulders away from him and analysed his facial response. He was enjoying this a little too much. *If this is an example of his bedside manner, no wonder he didn’t go into General Practice.* “I’m glad my brain excites you. So, there are no tumours, growths, anything that could kill me?”

“Not that I can see, but you do have a very high concentration of gyri.” Parth pored over the images once again on the screen.

“Is that bad?” She had palpitations thrumming in her chest.

“Not at all. They are the folds on the brain surface. More gyri and more fissures, or grooves, means larger surface area – bit like a dolphin.” He traced the pen tip along a fissure across her brain, illustrating his point.

“Marvellous. First, I’m Einstein, now I’m an aquatic lifeform.” She stood up, allowing the back of her knees to skid her chair backwards, making a harsh grinding noise.

“Oh, don’t be like that, darling. This is wonderful news.” He dropped the pen and stood up next to her.

“I’ll take your word for it.” Mary could not warm to his elation, particularly if it meant more tests. She stooped to reach her satchel from the booth floor and went back into the MRI suite to retrieve her clothes. Parth trailed after her and watched while she finished buttoning up her blouse.

"Don't you want to stay and see the electrical activity in your brain? We can hook you up to…"

"Nope. I'm going home." She pushed past him and thumped the door to the waiting room open with a clenched fist.

"Take care on your bike, love. See you later." He yelled, but she was gone.

***

Outside the Biochemistry Building, Mary looked up at Cyril's office window, but saw no signs of life. She gave a fleeting thought to collecting her helmet from her locker then dismissed it. Unlocking her bicycle from the stands, she rode it at speed right through the campus, scattering students and lecturers and ignoring the shouts of "Oi! Pedestrians only," on her way towards the park. Suddenly ravenous, she stopped at the supermarket and bought a veggie wrap, a drink and some porridge oats for the ducks, before steering her push bike along the cycle paths of Victoria Park. It was exhilarating. The smell of freshly cut grass, mixed with a tinge of diesel fumes, the late blossom raining in drifts and obscuring her vision and the slightly elevated risk of falling without protective headgear. All the sights, sounds and smells pummelling her senses as she free wheeled through giant puddles with legs splayed, giggling like a child. Muddy water soaked her plimsolls and caked on her brake blocks, but what did that matter? She was not dying. Her brain might be a cross between a genius and an echo locating sea mammal, but she was alive, invigorated and feeling refreshed.

Mary was also famished. She found a bench by the duck pond and dismounted, leaning her bicycle up against the backrest. The falafel wrap hit the spot nicely. Throwing a handful of oats onto the water's surface, she sat back down to wait for the ducks to notice her presence. The sun was high overhead and the light rays converted the pond into shimmering glass. She looked about for a bench with shade, but they were all taken by the elderly or young mothers with infants in pushchairs.

I shouldn't have been so snappy with Parth. She thought. I'll cook him something nice to make up for it. He was only trying to help and I did break his scanner. Oh God. I broke his MRI machine. How the hell did I do that? Faulty wiring perhaps? And the biochem heat lamp, centrifuge and photocopier? Not likely. I bet Einstein didn't have this trouble, Flipper neither.

The ducks paid no attention to the oats. They made themselves busy gobbling up chunks of wet bread from a little boy and his grandfather on the opposite side of the pond. *They prefer to swallow duck junk-food to healthy oats. Hey duckies – they are feeding you empty calories, in the same way that Parth is feeding me palatable lies. I'll make Parth a nice veggie lasagne, garlic bread, candles the whole nine yards. Then I will steer the conversation round as to why he and Yelena are lying to me.* With her plan fermenting pleasantly, she put the oats back in her bicycle basket and rode off to the shops for groceries.

***

The salad dressing sat in the centre of the dining table, separating into two distinct liquids. The garlic bread balanced on a baking tray waiting to slide next to the ceramic dish of lasagne, bubbling away in the oven. White wicked candles perched in their best crystal candlesticks and Mary stood on top of a step stool on the landing, cleaning the light fittings of dust. The bedroom door was open. She could see the time display of the alarm clock on Parth's bedside table. *He'll be home soon. I just have time to look up Out of Body Experiences on his tablet before he arrives.*

Aristotle lay sprawled at the foot of their bed. She tickled him between the ears as she passed. Nearing the bedside cabinet, Mary realised the iPad was no longer there. Neither was it hiding in the drawers. *He must have moved it to his office while I was in the shower this morning.* A mild feeling of déjà vu hit her as she descended the stairs and breezed into Parth's man-cave. For the first time in their marriage, Mary felt like an intruder in her own home, sneaking around her husband's spaces uninvited.

That's peculiar. His laptop isn't here either. She tried the drawers in his desk - locked. Pulling the door of his office closed on her way out, she went back into the lounge diner and located Parth's laptop, sitting on the side unit behind the settee. Lifting the lid, she pressed the power button and waited for it to spring into life.

The clicking and grinding and flickering LEDs woke the machine. She waited patiently for it to sort itself out, poised and ready to click the familiar desktop internet icon. To her dismay, Mary discovered that her husband had password protected the laptop, denying her access to any of its files or software.

Chapter Four

Mary stood watching the cursor fade in and out on the screen. In seven years of marriage, she and Parth had shared everything; food, money, fears, hopes, dreams and desires, their bodies and even during desperate times when they had been travelling, their underwear. It seemed inconceivable that he would lie to her, let alone shut her out of parts of his life altogether. The cursor flashed inside the password box in time with the beat of her stinging heart.

"Hi, honey. What are you doing?" Parth had arrived quietly through the back door.

She stood for a moment, unable to articulate her feelings, slack jawed and on the edge of tears. She blinked them back. "I was going to look something up on your laptop but I'm locked out."

"Ah yes, sensitive case study for work, one of the classified ones, darling. I'll create your own profile on it, then you can have your own password if you like." His answer felt rehearsed. He had pre-empted her surprise. "What were you going to look up?"

Considering her response carefully, she replied; "I wanted to see if there were any examples of people having an effect on electrical equipment."

Parth rushed to her side, dropping his precious rucksack to the floor in a heap. His tone altered, no longer the jaunty banter of husband and wife, his voice hardened to stone. "Did you switch the webcam on?"

She spotted the tiny green light glowing above the screen. "How could I? I haven't got your password."

Parth slammed the lid closed. "Maybe it just needs charging up. I'll sort it out later." He gathered up the laptop and carried it into his office. She heard it creak as he dumped it on his desk. A discreet chime sounded from his mobile phone, notifying him of a caller. Mary moved closer to the partly open door to listen in.

"No – you can't…" Parth blustered. "I need more time. It's too soon, you have to give me more time." He hung up and ran his fingers through his silken hair, reappearing in the hallway, with an enforced smile.

"Who was on the phone?" She shuffled backwards in time with his advancing steps.

"It was Yelena, she wondered if you wanted to go shopping sometime this week for a new ball gown. I said we were about to eat and that you'd call her back later." They moved into the kitchen and he watched her put the garlic bread in the oven. She played along, waiting till after she had plied him with a glass or two of red wine before tackling him with more serious matters.

"What's wrong with my black dress?"

"Nothing, you look lovely in it, but wouldn't you like a new one for a change? You always wear that one. People will think it's the only one you have." He grabbed a bottle of Zinfandel and applied his nail to the foil covering the neck.

"It is the only one I have." Mary twisted the dial of the kitchen timer to ten minutes and rested her back against the worktop.

"Precisely. We need to impress the investors. Let Yelena help you pick out a nice new one, matching shoes and what nots too." He fiddled with corkscrew, the metal arms flailing in balletic dance, then plunged the sharp point into the bottle top.

Mary bit down on her lip. *Choose your fights, Mary. Stay calm.* She chanted inside her head. "How did the meeting with Yelena go this morning?"

"Good, thanks. We discussed what approach to take at the ball with the potential new investor. Game plan all in order, so to speak." The cork popped. Parth opened a wall cupboard and retrieved a wine glass.

"Uhuh." *They obviously think I am moronic, a docile moron. At least I can use that fact against them.* "I'm sorry about your MRI scanner today, I really can't explain what happened…"

"Let's not talk about that now." Parth interrupted. He decanted a full glass of wine, sniffed it and took a huge gulp down. "Can I pour you one, honey?"

"What's got into you? You know I haven't touched a drop of alcohol for over eight years."

"I know. But you seemed a bit tense and I thought one glass might help to relax you." He took another slug and collected his bag from where he had dropped it. Reaching inside, he pulled out a brown plastic bottle filled with tablets. "Here, I got you some multivitamin and minerals from the department. You have been looking quite tired lately, perhaps you need more iron in your diet."

She peered with suspicion at the bottle. “They’re unlabelled.” A week ago, she would not have noticed the container. Her trust in him had eroded of late, like the band of her wedding ring where it had jostled against the soft gold of his grandmother’s handed down diamonds. Steadfast bonds wearing thin with time.

“Yeah?” Parth shrugged.

Mary took the bottle from him and put them on the kitchen windowsill with her migraine medication. Parth kneaded a knuckle into his tear duct, and waited for the raw lids to open. Standing there with his head tilted to one side and his shoulders sagging as if he had come home from years in the trenches. She relented. “Thank you, Parth. That was very thoughtful of you.”

The timer dinged. He lit the candles and poured his wife some Elderflower cordial, refilling his wine glass at the same time, almost to the brim. Mary served their food. As she placed his plate before him, he caught her hand and gave it a squeeze.

“You and I are alright, aren’t we? Have I done something to upset you?” Those rich dark eyes and sweeping lashes met hers and disarmed her.

“No, Parth. Everything is fine.” How could she confront him? She had no solid evidence with which to accuse him of anything. He clung to her, searching for a sign of contentment. The moment was heavy with expectation. He wanted more from her, reciprocal affection or a declaration of feeling. Mary knew what he wanted to hear but her devotion had emaciated to loyalty. She broke the impasse. “Are you all set for our next study session tomorrow night? What will you have us doing?”

Parth sighed and released her hand. “Yes, it’s all prepared. You’ll find out tomorrow. Did you remember your grandfather’s birthday card?”

“Oh blimey, no. I must sort that and order him a hamper for delivery. Thanks for reminding me.”

There were a few minutes of hushed eating, Parth gulping his down, eager to finish. “Would you like some more garlic bread?”

“No, thank you, my love. That was delicious.” He pushed his cutlery together on the plate and dropped the napkin on top.

“You’re welcome.” She scraped the last few mouthfuls of food to one side with her knife and lay the fork down. “Parth, I really think we need to discuss what is happening to me…” There was a hiatus of activity. Their gazes met, hers earnest and imploring, his alarmed and distressed. A rabbit trapped in a snare. “Why do I keep blowing up electrical equipment?” The wire snare tightened around his neck. He spluttered, unable to prevent her from speaking.

“I need a long soak in the bath. You don’t mind do you, darling?” He drained the contents of his glass and held the arms of his chair, awaiting her response.

“You have just eaten a heavy meal.”

“A long shower then.” He rose and pushed his chair under the table. Parth pecked the top of her head as he passed and made his way up the stairs. Mary rushed after him, but he was taking two steps to her one and he left her lagging behind.

He tried to close the door but she caught up and entered the bathroom with him. “Why won’t you talk to me?”

"It's been a long day, that's all, love. You could join me?" He pulled his shirt off over his head without unfastening it and held her in his arms, kicking the door closed behind them. He slid his hand inside her blouse and trailed his fingertips up her spine, unclasping her bra before turning his attention to the buttons at the front.

"But I need to talk about it…"

Parth kissed her into a silent, willing submission.

***

Mary woke, before the alarm clock sounded, next to a snuffling cat. Parth had risen early and engrossed himself in secret activities in the den. After her failed attempts at discussion ended in shower sex, she decided to bide her time and give Parth some distance. She bathed, dressed and grabbed a muesli bar on her way to retrieve her bicycle from the garage.

It had rained overnight and the roads were slippery. A double decker bus made her heart race when it overtook her, almost skimming her back wheel. The driver indicated left, stopping immediately in front of her to let passengers disembark. She swerved, just in time to avoid collision. Making headway along the bus lane, the same driver repeated the same dangerous manoeuvre again. Incensed, she screeched her brakes to a halt and kicked out at the back of the bus. Steering around the vehicle once more, she drew level with the driver's open window.

"You arsehole! Are you trying to kill me?" She roared, clamping her grip around the brakes.

"Roads are for vehicles, darlin'. Use the cycle routes and get out of my way." He wore a supercilious grin and a dated moustache, flecked with nicotine.

"Arrogant wanker!" She screamed, leaning on the rounded corner panel of the bus. The driver chuckled, pulling the lever to close the doors and putting the coach in gear. Mary could feel the fury brewing in her chest, her breaths shortening across her teeth. Balancing stationary on her pedals she balled up a fist and smacked it on the side panel of the bus in temper.

"Bastard!" The engine, choked, chugged and ground to a stop, jerking the passengers forward in unison. As she rode away smiling to herself, she heard the driver turning the ignition over and over again, trying to coax it into action. "Hah. Mess with me and I will fry your electronics. There might be some benefits to this after all."

***

The Biochemistry department was already buzzing with activity when Mary arrived a full half hour before her scheduled time. Locking her satchel away and putting her lab coat on, she wandered through the first-floor main prep room to see what all the commotion was about. Cyril Plender was in his office with a group of post graduates. An assembly of technicians dawdled around the bench near to the window in Cyril's office door. The discussion looked intense, with Cyril wagging his finger and looking stern at the students, before dismissing them with a clipboard of notes between them.

"Just make sure you keep me informed, of everything. Every tiny iota of progress." He hitched up his trousers by the waistband and pulled his lab coat closed.

Cyril spotted Mary. She winced and tried to make a run for it, admonishing herself for getting caught up in events.

"Ah, Mary. I trust you are feeling better today? Feeling up to work I hope?" He fiddled with his ID badge, adjusting its position on his lapel.

"Yes, thank you. I am terribly sorry about what happened." She turned away, hoping that would be the conclusion to his discussion.

"Good, good. Let's not worry about that now, shall we? Anyway, new project, Mary. Lab Twenty-Six needs a full spring clean. The boys have a new brief and will be putting in their glassware requests by lunchtime today. Can you make it a priority, please? Anything they need as soon as humanly possible. Also, can you fast track an application for a class one drug licence? Need to order quite a bit, very quickly. I've already contacted the Site Managers Office to get someone over to fit additional security to the lab door. Perhaps you could assign one of your team to be their dedicated technician?" He smelled of a mixture of antiseptic cream and bacon. It was overpowering.

She took a step back, trying to keep her expression neutral. "Any particular class one drug, Cyril?" Mary removed a notebook and pencil from her top pocket and stood poised to make notes.

"Yes, Dimethyltriptamine." A streak of encrusted egg yolk bisected the lateral stripes of his tie. He scratched a nail against the stain and then licked his thumb, rubbing the saliva into the weave. Rocking on raised heels in the doorway of his office, he regarded Mary.

"You are cooking up the hallucinogen DMT?" Mary raised an eyebrow at him. She didn't want to openly accuse her boss of creating recreational drugs in a British university. The parallels with a particular fictional television series about a desperate chemistry teacher, were evident to both.

"The new project is classified, Mary, and sanctioned by the board. Need to know only. If you could start the paperwork now, please. Oh, and they'll need you to order some MAO inhibitors, just the A form should do." Cyril closed his door in her face and returned to his desk, picking up the land line telephone.

With junior technicians dispatched to Lab Twenty-Six to begin the clear up, Mary settled down at a computer terminal to process the application. *I'd better check the University database first. There might be another department with a licence we can piggyback on.* The technicians' bible, a secure internal internet where conversion tables, hazard warnings, generic labels, chemical dilutions and waste removal advice could be sought or posted for all support staff to use. It also housed the electronic paper trails required for hazardous substances and drugs. A quick search for DMT yielded two results, both of which cited the Director of Biomedical Sciences as the originator. She made a note for herself of the database entry references, knowing full well that she would have to liaise directly with the department licensee.

Mary tapped timidly on Cyril's door. He looked up, holding the telephone receiver away from his ear and beckoning her in with his free hand. She thrust her head forward, clinging to the doorframe.

"What is it?" He held his hand over the mouthpiece of the handset.

"The University already has a licence for DMT, Cyril, but it is registered to the Director of Biomedical. Doesn't give a specific department."

"Well, well. Is that so? Go and have a snoop over there. See if you can't get the senior tech to give you the lowdown - I want to know who is using the stuff. I don't care if you have to beg the old walrus himself, I want a name." He returned to his telephone call and shooed her out with the flick of his hand.

"Yes, your majesty, anything else, your majesty?" She muttered under her breath. Cyril looked up, thinning his eyes at her as she closed the door.

Armed with her notebook and pen, she wandered down the stairs, across the courtyard and down the pavement leading to Biomedical Sciences. One of the largest faculties in the college, the Director had oversight of all departments that fell loosely under the heading of medical. The faculty therefore spanned many different buildings within the campus, with the creation of new departments over time. Mary knew exactly where to go for answers.

Enjoying the brief emergence of the sun from behind the clouds, she took the scenic route to the office of Professor Florian Haas, otherwise known as The Walrus. She remembered striking up a conversation with a kindly woman at last year's ball, who had introduced herself as the long-suffering PA to Professor Haas. If anyone would be able to find out who had the DMT licence, it would be her. *Patricia, Phillis, Phoebe – damn. What was her name? I'm sure it began with a P. Come on…what was it?* She knocked gently and opened the door onto an anteroom with a tall woman sitting at a desk. She rose and greeted Mary with an outstretched hand.

"Lovely to see you again, Mary. What brings you down to this neck of the woods?"

"Lovely to see you too…um…" Mary glanced down and caught sight of a name plaque sitting on the desk. "Caroline, I love your hair, have you had it cut?" *I knew it began with a P. That was close.*

"Yes, kind of you to notice. How can I help you?" She preened the short locks beneath her ears, thrilled that someone had spotted the change.

"I was looking for details regarding a Class One drug licence that is tagged to the Wal… to Professor Haas. Cyril Plender has me chasing it down to speed up an order for one of his studies." Mary slipped around the side of Caroline's desk to gain a better view of her monitor.

"Let's see what we can find." Caroline clicked on a few files in a private directory on her computer and frowned. "That's peculiar."

"What is?"

"I can find the file reference number for the physical copy of the licence but the department name is redacted. I have never seen that done here before." She peered at the screen, dipping her bony chin to her neck.

"Are there any names given or department references visible?" Mary bent low and studied the image, then faced Caroline with a pitiable look.

"I'd have to dig out the hardcopy for those." Caroline considered Mary and instantly caved in. "Oh, okay." She sighed, then moved from her desk to a door on the left of the office. Mary trailed her into a small room filled with filing cabinets. “There’s a lot of sensitive stuff in here. I could get into serious trouble doing this.” Mary nodded and tried her best to look humble and appreciative.

The room had no windows and was lit with a single fluorescent tube light overhead, that flickered and made a disquieting humming noise. Caroline pulled a set of keys on a retractable cord from her belt loop and began unlocking a cabinet at the far end. She heaved each drawer open on their corroded tracks, reaching into the suspended files inside and reading the labelling in turn. It was a noisy affair, the drawers had a momentum all of their own, clanging shut after only a small push.

“It should be in this section here.” Caroline pulled out a faded red cardboard wallet file and opened it. Inside was an official looking stapled document, with the UK Government’s Home Office crest at the top. The application bore Professor Haas’s name, but the copious redaction obliterated the name of the department in a similar way to the electronic version of the license. Turning to the second sheet in the bundle, they scanned through paragraphs of legal blurb. Mary caught sight of two scraps of incomplete information; the study name - *Project Sleepwalk* and the university study site - *Zone Six*. A short list of staff responsible for the drugs used was completely blacked out.

“I’m sorry, Mary, it doesn’t really help you very much, does it?” Caroline chewed at her nails.

Mary stood, lost in thought. She knew exactly which department within the University called sections of their building Zones, but was unaware that there were as many as six. She rubbed her eyes as her recent nocturnal adventure united with the study name on the license – *Project Sleepwalk.* Acid gurgled in her throat, her stomach rebelling against her muesli bar. *Get a grip.* She chided herself. *It's only a controlled substance license, not an order to kill.* Mary took the papers from Caroline and flicked through to the last page. The signature was her next surprise.

"Is that usual, I mean, for the Home Office Secretary, now Prime Minister, to sign these personally?"

"Really? No, it isn't. Let me see." Angling the document to afford Caroline a clear view, they huddled together poring over the paperwork in the dusty cupboard.

"Caroline? Caroline! Where the blazes has she gone now?" The Walrus was huffing his exasperation in Caroline's office.

"In here, Professor Haas." She knew that concealment was useless. He bustled in, wheezing with every nasal breath.

"What are you doing in… ah, Mary. Hello, my dear. I see this is not a social visit, how may we help you?" Haas fondled his enormous moustache, drawing her attention to its waxed bristles. It resembled a small woodland creature sleeping beneath his nose that was still in the process of shedding its ermine coat.

"Cyril Plender sent me over to see if he can be added to an existing drug license."

"Huh, that deviant little weasel. You know he's after my job, don't you? No? Well, he is. Can't wait till I bloody well retire. He's been to the trustees and told them that I am too old to be effective in attracting new investors. Egotistical little tosser." Professor Florian Haas may have been born and raised in Austria, but his accent was pure Leicester, including his fondness for using locally derived expletives. "I think I cut rather a dashing figure on the dance floor, especially when my partner is as delicious as you, eh Mary? You'll save me another dance at the ball this year, won't you?" He licked around his dentures, making a repugnant slurping sound.

"Really, Professor," Caroline interjected. "It is wholly inappropriate to address female staff in that manner."

"Oh, give over. Mary doesn't bother with all that Political Correctness claptrap, do you Mary?" Another whisker fondle and a sly pace forwards.

"I…um…" Mary shrank back into the cabinets. Caroline stepped between them, shielding her from his advances.

"See, she's a bloody good sport. Now then, which license is that back-stabbing retard after?"

Caroline took the paperwork from Mary and handed them to Haas. He squinted and raised his nose to see through the magnifying part of his bifocal spectacles. The sub-heading *Project Sleepwalk* came sharply into focus.

"This could prove problematic…"

Chapter Five

It was five minutes to five when Mary removed her lab coat and collected her cycle helmet and bag from her locker. The Walrus had taken charge of her license dilemma and had agreed to 'thrash things out' with Professor Cyril Plender directly. With no small amount of relief, Mary scarpered from the Biomedical Sciences building and stayed well hidden from Plender's fury for the rest of the day. She nipped to the canteen and grabbed a bite to eat, then made her way at a leisurely pace to her husband's department.

The Neuroscience Department receptionist, Yosef, greeted Mary and began the process of issuing her pass card. "That herbal cream you gave me for my eczema has done wonders – look…" He showed her the back of his hand where the scarred, dry tissue showed signs of healing. "Thank you so much for helping me."

"That's wonderful, Yosef. I'm glad it did the trick." She took a cursory glance at his skin and nodded. "Are any of the others in the study group here yet?"

"Just one, Dan Wildman. He always gets here a few minutes early. It's the undergrad participants who are always late." Yosef printed the pass and handed it to Mary.

"Great, thanks. Can you buzz me through, please?"

"No problem."

Making her way through the security door into Zone One, Mary walked the length of the main corridor and swiped her access card at the Zone Two scanner. Just beyond, was a door to the main psychology testing suite. Inside, a postgraduate student was busy setting up the evening's experiments and switching the power on in the glass booths used to isolate candidates. A quick peek through the door informed her that Dan was elsewhere, so she turned right into the medical wing, where the nurse's staff room had been set out with refreshments.

"Ah, there you are. Hello." She edged into the room filled with stacks of junk mail and circulars that propped up angle poise lamps and chairs that doubled up as desks. Plastered across the fridge were magnets from past holiday resorts and a sign attached by curling yellow Sellotape that read – Not for clinical use, in bold typeface.

"Hello again. Would you like some tea? I have just boiled the kettle." Dan enquired, making himself at home. He held up a cup to inspect the cleanliness of its interior before plonking it down next to his coffee and grabbing a teabag.

"That would be lovely, yes please." Mary laid down her bag and cycle helmet on an angular chair and sat next to them. "Milk, no sugar, thanks."

Dan pressed the hot teabag against the side of her mug and propelled it into a waste bin. "So how are things with you, since our last cuppa together?" He twisted around to face her, wagging the spoon in her general direction.

"Oh, you know. So, so. How about you?" Mary sprawled in the seat, twirling a loose tendril of hair around her index finger.

"Same old, same old." They snorted an understanding. "Anymore disembodied voyages?" Dan opened the fridge and reached for the milk.

"No, thankfully, but weird things do keep happening every so often." She sat forward, resting her elbows on her knees.

"Weird things?" He dribbled the milk into her cup, returning his attention back to Mary.

"I'm not sure I know how to explain. I get myself in a tizzy about something and the next thing you know, all the electrics are going berserk all around me." She threw her arms in the air and twizzled her hands around like she was avoiding a swarm of wasps.

"Have you been watching *Poltergeist*?" He chuckled, returning the milk to the cooler.

"I'm serious, Dan, it's frightening." Mary found herself laughing too. He was so easy to talk to. He reminded her of an aged oak tree, blessed with boundless assurance awaiting clement weather for their relationship to bud. She felt like a sapling by comparison, windblown against rigid restraints at risk of reckless pruning that threatened to stunt her growth. Dan was a rare specimen. An attentive listener, never judgmental, he would allow her to ramble and flourish. Why couldn't it be this light hearted with Parth? He was too intense, in every aspect of their lives. Somehow Dan made her feel like no problem was insurmountable.

"Does your husband know about this?"

"He knows about my electrical problem. I tried to talk things over with him at home, but he wouldn't discuss it. Kept finding ways to shut me up. There is something fishy going on, but I can't get to the bottom of it. Oh, I don't know. Maybe I am just being paranoid." Dan passed the cup to Mary.

"Why do you think that? You seem perfectly normal to me." He retrieved his coffee and sipped while he listened.

"He gets suspicious phone calls at odd times, he has locked me out of his laptop and he went very peculiar when he thought the webcam in its lid was active."

"Sounds more like the guilty actions of a man having an affair." He blurted it out without thinking then immediately regretted it.

"An affair! Oh God, I hadn't even thought of that. That could be it. And might be the reason why he wouldn't let me wait in his department yesterday. It could be someone he works with." Mary's face crumpled. She spilled some of her tea onto her legs, brushing at the spots ineffectually.

"You don't know that though." Dan backtracked. "It could be that he is just under a lot of pressure at work. There could be any number of explanations." He looked at her strained features, his own mirroring hers.

A neat looking blonde woman walked in and smiled at Dan. She paced a direct path to the bench where the kettle stood and smiled at him again. Dan sat down, avoiding an expectation to cater for all arrivals. They watched the young lady shovel two heaped spoons full of instant coffee into a cup, estimate the temperature of water sitting in the kettle with a quick touch to the back of her hand and then slop the contents over the coffee powder. Dan looked at Mary and opened his mouth to continue their discussion, but an infinitesimal shake of

Mary's head stopped him in his tracks. The blonde youth stacked several biscuits together and took them and her cup over to the seats. She perched on the edge of the chair, with her knees angled towards Dan.

"I'm Sophie." She pouted, dipping her chin and peering up at him coyly. "Has anyone ever told you that you have the most amazing jawline?"

"Um, no." Dan's six foot two frame withered into the back of his chair, his grip tightening on the wooden armrests.

"Shall we partner up for the experiment, tonight? I think you and I would make a formidable team." Sophie blinked as slowly and seductively as she could muster.

"I'm sorry Sophie, Mary and I have already agreed to team up for the remainder of Dr Arora's project." He tilted his head towards his friend. Mary smirked, revelling in the student's arrogant but thwarted attempt.

Sophie shot Mary a haughty glare. "Your loss." And in one swift move, she rose and spun herself around, gliding from the room with her coffee and biscuit stack.

"Dear God. When did young women get to be so forward?" Dan spluttered. "You didn't mind me using you like that, did you?"

"Not in the slightest." Mary tittered. "You had a narrow escape there."

"Shall we go and see what tests we will be doing this evening?" Dan said, keen to distract her thoughts from her marriage. Together, they crossed the freshly bleached corridor and into the testing laboratory.

The other participants had gathered around a desk packed with monitors and controls. The postgraduate student explained that Dr Arora was running late. His instructions were to conduct a series of warm-up tests until the scheduled break after an hour. He handed out packs of twenty-five cards that each contained a mixture of five symbols; a circle, a square, a triangle, a star and two wavy lines like water. One person in a pairing would act as the sender of thoughts and the second person the receiver. For each signal, the sender records whether an incorrect or correct symbol is received on the provided grid. After fifteen minutes, the participants had to swap roles and repeat the test. It was one that they were all familiar with and so the six pairs of participants, entered the glass cubicles and began the simple experiment.

Dan wiped his hands down his trouser legs and stepped inside a booth. It smelled of the plasticised sealant securing the tempered glass between him and Mary sitting in the adjacent soundproof cubicle. The theme tune for an old TV game show popped into her head. She signed the thumbs up to begin. Dan chose a random card from his pack and concentrated on its shape, making sure that his expression was neutral and could not influence her decisions. Mary closed her eyes and thought for a moment, the wavy lines of the water symbol flashed up on the inside of her eyelids. She picked up the water card and showed it to Dan. He smiled and recorded her response on his grid – correct. They repeated the procedure until Dan had run out of cards and then they began again with Mary sending the messages for Dan to receive. They spilled out of the booths, giggling and laughing eager to learn the marks of their test. All the other cubicles were still occupied by participants. Less than ten minutes had passed.

The postgraduate student, Simon, beckoned them over to his control desk. He recorded their results in his computer and it churned out a statement that Mary was correct for ninety-two percent of her responses and Dan was correct for a staggering ninety-eight percent of his. Believing that a small degree of cheating could account for the accuracy, Simon set them another challenge. He gave Mary ten sealed envelopes containing cards with random pictures on. Simon handed Dan, a pad of plain paper and a pencil and sent them both back into the booths.

Mary opened the first envelop. On the printed card was a line drawing of a guitar. She concentrated on the picture, her eyes wandering across the shape over and over until it etched clearly in her mind's eye. Through the window, her peripheral vision detected Dan's hand moving rapidly. She fought the temptation to look up at what he was drawing. Simon, moved from his desk to watch them, convinced that there had to be some underhanded trick. He saw Dan sketch a small circle, then an overlapping larger circle beneath. He scowled at the paper as he drew a thin rectangle through both circles and above the top of the smaller one. Scratching his head, the object became clear to him and so he filled in the details of the guitar. When the drawing was complete, he signed the thumbs up to Mary and they both held the paper and card aloft for all to see. Simon gasped. The next few cards were easier. Dan drew a flower, a banana, a cat and a key. They were not precise or accurate drawings, but they were easily recognised and all correct.

Excited and amazed, Mary and Dan tittered and snorted their way through nine correct drawings when Parth arrived in the testing suite. By now, the other participants had completed their warm up card tests and were crowding around Simon, watching Dan and Mary like a freak show.

"It's their final card," sneered Sophie. "I hope he gets it wrong." She flicked her long hair over her shoulder and into Simon's face.

"He's nine out of ten so far." Simon informed Parth, as he pushed his way to the front of the spectators.

Ripping open the last envelope, Mary stared at the shape printed on the card inside. Within a second, Dan had the object in his mind and sketched it in one single stroke - a large heart in the centre of his paper. He grinned and held it aloft. Mary held up a printed stylised heart shape on her card. Everyone except for Sophie and Parth applauded, astounded by their mind reading abilities.

"I really think we should get neural output readings of these two while they repeat the test, fresh images and everything." Simon enthused. Parth did not answer. He watched his wife leave her booth, hurry to the cubical next to her and throw her arms about the tall man inside, sniggering and bouncing around like a school girl.

"That was amazing, Dan, you are brilliant." Mary said, finally letting go of his neck.

"It took both of us you know, I can't take all the credit." He patted her back and followed her out of his booth.

"Parth, did you see us? Did you see what Dan can do? Isn't it wonderful?"

"Yes, I saw everything." Parth replied, with much less enthusiasm. "Sorry I am late, ladies and gentlemen, an unavoidable delay I'm afraid. Why don't you all nip to the staff room and have a short break while we set up the next experiment? Let's say... fifteen minutes?"

Simon wittered on about incredible results from their tests and how they should be recording the neurological processes of the paired activities, but Parth was not listening. He waited until the group had filtered into the nurse's quarters and were chatting animatedly, then he positioned himself near to the door so that he could observe his wife undetected. Mary made herself another cup of tea and sat beside Dan, who looked utterly enchanted by her unfettered zeal. Wandering back to the testing suite, Parth gave Simon new instructions for the remainder of the session, and waited for the group to reassemble.

Mary and Dan listened to the praise from the other participants and then returned to their own secluded conversation, describing the sensations they felt when the images formed in their minds. The euphoria waned and gave way to a more biological urgency, with Dan asking Mary the location of the nearest cloakroom.

"Oh, I could use the bathroom too. I know there are some by the main entrance, but we wouldn't have time to get there and use it. There must be one around here somewhere. This is the medical wing after all." She looked about her for possible clues to public facilities.

Dan trailed after Mary out of the nurse's room and down the corridor towards the rear of the building. Turning left, they came upon a set of double doors. Mary stood on tip toe, peering through the glass. She could see the foot of a staircase, a short corridor and a second set of security doors.

Dan stared over her shoulder. "There's a toilets sign through those doors on the far side. Try your access card."

She swiped the barcode of the pass card through the scanner; a red LED flashed up, denying her entry. Grabbing Dan's card, which hung from a fabric lanyard around his narrow neck, she compared his with hers. Both read Zones One and Two. Dan tried his anyway, "Just in case. You never know." The red light appeared once more. Taking the hint, he shuffled off in the direction they had come from. Mary cocked her head to one side, squinting at a sign above an entrance near the staircase. The angle was too acute to make any sense of it. Dan's voice was deep and forbidding. "Mary? What are you thinking of doing?" He spun back round, having read her thoughts. "Even if you could fry the circuits in the scanner, it would alert security."

"How did you…? Wow, we really are in tune, aren't we? If we get caught, I'll say it was an accident. I'm just not sure how to make it happen. It usually takes me by surprise."

Bemused, Dan stood by and watched as Mary placed both palms squarely on the scanning device. She closed her eyes and imagined energy flowing from her to the panel. Nothing happened. Dan chuckled. "Come on, let's go back."

"No. I can do this." Gritting her teeth, she adjusted her grip.

"There are bound to be loos elsewhere." He let his arms swing, meandering back the way they had walked. "Come on…"

"Wait… I can do this." She felt a challenge was being set, a thread of disbelief detected in his tone. *He thinks I'm making all this up.* "I'm not mad, I promise you."

"I believe you. Come on." His speech altered again. Now it was soft, an intonation reserved for confused old ladies in care homes. Mary felt her temper mounting. She was accustomed to her husband patronising her. She couldn't bear it from Dan too. Distilling her indignation into a pure fluid force, she directed it through her hand into the access panel. There was a loud pop, a fizzle and a thunk, as the door catch released.

"See, I told you I could do it."

"Bugger me – You really did! You are going to get us into so much trouble." He pushed her through and closed the door behind them. They rushed past the staircase and opened the second set of doors, keeping a watchful eye for any evening security teams. "Here, grab that fire extinguisher to prop the door open. I don't want you to break anything else with your laser vision or whatever else you can do."

"Just a minute…" Mary stopped in front of a cardboard sign, tacked on the skew above the entrance she had spied earlier. In marker pen, someone had scrawled "THE CRYPT" on the corrugated board, concealing the official insignia.

There was an additional sheet of frosting on the reinforced glass panel of the door. It obscured all but the edges from sight. Peeping through the slim gap, Mary recognised a wall mounted collection of trip switches, power circuits and gas connections familiar to any well-equipped laboratory.

"Must be more labs down there." Mary remarked, catching up with Dan in the doorway.

Something was nagging at her; the bat of bad omen taking flight during her waking hours, goading her to release it from its underground cave. Something incongruous about the makeshift sign, amongst all the high tech gleaming white sterility, spurred her curiosity. Something was forcing her to investigate, the growing sense of foreboding sneaking into her mind. "Dan, can you pull that sign down for me, please? I can't reach it."

A tired request, perpetually made of the lofty, his response was one of instinct. Reaching up, he dislodged the cardboard and handed it to Mary. They scrutinised the printed label hidden beneath.

ZONE SIX – SACMILL

"Mary? What are you doing down here? This is a classified area. How on Earth did you get past security?" Parth was standing behind them, hands on hips, incensed.

Mary slid the card behind her back. Dan quickly mastered the situation. "We were trying to find some toilets and saw the signs through the windows."

"The toilets are behind the nurse's staff room. You had no need to come poking around in this Zone."

Parth herded them out of the corridor and back into Zone Two, examining the charred remains of the security scanner as he passed. She could sense his fury, as he marched into the nurse's quarters.

"The toilets are that way and to the left. I'd like everybody to return to the testing suite in five minutes – please."

In the Ladies' Restroom, Mary took the opportunity to collect her thoughts. Having thrown 'The Crypt' sign in the waste bin, she sat clumsily onto the toilet, rubbing her face in her hands. *Well at least it's definite now. Parth's classified studies involve the use of hallucinatory drugs in a basement. So, his big secret is Project Sleepwalk, is it? What the hell is SACMILL?*

Inside the lavatory cubicle, Mary listened to the sound of depressed taps and water gushing out. A metallic handbag zip fizzed and the unmistakable hollow popping noise of an unsheathed lipstick.

"Don't you think Dr Arora is well fit?" Sophie proclaimed. The taps squeaked again. Paper towels rustled from the metal dispenser.

"S'pose. Not really my type." Her friend replied.

"What does he see in that dowdy old wife of his? Do you think she even brushes that mop of hers? Bet she hasn't shaved her legs all summer." The lipstick clicked shut.

"Huh, yeah. Probably. I like that bloke she's partnering though, Dan, is it? I reckon his shoe size is a promise of things to come" there followed shuffling boots on granular flooring and a giggle.

"Wasting your time there. I think he's gay." The door creaked open.

"Pity."

Mary waited until she heard them leave before flushing the loo and venturing out to wash her hands. She stared at her features in the mirror. The blue capillaries visible through the rice paper skin under her eyes, the scattered white hairs highlighting the contrast of her dark curls. Her hands ravaged by the spilled chemicals and multiple handwashing throughout an average workday. *Well Sophie, I can't argue with you there – dowdy is an understatement. I look old, I feel older. Maybe I should let Yelena take me for a makeover. Can't go to a ball looking like a sea hag in my one and only black dress – no, that won't do at all, would it Parth? Perhaps he'd prefer to go with one of his nurses, or Sophie or whomever he is having his affair with.* She threw a scrunched up paper towel in the swing bin and returned to the testing suite.

Mary was last to arrive back at the psychology suite. Simon was orchestrating the test that she and Dan had conducted prior to the break, with the remaining participants. Dan was standing with Parth. They both wore serious expressions and the light-hearted giddy atmosphere had long since evaporated. Parth handed Mary a two-way radio and sent her out of the Neurosciences building.

Grumbling to herself in the twilight, she wandered down steps, across grass patches and jumped over raised flower beds until she was at the opposite side of the campus. Some of the street lights carried cost cutting motion detectors, restricting illumination to paths that were in constant use. A delay between detecting movement and switching on the light left Mary in darkness for some of the alleyways between buildings. At this time of the year, few students remained on campus beyond five in the afternoon. Amid the dank isolation, she could hear leaden footsteps echoing behind her. They fell out of sync with hers, a man's stride.

The only buildings she could access without security hassles, was the Student Union bar or the Library. She chose the library and pushed her way past the turnstile into the main foyer of the seven storey structure. *Random, he said.* She walked into the lift and chose the sixth floor. *Random, pick something at random. Phew it stinks in here. A whole day of smelly, sweaty students enclosed in a metal cube. They should be automatically sprayed with deodorant before gaining entry to the lifts.*

"Mary? What are you doing?" It was Parth's crackly voice on the radio. She pushed the button on the side of her walkie-talkie to reply.

"What do you mean? I'm finding something random like you told me." She breathed in through her mouth to mitigate the smell.

"You are making Dan laugh. What are you up to?"

"Oh, um…nothing. Nearly there, won't be a tick."

On the sixth floor, she wandered into the shadowy isles. It was not a floor she had ever visited. The seventh floor housed science related books. The body odour gave way to a musty smell of hardback books. Volume after volume of enormous texts, encyclopaedias and periodicals. The age of the tomes, set the atmosphere to sombre.

Mary felt uncomfortable. From the silence, she surmised that she was all alone amongst the texts on architecture. There were no other noises apart from the mechanical workings of the elevator, grinding and halting in a repetitive and predictable way, and her own muffled footsteps on the worn carpet. Her scalp tingled and the hair on the nape of her neck bristled, making her shudder. Was someone watching her? She lowered her head, squinting between the shelves in the dimly lit racks, but all she could see was the dusty ridges of hardback books. Picking out a large tome with a navy blue cover, she flicked through the pages until something caught her eye, a black and white print of London's Tower Bridge. She clicked her walkie-talkie button.

"Ready."

"Okay, concentrate, Mary. We'll let you know when to come back."

Mary sighed and stared at the image of the bridge. The photograph was old, faded around the edges and the cars looked like something her Grandfather would have driven in his heyday. *Don't think of Grampy - that will confuse things. Think, Tower Bridge.* She closed her eyes, concentrating on the image to send to Dan. She shivered, opening her eyes again and checking around her for onlookers. *Maybe I could just take the book out and go somewhere more public, less eerie.* A waft of strong aftershave hit her sinuses, the kind that required moderate use or not at all. She could taste the chemicals in the air. *There is someone here.* She was just about to quit the experiment altogether when the radio crackled into life.

"Okay, honey. You can come back now."

About bloody time too. Returning the book, Mary rushed to the lift and hit the 'down' button several times in rapid succession. Fidgeting and biting the edge of her fingernail, she hopped from one foot to the other, waiting for the elevator to announce its arrival with a ding. She threw herself in the moment the doors started to open, scraping her arms on the retractable seals. Hitting the ground floor command, Mary pressed her back against the dirty walls, begging the lift to speed up.

There he was. A thick thatch of grey hair and green, almost feline eyes, smiling at her between the narrowing gap of the lift doors. Wide eyed, terror rising in her chest and panting hard, she was dizzy by the time she reached the lobby. Bolting as fast as her canvas shoes could carry her, she dropped her radio on exit through the turnstile making her scrabble around on the floor trying to grasp hold of it. Clearing the library building she ran and kept running all the way back to the relative safety of the Neurosciences building. Wrenching open the main doors, she ducked into the Ladies' Cloakroom and just made it to a cubicle before retching and vomiting her panic into a porcelain receptacle.

Chapter Six

"No need to be nervous, honey, you look terrific. Told you Yelena was the woman to spruce you up." Parth kissed the end of Mary's nose, scanning the foyer for investors worthy of approach. "Oh, here…you forgot to take your vitamins."

Mary grappled with the midnight blue fabric of her gown, yanking the bodice higher to better secure her bosoms. "You brought my vitamins to a ball?"

He handed her the brown unmarked bottle from the pocket of his Dinner Jacket.

"Well, I'm not going to take them now, am I? Put them away. Oh there's Dan."

Mary waved, inelegantly. Parth glued himself to her side as Dan piloted his slender Parisian girlfriend over to meet them. He bowed low to kiss Mary's cheek and offered his hand to her husband. Parth eyeballed the tall man, constricting Dan's fingers in an enduring warning.

"Mary, Parth, I'd like you to meet Constance Cadot. She's a freelance journalist. Connie, this is Doctor Parth and Mary Arora, I met them through the study I told you about." Limp handshakes all round.

"Your dress is stunning, Constance, is it from Paris?" Mary examined the blushed silk. It slipped and caressed her form when she moved, a living lamina, accentuating Connie's understated grace in a symbiosis of beauty.

"How kind. Yes, it is. Your gown is very nice too." Constance paused, allowing the men time to deduce the disparity between Mary and herself. "Tell me, Parth, what are your views on vivisection?"

Disarmed, Parth coughed. Dan's face coloured.

"Really Connie, you can't go ambushing a man like that." Dan berated.

"Are you interviewing me?" Parth said, regaining his composure and switching to a charm offensive. "Surely there are much bigger fish here for you to fry?" Constance looked perplexed, taking time to process the meaning of the English expression. "Won't you allow me to introduce you to some very big fish indeed?" Parth took Constance's arm and led her into the main hall, deflecting her attention on to Professor Cyril Plender and his wife, Yelena, who had already dispatched several glasses of champagne and a couple of neat vodkas.

Mary took her shawl to the coat check and allowed Dan to escort her into the ball on his arm. "This is going to be a lonnnng evening." She said, trying hard to walk with poise on her new strappy heels.

"Uh-uh, but at least we can keep each other company. Are you feeling better today? You looked positively grim after that daft experiment we tried the other night. Parth whisked you away before I could ask if you were okay."

"Yes, thank you, much better. I'm sorry about that. I got spooked by something, that's all."

A waiter floated around them with long glasses of bubbled and still liquids on a silver platter. They both took the soft drink option. “I don’t drink alcohol.” She said, sipping the berry cordial.

“Driving.” He replied, in answer to an unspoken question.

“I never thought to ask. What did you draw that night?” She swept a lacquered tendril behind her ear with a gloved hand. It sprang back onto her cheek.

“It was a sort of chunky looking old bridge. I tried to draw it but it didn’t come out quite as I saw it. Was I right? What was it that you picked?” He ruffled the edge of his jacket up and sunk his hand in his trouser pocket.

“Tower Bridge.”

“No way. You’re kidding…Tower Bridge?”

“I know. You have a rare gift, Dan.”

Dan snorted into the fruity concoction. Sticking out a finger from the glass edge, he said; “I looked up that sign. The one beneath the cardboard about The Crypt…”

“Oh good. What did it mean…*SACMILL*, wasn’t it?” She pulled at the bodice of her dress again.

“Uh-uh. It stands for Scientific Advisory Committee on the Medical Implications of Less Lethal Weapons. It’s an MOD funded body.”

“Ministry of Defence? That must be why Parth is so cagey about some of his studies.”

“Indeed. What is your husband cooking up for the government in his basement, Mary?”

She tried to fully inflate her lungs but found her chest restricted by the tight bodice of the dress. “I shudder to think.”

At the front of the hall, musicians filed in through a stage door and mounted the band stand. Their instruments reflecting the polished smiles and Art Deco stripe of their jackets. Piped background music ceased as the band took up their positions and started to play. A trio of trumpets blasted short notes to begin an agile number, summoning the smokers from the botanical gardens and coughing onto the dance floor.

"A jazz band? That's unusual at these kinds of affairs." Dan remarked, pleased at the change from 1940's swing.

"That'll be Yelena's doing. She organises these dos." Mary balanced on tiptoe at his shoulder, straining to make herself heard.

"Who is Yelena?" He yelled back, craning his neck down to her ear.

"That's her, over there. That's odd…" Mary pointed out her friend, who had extricated herself from the conversation with Constance and her husband, Cyril, and was talking intimately with a man that Mary recognised.

"What's odd?" Dan was gazing in the general direction of Mary's outstretched finger.

"That man, I've seen him before. He was in the canteen when we had tea together the other day. He barged right past me." The balls of her feet burned with the renewed pressure from tipping forward from her heels, and her throat was dry and croaky. She sipped at her squash. Dan dipped to her ear once more.

"I saw him too. In fact, I've seen him around a lot, recently. He's got…"

"A finger missing."

"Yes, just like…"

"Terry Nutkin..."

"From the Really Wild Show!" They erupted in laughter. The musicians bowed to grateful applause and shuffled the sheet music to a more sedate rendition. Now swathed in a tolerable volume, they sauntered to the buffet table and picked.

"I loved that programme as a child. Poor Terry, losing his finger to..."

"An otter. Except it was a finger and a half." Dan corrected, choosing an enormous curled prawn that garnished a bowl of gloopy pink sludge and holding it high.

"Was it really? Oh, I didn't know that. I wonder how that man lost his?" Wrinkling her nose up at the smelly chicken satay sticks and pausing over the spring rolls.

"You could ask her. She seems to be heading this way."

A vision in sage green, Yelena glided across the dance floor on her golden stilettoes. Five hundred hateful, lustful and admirable desires, projected on her as she undulated passed. She commanded attention. Her obvious lack of underwear sent the older professors into paroxysms. Some reached for angina pills, others cleaned their varifocal lenses for a clearer view.

"What are you and your handsome friend finding so amusing, Mary?" Yelena overtly scrutinised Dan, taking in his entire height in one toe to head sweep.

"We were wondering, rather unkindly I suppose, how that man you were talking to, lost his finger." Mary considered what to do with the spring roll. A bite would hinder speech and now that she had touched it, returning it to the serving platter was no longer an option.

"Ah yes, him. That is Flynn, my lover."

Trying not to look shocked, Mary couldn't stop herself from inquiring further. "Does Cyril know?"

Yelena shrugged. "Who cares? Flynn is very pleasing to me." She looked up at Dan, with a forced expression of interest.

Mary took the cue, resting the Chinese roll on a napkin and wiping her hand on her midnight blue hip. "Sorry…Yelena, this is Dan, Dan – Yelena."

"Pleased to meet you." Dan chanted, dutifully. She nodded.

"Don't you think Mary has washed up wonderfully tonight? It is my doing, you know. She would be happy in a sack if you let her." Yelena scooped up a glass of bubbly from a passing waiter and chugged a third of the liquid down.

"Mary always looks lovely. She doesn't need fancy clothes to be radiant." The sincerity incapacitated Mary. Her ivory skin bloomed with embarrassment. "I should probably go and rescue that chap from Connie's interrogations." Dan returned his half empty glass to the table and unbuttoned his dinner jacket.

Constance was holding court with Professor Cyril Plender. In her black suede heels, she was a good three inches taller than him, angling her eyes away from the glare of his bald pate. Cyril fondled his goatee, a compliant puppy, eager for praise.

"I'd say that Connie needs rescuing from my husband, but she is doing a fine job keeping him out of my way." Yelena said, slipping deeper into her St. Petersburg drawl.

Parth reappeared, insisting on taking Mary for a dance and ignoring her protestations. Burying her face in his shoulder, she allowed him to waltz her around the empty parquet floor. Dan sensed her discomfort and politely asked Yelena if she wanted to join them. More couples found their confidence, much to Mary's relief, until the polished floor was a tangle of taffeta in sweet wrapper colours.

"You are so quiet today, is anything wrong?" Parth dropped his head towards hers and slipped his hand lightly beneath her chin, raising it to meet his gaze.

"I'm fine. Just have a lot on my mind." She tried to lower her face but his soft fingers against her jaw prevented it.

"Tell me." This was the Parth she had fallen in love with - the Parth that wanted to understand her, to sink into the abyssal depths of her soul and memorise every event that had shaped her. He moved his free hand to the small of her back where the low cut of her gown exposed warm skin. His irises had tiny beguiling flecks of amber running through the chestnut brown. He locked them on hers. "Tell me." Summer heat and mild exertions released his pheromones, combining them with his aftershave into a heady mixture that tugged at her resolve. He traced little circles on her spine with his thumb, sending a ripple of desire through her core. "Tell me."

A dozen or more questions flooded her mind. *Where do I start? How can I express feelings and hunches, all the doubts and fears that have plagued me for the past few weeks? How can I sound sensible and coherent with no proof supporting my accusations? How can I ask about projects that I know are secret, even from me? Why wouldn't you talk to me in the safety and privacy of our home, where I can cry freely?* She inhaled slowly and framed the one question that mattered the most.

"Do you still love me?" Her bottom lip trembled, waiting for his reaction. Astonishment shook him from their intimacy.

"How can you even think otherwise? Of course I do. I have been a bit neglectful of late, and I'm sorry for that, but you know how it's been with work, honey." He loosened his grip as she pulled her body further from his.

"So, you're not having an affair?"

"An affair? Where would I even find the time for one? Is that what all this silence and stomping around has been about? You think I could have eyes for anyone but you? After everything we have been through together, you are still the most interesting person on the planet to me." The highest compliment a scientist could pay to their partner. She couldn't help but smile. "How about we go for a picnic in the park on Saturday, just like we used to and you can tell me everything that has been bothering you." Mary liked the idea and nodded.

Parth picked up the speed, using the music to rock her in his arms. He rested his chin against her temple, catching sight of Yelena leading Dan a few feet away.

"I have decided to move Dan to another study group for the rest of the project."

Mary pushed him from her, stopping in the middle of the dance floor. "Why? What for?"

"Shush." He pulled her in again and swayed to the popular tune. "I think he is a suitable candidate for my augmentation group."

"Augmentation? You mean drug trial? You are going to pump him full of drugs? You can't. I'll tell him to drop out. Why would you do such a thing, when he and I were making such enormous progress?"

"Well that's just it. He has been a negative influence on you. Encouraging you to snoop around classified areas of the department, damaging equipment in the process, I might add."

Mary thrust her hands against his chest, forcing him to let his arms drop from her back. "We told you, we were looking for the toilets. I mean it Parth, you leave him alone, or I will tell him to ditch your project altogether." *Why did he have to spoil it? We were just getting along nicely and he ruins the moment.* "I need to powder my nose." She left Parth standing amongst the revellers dumbfounded.

Weaving between the crowds, she passed Cyril Plender and Connie, who were greeting a larger gentleman with tufted grey hair. Hurrying past, Mary glanced back at him, those distinctive green eyes, and the nauseating aftershave lingering in her lungs, that bullish neck supporting wide jowls. She stopped breathing. *Get a grip, Mary. Stop being so jumpy the whole time.* She chastised herself. Within seconds, Dan was at her side.

"Is everything okay? I felt...you felt, something told me to make sure you were alright." He flustered, moving his hands to his pockets and back out again. He then adjusted his bow tie, aware of his over-reaction.

"Have you ever met anyone that gives you the willies? You know, sends a chill right through you, but you don't know why?" She toyed with her wedding ring, turning it around her finger and slipping it over her knuckle.

"Yelena introduced me to her husband, Cyril, on our spin around the dancefloor. He creeped me out, if that's what you mean?"

"Ha-ha! Kinda. He's my boss. You get used to him."

"Poor you."

"That man with Cyril and Connie. He frightened me to death in the deserted University library the other night – when we were doing that experiment. He seems to pop up when I least expect it and there is something not right about him." She gave Dan a look, one that seemed to convey an expectation of trouble.

"I'll retrieve Connie and grill her for what she knows. Just need a Walther PPK and an Aston Martin and I could be the next James Bond." They tittered. He had such a way of lightening the mood. She felt better knowing that he was near.

Mary watched Dan saunter over to the group, make polite apologies and guide his girlfriend towards the dance floor. The grey haired man called after her, waving his business card and telling her to get in touch. Connie took it, securing it in her clutch bag for safe keeping. As soon as she had turned her back, Mary noticed him slip something small and silver coloured into Cyril's hand. She watched her boss tuck the object nervously into his jacket pocket, then take a large guzzle of fizz as if he needed fortifying.

A pit stop in the Ladies' Powder Room and Mary reappeared in search of her tall conspirator. The Walrus was bearing down on her, all breath and hairs. She glanced beyond his frame, seeking her gallant knight. Dan whirled Connie around like she was made from tissue paper and Parth was in the throes of investor negotiations. There was no escape.

"You look devastatingly beautiful tonight, my dear. Ready for our dance?" Professor Florian Haas slurred. There were dewdrops of scotch embedded in his whiskers that transferred to her hand as he kissed it. She forced a smile, but her knotted brow proclaimed her distaste. "New dress, new hairdo, new shoes, you're like a debutant – ravishing. Parth doesn't appreciate you, my dear, and what you are doing working for that biochemical pond scum is beyond me. You should defect. Come over to Biomedical. I looked up your particulars. Why are you wasting your talents being a technician? You have a first from Cambridge, no less, and in biology too." He twirled her under his outstretched arm and used the moment apart to obtain a tighter grip on her waist as her pulled her close.

"Yes. It's where Parth and I met. He was just completing his PhD when I was an undergrad." She arched her spine, thrusting her head and pelvis away from his body.

"Hmm, yes, lucky chap. But why come here to be a technician? Why did you stop studying?"

"It's a long story, Professor Haas."

"Florian, my dear. Call me Florian, or Florrie if it pleases you?" He flicked his bushy brows.

Mary ignored the invitation. Not content with her answer, he waited, swaying her from side to side, allowing him to look into her doleful eyes.

"Parth and I travelled after I graduated. It was his way of helping me through a very difficult time. He was offered a research position here shortly after we got back. I followed." Mary straightened her back, her jaw rigid.

In her mind, she imagined the bricks of a turret surrounding her. Turning from his gape, she built herself a drawbridge and raised it, barring him entry. Haas took the hint. Do not delve any further. Marauders are not welcome.

"Consider this, my dear. I have a couple of funded PhD studies in the faculty that might interest you. Give me the nod and I could negotiate a release from your contract with that aberrant social climber you call a boss, and Bob or rather Florrie's your uncle. What do you say?"

Despite her revulsion at the thought of swapping one odious boss for another, she tingled with excitement. Parth had taken a whole year of his life and devoted it to stabilising Mary's fragile state following a deeply emotional event. The least she could do was to repay his kindness and resign herself to routine in favour of her husband's accomplishments. No one had identified her potential in many years. The compliment was exhilarating.

"I would have to discuss it with Parth, but I thank you for your kind offer, Professor Haas."

Encouraged by her response, Haas spun her around and dipped her over his arm, making Mary squeal in alarm. He looped his arm above her head, whirling her like a spinning top. Mary winced at the bitter scent of smoker's breath as Haas wheezed with his exertions. Haas trotted her across the ballroom, close to a group of bemused onlookers. Cyril Plender moved towards them, touching his hand to the Walrus's back.

"Ouch! Static shock." Professor Haas jumped back, releasing Mary from his grip.

"May I cut in?" Plender smiled at Mary, a disturbing smile that displayed too many teeth. He reached in his inside jacket pocket. The fabric dropped a fraction, bearing the weight of something deposited. He reached for Mary's hand. "Shall we?"

"Wait, something is wrong…" Mary watched Professor Haas, grasp his left arm and then clutch at his dress shirt across his chest. His face reddened, veins bulged at his temples and he was panting hard. "Professor?" Mary slipped around Plender just as Haas lost consciousness and collapsed on the floor. "Somebody call an ambulance - quick!"

Mary knelt at Haas's side, trying to find a pulse in his neck. "Cyril, find Parth. NOW!" She shouted. The Jazz band stopped playing, alerting everyone present to the situation. Parth made his way through the gathering crowd, as a few fumbled with their smartphones dialling emergency services.

"There's no pulse. We were dancing too vigorously." Mary informed him. Fear crept into her lungs and compressed them into ragged sobs.

Parth began CPR, counting his chest compressions in a rhythmic whisper and stopping to administer the breath of life. On the fourth round of exhalations, Parth asked aloud if the hall had a defibrillator. Two waiters dashed out of the room to locate one hanging in the first aid unit near the main entrance. On their return, Mary took over the compressions while Parth unpacked the machine and unwound the cables connected to the paddles. To his astonishment, he found the wires severed. Holding the inoperable paddles mid-air, he stared at the waiters for an explanation.

"The hall suffered some vandalism a couple of nights ago, sir. No one thought to check the first aid cabinet for damage." One of the young gentlemen said, by way of an apology.

Mary checked again for a pulse in Haas's neck. "I can't get him back. I've killed him. I can't get him back…" She wept hysterically and pounded on his chest. He may not have been the most likeable colleague in the University, but the thought of him dying was too much for her to contemplate.

She closed her eyes, felt her arms stiffen and upper body tense, leaning both hands down on Haas's ribcage. A surge of extraordinary power rushed through her, electrifying every nerve in his body and sending his torso skyward in a giant arc from the floor. As he crash landed, sending his legs skating across the slippery floor, Haas took a massive gasp of air.

Chapter Seven

"Congratulate me, Mary. You are looking at the new Director of Biomedical Sciences...well, Acting Director, until the whole Haas situation gets sorted." Professor Cyril Plender puffed out his chest and tucked his gold tipped, vintage fountain pen in the top pocket of a new white lab coat.

"You mean until the poor chap has fully recovered and has decided whether to fight the trustees plans to retire him?" She opened her locker and let the door swing, clattering her distaste against the adjoining compartment.

"Well, yes. Of course, it's a shame for the old boy, but retirement is his best option now." He tried hard to look concerned but failed. "Can you take what's-her-name...um... the one you designated as dedicated technician to the boys in Lab Twenty-Six...?" He angled his face to one side, inquisitorial eyebrows lifted and demanding an answer.

"Jill." Mary snarled, turning her attention to the contents of her satchel.

"Yes, that's the one. Can you take Jill through the controlled substance protocols? She will be handling all of their requirements from now on." Plender examined his fingernails, then picked at a loose flap of skin with his teeth.

"Which budget will she be using?" Mary stopped buckling her bag and snapped a scowl across his pudgy face. Up until then, he was oblivious to her malcontent.

"I've assigned them a separate account. You won't have any involvement in that Lab at all now, only...um...Jill." He took a pace backwards, smoothing his lab coat and unconsciously fiddling with his pocket pens.

"You've promoted her?" She could feel her fists tightening, hot acid swelling in her gut.

"Let's just say that she will be directly under my line management from now on."

"Fine." The word came out spitting venom. She shocked herself. It was difficult to find any goodness in Cyril Plender. Suspicions were new concept to her, but in light of Professor Haas's rapid onset heart attack, she found herself quite plausible in her eccentric theories. Conspiracies were more her late father's obsession.

Mary recalled sitting in the hospital corridor, pondering the ramifications of the night's events. She had volunteered to travel in the ambulance carrying Professor Haas to the cardiac unit from the ball, mostly to avoid the aftermath of what she had done. People reacted strangely to her theatrical performance of jump-starting a dying man on the dancefloor. Some onlookers grappled with their phones in an attempt to capture a digital recording of the phenomenon. The whole process lasted only moments and so no one caught the actual event, much to Mary's relief. Others avoided her and gossiped behind Mary's back, trying to vocalise a description that captured the essence of a modern day witch.

It was rather convenient that the Walrus had a heart attack just when he was in the middle of an employment battle with Plender. An ongoing power struggle for the oversight of the entire Biomedical Faculty, which afforded him generous control over project funding and the direction of many peoples' careers. Mary convinced herself that Cyril Plender was at the root of something malevolent, something far reaching, something vile.

I need to stop these silly accusations. Plender had no way of making Haas have a heart attack – unless that static shock was more than static. Plender did have something in his hand. That green eyed creepy bloke gave him something metallic or electronic. What is wrong with me? I never used to be this suspicious. Why am I always so ratty all the time? Why is my head splitting again?

Plender drifted off to gloat to any and all he could find in the vicinity. She swallowed a couple of pain killers with some bottled water, grabbed her cycle helmet and bag and closed the locker door.

"Glad I caught you," the technician from Lab Twenty-Six, Jill.

"Plender told me. Can we go through the protocols tomorrow? I'm just heading out." Mary massaged her right temple with fingertips in a circular motion but the dull ache persisted.

"Yes, of course. I was actually hoping you would help me with this fund raiser? It's for the victims of today's disaster." Jill cleared her throat and swiped at her nose with a tissue that she had balled up in her hand.

“What disaster? I haven’t seen the news today.”

“Another Earthquake in the same spot in Japan. Eight point two, they said earlier. Only this time, it hit a nuclear power station.” Jill’s face slackened and the corners of her mouth twitched.

“Oh God, that’s awful. Those poor people.”

“They have evacuated as many as they could, but … well… radiation burns and…“ Jill drew a breath, steadying her emotions. “The news footage is grisly, so upsetting.”

“I imagine it is.” The empathy for the disaster victims had already overwhelmed Jill and was threatening to permeate Mary. It diffused across the ether as an escalating smog of grief, enveloping and smothering, poised to render them incapable of clear impartial thought.

“I have started a collection for one of those Survival Boxes for a family over there, more if we can raise enough.” It was too late for Jill. The charitable fervour consumed her. Mary had to leave or risk equal consummation.

“Right, yes.” Mary located her purse and handed over a twenty pound note. “Might be an idea to contact the Student Union President to see if there are any larger fund raisers planned.” Stuffing her purse back in the satchel, she edged backwards towards the door.

“I will, good idea. Thanks. Night then, Mary, see you tomorrow.”

***

The wind picked up as she wheeled her bike through the campus to the Neurosciences building and leaned it against the railings at the top of the disabled access ramp. Noticing her through the windows, Yosef picked up the phone and dialled the extension for her husband's department.

"Hello. Mrs Arora, are you well?" Yosef held his hand over the receiver as he greeted her. He was listening to canned music, on hold. Mary felt too tired for pleasantries. She leaned on the reception desk and waited. "Yes, sir. I'll tell her. Okay. Bye." He looked up at Mary.

"Dr Arora has asked me to tell you that he'll be late home this evening and suggests you get a takeaway on your way home." His smile undiminished.

"Was there anything else?" She looked up at Yosef, her cheek squashed by her knuckles. Her elbow clicked against the lacquered wood under the pressure of supporting her propped up head.

"Do you want me to call him back?"

"No. Thanks, Yosef." She turned away, the weight of melancholy compressing her spine. *He's forgotten what day it is again. Parth used to be so thoughtful.*

"See you soon, Mrs Arora. Take care." Irrepressible cheerfulness, his smile remained plastered on his face.

"You too."

In the distance, Mary watched the newly graduated, returning their hired gowns and mortars, having spent their day in ceremony and celebration. Their fresh faces chapped pink with the cool breeze, their gowns lifted and billowed for the obligatory group photographs. A glorious day for so many students and families. The culmination of years of stress, toil, and financial uncertainty, followed by the excitement of greater things to come.

Few would look upon the scene with sadness, as Mary did. She mounted her bicycle and rode away, letting the tears streak across her face unimpeded. She cried all the way home to a house devoid of all heartbeats. Even Aristotle had failed to appear at her calling. Putting the kettle on, she ripped a sheet of kitchen towel from its roll and blew her nose.

It was almost six o'clock. She poured the hot water over the teabag and collected the milk from the fridge. Discovering the mug too full, she emptied some out in the sink. *Can't even make tea properly. Pathetic. It's been nine years. Move on. I can't... It still hurts.* Mary took the phone from its cradle and dialled a number from memory. It rang twice.

"Grampy?"

"Hello, sweetie-pie."

"Did they arrive in time?"

"Yes, my love. A beautiful spray of white roses. I put them right between the two headstones."

***

Red, amber... at last, green. Should have taken the route along the park and avoided the traffic. Did Parth put the dustbin out? Oh well, too late now. I wish that van would just hurry up and overtake. It's so close he's gonna clip my back wheel.

Mary changed gear and peddled faster, dodging static cars queuing in their lanes for the next junction. She sneaked up the passenger side, one foot on the kerb, propelling herself to the front of the line. The offending black van was three vehicles away and she was sure she could make it across the junction before it caught up with her. When the lights changed, she set off at a determined speed. As she reached the opposite side of the traffic lights, the van drew level with her back wheel and stayed there. Peering over her shoulder, she wobbled, hit a pot hole in the tarmac and steadied her handlebars to recover her trajectory. *Why isn't he passing me? Such a jerk.*

Ahead, the traffic was grid locked. Some vehicles had pulled up onto the pavement to allow the ambulance and fire brigade through to an accident site. Chilling soundbites of siren wailed, stilling the hearts of parents across the district. Mary stopped and stood at the kerb on tiptoe to view the scene, but a tall four wheeled drive blocked her view.

The emergency crew began to unload equipment and position themselves around the wreckage. A pang of recollection stabbed her in the chest, inducing a rapid inhalation. The van edged ever closer to her, nudging right up to the rear bumper of the car in front.

A large side door on metal runners, slid open in the van. Within seconds, two muscular men hopped out. One took hold of her handlebars and the other slipped an arm around her waist and clapped a hand over her mouth. Shock stunned her. The man hoisted her from the bicycle and thrust her into the van. Her attacker's firm grip bruised her cheeks and restricted her chin as she tried to bite his hand. In her peripheral vision, she saw second man ride away on her bicycle. A third man, crouched low at the back, was holding a syringe.

Terror took hold of her logic. She flailed her limbs about, punching and kicking at them with as much force as the space would allow, but to no avail. The man forced her arm down and raised her sleeve. The needle punctured her bicep and a cool liquid seeped into her tissues. Her world grew darker, till nothing existed but a dreamless sleep.

***

Mary woke in unfamiliar surroundings, groggy and disorientated. Her leg muscles were cramping and she smelled ripe. A cold, clinical room, tiled half way up the walls with a sink unit by one of the two visible doors. Her first inclination was that she was in hospital, till the memory of her abduction came skidding back in her mind. Panic rose in her throat, hot bile and an erratic heartbeat, adrenalin coursing through her circulatory system.

How long have I been asleep? I'm fully clothed still, thank God. Although who knows what these bastards have in store for me. Her arms were bound at her sides and strapped to the small bed. She tested the strength of the bindings, tugging till her wrists were raw. Raising her shoulders as much as her restraints would allow, she searched the room for any aids to escape. A steel trolley supporting a tray of wrapped syringes and empty vials stood at the side of the room. Mary shuddered. *Organ snatchers.* She had read reports of drugged people in nightclubs, waking up in cheap hotels with their kidney missing.

They are going to take my innards, leave me to bleed out then throw me in an incinerator. I bet one of those syringes contains more sedative. They'll wheel me to an operating theatre strapped to this bed. A camera winked a little red light at her from the corner of the ceiling, as if confirming her hypothesis.

She heard the noise of a tumbling mechanism as a key turned in a lock and a bolt slammed across in its housing. Her breathing accelerated. She tried to hold herself still, but she was trembling right through to her core. The muscles in her throat went into spasm, absorbing the air-born particles of pungent aftershave. Clenching every muscle in her body, she held her breath as the door swung open. There he stood - her green eyed stalker from the library. He strolled across the room to the foot of the bed.

"I expect you are wondering why I have brought you here." He tucked a thumb into the tiny pocket of a fawn waistcoat that retained his expanding waistline. The fine woollen material looked expensive and matched his trousers. It seemed lost without the accompanying jacket.

"Let me go. Please. Let me go and I won't report it to the Police. I won't tell anyone, I promise." Her voice cracked.

"Now, now, Mary. Don't get yourself in a state. Cooperate, and no harm will befall you." He looked pleased with himself, like he had just landed a record breaking marlin. *Befall? Who uses the word, 'befall'?* It reminded her of when Yelena would use an English expression, but not quite get the words right.

"There's not much money in the family, if that is what you are after." Mary's mental faculties were starting to return to her.

"Money? No, child. Nothing so petty. My motives are in the highest order of magnitude."

She couldn't place his accent. His English was perfect, a little too perfect but there was a detectable cadence. An inflection in the spaces between the words and a lyrical upward sweep to the tone at the end. Her trembling increased to a noticeable shake. "I will send someone to take care of your comfort, presently. Make yourself at home, Mary. You will be my guest for quite some time."

"But my husband…?"

"Thinks you are dead, child. Mary Arora died in that accident you saw just before we collected you."

"No, you can't… It will crush Parth. Grampy will be devastated. Why are you doing this? What do you want from me?"

"Rest now. We will talk later."

A slight man, dressed in surgical scrubs appeared in the doorway, holding a bundle of white cotton towels and a wash bag. Fear returned. *Is he going to give me a bed bath? What are they preparing me for? Is he the surgeon?* The two men exchanged a few words that were unintelligible to Mary, but the guttural tones sounded distinctly Russian. Whatever he said, the man in scrubs bobbed his head in an abrupt nod, as though obeying his commanding officer. The wafts of aftershave followed the older man from the room, but took some time to disperse from her senses.

The small man pushed the steel trolley towards the bed. He slipped on a pair of latex gloves and removed a syringe from its sterile wrappings. As he drew near to her, she stretched her restraints to their limits, leaning further away from him.

"Blood. No hurts. I good."

She was not reassured, but had little power to stop him from drawing several full phials from her veins. Upon finishing, he pushed the trolley through the doorway, delivering it into the hands of a guard. She heard the bolt clanking across, a sound that would haunt her for a long time to come. The gaoler's taunt. She would listen and track its movements. One day her gaoler's complacency would mark the start of her route to freedom.

He returned to her side, loosened the restraints and assisted her up from the bed. Her back creaked and clicked as she straightened it. The man picked up the washbag and towels and handed them to her.

"Wash." He walked to the second door and opened it, revealing a utilitarian shower room. He smiled again, and gestured for her to enter the bathroom. Mary folded her arms across her chest in defiance and jutted her hip out to one side. She hoped she looked more confident than she felt. He shrugged, then tapped lightly on the bolted door. The guard entered with a tray of hospital food; liquid mash potato, an anaemic looking veggie burger, boiled cabbage and a bottle of water. Setting the tray down on the bed, they left her alone with the blinking light of the camera and her tumultuous thoughts.

Despite the futility in the action, she rushed to the door and rattled the handle. It refused to budge. She darted into the shower room – no window. She checked in the vanity unit beneath the sink – empty. Her satchel hung from the bedframe. She snatched it up and searched through its pockets for her mobile phone. She had left it on the dining table at home. Sinking down onto the bed, she wept; tears for her husband, tears for helplessness, tears for her future.

Puffy eyed and dehydrated, an agonising pain like a pick axe driving into her skull just above her right ear, warned her to prepare for an intense migraine attack.

She raised her head from the pillow, blinking against the flashing zig zag lines in her vision, to locate her handbag.

Mary felt her way around the satchel's contents, unzipped a smaller bag inside and found a plastic sheath that protected her medication. Sliding the tablet under her tongue she let it dissolve in the moisture, immune to its acrid taste, and let the drug absorb into her bloodstream. She struggled to the bathroom to urinate, noting that there was no lock on the door. The irony was not lost on her. Tears surged again, pouring from her eyes with no accompanying sound or effort, fuelled by a cavernous ache welling up inside her abdomen.

Moving the tray of congealing food to the floor, she climbed onto the bed and buried her face in the pillow. *Think, Mary.* She told herself, partly to regain control and partly to rationalise all that had happened. *If they were going to hurt me, they would have done that already. I am still wearing the same clothes, so there appears to be no sexual intent, thank Christ. But don't rule that out. You hear of women being abducted and sold to foreign millionaires. That can't be the case here, I'm too old and married to be worth anything. They are trying to feed me so they don't want me to die, but they claim to have faked my death. You can't feed preoperative patients in case they choke on regurgitated food under anaesthetic. If they are after my organs, they won't be taking them today.*

He said that they don't want money, so what the hell do they want? Hang on, I still have my satchel. Parth knows I never go anywhere without it. Unless they gave my fake dead body a copy of it. They could have done that. What would anyone want with me? I'm nothing special. I'm... 'Docile as a kitten'. The words were bullets finding their target with military precision. The phrase rattled around her subconscious, till the medication took effect and Mary drifted into an exhausted fright filled slumber.

Chapter Eight

Mary awoke to find her arms rebound to the bed and attached to an intravenous drip. Desolate to discover that the events of the night before had not been a dream, she wrestled against the wrist cuffs with renewed vigour. Her scalp prickled with the remnants of her headache. Cologne filled her nostrils. He was sitting on a plastic chair near the foot of the bed.

Looking up at the bloated bag of liquid hanging from the metal stand, she struggled to free herself.

"It is a saline and glucose feed. You would not eat. You would not drink. You induced a migraine with your stupidity. Cooperate and we will remove the restraints." He sat passively, arms folded in his lap.

"Just let me go. You could have no possible use for me. I'm not worth your trouble." Her muscles had stiffened from her struggles and from holding an unnatural position for too long. The bindings had scuffed her wrists beyond the pale epithelial layer, biting into the raw meat beneath. The pain would surface later, when the chemicals of fear no longer masked the injury.

"Dear me, Mary. You have no idea of your value," a hint of perplexity waivered on his face, as though he could not quite believe her naivety.

"What do you want from me?" Her voice rasped and her tongue stuck to the roof of her mouth.

He paused, weighing her words for their authenticity; analysing her features for a veil of pretence. "You are going to help me to reshape the world." Still he did not move. He was the granite boulder barring exit - the Immovable Object.

"That's absurd. I'm just a technician. I don't even understand what the research fellows are doing most of the time. I fetch and carry chemicals. That's my job." Mary saw her truculence chip away at his patience. A glimmer of menace flickered across his expression. She changed tack. "You have kidnapped the wrong person. Please, let me go." The taut wrinkles in her forehead dissolved. She tried to mellow the timbre of her plea, an imploring cherub at his mercy.

"No, Mary. You and I are going to make history together."

"You talk in riddles."

He smiled at her. "The rules of your incarceration are simple. Comply with my requests and you will be rewarded." He was analysing his fingernails, a message of superiority that Mary failed to notice. Kidnapping was a minor, every day event in his life. The situation hardly needed further evidence of his control.

"You'll let me go?"

He chuckled. It was a sinister kind of snort, one filled with a gnarled self-assurance. "The quicker you grow used to this arrangement, the happier you will be. Your old life is gone. Although it is refreshing to see you finally crawl out from beneath your husband's shadow and find your voice."

What is this mad man talking about? Of course my life hasn't gone. I just need to get back to the people who love me. Play along until the Police, or Special Forces or whatever, are able to find me.

"I'll eat, drink, I'll do as you say. Please take these cuffs off." She tried to adopt the tone of a broken woman, submissive. "What do I call you?"

"I am Lars Visser. You can call me Lars." He leaned forward on the chair, his thin green stare fixed on hers.

"What do others call you, crazy?" She rebuked herself for unleashing her belligerence.

"No, Sir, mostly." He raised an index finger at the camera, as though calling for a waiter in a restaurant. The bolted door opened and the little man in scrubs reappeared. He detached the intravenous feed and removed the cannula from inside her vein. Releasing her arms from the restraints, he handed her a tray of warmed pain au chocolate, croissants and a mug of tea.

"I thought you might like something a little more appetising." Visser watched her grab the mug and swallow the hot liquid down. "You'd like some more?"

She nodded, emptying the cup in just a few gulps.

"Alexi will take care of you. You must tell him what foods you would like to eat, although his English is quite poor. You could teach him while you are here, Mary."

She glared at Visser, then lowered her eyes. Alexi ducked out of the open door with her empty mug. She took a croissant from the plate and stretched her legs to the floor. Her ankles cracked as they bore her weight. Mary made a show of extending her limbs and walking around the room, all the while trying to gauge the likelihood of escape. Ripping the pastry into smaller pieces she fortified her strength, munching quickly and peering through the doorway at a long empty corridor as indifferently as she could feign. "I will eat and drink, and try to stay well, but I will not be working for you."

"I think you will change your mind. Remember, child, the more you cooperate the more rewards you will have. We are not barbarians. We can get you nice foods, books to read, perhaps a television."

"Can I have a telephone?"

He shook his head, grinning. "Neither can you have access to the internet, before you ask."

Mary looked at Visser, sitting calmly with his legs crossed and his arms resting in his lap. His scent blended with the molten chocolate in her throat. She forced herself to swallow. Returning her attention to wandering around, she kicked out, stretching her legs and rotating her feet mid-air. She drew level with the open door once more. The way was still clear. Although weak from days without food, she gauged the likelihood of escape against the probability of encountering a second opportunity to flee. She dropped the pastry and bolted through the door. Slipping on her socks down the linoleum, she ricocheted off the walls with her unsteady gait.

A massive guard, dressed in camouflage army fatigues, stepped from his station on the other side of the door and hurried after her. His giant strides caught up with her in fewer than ten steps. He grasped at her clothes, bunching her top into a fistful of cloth mingled with her hair and tugged her to a standstill. Her head snapped back. She squealed in pain, arching her spine to relieve the pressure. The guard seized her arm, letting her hair go and spinning her around, dragging her body as though it was weightless, back towards the room.

Visser was in the doorway, watching her reaction. The sight of him standing there all smug and superior woke a long dormant feeling inside her. The more he smirked, the greater the feeling. It was like the torrent of revulsion bathed her brain in a hatred so concentrated, it dissolved a wall of compliance that had secured her temper for nine long years.

The guard's fingertips dug into the flesh of her arm. As she struggled to free it, the guard's hand slipped. He countered by clutching both upper arms with greater force. He was so enormous; her head barely reached the height of his chest. Mary kicked at his shins, but with no shoes to protect her toes, they crumpled ineffectually against his legs. He was laughing at her.

Anger rose from the pit of her stomach. With clenched teeth, she mustered her strength and forced her leg skyward, connecting the top of her foot with his unprotected genitals. She felt them crush against her bones. He screamed, a surprised high pitched yelp.

The discomfort he endured, was not sufficient to lessen his grip. With a few angry words in Russian, spat out in her direction, he released one of her arms and smacked her across the face with the back of his knuckles.

"Cyka!" The guard yelled at her. "Bitch!"

Her face exploded in pain, her nose pouring with blood, she collapsed to the floor. Visser stepped over the threshold and walked towards the guard. He leaned across and removed a pistol from the man's military holster, aimed it at the guard's forehead and pulled the trigger. Blood, mashed brain and skull fragments splattered the wall behind him in a biological collage worthy of Damien Hurst. The hulking mass of guard, crumpled to the ground moments later.

"See, child. There are consequences to your petulance." He waved the gun barrel at the bloody mess streaking down the whitewashed walls.

"Fine by me. Kill all your henchmen for all I care." She gently fingered the bridge of her nose to ascertain if it was broken.

"Cooperate, Mary, or you will find your husband decorating walls in a similar way."

Mary looked at the dead man with dispassion. He mattered less than an animal. It was not her first experience of seeing mangled flesh, but the thought of Parth being in Visser's line of fire stopped her from further retaliation. She swallowed hard, her life for his. That is the bargain. To save her best friend, her confidant and protector, the love of her life from this stone hearted sociopath. She imagined Parth pleading for his life, Visser standing over him, aiming that pistol between her husband's eyes. Nausea clawed at her throat.

Visser held the gun against his thigh, waiting for some confirmation of her obedience, his stare tunnelling into her head. An odour of butcher's waste tinged with aftershave made her balk, the association forever embedded in her memory. The guard's blood was travelling along the tile grout channels and threatened to join the splashes of red on her clothes where she sat. She watched it trickle and ooze towards her, resisting the urge to move. She would cooperate up to a point. Finding that threshold would be a tightrope of considerable risk, but one she must take to secure her freedom. Alexi broke the stalemate. He scurried down the corridor and pulled

Mary up, handing her a wodge of tissue for her bloodied nose and leading her back to her room. "Ice? I get ice?" He fussed about her, moving matted hair from her eyes and patting her shoulder.

Sealed back in her room, Mary took time to steady herself. To her relief, Visser had remained on the opposite side of the door. Alexi scurried around the room, pleased that she seemed receptive to his care. He bustled about making and remaking the bed and issuing commands to the guards to fetch items to make her more comfortable. "Eat? Wash? Clothes?" Each question punctuated with hand signals to items left on her bunk. Mary nodded. It was not Alexi who threatened her or Parth's life. For all she knew Alexi and perhaps his family, were living with the same sword dangling over their heads. And he was quite possibly her best potential ally to aid in her escape.

Alone once more, she ate the remaining pastries, sank the cool tea that had grown a taupe film on the surface and went into the bathroom to shower. She could not find a speck of daylight anywhere. Mary pulled the cord that controlled both the light and extractor fan. No method for estimating the time of day, or which day it was even. How many days had she already been there, drugged into a state of unconsciousness? The air in the bathroom was stale. Mould spores left a rank black crust in the damp corners.

Scanning the room for any sign of covert cameras, she stripped off her filthy clothes and left them in a heap on the floor. A lukewarm shower washed away the congealing blood and sweat. Acutely aware that any of her captors could walk in at any moment and find her naked and vulnerable, she scrubbed herself clean and dressed in haste.

The jogging bottoms and T-shirt Alexi had left for her soaked up whatever moisture she had failed to dry. She found a new tooth brush and paste in the washbag and set about removing the woolly feeling in her mouth.

The only time she could ever remember her teeth feeling that caked with detritus was following the operation on her wisdom teeth, when it had been far too painful to brush. A salt water rinse kept bacteria in check back then. Now the pain was from the bruising that deepened following the guard's assault. The mirror showed her a gaunt and harrowed woman, aged overnight, with purple welts of receding blood beneath the skin.

Mary looked at her room afresh. As prison cells went, hers was not uncomfortable, but the lack of privacy disturbed her. She sat on the bed and watched the little red light flashing on the side of the CCTV camera. It stared back at her, goading her, sneering in the same self-satisfied way that the guard had done. They would be watching her now, sitting in a room nearby, pointing at their screens and judging her. Would they be giving her marks out of ten for her appearance, for her courage and strength, for her figure? Would they be making bets over her actions, or worst still, her fate? They must know what Visser had in store for her. She was at their mercy. The trembling started again. Knowing that their critical eyes focused on every movement she made was unbearable.

Visser had left his plastic chair in the room. She got up from the bed, grabbed the chair, positioned it directly beneath the mounted camera, and sat down.

Above her head, she could hear a tiny motor whirring frenetically while the guards tried to reposition the sight lines of the lens - a moment of peace.

Alexi returned with more tea for her. He looked at her balancing her head in her hands, elbows resting on her knees. “I bring you more food?” He tilted his head towards her in pity.

“No, thank you, Alexi.” He turned to leave. “Could I… please could I have something to read?”

His expression was one of puzzlement. She placed her hands together as if in prayer, then opened them wide to symbolise a book. “Book? Reading?” She peered into her outstretched hands, miming the action of reading. A spark of recognition formed in his eyes.

“Da! I bring.”

Sipping her tea, she waited. It tasted of long life milk. She could always tell the difference. Ultra-heat treated milk had a mild bitterness to it. Did they have cupboards full of long life supplies to keep her there indefinitely? The thought was chilling. Alexi returned, waving a rolled up newspaper. “Book, Da? You book?”

Mary thanked him and took it, momentarily diverted by his noun confusion. She didn’t correct him. Unrolling the pages, she glanced at the date of publication. A full week had passed since her abduction.

“Alexi, is this today?” She pointed at the date. “Today?”

“Before today…um… it is when? Before today?” His face pinched in confusion.

“Yesterday?”

“Da. Yesterday.” He left the room muttering, yesterday, mastering its pronunciation. The bolt slammed across and down.

The headline was standard for local papers; Council tax rise furies followed by photographs of the mayor looking regal in his flamboyant garb and chain. Page two documented the contested plans for a new traveller community on the outskirts of a market town in the south of the county and the threats of another cottage hospital closure. There, on page three was a more shocking headline. *University Technician Named as Crash Victim.* Her heart stopped for a moment, like a bubble of trapped air inside the chambers had worked its way out of the plumbing and popped in her chest. She read on.

"The victim of a recent fatal accident on London Road has been identified as local University Technician, Mary Arora, aged thirty. The crash happened last week on a section of the A6 close to Victoria Park. Witnesses state that the gravel lorry was travelling at speed and appeared to clip the Kerb and lose control, careening into Mrs Arora's bicycle, as she was riding to work.

Other witnesses took to social media, claiming that the driver was using his mobile phone just prior to the accident, who was himself severely injured in the crash. Police have charged the driver, whose name is being withheld, of causing death by dangerous driving. When questioned regarding the length of time taken to release the identity of the victim, a police spokesperson said; "Unfortunately, the accident caused such irrevocable damage that conventional methods of identification have not been possible." Funeral arrangements are delayed until the body is no longer needed in the ongoing investigation."

Mary felt her chest constricting. She couldn't breathe. A searing flush of fear and grief welled up inside her, burning her neck and face. That tiny thread of hope that she had fostered since her capture frayed and snapped. A single line of spider's silk dangling down into her personal abyss of dread had gone. Parth would not be moving mountains to find her. No cavalry would be hammering down the doors of her prison.

Parth will frequent a personal form of confinement, a pit of sorrow, lamenting her loss. She had little doubt that Visser would do more than threaten to kill her husband if she failed to please his every whim, whatever that may entail.

The newspaper embodied reality and it was all Mary had to cling to, a small token of the outside world. She folded it, with a degree of care and reverence and tucked it beneath the pillow. Her dash for freedom had expended more energy than she realised. She felt emotionally and physically drained. Lying back on the bed, she closed her eyes and tried to sleep.

The overhead lights were stark and glowed pink through her eyelids, highlighting the images playing in her mind. She pulled the covers over her head, but the air became humid and uncomfortable. Rolling out of the side of the bed, she examined the walls for a light switch, but found none. Standing in front of the camera, she pointed to the ceiling and then covered her eyes. She then mouthed the word, *please*. They took pity on her and the lights dimmed, not fully, a half-light allowing the guards to continue their watch.

Horizontal once more, she thought only of Parth. Were they following him, ready to shoot him at any time Visser gave the command? Was he alone in his grief or had her Grandfather travelled up from Brighton to mourn with him? Was Parth busy arranging a traditional funeral or was he carrying out her wish for cremation, as she had once expressed to him on their journey through his homeland in India?

Mary allowed her thoughts to wander back eight years to their days of travel; a few moments of indulgent escapism. It was during the trip to visit his family that Parth had found the courage to propose to her. She recalled the joy of people on the streets revelling in the first rains of the monsoon, overdue and eagerly awaited. Puddles splashed against leather sandals and the dust pitted with heavy raindrops. Children danced in the natural shower and the water flattened their hair against smiling faces.

She remembered the steam rising from corrugated metal sheeting protecting shacks and houses from the elements. The smells of rotting excrement washed down gullies and into drains, cleaning the streets anew. Street vendors erected beach umbrellas over their vats of spiced offerings, broadcasting their wares in raised regional dialects.

The Arora family home was beyond the markets and taverns, far from the ghettos and poor districts of Mumbai. Theirs was a former Victorian building, situated in the tree lined suburbs of Colaba, overlooking the yachts in the bay and a mere stone's throw from the golf course. Mary overcame the intimidating meeting with his parents, who were a little perturbed by Parth's refusal to marry a local lady from a well-respected and wealthy family.

They had welcomed Mary as their esteemed guest, dressing her in fine silks, dining out in style and indulging in beauty treatments and henna tattoo sessions with his female relatives. None but the eldest of two sisters had treated her with anything less than kindness. She had sensed in him a partiality for Mary that transcended duty. She knew that he had set his sights on marrying this British girl who had lost all but one member of her family just months before their travels.

One sultry evening, Mary sat on the veranda drinking a cool glass of homemade lemonade, watching the boats bobbing up and down in the bay. Parth approached, bent one knee beside her and uttered the immortal words.

In her prison cell, she whispered them into the pillow, damp with her tears, hearing not her own voice, but his deep masculine intonation instead. “Marry me, Mary. I cannot imagine life without you by my side.”

Chapter Nine

"Try again, Mary, and I will get you some nice fruit to eat." Alexi read the translation from the smart phone application. It was slow and laborious, but at least he could now communicate with her. Mary was content to wait for him to type in his statements. It gave her time to think of a way to get the phone from his grasp and call for help.

Alexi had risen early, delivered her breakfast of boiled eggs, toast and tea, and set up the laboratory a short distance from her room. Mary had taken her time getting ready. She was not going to let them call all the shots. She had sacrificed the sports pages of her precious newspaper, folded them into a tight tube and wedged them beneath the bathroom door. She let the hot water pulse on the back of her head, telling herself to relax and think logically, but the knotted muscles in her neck and shoulders refused to ease.

In the lab, Alexi had placed a peculiar hat covered in electronic nodes on her head and connected trailing cables into a computer. On the bench, he placed a standard Boy Scout compass in front of her. "Please, try again." Mary touched her index finger to the metal casing of the compass. The needle trembled and then returned resolutely north. She sighed, raising her hands in defeat. "Why must I do this Alexi, it makes no sense?"

He listened to the phone verbalise her words in Russian through an earbud perched in one ear, then tapped in his response. "You have a great power, Mary. We must make it stronger, easy for you to use on command."

"But why? What for?" Exasperated, she let her arms drop, thumping them down onto the bench in front of her.

"You do what Visser say, or he hurt your man." Alexi wagged a finger at her.

"Yes, I understand the threats. What I don't understand is what he wants me to do and why?" She scanned the lab for potential exits or methods with which she could contact Parth - a landline telephone perhaps or another internet connected computer. None were visible.

"He wants you to lead a team of special people like you. You are very strong. You learn to control power." He finished reading out his response and raised his face to her. He smelled of baby powder and his thinning hair revealed dry flakes loosely covering a sore patch on his scalp.

"And what is this team supposed to do exactly? She noticed his creaseless lab coat bore no telling stains, unlike her own back at the university.

Alexi returned his attention to his computer monitor. "I not allowed to say."

Mary considered his response. She knew that Visser had been present in Cyril's lab when she blew out the fuse board and also at the ball when she jump-started Professor Haas following his heart attack. There was a good chance that he had no idea about her being able to leave her body and spy on people. If she learned to strengthen and control all her abilities, they might assist her escape.

"We start small, yes? You make compass move." Alexi was nudging her to try again.

She settled herself to the task, scratching the fabric on the cap where tiny thunder flies were tickling her skin. "It's sweltering in here. Can we have the windows open?"

Alexi hopped off his chair and walked between the benches to the windows. Grabbing the mechanism on the wall, he wound the metal handle, cranking all the vents open at once. Mary waited until he diverted his gaze and grabbed the smartphone. She clicked the green icon and started typing in Parth's mobile phone number.

"No, no, no! Very bad, for you and me. No telephone, Visser say." Alexi rushed back to her side and snatched the phone from her hands, securing it in his shirt pocket and wagging his finger at her again. "You very bad. No fruit."

"You can't blame me for trying. I want to go home." She sagged on the stool like a petulant child.

"This new home. I your family now." He banged his chest with his hand and returned to his seat.

"If I make the compass move, you'll give me fruit and a television in the room?" Mary glowered at Alexi. The sternness of his tone did not match his open body language. Was that a faint smile as he chastised her? Did he admire her?

"Move compass, you get fruit."

"And the television." It was not a request.

"Okay."

It was in her own interests to master her gifts. Concentrating on the floating needle inside the steel casing, she touched the side with her index finger once more. Imagining energy flowing from her digit into the compass, she willed the red tip away from North towards her finger positioned at the South Easterly point. The needle moved. Mary anticipated a move towards her. Instead, it was repelled, resting in a north westerly direction. Alexi laughed and clapped his hands together. "Good, good." She moved her finger around the circumference of the case, the needle keeping equidistant from her touch. He barked an order at the guards positioned at the entrance to the lab. One of them entered with a bowl of fruit. She seized a Granny Smith and sunk her teeth into it, relishing the crisp texture and tart juice on her tongue. *I'm a performing monkey. Be a good chimp and you'll have a banana.* She did not articulate her thoughts.

Turning to the computer monitor, Alexi used the mouse to navigate the software recording her brain patterns. A few more taps and a simulation of the electrical and neural activity in her head played back like an animated video of a cuttlefish, rippling the colours of its skin in rhythmic pulsations.

He changed the settings again and replayed the simulation. This time, the computer showed them the most active sections like a heat map. While Alexi *oohed* and *aahed* over the images, Mary recognised the section of her brain that had recorded the most activity. It was the area containing the same gland that Parth had shown to her after her MRI scan – the Pineal Gland.

Alexi's top pocket vibrated and pinged. He took out the phone and read the message. "Ah. Visser returns.

You go back to room. Guards will bring television and fruit."

Mary pouted. The lab had daylight and fresh air, and although the view looked out upon a quad surrounded by tall concrete and glass structures, there were a few trees and some flower beds between the patches of grass. Her room was oppressive and enclosed. She sauntered back down the corridor, flanked either side by scary men in military attire and sat on the plastic chair under the camera. One clumsy guard slammed down the bowl of fruit onto a newly added table so that the grapes slid off and onto the floor. Another carried in a flat screen TV and attached the cables to the sockets in the wall.

Hugging her legs and balancing her heels on the edge of the plastic chair, she listened for the *thunk-click* sound as the bolt slid across into the metal sheath on the doorframe and the handle angled down. She rose, twisted the TV to face the chair and flicked through the channels. Daytime chat shows, quizzes and black and white films were now her staple diet.

Mary switched to a channel playing a war film. The noise was comforting. It reminded her of when her grandfather babysat so that her parents could sneak away for romantic weekends together; trying, no doubt, to patch up their fraying marriage. Grampy would sit patiently for hours playing *Cat's Cradle* with a loop of wool wound around his arthritic fingers, *Where Eagles Dare* or another of his favourites blaring in the background. She would sit on the footstool by his knee and eat his grapes, or cherries if they were in season. Mary scooped up the bunch of seedless grapes that the guard had knocked to the floor and brushed the film of dust from them.

Reminiscing filled huge reservoirs of emotion within her. The weight of memories forcing her muscles to tense, as they pounded against the dam that held her feelings in check. One sudden deluge of fear or sadness would unleash all her latent powers and if recent events were anything to go by, her intense emotion could yield catastrophic results.

Mary could hear voices in the corridor beyond her room. She grabbed the TV remote and hit the mute button, straining to hear the conversation. Standing close to the door, she turned her head to one side. They were speaking English. She recognised Visser's peculiar pitch, but it was growing quieter – they were moving further away.

If she could get a message to the new visitor, they could raise the alarm and fetch help. How could she signal their attention? Her newspaper might have sufficient headlines to tear out words that asked for help, but there is no way of getting the message to them. That is assuming they are not already part of Visser's crew of captors.

Hammering her fists against the door, she shouted till her lungs burned. "Hey! Let me out of here! Someone help me…I'm being held against my will. Please, help me!"

A large guard unbolted and pushed open the door, forcing her to take a few steps back. In heavily accented tones he said, 'Quiet! You want a slap, eh? Like before?" He raised his hand close to her face.

"Visser would kill you if you lay a finger on me. Just like he did your friend." Her eyes filled with malicious intent. He rose to her challenge, pacing forward and towering over her.

"A finger, perhaps. But keep this up and I will put you back in your restraints. Then I could do exactly what I like with you. Easy to turn off the camera tonight." He grinned a repugnant, salacious smile.

"Visser would kill you." She repeated, with less vitriol.

"Maybe, maybe not. Your word against mine." He clutched her face roughly, squeezing till her mouth puckered up. "Save a kiss for me."

Mary shoved his hand away and threw the TV remote at his head. It bounced off and smashed on the wall, spilling the batteries across the floor. The guard laughed and re-bolted the door behind him.

Well done, Mary. Full marks for pretending to cooperate. I have got to find a way out of here. I need to know what is going on out there and where the exits are. If I could just make myself travel without my body again. Although I don't know how to make that happen. She paced up and down the room. Reassembling the TV remote, she pressed the EPG button and the electronic programme guide popped up on the screen. It was 12.30pm. She estimated that she would have approximately eleven to twelve hours, before the guard would attempt anything. Taking a deep calming breath, she sat on the edge of the bed, thinking back to the occasion when she had spied on Parth. She had been asleep, but had woken up not being able to move. That had been the start of her extra corporeal journey.

If I am to have any chance of repeating the experience, I need to be relaxed and semi-conscious. Ha! Relaxed? Under these conditions? OK, music. Music might help. She trawled through the channels on the TV. Chart Hits from the Eighties, was the closest she could find to a music channel. *That is more likely to rev me up, not calm me down.* Turning the television off, she cast the remote aside.

Using a rolled up T shirt to cover her eyes, she lie on the bed and tried to still her rapid pulse. *Grampy would stroke my forehead and sing to me when I was a restless child. I could try singing, something soft and lyrical. I could try the Beatles number that he used to sing.* With her arms loose by her side, she concentrated on her slowing her breath and pushing her thoughts to one side in her mind. The song began, softly out loud, no more than a hum.

It was the song about her namesake, *Let it be.* As the song progressed, her voice petered out until the final chorus played inside her head, a synergism of melody and the torpid frequencies of submission. The vibrational beat of her song, tuned to the alpha waves of her psyche, carrying her into a focused state of existence. As she imagined the instruments playing the final chords to the song's conclusion, she told herself to fly.

Her consciousness percolated out of her body and amassed high above. She glanced down at herself, making sure that her physical form was safe before moving towards the bolted door. Since wood had not prevented her movement in her last travels, she pushed through the grain and emerged in the corridor beyond. Staying close to the ceiling, she swept along the passageway, stopping briefly to assimilate the situation in the guard's station next to her room.

The small alcove, had several mounted screens showing multiple aspects of the base. It was far larger than Mary had predicted. As the pictures changed between camera views, she saw outside images of derelict brick and concrete buildings, surrounded by scaffolding and security fences.

Above the central monitor that showed her prone body, lying in bed with a T shirt covering her face, was a line of screens all showing darkened hospital wards from different angles. She bobbed closer. A silent patient occupied every bed, still as though preserved in aspic and attached to an intravenous feed. The image changed again, showing a man wearing scrubs rolling a patient onto their side, while another changed the plastic bag of fluid. *What is Visser doing here? Are all these people in comas? Where the hell am I? This cannot be a proper hospital.*

Fearing that she would not be able to sustain her present form for long, she floated back over the guard's head, noting that only one person manned the screens, while another stood outside her room. A quick look informed her that neither of those currently on duty, was the one that had threatened to call on her later on. She turned and peered down the corridor. Alexi was crossing from the laboratory to an office opposite. She followed him, hurrying towards the room before he could close the door.

She commanded her presence to rise above their backs, reaching up to see the visitor. With the three people packed inside and all the furniture, space was tight. Her vision panned up Visser's sport's jacket and over the thick waves of grey hair.

Sitting opposite them, stroking his goatee, was a face she knew well. A man who had directed all her working hours for the last seven years of her life. Her boss, Professor Cyril Plender was talking to her captors. Mary froze. She chanted in her head, not to feel shocked. Any burst of emotion and her consciousness would zip straight back into her body. Did Cyril know that she was there? Was he part of the conspiracy to abduct her? Was that the reason why he had given her most confidential tasks to another technician? She needed a few moments to compose her thoughts but she sensed there was no time to waste. From Plender's expression, the meeting was not going his way. If only she could hear as well as see what was happening. How could she get her ears to work in conjunction with her sight? If she could pick up anything from lip reading it might help.

Cyril's countenance conveyed his fury. His tone of voice would be irate. Mary watched his lips. He was talking about the ball. She picked up the words 'bloody', 'man' and 'die'. She assumed they were referring to the Walrus, Professor Haas, and his miraculous recovery from a sudden heart attack. Plender fished in his pocket, withdrew the tiny steel device and handed it to Visser. Without warning, her hearing kicked into action. "You said one touch from that bloody contraption would kill him without any trace of foul play. You promised me his job."

"Nobody could have predicted Mary's involvement in saving his life. You have to hand it to her. She is more powerful than even we could have guessed. And anyway, you did get his job." Visser was examining the device with a degree of insouciance that clearly annoyed Plender.

"Only temporarily. That infuriating old git is fighting the board. He is refusing to retire."

“That is your problem, not ours. Have you brought the test results with you?”

Plender stopped fuming long enough to grab a portfolio from the desk top and remove a bundle of papers secured in a plastic file. He handed them directly to Alexi, who pored through them with eager interest. Cradling the file in one hand, Alexi trailed his index finger past the paragraphs of explanations, down to tables of raw data and graphs. Alexi stopped and looked up at Plender, mystified.

“What is it, Alexi?” Visser asked, taking the folder from his grasp.

“I not understand. Data says no Di-Methyl Tryptamine, no MAO inhibitors?”

“That’s right.” Plender confirmed. “Mary’s blood is clean. She’s a little anaemic and could do with a good multivitamin and mineral supplement, but otherwise there were no enhancers in her blood.” He went back to playing with his beard.

“But that can’t be right. Are you sure these tests are reliable?” Visser scanned the conclusions drawn in the paper.

“I’m certain. I had my best post grads conduct the tests in Lab Twenty-six, the one that you are paying for.”

Chapter Ten

Mary was spinning. Her consciousness struggled to maintain focus on the scene before her. She could feel a dragging sensation, pulling her back towards her room. Her sight grew grainy around the edges, the corridor reduced to a few blurry pixels as her energy reinserted itself back into her body.

Gradually, the physical sensations of her limbs returned, accompanied by the familiar nausea. The scale of verisimilitude in her life was beginning to reveal itself. How far did the deception extend? Was Yelena Plender part of the treachery, along with her husband, Cyril, or was she working with Parth? At least the tablets Parth had been feeding her, were just multivitamins after all. Small comfort.

Perhaps the relationship between him and Yelena had all been innocent and work related, despite her suspicions. Parth would never have put her in harm's way, of that she was sure.

How could Cyril Plender, her employer, have betrayed her so easily? She though back to all the occasions when she had worked overtime and not claimed for the hours, fearful of his budget. Of sacrificed weekends when he deemed a project too important to wait until Monday. Of all the times he had abused his power and sent her on personal errands, picking up dry cleaning or shopping for anniversary and birthday gifts.

How many times had she defended him to Yelena in a misguided attempt at saving their marriage? He would whine at Mary like a bird that follows the gardener, jumping from branch to fence as she worked, chirruping his woes and engendering pity.

Plender ingratiated himself by stealth, feeding on her goodwill and placid nature, all the while hiding a predatory raptor inside. It was pointless to mourn the loss of the PhD offer that Professor Haas discussed with her when they were dancing together, but it gouged at her ego nonetheless. She would be lucky if she escaped with her life, let alone further her career. All the same, the barrage of emotions left her bewildered.

Regrets were never an indulgence Mary subscribed to, but in this moment, her heart ousted all rationality. She should have carried on travelling when Parth had insisted on returning to England for their wedding. She should have applied for post graduate courses following her graduation. She should have started a family with Parth years ago, before his work became his reason for living. She should have spent more time mourning with Grampy instead of leaving him to fend for himself and running off around the World. She should not have argued with her parents the day of her graduation ceremony when they were driving home to Brighton.

The bolt slid and rattled. She wiped her damp eyes with the T shirt and sat upright, trying to feign an unperturbed air. Visser strolled in looking stern, his hair unusually ruffled. She watched him settle on the plastic chair and arrange his legs, smoothing the wrinkles in the cloth as he sat down.

Raising both hands to his head, he tamed his locks, and then looked up. Those stony, discerning eyes scored a pathway into her thoughts. They bored into her, tethering an intense connection along her optic nerve. It felt like he was physically extracting the information he desired. An ethereal memory drive, plugged into her consciousness ready for the download. The invasion felt surreal. For a few moments, she sat transfixed, his hold on her binding. The intrusion prickled the right side of her brain, spiking the neurons and increasing blood flow. Mary shut her eyes. These symptoms usually preceded a migraine.

"Please may I have some tea? I need to take my medication." Mary broke Visser's concentration, rising from the bed and walking across the room to her handbag. "Stress is a known trigger for migraines and you are making me anxious." She could sense he was attempting to re-establish the connection, trying to catch her stare and refusing to answer her request. "Fine, if you are just going to sit there like a spectre, I'll have water, or I'll ask Alexi. He at least is human enough to take care of me." She needed him to go. If that guard was going to carry out his threats of visiting her room and overpowering her, she needed to find a way out, and fast.

"Tell me about your husband's work, Mary. What project is he currently running?" Visser folded his arms across his chest, determined to appear unfazed.

"He doesn't talk about them. Most of his work is confidential." She carried the satchel back to the bed and sat with it balancing on her knees.

"But you are involved in one of his studies, are you not?" He watched her closely, biding his time till she would look up at him.

"Well, yes, but that was just to make up the numbers in his study group. It's only basic psychology stuff." She located the plastic case containing her tablets in her handbag. Mary spun the package idly in her palm, considering whether the migraine alarm inside her head was worthy of expending one of her few remaining tablets.

"Like the one you were conducting in the University Library that night you saw me?" A disturbing smirk spread between his drooping jowls.

"Um, yes." She shivered. It rippled from her neck and down the length of her spine in recollection of the experience.

"You attempted to recreate Ingo Swann's famous remote viewing experiment. How did you fair?"

"How did you know that?" Mary barked, regretting her response the moment it had left her lips.

His implacable façade registered her discomfort. He had rattled her. A cool smugness radiated from him as he unfolded his arms, flicking each wrist outwards in turn, to adjust his gaudy cufflinks. "I have my sources."

Sources indeed. Now Plender is Temporary Head of Faculty, he can snoop into all of Parth's studies. Hateful little man.

"So… was it a success, Mary?" Visser's shot at charm was making her ill at ease, missing his target by a country mile.

"I wasn't the one being tested. It was another participant. He was quite accurate." *Careful now, don't implicate Dan. Tell him just enough to pacify him.*

Change tone. If he thinks you are being obstinate he might resort to violence.

"Hmm, perhaps. And during this study, did Dr Arora give you any tablets or injections prior to the tests?" He refolded his arms, allowing the upper hand to stray to his face, tapping his lip pensively.

"No of course not. They were simple preliminary experiments." *Too pushy - be the harried victim.*

"Preliminary to what, exactly?" He snapped, shuffling more upright on the chair.

"I don't know. You would have to ask my husband." She opened the plastic sheath of her migraine treatment and removed a foil covered blister pack.

"And you are sure that you neither imbibed nor injected any kind of drug?"

"Imbibed? Where did you learn your English?" *Stop goading him. What is the matter with you?* She couldn't help herself. Her new found gifts were giving her a confidence that she had never possessed before. It was a heady rush. In any other situation, she would have time to reflect on her actions - to take stock and learn to curb her more audacious inclinations.

It felt like the first time she rode her pushbike without her father holding the saddle; the exhilaration of mastering the balance and control completely unaided. The freedom of movement it represented. The proud look on her father's face as she turned in a huge arc in the park and peddled closer. His features set in a sustained smile. Her first steps towards independence.

Her second solo ride was less graceful. The conceit of youth, fooling her into believing that one successful trip equalled mastery. Her father had been there on that occasion too, ready to scoop her into his arms and sooth the bumps and grazes. He had always been her set of stabilisers. Now she rode fate alone.

"Forgive me if the Dutch are better at educating their children, Mary. Please answer the question."

"Dutch, I thought that you were Russian?"

Visser sighed. "I have been very patient with you, Mary. I have explained the rules. I'm sure that you would prefer the carrot to the stick. I can have one of the guards remind you of the penalties for non-compliance, or perhaps we can arrange an accident for your husband, if you prefer?"

"That won't be necessary, thank you. I'm just curious. It helps to pass the time. No, Parth has not used any drugs on me during the experiments." The threat pulled her up sharply. This was no game. These people meant business. Despite the risk, she felt the need to pry and to gather intel for her cause. It was a gamble, but if she could just act a little ditsy, it might throw him off the scent.

She must pretend to be captivated by his authority and let him ramble. "Dutch you say? I loved Amsterdam when Parth and I visited. Such a beautiful city and the people are so nice; so tolerant and welcoming. So, you are not Russian, but you speak it so fluently. You must be very talented with languages. I never really got the hang of them myself. I gave up learning French in my third year at school."

"I speak a number of languages. I find good communication is a vital key to success." He straightened his collar and adjusted the cuff links of his crisp white shirt once more.

"I imagine it is. And particularly useful here, since everyone else seems to be Russian." She moved the satchel and pill case to the bed, swinging her limbs up and into cross-legged position like a school girl on an assembly hall floor.

"Mostly they are, yes. I think of myself as a citizen of the world. A world in which the balance of power is changing, and you, dear child, will be the instrument of change."

"Me? Don't be silly. I'm not involved in politics. I forgot to vote during the last general election." *Careful... not too ditsy.* Mary ran her fingers through her hair, gathering the curls into a bunch and pulling them down over one shoulder, distraction being her main aim.

Visser stood up and paced around the room, puffing out his chest and bolstering his posture. He peered down at Mary's tiny frame, perched on the edge of the bed. "You will see. A great change is upon us. It will begin in Japan and then in the US, across Europe and the antipodes and soon every continent will see a profound difference. A new and sustainable world." There was a sparkle in his eye; a glint of devilry that disturbed her. He was ambitious and calculating and his cool reaction to killing the guard showed her that beneath the poised façade, there was an unequalled ruthlessness.

"You plan to stir up a third world war? That's ridiculous." *Don't anger him. For God's sake, hold your tongue.*

"War? No, child. Wars are so last century. Countries are won and lost on debt. Debt is an affluent nation's power. Politics become irrelevant when you control the world's resources and the key to that is data." His perpetual use of the term 'child', reassured her that he felt she posed no threat. His affirmations seemed to her no more than the rantings of a madman. How he had persuaded her boss, Plender, to become involved was baffling.

Alexi came in with a tray. On it, he carried a mug of steaming tea, some plain biscuits and a bag of salty crisps. He placed the tray beside Mary on the bed. “For headache. You wish for ice pack or hot bottle?” It didn’t surprise her that the guards were listening in on their conversation. The sentiment was kind, were it not for the realisation that Alexi knew about her individual requirements of symptom relief. Only Parth knew her well enough to know that sometimes she needed a cold compress on her head while other times she required heat. Only her husband knew that sometimes a salty snack and hot tea would relieve the tension and other times a plain biscuit would do the trick. Not even Grampy knew of her preferences. Visser continued to waffle on about the greatness of nations but she heard none of his impassioned speech.

Her mind reeled. Had they bugged her home? Was Parth aware of the wiretap in their house? Was that why he refused to discuss the bizarre events that had happened to her when they were together in the lounge? Was he part of the scheme to abduct her? That one didn’t bear thinking about. He was her most beloved. It was unthinkable. Alexi was urging her to take her medication.

“You feel well. We have more work to do.”

What were they training her for? Why was she so crucial to their plans? It was some assurance that she was going to live, at least while she was being useful to them. It gave her a measure of command, an ounce of leverage. How she could use it to aid her escape was not yet clear to her. It did not, however, convince her that she would remain unharmed if she failed to comply with their demands. What would they make her do?

With such global goals, Visser could be planning something catastrophic, something of immense magnitude. But what role could she have in that? So far, all she was able to achieve was to fuse a few electrical appliances and empathise with an Earthquake victim. Visser could not possibly know about her recent endeavours in leaving her body behind. She had only told one person in the whole world and Dan Wildman, her study partner, had no ties to Visser at all. Had he?

Mary sipped the tea and dissolved the migraine medication under her tongue. She made a mental note that there were only two doses left. Keeping calm and well hydrated were methods known to reduce the frequency of attacks in most sufferers. She would need to ration herself until she could escape.

"So you see, Mary, a few eggs must be broken in order to create a better omelette." Visser had not noticed her lack of attention. He had lectured for a couple of minutes on the state of world politics and national debt and assumed she had kept up with his monologue. "And you maintain that your husband does not augment your abilities with any drug use. So how did he initiate your gift in the first place?"

Augment. That was a most familiar word. Parth had mentioned an Augmentation Set when he threatened to move Dan out of her study group. He had wanted to test Dan with dangerous drugs to see how they effected his abilities in Psychology tests. She remembered that there had been close to a full blown row over it. One of very few rows that they had ever had during their marriage.

The acid in her stomach erupted high into her throat. For a moment, she forgot her subterfuge. "How many times must I say it? Apart from prescription tablets, I take no drugs what so ever. You should know, you have my blood test results. There was no initiation, no augmentation. You have kidnapped the wrong person." As soon as the words passed her lips, she was furious with herself.

"You know about the test results?" Visser returned calmly to the chair. He sat as still as an alabaster tomb carving, more gargoyle than angel. The colour leached from his already pallid skin. Those lifeless eyes locking on to hers once more, probing her thoughts for answers.

So, this is his skill, is it? To extract information by creeping the bejeezus out of me. He is trying to read my mind. Well it's bloody rude to stare you nasty, eerie, Dutch freak! Mary squinted her eyelids, turning the direction of focus to his pale irises, locking him out of her mind and intensifying her gaze. The animosity welled up inside her, a level of hatred she had never experienced before. A cogent intention to preserve herself at all costs, even at the risk of harming others.

Alexi fussed about tidying things and muttering anxious worries in a quiet Russian vernacular as the stare down continued. The whites of Visser's eye balls were flecked with capillaries, as the blood pressure in his head rose, bursting a vessel and coating the outer rims of each iris in a layer of crimson. The more he concentrated, the bloodier his eyeballs became, until she could see a picture forming in her thoughts. Like a 'magic eye' image, she immersed herself in the jumble of mixed messages, until she could make out a three-dimensional vision forming in her mind.

Visser fought against her penetrative scan; flooding his thoughts with random pictures and images from his past. A framed masterpiece, a girl with a pearl earring, her luminous face fading into a monochrome skull on a pirate's flag; the Black Pearl from Jonny Depp movie fame. Depp's pirate dreadlocks shrinking and then vanishing beneath a beanie hat as he peeps through the Secret Window, Stephen King's haunting tale of a writer's dwindling grasp on reality. Secrets… a playground full of children, encircling the young Lars Visser, all chanting *Vis Jongen, Vis Jongen – Fish Boy.* The young Lars standing in a scalding bath, tears spilling down his face and scrubbing his body raw with a nail brush. The series of medical tests confirming his rare disorder. A large bottle of potent cologne on Visser's dressing table.

He snapped his mind back from the rolling train of thoughts. He had strayed into his own personal realm and was fearful of what she might discern. In the spaces between his thoughts, she locked on and located the images he was desperate to conceal. In that one instant, he knew what power she had acquired. She had progressed farther than he and Alexi had anticipated. This was no docile captive. She was rapidly becoming a threat.

Mary sensed his apprehension, the resistance visible in those feline eyes. They darted about the room, first at Alexi, his expression deeply troubled, then back to Mary. It didn't matter. He could not break the connection she had forged into his stream of consciousness.

And there lie her mistake. In her pursuit to gain an insight into their scheme, she had laid bare her abilities. Training her was no longer an issue. Channelling her power for their own ends was now their primary goal. She knew that they would increase security as a precaution from her attempts at escape. Visser would enforce a tighter rein of control to assure her cooperation. That would inevitably put her loved ones in greater jeopardy. Mary lost focus for a split second, her mind drifting to those she loved most.

A pang of separation pierced her heart and induced a jagged intake of breath. If she could just get away from this megalomaniac, she might be able to protect her husband from harm. She had to get Alexi on side. He seemed a reasonable sort of person. Maybe she could persuade him to stand up to Visser's demands and help her to flee.

Before she released her captor's mental state, she extracted a scene from his thoughts. It was a confusing and disconcerting vision, resembling the one she had viewed on the guard's monitors. Row after row of motionless people in hospital beds. Men in scrubs, unhooking intravenous bags of fluids from patients and zipping those that had perished into opaque body bags. Each of the remaining unconscious people, were being physically turned on their medical cot and injected with more drugs.

Above them, she saw a large electronic wall chart showing exact positions of the world's tectonic plate boundaries. The great seams of the Earth's crust where volatile shifts and upwelling from the core result in volcanic eruptions and earthquakes. Japan, was lit up like a beacon.

Chapter Eleven

The lights dimmed in her room. They left Mary to sleep off her migraine, which in truth, was not severe. She could hear Lars Visser and Alexi in a fiery debate down the corridor. If only she had paid more attention to language lessons at school. Not that they would have taught her Russian at the time, but she might have developed enough of an interest to learn later in life. Mary assumed that they would be discussing how she had blocked Visser's attempts to read her mind and how she had caused him physical harm when she had turned the proverbial tables on him.

Three peculiar abilities, as a result of recent traumatic events. Three potentially useful gifts, plus an over developed sense of remote controlled empathy. And yet, she could not fathom how best to use those abilities to escape. She could fry electrical circuits, which is fantastic if they had used digital keypad locks. The huge iron bolt, supplemented with the mortice lock inside the door cavity was enough evidence to support their knowledge of that ability.

Travelling without a body and being able to look into other peoples' minds are handy gifts if your occupation just happens to be an international spy. It is not especially useful to a kidnapped senior lab technician. She was tying her brain in a knot thinking of possible routes to freedom, all the while aware of how time was plodding its weary steps closer to the night guard's duty.

There was no possibility of sleep. There was far too much at stake. Perhaps there was more chance of freedom from Alexi's lab. She munched on another apple while she pondered upon how to get Alexi on her side. Perhaps she could flirt with him. Seduce him into letting her go. He was only small. Mary felt sure that he could be no physical threat to her. Not like Visser and the guards. They were seriously imposing figures. If she could get him into that courtyard, away from everyone else, out in the fresh air, there might be a way out. Finishing the apple, she balanced the core on the table next to the TV. She pressed the power switch on the television and checked the time – 4.35pm.

"I'm feeling ok now, Alexi." She said to the camera. Within a couple of minutes, he appeared through the door.

"Good, good. Ready for work?" He was wearing his white lab coat over green scrubs. A pair of black rim spectacles poked out of the top pocket. Mary analysed his face. He had fine features, delicate and well groomed. Big blue eyes and soft mousey hair that was once referred to as *fly-away*, before the big commercial ad campaigns for shampoo rebranded it, *lifeless*.

Alexi was neither attractive nor unattractive. He was simply not the kind of man that she had ever desired. Mary wasn't sure that she had ever managed to pin point a type, but she knew the moment she met Parth, on that undergraduate field trip to South Shields, that he was someone she found highly desirous. The falling hopelessly in love part was gradual, spanning more than a year.

Occasionally, she wondered how her life would have turned out if Parth had not assisted her biology lecturer on that trip. They might never have met, had it not been for a minor bout of food poisoning that the department's research fellow had suffered the night before they were due to leave. Thirty undergraduate students in two minibuses travelling north, with only one qualified lecturer between them. Parth had just completed his doctorate thesis in Neurology and was contemplating moving back to India when his supervisor begged him to rescue the trip. Parth and Mary's relationship bloomed over the identification of marine wildlife.

Mary followed Alexi back down the corridor to the laboratory. A tea tray was waiting for her, pre-empting her request. Guards stood motionless either side of the exit and another inside the room itself. Alexi began attaching sticky pads to her forehead, connecting the wires to the metal contact points and checking the calibration on the computer. As he leaned in she whispered to him.

"I need to talk to you… alone." Mary flicked her head towards the guards, raising her eyebrows to stress the importance of confidentiality for their discussion.

"We are alone, Mary." Alexi continued his task, repositioning errant electrodes.

"Let's go outside for a breath of air. How do we get into that little quad over there?" She pointed through the window to the courtyard of abandoned flower beds.

"Work now. Outside later."

"Do you promise? If I do whatever it is you want of me now, you will come with me to the garden?"

"Yes, garden is reward." He sat on a high lab stool and poured her tea. From his pocket, he withdrew the same compass as before. Mary tried to hide her surprise. She was sure that he would be giving her a task with more challenge after witnessing the drama with Visser just a few hours ago. He placed the compass down in front of her. "Move needle with no touch."

Mary raised her hand next to the compass. Alexi grabbed her wrist and moved it behind her back.

"No! Hands away. Like this…" He put both his arms behind his back. She copied him, then concentrated on the red tip of the needle. As she imagined the metal shard facing the opposite direction, it started to move. Slowly at first, and then with a swing, it obeyed her command. Pleased with herself, she hopped down from her stool.

"Can we go to the garden now?"

"Work not done. We have only just started." His manner had altered from the morning. It could be her imagination, but Alexi seemed gruffer and stricter than before. He moved his computer mouse about the screen, clicking icons, saving files and then opening a video link. The screen showed a grey gravelled surface with another compass, glinting in the sunlight. "This on roof, here." Alexi pointed up, his eyes mirroring his finger. "You make it move."

She frowned. What was the purpose of all this? She needed to speed up the challenges, to get him alone to beg him to release her. *Okay. I can do this. Think of repelling that needle at my command. I can do this.* Mary focused. She imagined herself up on the roof, channelling her electromagnetic touch to the compass. The screen on the computer showed the needle vibrating, then it wobbled till finally it lurched in a full one hundred and eighty degree turn.

"Is that it for today? Can we go now?" She was impatient to investigate the garden quad.

"No. More to do."

"What is all this for? You cannot possibly have abducted me to move a few compasses?" She slumped on her stool, exasperated.

"You learn to combine your gifts. Use all at once. You very powerful." Alexi did not take his eyes from the screen. She laid her hand on his arm, trying to catch his attention. He looked down at her hand.

"Alexi, look at me."

He kept his gaze low. "Why won't you look at me?"

"You very powerful."

"You think I would hurt your eyes if I look into them? I'm not going to hurt you, Alexi. We can be friends. Let's go for a walk in the garden together."

"We have much work to do. We go later."

"No! We go now!" Mary's temper flashed. She banged her fist on the bench in front of him, sending a surge of power along the cables of the computer and blowing out the electronics. The screen went dead. The guard by the door fell to one knee, aiming his rifle directly at her. He paused, waiting for the command to fire. Alexi waved him to stand down.

"You were going to let him kill me?" Mary was shaken. She had convinced herself that she was more valuable to them alive than dead, allowing her a small degree of leverage. Fear took hold. Her motor neurons fired randomly, sending her core muscles into an uncontrollable tremor. Timid once more, she leaned her elbows on the table.

"Not kill. Gun has tranquilizer darts. Guards orders are to sedate you and restrain you on bed." Alexi pressed the power button several times on the computer base unit. It emitted no signs on life. "Come. We get fresh air."

The guard followed them through a preparatory room, down three concrete steps and through a fire door. Mary took that as a good sign. A fire door would never direct staff fleeing from a blaze into a dead end. There had to be a route to freedom somewhere beyond the garden quad. Alexi led the way towards a wooden bench situated beneath a silver birch tree. The slight breeze tickled the downy hairs on her arms. The dappled shade warmed her face. If she closed her eyes, she could almost be back at the duck pond in the park - almost.

The man with the gun, clicked his radio and muttered something Russian, before standing at the fire door threshold. Mary heard a noise like clanging metal – a closing gate perhaps, then booted steps marching into view from behind a corner of a building. A second guard arrived to block any attempt at escape. *So, that is my route to freedom. Just a matter of getting past armed soldiers first.*

"Alexi. You want me to cooperate, don't you? To use my gifts to help you and Visser in some way, yes?"

Alexi nodded.

"Then you have to keep me safe." She was clutching the sleeve of his lab coat. He edged away from her, pulling his arm away from her grasp.

"You are safe. Many guards keep you safe." He leaned away from her, pulling his white coat close around his legs, as if he could use it as a defensive shield.

"And who will protect me from the guards? One of them has threatened to come to my room tonight and hurt me." Her voice hushed to a rasping whisper.

"Not possible. Visser kill them if they harm you." He looked into her eyes, then immediately shrank back, physically turning his head away from her face.

"He said he could disable the camera and overpower me." She sat on the edge of the bench, her knees turned towards Alexi, imploring him.

"No. None of the guards would dare. Visser find out, kill them."

"But Visser would not find out if the camera was not switched on. Don't you see? You have to let me go or they will seriously harm me. Please Alexi. You know it's the right thing to do. How could you live with yourself if they raped me and you could have prevented it?"

Alexi shook his head unconvinced. His mobile phone rang. He listened to the person on the other end and hung up without a reply.

"New computer. We go back to work, da?" He stood up and beckoned her to follow him, noticeably avoiding her gaze. Mary sighed, taking in a last look at her surroundings. The windows on the buildings opposite all had drawn blinds except one. A roller blind extended less than halfway allowed the breeze to enter the open window. Mary stared, trying to gauge the height of the windowsill.

"I need to stretch my legs for a minute or two. Can I have a few minutes while you go and sort out the software on your new computer?" Mary flicked her eyelashes at him, adopting her best and most innocent expression. Alexi folded his arms, resisting her allure. "It's not as though I can go anywhere, can I?" Mary pointed at the armed guard in the doorway.

Alexi relented. "Five minutes. No more."

As soon as Alexi was out of view, she kicked her legs out, stretched and wandered around the flower beds, all the while keeping one eye on the guard. She crouched to tie and retie the laces on her old canvas shoes. They had seen better days. They still wore the mud stain from her bike ride through the puddles. Mary snapped her attention back. The guard drew a cigarette pack from his top pocket and slid one between his lips. She pretended not to notice, scuffing the rubber soles along the edges of the paving slabs near to the windows.

Mary watched him in the reflection. He tilted his gun down, pushing it out of his way on its shoulder strap and then fumbled with a box of matches from his trouser pocket. The breeze caught the first flame. It guttered and extinguished before he could light the end of his cigarette. He stepped backwards into the stairwell of the preparatory room, to shelter himself from the airstream.

This was her chance. Mary hopped across the flower border and trod on the concrete plinth below the open window. It was higher than she had estimated, but not enough to dissuade her attempt. Sliding her top half beneath the swinging window, she grasped the sill and readied herself to lock her elbows above the frame. Bouncing twice on tiptoe, she hoisted herself up. The metal dug into the palms of her hands and the weight of the glass swinging against her back bruised her spine, but she gritted her teeth long enough to hook her leg inside and heave the rest of her mass over the ledge. The drop on the inside was shallower, allowing her to reach down one leg at a time.

Mary scanned the room for reorientation. Her pulse was hammering in her throat and her mouth was dry. She could hear the guard yelling in Russian and heavy boots heading in her direction. Surrounded by rows of beds, each containing an unconscious patient, she crouched low to avoid detection from the teams of men wearing scrubs, who she knew would be making their rounds.

They were all so uniform, so still. Each patient wrapped tightly in surgical stockings and pressure bandages to prevent deep vein thrombosis. It was hard to tell them apart, or even which sex they were. Their slim gurneys equidistant and encasing the victims in familiar restraints. Chains of larvae in a bees nest. Was she supposed to become their queen?

The guard noises were approaching, and she had no doubt that they would radio for assistance. There could be more of them waiting for her beyond this hospital ward. It was a risk she had to take. Weaving between the trolleys of comatose people, Mary dashed towards the double doors at the far side of the room and into a corridor. Her plimsolls dampened her footsteps as she hurried along, searching for an external door to freedom. She could hear someone speaking English, a voice that made her shudder. Cyril Plender was close by. She edged nearer to an open door.

Mary peeked through the gap near the hinges. Inside the room, one patient lay attached to heart and blood pressure monitors. Cyril was barking orders at a Scrub Man. He passed Cyril a loaded syringe. Holding the plastic tube that delivered fluids via an intravenous line into the patient's neck, Cyril opened a valve and squeezed in a chemical from the syringe. They waited, watching the monitors trace a path across the black screen. If Mary dashed past the door now, they would definitely see her. She looked behind her. The corridor was empty, but she knew it wouldn't be long before the guards caught up.

"So far so good..." Plender said, a smug grin plastered between his straggly goatee. The monitor's trace lines wavered and an alarm sounded. The patient shook violently within the confines of the bindings, the seizure testing atrophied muscles to their limits. Within seconds, the trace flat lined.

"Bollocks. I was sure they had cracked it this time." Furious, Cyril turned and threw the syringe at the back wall.

Mary crept past and broke into a jog. Despite the late afternoon sun, the corridor was dim. As she scurried past each set of double doors, she peered through the window slits at shadowy wards of insect people, cocooned in their larval stages.

The labyrinthine network of corridors was disorientating. She made a series of left and right turns, passing empty nurse stations and several adjoining passageways. She was no longer sure that she was heading away from danger or towards it. Her sense of direction failed her and panic was creeping in.

Footsteps and muffled voices seemed to be echoing all around her, making her head spin. Her ribs ached with lactic acid and hyperventilation, the dizzying effects neutering her judgement. Mary found herself at a four-way junction. She looked around at the faded and torn notice board posters for anything remotely familiar; something to give her a clue as to which direction she had come from, or a sign to guide her to safety.

The choice of direction was random. Mary knew she couldn't afford to stand still and deliberate her options. She ran down the corridor that seemed the brightest. There was a window near the terminal point, next to another set of double doors. Perhaps she could orientate herself if she could see what was outside. In an acute state of anxiety, she ran. Holding her hands up to the glass to cushion her propulsion, she ground to a halt. She checked all around the frame for a mechanism with which to open the window, but it was a fixed pane.

Outside she could see that a left turn ahead, would take her to an ambulance bay and a set of external doors. A brief moment of elation washed through her mind, diluting the adrenalin in her veins and crystallising her thoughts. Mary bolted through the doors, letting them swing back into the metal doorstops with a loud bang. Reaching the corner, she held out her hand to the wall to aid her course correction and slammed right into the chest of a broad shouldered guard. He grabbed at her arms and held her close.

"I knew you couldn't resist me." He said, licking his teeth. "You couldn't even wait till tonight to get your hands on my body."

Chapter Twelve

It had taken a great deal of pleading on Mary's part to persuade Alexi not to return her to the bed restraints. She could tell that he was angry with her. He removed the bowl of fruit and stormed out of her cell without uttering a word. His demeanour said it all. She assumed that Visser was away from the building during her bid for freedom or the punishment would have been far more severe.

Mary's evening meal consisted of a lukewarm bowl of porridge, presumably to reinforce Alexi's displeasure with her. It tasted sickly and had a weird tang to it, like they had used spoiled milk to make it and hidden the fact by adding too much sugar.

The television informed her that it was past ten o'clock. She left it on mute and considered her options. That brute of a guard was clearly sincere in his threat to visit her room. In fact, he had announced it in front of several other guards, leading her to assume he had some authority over them. That being the case, the lower ranking soldiers would take no part in preventing him from overpowering her, forcing himself upon her.

They could switch off the camera, or worse still, be passive spectators of the crime. They had the ability to remove any recordings or disable functions as they egged him on. *Might I have to endure not one rape, but multiple offences?* Her thoughts rewound to the sensation of his fingers digging into her arms. The rank smell of layer upon layer of old sweat, dried and reanimated by his body heat.

Mary trembled. Her helplessness manifesting in uncontrollable muscle twitches. She sat crossed legged on the bed, her hands cradling her head, rocking her torso backwards and forwards. *Pull yourself together. There has to be a way to fight back. If you can hurt one of them, it might make the others think twice about joining in. They cannot kill me, or Visser would shoot them in the head. They can injure me. They are more than twice as strong as I am. I won't be able to overpower them.*

I need to keep moving, don't let that bastard get me on the bed and in those restraints, no matter how much he slaps or punches me. Just take the pain. The last cuff across my face from the guard that Visser killed, was no more painful than a bad migraine. Bear the pain and resist. But how? He could crush me. Find something sharp...

Rushing into the bathroom, she rummaged in the toiletry bag for the aerosol can of deodorant. Holding it securely in both hands, she turned her face away and thrust it against the mirror. It sprang back, leaving a small dent in the reflective surface. *What the...?* A stainless steel, anti-vandalism mirror.

Mary considered her toothbrush. She had watched all those series on TV about women in prison making *shivs* by grinding down the end of a snapped toothbrush on a brick wall. She analysed the brush that Alexi had provided. It was bendy at the narrowest point of the handle. No amount of manipulation would induce the plastic to snap.

The hairbrush was solid wood with stiff plastic bristles. She leaned it at an angle between the floor and the wall and stamped down on the shaft. It slid down, horizontal to the floor. The bristles crushed under her shoe, but it was otherwise intact. Mary picked it up and bounced the head against her hand. The uniform bunches of nylon jabbed her palm. It might inflict some pain if she could swipe it with enough force against his face. It would have to do.

Mary's stomach gurgled, pushing the half-digested food up her gullet. She swallowed the acid back down and held her mouth under the running tap, slurping at the cold water. Facing the mirror again, her vision blurred and focused alternately. She staggered back towards the television. The weatherman turned into a smudge of blue with flecks of red that had minutes before been a tie. Rubbing her eyes with a free hand and clutching her hairbrush with the other, she misjudged the height of the chair and thumped her bottom down heavily. *They have drugged me… shit. Stay awake. Walk up and down. Must stay awake!*

Using her hands to push herself up from the seat, she fought against her buckling knees and weighted eyelids, forcing herself to pace between the door and the corner that contained the mounted surveillance camera. Her head felt inordinately heavy. It drooped down to her chest, pulling on the muscles in the back of her neck. Saliva pooled at the corners of her mouth and oozed down her chin. Her foot dragged across the floor with each step until the weariness seeped throughout her entire body. She tried to make it back to the chair, the last of her common sense telling her to avoid the bed. Her knee gave way and she crumpled to the floor, one elbow hooking the chair seat. Mary was still holding the hairbrush in her lessening grip when she passed briefly out of consciousness.

Her chin connected with the hard plastic of the chair as her head fell, clenching her teeth around her tongue. The pain woke her, not fully alert, but to the echoed sound of the key turning in the lock. Her mind told her body to move, to wake up, but nervous control of motor function was jerky and uncoordinated. The bolt slid across and the door creaked ajar.

The brute surveyed his handiwork for a moment, chuckling at her undignified state. Through the blurred veil of eyelashes, she could see him gesturing to the camera. He swiped a flattened hand across his neck, indicating that they should switch off the device. Contra to her notions of voyeurism, he did not want an audience. She wasn't sure whether this was a good or bad sign for her fate. Did he mean to abuse her all night? He could still bang on the door and his co-conspirators could let themselves in later. They secured the lock and bolt once more. There was no escape.

He grabbed the remote control and raised the television volume. Every brain cell in her head was telling her to fight, to keep moving, but her physical actions were too delayed to be useful. She waved the hairbrush in his general direction, making him snort in humour at her ineptitude.

"Very powerful. That is what Alexi said. Ha! That is funny." He stepped closer and slid an arm beneath her limp legs, his other around her back, and lifted her as though she were a rag doll. Dropping her onto the bed roughly, he grabbed at an ankle and pulled off a shoe. "I don't think I will need to bind you. It will be like fucking a corpse as it is. You like it in the arse, little girl?" Her second shoe came off and hit the floor. He was tugging at her sweat pants.

The theme tune for a noir comedy drowned out her muffled cries for help. She pleaded with him to be merciful, but the speech pattern was unrecognisable. It amused him. "You want I should slap you about a bit first, eh? You like it rough?" He twisted her by the legs, pulling the trousers down and revealing her cotton underwear. Her face was buried in the folds of the pillow. He slapped her across the buttocks, hard, the pain radiating through her pelvis. It revived her senses.

"Enough foreplay." He yanked the jersey fabric over her feet and dropped the trousers to the floor. "I think I will have both holes. Which do you want me to do first, eh?" He rolled her onto her back and grabbed at her knickers, the stretched elastic cutting into her skin. He tried to rip the material, but they were too well constructed. Annoyed, he wrenched them down towards her feet.

God, no. Please stop this. Mary's intentions to plead with any vestige of kindness that the guard might have, remained inside her head. Her mouth could not form the words audibly. He unbuckled his belt, unzipped his army fatigues and let them ruche around his ankles. Waves of revulsion rippled through her body, as he knelt between her legs and considered her most intimate parts.

I cannot let this happen. Where are Visser and Alexi? I can't believe that I need my captors to rescue me. This is too cruel. He is looking right into me. I feel sick. Perhaps projectile vomit all over him would make him stop, or it might anger him. That slap across my bum was painful enough. A punch to the face would give me brain damage or kill me. I don't know what to do…

The guard hovered over her body, knocking her legs apart with his knees and resting his hips against hers. "You like this, eh? You feel how big I am? I am going to split you apart."

Mary battled the effects of the sedation. Every reviled muscle that could still respond to her command clenched. He reached down and jabbed two dirty fingers inside her, his jagged nails tearing her delicate tissue.

That initial act of defilement, triggered a series of chemical reactions in her brain, which in part neutralised the effects of the sedative. Mary summoned the strength to move her arms, forcing them to bend; her tightened fists tucked beneath her chin. *Bastard! He will pay for this…* From the depths of her abdomen, a swirling force of energy built momentum, coursing through her body, heating her torso and surging through her arms. Mary spread out her hands and connected them around his bullish neck.

Visible sparks flew. A bolt of enormous voltage jolted through the guard's body, sending his heart into uncontrollable spasms and overloading the neural pathways in his brain. The skin on his throat charred and the smell of grilled meat, overpowered the stench of sweat. Her hands felt like glowing embers, yet they did not burn. His body shook violently, all muscles contracting in time with the powerful electric current cooking him from the inside out. The brute wailed just once, a prolonged and agonising howl, before all activity ceased and his limbs gave way to gravity.

The dead weight pinned Mary to the mattress. She shook in terror from head to toe. She had killed a man. A soldier had died at her hand and without the use of a conventional weapon. That was not something you could shuck off lightly. She pressed her fingers against his blackened jugular vein. There was no detectable pulse. Wriggling sideways, she lifted one of his arms over her head, and pushed his ribs until he slid from her body and hung off the edge of the bed.

The energy surge restored most of her faculties, enough to kick his legs from hers until he slipped off the cot and on to the concrete below. Mary located her knickers, which were encircling her left ankle and put them back on. She stepped over the body and did the same with her trousers.

The tremor in her stomach subsided and she looked impassively at the dead body. Why didn't she feel remorse? She should feel horrified – she had killed another human being. Vegetarian, humanitarian Mary had snuffed out a person's life. He may not have been a good person, he may have deserved punishment, but she had with deliberate, wilful intention, killed him. She was a murderer.

These thoughts and many more trickled calmly through her mind. It was not a skill she intended to use often, but the sudden realisation that she could kill, or perhaps seriously harm if she could learn to control it, formed the basis for a new plan of escape.

***

Mary contemplated her options. Firstly, she had to avoid any punishment and secondly, she was not yet ready to implement her plan. The thought of the arm restraints or the possibility of guards' retaliation horrified her. Mary decided that she must stage the crime scene to deflect attention. If they accused her of being the cause, she would deny it and adopt a flaky and pathetic tone to some well-timed feminine histrionics.

The red light on the camera was still off, but she had to act fast. Post-mortem urine was already soaking into the guard's underwear. A pool of the acrid liquid in the wrong place would ruin her pretence. It sickened her to touch him. Mary forced herself to inch his trousers up, yanking one side then the next in turn, until the waist band was above his posterior. Using the loose belt as a strap, she pulled it until the body twisted onto the side allowing her to fasten the zip and buckle.

With restricted meals and no access to exercise, her incarceration had reduced her muscle mass. She felt weak and could not shake the dizzy spells in the aftermath of the drugs leaving her system. With both hands gripping the guard's wrist, she leaned her shoulders back and hauled him close to the power socket supplying the television.

Now what? A television wouldn't blow itself up. A short circuit in the plug would trip the fuse board switch and alert the rest of the guards. Then there is his scorched neck. How can I explain that as the obvious point of contact? The problem required a clear head and more careful thought that she felt able to give. Mary's mind drifted, lamenting the need to sacrifice the television. She would be unable to tell the time in its absence.

Maybe the brute has a watch or even a mobile phone. Mary searched the body for anything useful, stripping him of his cheap Timex and hiding it in her washbag. She found no phone, but during her rummage in his pockets, his combat trousers slid up his leg, revealing a small knife tucked into an ankle holster. Result. She used the remote to switch off the television and then unplugged it. Scraping and fraying the power cable with the knife, Mary exposed the bare metal near to the base of the plug, as though the plastic clasp had worn the wires.

Where could she hide the knife? Alexi changed the sheets on the bed often, she couldn't hide it under the mattress. She needed it close by for protection. There was plenty of room to hide a small knife in the sports bra that Alexi had provided, were it a penknife with a covered blade. The leather ankle holster would be visible if she wore it under her jogging trousers. She quickly cut the straps away from the holster, leaving just the sheath and stowed the knife carefully beneath her left breast. It was uncomfortable and the pointed part of the leather dug into her upper arm, but it was worth it for the security.

Mary was almost ready. Returning the television plug to the socket, she angled the guard's arm until his hand connected with the bare wires. His other hand, she positioned on the back of his neck, resting his elbow on the floor to hold it in place. She flicked the switch and jumped back. The television blared into life. Alan Yentob was analysing a post-modern painting and gearing himself up to interview the relatives of the deceased artist. *Damn. It was supposed to short out. I will have to boost the power myself.*

Reaching over the body, she leaned down and sharpened her mind. *Come on… you did this before with Dan, when you blew out the security panel in Parth's department. Be calm, Mary.* She told herself. Closing her eyes, she steadied her thoughts and visualised the energy flow. Holding her hand a couple of centimetres from the exposed wires, the voltage skipped from her palm via a blue vein of light, overwhelming the circuits.

The television tripped out with a loud bang; Yentob cut off in his prime. The overhead lights went out, pitching the room into darkness. Mary waited a moment for her eyes to adjust. She scrambled back to the bed, sitting cross legged and trying to look blameless. Voices and loud boots clamoured down the hallways, workers and soldiers all busying themselves like frenzied fire ants in restoring power and finding the root cause.

There was a distant clunk through the walls as they found and flipped the mains trip switch, and then a buzz as the strip lights above her head choked back into life. Her room smelled repugnant, a mixture of body fluids and singed plastic and flesh. The bolt clanged back, the key turned and two armed men bowled through the door. They looked in horror at their superior officer smouldering on the floor and then at Mary.

"Cyka! You bitch. You killed him." One of the soldier ants yelled.

"It wasn't me. He electrocuted himself." Mary creased her face up and started to cry, a whiny, feeble, dry-eyed whimper.

"Lezha suka. Lying bitch!" The second guard stormed over to her on the bed and threatened to hit her with the butt of his gun. Alexi wandered in, wearing pyjamas and a dressing gown, scratching the back of his head.

"What is happening?" Alexi froze as the guard threatening Mary drew his gun back and was about to strike her. "Ostanavlivat'sja! Stop!" Alexi growled a full sentence of Russian that Mary had no hope comprehending, but the guards' response was explanation enough. Both men, hung their heads in shame. Scalded, they left Alexi alone in the room with Mary.

Alexi turned to face her. "What has happened here?"

Mary stepped up her tears a notch and threw her arms about the little man, stretching up from the bed. "Oh Alexi, it was so awful…" She sobbed into his shoulder, half theatrics but with a significant proportion of truth.

Chapter Thirteen

Alexi ordered three soldiers to clean Mary's room. It took some time for the noxious smells to dissipate, so it was late when Mary was able to shower and climb into the bed. She harboured a mild feeling of empowerment. She was not sure how much of her story Alexi believed, but the guards were in no position to give him a factual account.
The red flashing light resumed as they switched off the overhead lights, leaving the dim wall mounted lamps with which they could spy on her nocturnal habits. Whether the drugs were still active in her system or the mental exertion of the evenings events had drained her, Mary slept. A profound rest, stemming from a new found security. The guards would not be attempting any further efforts to violate her. She had them running scared.

The following morning, Alexi woke Mary and encouraged her to eat the hearty breakfast he had prepared for her; poached eggs, toast, cereal and a large pot of tea. She showered again, scrubbing away the flashbacks of the night before. It was clear that the guards had been talking. As she and Alexi walked down the corridor to the lab, the soldier ants edged further away from her, their fingers twitching over the triggers of their tranquiliser guns.

Alexi had prepared a translation on his phone. "Now that you have seen the other patients in this hospital, you will have some idea of what we expect of you."

"No, not really. I know that you have a large number of people in chemically induced comas. I know that some of them are dying." She was careful not to mention her knowledge of Plender's involvement. Alexi listened to his phone and then pasted another Russian sentence into the translator application.

"Those people are special, like you, but much less powerful. They need medication to help their abilities. Long term drugs make them ill."

"Easy solution then, stop medicating them." She shifted uneasily on her lab stool.

"That cannot happen. They are needed for a mission." More tapping and listening on his phone.

"Mission? What mission?" Mary tried to gain Alexi's attention. He kept his line of sight on his mobile screen.

"That is confidential at present, but know that you are necessary for its success." He glanced furtively at her face for a second, lowering his eyes from her gaze.

"Why would anyone volunteer to be subjected to a chemical cocktail that puts them in a semi-permanent coma which could kill them?" She threw her arms in the air. There was a long pause while Alexi thought carefully about his choice of words to type into the application.

"They did not volunteer. Most were conscripted. Russian military screens for potential candidates. The rest Visser found, like you but younger, then paid off their families."

"That's disgraceful." She did not hide her look of disgust.

"Perhaps. They are serving their great nation." His expression had not altered throughout their conversation. Alexi's implacable stance being part of his upbringing.

"But why must they stay in a coma? Can't they meditate or something instead?" She could see that Alexi was losing patience with her. His agitation manifested in his strident phone tapping.

"Hive mission very intense. They stay a focused unit at all times, ready for commands. Coma is only way to maintain cohesion of their minds. Individually, none are strong enough to affect changes and lose valuable time in trying to coordinate brain rhythms."

"What do you expect me to do?" Mary grasped the edge of the bench, tightening her grip with a sense of foreboding.

"You will lead them. Guide them, be at one with them and direct their powers." This was another pre-prepared sentence Alexi pasted.

"I will not!" Mary hopped off the lab stool and marched towards the door. Lars Visser arrived and blocked her path. Instinct prompted her to cover her mouth and nose, shielding herself from his resilient cologne. Despite holding her breath, the vapour inveigled its way around her digits and adhered to the linings in her nasal cavity. Beneath the chemical tang, she detected a fishy note. Mary recoiled, her gag reflex summoning the remnants of her breakfast.

"Are you being quarrelsome again, Mary? Tut, tut. That will never do." Visser removed a thin piece of red leather from his jacket pocket and shook it till the little bell dangling from a buckle on its end, tinkled. "Shall I give Aristotle your regards?"

Mary wobbled. Sudden confidence in her abilities had made her temporarily forget Visser's threats to harm her loved ones. She had pushed at the limits of her captor's patience without regard for Parth's wellbeing. They would still be monitoring him and perhaps her grandfather too.

A swell of emotion engulfed her, her soft palate acidifying and making the space behind her nose tingle, foretelling the tears. Mary fought to gain control. *Be compliant*. She told herself. Information was power, and the more amiable she was, the more he talked.

"What do you want me to do?" Mary tried to extinguish the animosity glowing in her eyes. Visser had gifts; considerably more than intuition to fall back on. She could not afford to let down her guard. Visser guided her back towards the stool where Alexi was sitting. Mary flinched at his touch.

"You must learn to tune into my Hive Mind…" Visser flashed a beatific smile in her direction. *His* Hive Mind. *His* proud creation. *His* megalomaniacal whims directing perhaps hundreds of gifted minds. A cold chill permeated her spine. *Compliance.* She reminded herself.

"How do I do that?" She dampened her voice to a whisper.

"Do you remember the first time you saw me?" Visser waited for her to recollect. "When you synchronised your thought waves to that little boy in Japan, the trapped earthquake victim?" He was standing too close. Mary could taste the seafood and aftershave cocktail with every inhalation.

"Synchronised? You mean that I was feeling his pain because my brainwaves mirrored his?" She leaned away from him, restricted by a bench top.

"Precisely. You did the same thing when you read my mind too. Although I should have been prepared for that and stopped you. In both cases, you were emotionally charged. Pity for the little boy and hatred for me." Mary could not stop her eyebrows from rising and a demi-smile of agreement formed on her mouth. She did not deny it. "Now you must learn to do the same thing but at your command. To tune into their rhythms and feel their collective energies."

"How?" Mary could see sense in the theory of channelling frequencies. It sounded like tuning a radio or television. But they were receivers of a broadcast, in the same way that she became the receiver of the little Japanese boy's broadcast of pain and distress. She was in no position to alter the subject of transmission.

"I think we should begin with you being in close proximity to the Hive, perhaps… Alexi, could you take Mary into one of the wards? I have a meeting shortly, elsewhere, and it might be less confusing than having my thought patterns in the mix too."

"Yes, yes of course." Alexi slid from his stool and took Mary by the elbow. "We go the proper way. No climbing through windows and running away." He admonished.

***

"Do they know what is happening? Are they aware that the drugs are killing them?" Mary looked closely at the neutral expression on the young man's face. A thin hospital sheet and gown were all that kept his dignity intact. Alexi began typing into his smartphone.

"They are one. They are all in constant communication with each other. A community within their linked subconscious minds. I suspect that they are no longer aware of their physical bodies, but I am not the one who talks with them. Visser is their director at present."

"But they are all so young. They should have their whole lives ahead of them – to work, fall in love, have families and experience the world… Alexi, how can you stand by and let this happen? Can't you see how wrong it all is?" An empathy and sadness filled her, an intense compassion meandering through her thoughts.

"Only the mission matters. Can you detect their stream of consciousness?" Alexi scanned Mary's eyes. The pooling glaze of liquid accentuated the rich mahogany tones of her irises. One drop escaped her lids and nestled between the lashes. Alexi looked away. "You can feel them, yes?"

"No. I can't, and I won't either. This is barbaric." Mary turned towards the entrance to the ward and started walking.

"Visser will hurt your husband. Parth is in grave danger. Visser does not enjoy killing people, but he does like reading their minds while he tortures them slowly." He waited, poised with his phone, waiting for her obedience.

Mary stopped and sauntered back to the gurney supporting the comatose Hive Operative. Maybe she could find out enough information to free these victims or at the very least, defeat Visser and compromise their operation. It had to be a mission with deadly consequence, or they would not have gone to such lengths to ensure her collaboration. How could a Dutch born sociopath use a Russian Hive Mind to cause monumental changes in the economic and political landscapes of great nations?

Mary listened to Alexi's instructions. A guard collected a chair with soft padding from an office and wheeled it into the ward for Mary to sit in. She made herself comfortable and closed her eyes, concentrating on rhythmic breathing, slowing her movements and thoughts down until she could almost fall asleep. Alexi and the guards crept further away and watched.

Inside her head, eddying thoughts alighted on an image of Parth, like a butterfly landing on an exotic flower to drink in the nectar. He was sitting at his office desk, typing away at his journal, periodically slurping from a large coffee mug. A pang of sentiment and fear broke her attention, stirring her fully alert. Alexi scurried over to her.

"You could sense them? Yes?" He shook his clasped hands towards her in elation.

"No. You are wasting your time. I couldn't sense anything other than my own thoughts."

Alexi frowned, turned to a guard and bellowed a stream of Russian at him. The guard ran off out of the ward and into a room close by. Mary heard a mechanical clunk – the sound of a thrown lever and a high pitched whine that she had not noticed before, wind down into silence.

More tapping on the smartphone. "Stupid guards left the solenoids switched on. It should be easier for you now." Alexi touched her shoulder, gesturing her to lean back and try again.

"What do the solenoids do?" She perked up. *Could this tech somehow aid my escape? Keep him talking.* Alexi started the laboured phone translation process again, while she spun from side to side in the office chair, analysing the ward for potential routes to freedom.

"We use them to hide any electromagnetic flux emanating from the Hive Mind. We don't want intelligence agencies to find us, do we?" Alexi gently pushed her shoulder again, indicating that she should try again.

"No, of course not. That would never do." She failed to hide the sarcastic tone. Alexi realised his mistake in telling her. He muttered a command to the guard on his return from the room containing the solenoids. He removed a key clip from his belt and rushed off to secure them. *Think before you open your mouth, Mary. You are your own worst enemy.*

"You try again. Perhaps better if your hand connects with Hive Man?" Alexi was moving her by the wrist closer to the Operative. Mary pulled her hand away.

"No, thank you. I will try without having to touch that poor young man." She sat back in the chair, arms resting in her lap and cleared her mind. Behind her eyelids, blobs of colours faded in and out of her vision, moving randomly. There was a low hum in the back of her head. It should have been alarming, like the ominous buzz of an overhead pylon in the early morning mist. Instead it felt strangely soothing. The reassurance of a supportive presence surrounding her – safety in numbers, a collective intelligence.

Next came the voices, low at first, then louder. Shrieks of laughter, murmurs, shouting and singing, filled her head in a massive cacophony of noise that was so voluminous, it was painful to listen to. Too many voices, some deep, some higher pitched and all in a language which sounded aggressive and incomprehensible. She opened her eyes, gasping.

"I can't, Alexi. They are all shouting. It's so very loud in there."

"But you could hear them, yes?" his expression, gleeful.

"Yes, but they are mostly Russian. I cannot understand a word they are saying. This is pointless. Whatever you expect me to do with them, is impossible. You may as well let me go now. I'm going back to my room." Mary stood up and again made for the exit. The guard placed his gun across the opening, shaking his head.

Patting and swiping the screen of his phone, Alexi placed a call. "Visser, she did it… yes, I know. Very quick. Told you she was powerful. You come back now." He turned to Mary. "You get fruits, chocolate, films to watch…treats. You did well, Mary. Very good."

"Yay. Well done me." Mary grimaced. "Can I go outside again? I miss the sunshine. I promise I won't climb through anymore windows."

Alexi narrowed his eyes, then nodded. "Half an hour only."

***

There were grey clouds scudding by and a breeze that carried a bite, making the gooseflesh on her arms prominent. Mary breathed the cold air into her lungs and let the particles of hospital stink blow away.

How did Visser find me in the first place? If all the other Hive Operatives are mainly Russian, what prompted him to search for me in the Midlands of England? Had Plender assessed my abilities when I first started shorting electrical equipment in the Lab? Did he tell his wife, Yelena about the oddities and she informed Visser?

Which one of them is to blame for my predicament? Yelena has been my friend for years. How could she suddenly turn against me like that? And now, she is infiltrating Parth's life too. Is she Visser's trigger man? If I fail to do as he asks, will it be Yelena who fires the shot into Parth's head?

Mary rubbed at her eyes and told herself to concentrate. She longed for her husband. She missed his voice, his kindness, the intimate touch of a spouse. He would still be grieving for her. Parth had been quite pragmatic about death when he lost a much-loved uncle. He grieved quietly, alone in his office, sent flowers and attended the funeral with deep respect. Mary wondered if he was equally calm when they informed him of her death.

The wind changed direction, bringing a faint smell of diesel and muffled traffic noises. A siren blared, confirming her suspicions that the 'disused' hospital she was sitting amongst was on the outskirts of a town or city, perhaps even her home town. The way that Visser popped out for half an hour or so, and then returned promptly, suggested that they were not far from civilisation. This revelation sparked an idea to travel without her body again, to search for her escape route at the earliest opportunity.

Alexi stepped out onto the courtyard to join her, bringing packaged sandwiches and cartons of juice. Mary accepted her cheese and pickle offering, ripped open the cardboard and took an enormous mouthful.

"I think you very hungry, yes?" Alexi chuckled.

Mary chewed, swallowed and then tucked the remaining food into her cheek to answer. "I don't understand why. I haven't exercised at all since you locked me up, yet I am constantly ravenous."

"Normal brain function makes up twenty per cent of body's energy needs. When brain is being used to do complex things, energy consumption is more." He unsheathed a plastic straw and pierced the foil covered hole in the juice carton. He offered it to Mary. She shook her head, wrinkling up her nose. "Ah. You drink only tea. I make you one in a little while." They sat together in silence, munching on their lunches. Mary pulled stray strands of her hair behind her ears when the wind caught it.

"I know you killed that guard." Alexi said, not looking up from his sandwich. Mary half expected this. She froze waiting for him to give her bad news or some form of punishment. "I did not tell Visser."

"He was trying to rape me, Alexi. I had no other choice. They drugged my porridge. It was all planned in advance – I tried to tell you." She put the half eaten sandwich back in the wrapper and swivelled her body to face him. "You have to believe me. I had no other choice."

Alexi stopped eating, listening to her appeal. He did not face her, but bowed his head slightly. “Then you understand that sometimes we must do whatever it takes to survive.”

“Are they threatening too? Is Visser forcing you to hold me here?” Mary brightened at the prospect of forging an alliance with Alexi.

“Visser? No. Not him. Come… I make you tea and then back to work. Visser is talking with Hive Mind. He is giving them orders. You are new director, English only.” He stood up, indicating that the discussion was over. Mary wanted more information. She had to get him to sit down and confide in her.

“Are you married, Alexi? Do you have children?” She stayed resolutely in her seat.

“No time for talk. We work. Come.” He beckoned her with his hand to follow.

“We have all day. Sit with me for a while. You must have someone you love back home?” Mary continued to eat her sandwich.

“Not all day, deadline has been set. We must work now.” He gestured again.

“Deadline for what? Who has set it?” She moved from the bench on his insistence. “Is Visser planning something dreadful?”

“Come. Must show progress, and soon.” He scuttled into the prep room through the fire door, leaving the guard to round her up like a Border collie. Mary finished her sandwich and thrust the packaging at the guard. He glared at her, but took it. Alexi led the way back into the laboratory where Lars Visser sat waiting for them.

"Ah there you both are. I was going to send out a search party. I have given my Hive implicit instructions, Mary, but you will do whatever Alexi commands. Is that understood?" Visser paused for her acceptance. Mary waited for a moment, pretending to contemplate his demand, then nodded. Visser grinned at her power play. "Good. Now then. I have to go for my interview with a stunning French blonde. You remember the one, Mary? From the Ball?"

"Connie? You are meeting with Constance Cadot? What for?" Mary's mind raced, linking all the possible reasons Visser could have for meeting with Constance. Did they already know one another? And by logical extension, did Visser know her boyfriend, Dan Wildman? The man with whom she had shared her secret regarding out of body adventures, the friend who had read the picture from her mind of Tower Bridge in the University Library? Was there anyone left in her life whom she could fully trust?

Chapter Fourteen

"Hello? Can anyone hear me? This is a weird sensation. My head feels very full". Mary sighed. How could she introduce herself to a Hive Mind? Worse still, Visser expected her to guide them. Her mind wandered into a vision of her handing over a key to all her thoughts. Her most intimate dreams and wishes, locked away from even her husband.

What if I am not strong enough to pull myself back out, will I be assimilated into the hive too? Her mouth was dry and a tremble that began in her stomach, radiated out to the tips of her extremities.

"It is better than having an empty head, is it not?" Several voices laughed. Mary could hear them all muttering in the background. It was like the intermission bar at a theatre, the hushed voices of polite people, echoing from the vaulted ceilings.

"Who said that? What do I call you?"

"I am Thirty-Four. Captain." His intonation was soft, but his words were abrupt, as if years of military practices had hardened his tongue.

"What is your...um...name, Captain?" Mary tried to affect an authoritarian tone, but the result sounded more like a backfiring campervan. The thought

of commanding anyone was bizarre to her, let alone hundreds of professional soldiers.

"Thirty-Four. Captain Thirty-Four. Traditional names were relinquished at the start of this programme, ma'am."

"Are One to Thirty-Three your subordinates, Captain?" The image of their physical state flashed through her thoughts. She dismissed it as fast as she could. Mary had no desire to upset these soldiers with a reminder of their bodies. Another thought occurred to her. What if she accidently angered the Hive? Would they swarm into her head and do irrevocable damage? What if they receive the idea of attack through her and that initiated action? In her semi-conscious state, she shook her limbs, drifting her attention back to the laboratory.

"Are you alright, Mary? What is happening?" Alexi panicked, fiddling with the neural mapping cap on her head. Mary waved him aside, closed her eyes and refocused.

"Captain?"

"Privates Thirteen and Twenty-Two are still here and under my command. The others you mentioned timed out. Their conscription or contract ended, Ma'am." Thirty-Four issued some Russian orders at the rising voices of discord. The clamour ceased. Mary had opened a festering sore of contention.

"And how long have you been serving for, Captain?" An honest question, innocently framed. She had seen television footage of her Majesty Queen Elizabeth inspecting the troops. She had asked similar of her personnel. The voices rose once more. Thirty-Four

put them sharply in their place. *"Have I said something wrong, Officer?"*

"No, Ma'am. It's just time is a difficult concept here. Some of the soldiers think they are being cheated out of their pensions or forced to serve longer than their contracts."

A damning thought occurred to her that she did not know how to conceal. She pulled herself out of the Hive Mind, shaking her limbs. Blinking fully alert, she turned to Alexi. "Visser hasn't told them they are dying."

"Shush, shush, Mary. Do not upset yourself." Alexi poured her another cup from the teapot.

"Upset myself? It's inhuman the way they are treated. We have to stop him." She raised her hand again, this time dismissing Alexi's offering.

"Cannot stop. Only the mission matters. You must not tell them they are dying. Do only as instructed, Mary. That is very important." He faced his computer, trotting out the lines he thought she needed to hear.

"But those poor men. Can they read my mind while I am away from them?" Mary's urge to escape was all the more desperate. She stood up from the comfy chair and stretched her legs.

"I don't think so. No one else has ever been as powerful or controlled as you. Even Visser has to be physically close to talk with them. He must meditate to find their frequency. You can dip in and out when and where you like, it seems. Quite amazing." Alexi was talking through his smartphone app and clicking the computer mouse at the same time, trawling through images of neural activity in the simulation programme. "You need to get their full cooperation, Mary. Then we will try a little experiment."

"But I have no idea what to say to them."

"General chit-chat. It is good word, eh? Chit-chat. I like very much. Go on." He gestured for her to sit down and try again. She complied, reluctantly.

Closing her eyes and slowing her physical movements, she tuned in again to the rumblings of the Hive.

"Captain Thirty-Four?"

"Da? Yes, Ma'am?"

"Tell me a little about yourself."

"What would you like to know, Ma'am?"

"Are you married, Captain?" Mary tried to keep her thoughts neutral. Any emotional outburst could destabilise the men. She needed them to trust her. The sight of their comatose states kept floating back into her mind. She swiped at them with a metaphorical hand.

"I am, Ma'am. We had five wonderful years together before this mission."

"Any children?"

"We had a boy, Ma'am, but he didn't pull through from..." Thirty-Four struggled to find the English words for a childhood disease. Mary didn't wait to prolong the agony.

"I am very sorry to hear of your loss, Captain. Are many of you family men?"

"Quite a few, yes Ma'am. There are a few women amongst us too. Not many though." The other voices were silent, but still listening intently. Of that she was sure. Had she provoked a dangerous level of introspection? Perhaps she should change the subject. Focus the Hive back on military matters and steer away from personal queries.

"Can you tell me what you know of the mission, Captain?"

"Our orders are to influence and infiltrate, Ma'am."

"Infiltrate what exactly?" This was it. Thirty-Four was going to give her the exact nature of Visser's plan.

"Whatever Colonel Visser commands us to do, Ma'am."

"Such as...?"

"There is a smaller group who have infiltrated areas of global stock markets, Ma'am, but the majority of us direct our energies into whatever Colonel Visser is working on at the time."

"Stock markets? How are they influencing them?"

"Our strongest team can persuade weak minded capitalists to sell shares at a time that benefits Colonel Visser. His agents then buy them at a fraction of the cost."

"So Visser is a common thief?"

"Ma'am, you cannot slander the Colonel. He is a war hero, a legend."

"Hmm, if you say so. Has the Colonel given you orders regarding me, Captain?"

"Yes Ma'am. We are to channel all energy into your conscious stream. Would you like us to begin now?"

"Gosh, no. Not yet. Let me get back to you. At ease, gentlemen." Mary brought herself to full consciousness and drank her cooling tea. *So, this is how Visser is funding this operation.* Making a killing on the stock market suddenly had new meaning.

"They understand what to do, yes?" Alexi clicked his mouse, bringing Google Earth up on his screen. He grabbed the globe and dragged it until it showed the furthest reaches of Russia and the west coast of Alaska. "Come, look." Mary got to her feet and ambled across the lab. This was where it got real. The sense of menace weighted her limbs, a deep sea diver running out of oxygen and hope. She perched herself on the lab stool at Alexi's side. He zoomed in on an area in the south of Alaska, bordered by snow-capped national parks and gigantic winding rivers.

The entire area looked to Mary, like a transverse section of the brain, the peninsula and islands forming the brainstem, the glaciers branching like arteries and veins. Alexi kept zooming. In the central point of the Alaskan brain, at the site of its imaginary pineal gland, was an almost perfect square.

"You see this? Da? It is American research facility." Alexi jabbed at the screen, making the surface bow and leaving a dent where his fingertip had been. "It emits big, big waves. Sends up into atmosphere."

"O-kay."

"You make it switch on. Hive will help you. You direct wave. Hit certain part of atmosphere." He continued to prod the monitor.

"Can't you just ask them if you can borrow it? Or hack into their mainframe or something?" Mary yawned. "This seems an awful lot of bother just to use a research gizmo."

Alexi turned to face her. His eyes burned into hers. It was the first time he had looked directly at her since her standoff with Visser in her cell. "You do as told." His voice rose along with his temper.

"Okay, I was only asking." She moved away from him. This was a side of Alexi he had kept well hidden.

"Hack can be traced. Important that no one knows who is controlling beam. Time for experiment." Alexi continued to growl. "Deadline very soon." He twisted back on his stool and keyed in a series of calculations, his typing rapid and his concentration intense.

Mary sat by his side, watching his keystrokes and trying to decipher their meaning, without success. "Alexi? I don't want to upset you, but why do you need me to do this when Visser has been working with the Hive all this time?"

He didn't look up from his keyboard. "Visser not powerful, he gets tired before mission complete. He is not accurate." She mouthed an 'Oh, I see.' Silently. It made her smile. Alexi thought her to be more powerful than Lars Visser. A dose of dopamine dribbled into her bloodstream, fuelling a little mind tickle in the reward centres of the brain.

"Here. You must memorise these coordinates, this frequency and the face of this man." Alexi was all business-like. The mantle of kindness he had shown her all but gone. He collected a colour printout from the machine on a nearby bench and handed it to Mary. In the top corner of the page was a fair haired man, approximately forty five years old, with rimless glasses resting on the bridge of his squat nose. "This is the man you will synchronise with. He controls the IRI." Mary lowered an eyebrow. "It's the Ionospheric Research Instrument. High powered radio frequency transmitter."

She glanced again at the man's picture. He looked a kind soul. He had freckles on his cheekbones.

"When you have synchronised your brain waves to his, you will command him to enter those coordinates and frequency settings into the terminal on his desk. The Hive will boost your power over him. Then you tell him to activate the IRI."

"And then what?" Mary looked into the paper face. She was about to try and take over this man's mind, to force him to participate in an unlawful act. This was not an attack on some faceless bureaucrat or massive conglomerate. This was a personal invasion. Her stomach bubbled and eddied. She blew out a slow palliative breath.

"And then we wait." There was a long pause while Mary processed the information. A part of her was beginning to think that Alexi has lost his grasp on reality. Another, more sinister part of her, hoped that the experiment was a success. She returned to the padded seat and wriggled till she felt comfortable. The page of figures and the man's photo rested in her lap. Once again, she slowed her breathing and relaxed.

"Captain?" I can do this, I can do this. She steadied her nerves.

"Yes, Ma'am. Awaiting your orders."

"I'd like you all to help me reach this man in Alaska." Mary recollected the image from the page, displaying him in her mind for the Hive to concentrate on. *"We need to make him fire a beam of radio waves at these coordinates and on this frequency."* She presented the digits for the Hive. The captain repeated her command in Russian, to allow those without the ability

to speak English to catch up. *"Is everyone ready?"* A great chorus of different pitches, voiced their assent.

The sensation was exhilarating. Her supercharged entity reacted immediately to her directives. Mary's mind rushed out of her body, travelling at tremendous speed over land and seas to the subarctic landmass, cocooned in a bubble of energy. She slowed above a massive, almost square field. There, standing sixty feet above the icy ground, were one hundred and eighty aerials, each supporting a web of cables, parallel to the sky. They looked like umbrella frames, equally spaced, their waterproof fabric torn and blown away to the furthest reaches of the tundra.

Mary's mind travelled along the service road, whizzing through walls and floors and alighting inside the research facility, over four thousand miles from her body. Her consciousness rose and fell through each floor, scanning for her target.

Mary caught sight of the fair haired man. She hovered near the ceiling above his computer terminal. He sat scratching his nose and readjusting his glasses, updating his status on Facebook. He lingered on a photograph of a woman wearing an ivory dress, dancing with her dark and handsome groom. A colleague walked past his desk, prompting him to minimise the window and grasp a plastic ring binder of notes from a tray.

"Okay, how do I synchronise with him?" Mary muttered it absently to herself, forgetting her connection to the Hive.

"Try looking into his eyes, Ma'am."

"Oh, right. Good idea. Thank you." In effortless flight, the Hive's energy maintained her buoyancy close to the man's face. Looking into his unsuspecting blue

eyes, she tried to see his thoughts. She drifted closer and closer, until all went dark. Eyelids opened and the light poured in once again, but they were not her eyes. She had fused herself with the man's mind. Her consciousness had entered his.

Automatically, her brain informed the motor functions to lift an arm. Mary analysed the man's soft hands, his clean finger nails, and the wedding ring. She relayed a neural transmission to the right arm, to put the folder down and hold the computer mouse.

"Now, Ma'am. Type in the coordinates."

Mary looked at the bottom toolbar on the screen for minimised programmes. She steered the man's hand on the mouse to open each one until a complex looking interface popped up. An I.R.I. logo appeared at the top of the window and empty white boxes with formal scientific labels filled the screen. Scanning down the list of variables, she typed the coordinates and frequency settings into the most probable boxes and hit the 'OK' button. The following pop up window, asked for an authorisation code.

"His access code will be on the back of his ID card - round his neck, Ma'am."

"I wish you would stop calling me that. My name is Mary." She located the card, his code and typed the numbers into the computer. Another window, more coded instructions required. *"I don't know what to put in this bit. Alexi only gave me the information I have already put in."*

"One moment Ma'am. One of our operatives worked at Sura in Vasilsursk."

"I don't understand." The note of panic, reverberated in her consciousness. For a second, she lost

control of the man's arms and they crashed onto the keyboard, wrists first. The clattering noise jolted her composure further still, anticipating discovery from the man's co-workers.

"Remain calm, Ma'am. Mary. These are the numbers you must type." Captain Thirty-Four soothed Mary, his serene voice modulating her biorhythms, helping her to regain her poise. She could feel his strength of character supporting her, his fierce intelligence and courage. A confidence that only combat experience of a tightly connected military team could forge, all at her disposal. She directed the man's fingers onto the keyboard and punched in the remaining figures.

"Now what?"

"You hit the big green button, Ma'am."

The man's finger pressed the mouse button, activating the antennae array with a high frequency beam into the upper atmosphere. The sound was deafening. The radio waves connected with the Ionosphere, some seventy kilometres above the Earth's surface. There was a roar as it broke through the sound barrier, then a crescendo of acoustic feedback similar to the end of a Jimmy Hendrix concert, as he smashed his electric guitar through an amplifier on stage. The discordant squeal and trumpeting eased, then pulsed again with renewed intensity.

Men and women across the base looked skyward, recognising the unmistakable noise of the I.R.I. beam. Some made frenzied telecommunication calls with colleagues or ran into the offices of superiors to ascertain the cause of an unscheduled use of the instrument.

"All done, Ma'am. We can leave." Captain Thirty-Four gave her consciousness a verbal nudge.

Mary released the man's nervous system and floated back towards the ceiling, observing the pandemonium in the office building. The bespectacled man beneath her nebulous form, fluttered his eyelids and peered at his screen in puzzlement.

"Poor chap. He'll probably lose his job for this, or worse." Mary felt the Hive's energy, cushioning her psyche and transporting it back over the tundra, across seas and mountains, delivering it safely back to her body.

When Mary came to, Alexi was standing over her, watching her features. Detached from the Hive Mind, Mary felt an acute separation. Her brief interaction, released large quantities of endorphins into her bloodstream. A natural high that could easily become addictive. The subsequent crash left her with an emptiness in knowing that alone she would have to rely solely on her own wits. To keep her own counsel and make decisions based purely on self-preservation. The rapid attachment to the Hive surprised her. She was bereft of their company. Now she understood Visser's pride in *his* Hive Mind.

Alexi had a variety of snack foods waiting and the kettle was boiling. He removed her neural activity cap and touched his hand to her forehead, testing her temperature. "Headache? Nausea? How do you feel?"

"Starving."

"Remarkable. Here…eat, eat." He returned to his lab stool and clicked away at the images of her brain on his monitor. His fascination of her cerebral cortex reminded her of Parth. He should be the one looking at those images of her brain, not Alexi. She reached over to the tray and selected a packet of salt and vinegar crisps.

If Parth could see what I can do now, he would be so proud of me.

"How will we know if the experiment was a success?" She opened her mouth wide to receive an oversized golden crisp.

"Visser has agents all over world. Should get a text very soon." Alexi removed his mobile phone from his top pocket, slid the button back from the mute position and laid it on the bench. They both looked at it expectantly. As if by command, it beeped. Alexi opened the text and read it.

"Well?" She said, through globs of wet crisp.

"It was successful. Very good. On schedule too." He replaced the phone back in his pocket.

"So, what happened?" She paused her crisp munching.

"Earthquake in New Zealand, North Island."

Chapter Fifteen

Congestion in Mary's sinuses made her breathe through her mouth. It rendered her tongue dry. She ran the corner of the bath towel under the cold water tap and dabbed at the raw lids of her eyes. Her reward for obeying Alexi's commands and inducing an Earthquake in New Zealand, was a new television on which she could view the devastation in the comfort of her prison cell. Her first reaction to Alexi's statement had been laughter. How could she have initiated an Earthquake with radio waves? That was absurd.

When the national news bulletin announced the quake, it was the top story. The people of New Zealand were fully prepared and more than used to frequent tremors. What had made the headlines was the strange noises that preceded the Earthquake. Witnesses described the oscillating screeches as being like a rock band tuning up and adjusting the acoustic feedback. As if to confirm Mary's worst fears, a New Zealander had captured a video recording of the deafening sounds on his smartphone. The BBC obliged their audience and played the footage.

At this point, Mary stopped watching the antipodean video showing back yard swimming pools sloshing around like a massive invisible hand was swilling brandy around its glass, and made a dash to the bathroom to vomit. The tears flowed shortly after when the newscaster announced the deaths of ten people, killed during the quake, mostly due to falling objects and vehicular accidents.

All those years campaigning against cruelty to animals, the struggles to maintain protein in her vegetarian diet and nightly preponderances trying to justify the consumption of dairy products and the purchase and wearing of leather. The day she cried herself to sleep after an argument over whether King Prawns would be self-aware following a mouthful of her friend's Thai prawn curry. All blanched into insignificance in the light of her being responsible for the deaths of ten innocent human beings and the slaughter of one brutal guard.

She was a murderer. She had ended their lives, destroyed families, their hopes and their dreams. Mary could rationalise killing the guard, to a certain extent. His ruthless treatment and intentions towards her had incited actions in self-defence. She felt no remorse for his loss of life, but ten decent, hardworking people, were mortally wounded as a direct result of her activities.

Mary squeezed more toothpaste onto her brush and scrubbed her tongue and teeth. The stomach acid seemed determined to loiter on her taste buds. She looked at the shadows beneath her eyes in the mirror. She counted at least eleven more crow's feet, a wrinkle for every death she had caused.

If Visser and the Hive had been responsible for all the other recent Earthquakes, the death toll was incalculable and set to increase further still. So many lives in danger. There was more at stake than Parth's safety. She had to escape and warn the authorities, even if that meant killing another guard or two.

Alexi would be coming in soon, to check on her phantom migraine that she claimed to be suffering. She demanded a rest after her expedition with the Hive. Mary needed breathing space, time to think. Alexi wanted to forge on, muttering half Russian, half English sentences regarding timescales and schedules. She needed to fake her illness for long enough to formulate a plan to prevent Alexi forcing her to hurt others. Mary ached to go home, but that was not an option. That would be the first place Visser would look to hunt her down.

Muting the television, she lay on the bed and put the damp towel across her eyes. It was an effective blackout, albeit rather humid. She figured that Alexi would have ordered the guards to switch the solenoids that surrounded the hospital wards back on. The electromagnetic charge from those, would effectively shield the Hive Mind from any detection device. It would also shield her mind from theirs, allowing her an opportunity to snoop.

Oh come on... relax. This is never going to work if you can't slow your breathing and heart rate down. The pep talk failed. Her short, rapid breaths continued. Try singing again, that worked before. In an almost imperceptible whisper, she began. The hum at the back of her voice box, reverberated her backbone, the waves travelling up to her skull and modulating the soft tissues within. By the second chorus, Mary was tranquil, in harmony with alpha waves produced by her brain and the resonant frequency of our much beleaguered planet.

Without the boost of energy from the Hive, Mary's consciousness travelled at a sedate speed through her cell door, down the corridor and located the fire exit leading to the courtyard. She turned the corner of the building leading to a passageway. There was a guard standing next to a high, metal gate, an entrance to a makeshift car park and a demolition site beyond. She recognised him as one of Visser's henchmen. Instead of a military attire, he wore a standard security guard uniform.

That would be right, army fatigues would draw the attention of any police on patrol. Further on from the car park were a few trees, tall buildings, factory units and somewhere in the distance her home, her husband and her affectionate cat. Mary directed her mind to ascend, surveying the view from above. A large golf course lay behind the building site, its tree lined fairways like bacterium huddled together on a microscope slide.

Hang on, Mary. In the absence of companionship, she grew fond of talking to herself. *I recognise this area.* Her energy responded to her commands and she flew down the street adjacent to golf course, turning left at the first opportunity. *Visser has some bloody nerve, setting up a secret base so close to a Police Station. The gall of that man. I'm just a few miles from the university, and our house.*

The use of the word *our* sent her mind spiralling to thoughts of Parth. How many days had they been apart now? Would he still be publicly mourning for her? *I bet he isn't taking good care of himself. Probably living on junk food and old freezer burnt meals for one from the bottom drawer of the fridge. What if no one is visiting him and he is all alone in his grief, wearing the same shirt for days on end and screening everyone's calls? What if he is sitting in front of daytime telly every day and slowly losing the will to go on? I have to see that he is alright. I have to know that he will survive until I can escape and get back to him. He would still be at home on compassionate leave – desolate, poor sweet man. Maybe I can get a message to him that I'm alive.*

She soared into the afternoon sky, taking the most direct route to her house, a homing pigeon, in a desperate bid to unite with her mate. Unlike a pigeon though, her sense of direction failed her. She flew over the golf course and housing estates and headed towards a large cluster of buildings she recognised as the General Hospital. Veering past it on the right hand side, street after street of similar looking houses zipped past beneath her, muddling her bearings. *I'll have to get lower and read the street signs. Then I can find my way home.*

Hovering above the tarmac in her road, the excitement of seeing her house tingled her neurons. The days of captivity felt more like months. Despite her physical incarceration, Mary felt a modicum of peace. Like returning from a particularly stressful and disastrous holiday, when all parties present had argued and fallen out of favour, and the remaining time together endured in the confines of a shabby hotel room. That moment when, dragging the luggage to the front door step, and fumbling in bags and pockets for keys that remained hidden for two long weeks, you finally set a foot across a familiar threshold and all antagonism fades.

She viewed the scene. The wilting pots of Michaelmas Daisies, and hanging baskets by the front door; the wheelie bin, all alone in the street, leaning against the railings of their drive, the neighbours having retrieved theirs days ago. *Bless him, he hasn't bothered keeping up the household chores. I'm not surprised.*

Aristotle, her beloved feline companion, strolled across the grass patch of a neighbour's house and let himself in through an open window. *Turncoat. A few days away and he moves in next door. Wait, all our windows are closed, on a warm day like today. Where is the car? Parth is not here.* Mary pushed her consciousness through the roof and made her way through each room, searching for evidence of her husband.

The bedsheets neat, their en-suite spotless and dry, with no clothes piled haphazardly around the washing basket. Mary moved downstairs. The rinsed bowl and spoon she had used to eat her cereal from on the day of the accident lie upside down on the draining board. It was all precisely as she had left it on that fateful morning. She turned and drifted into Parth's study. His folders of papers lie stacked in a tray, his chair tucked under the desk. A sudden flash of anxiety came over her. Had Visser arranged for Parth's abduction too? Searching around Parth's den, she realised that not only were his laptop and iPad missing, but also the power chargers.

Oh, thank God. There is no way that Parth would go anywhere without those. I wonder whose house he has been staying at. Who would have taken a grieving widower in? Mary's mind strayed to Yelena, and shuddered. It was a possibility that she did not want to believe. Her beautiful, intelligent Russian friend, who was in frequent communication with Parth, had blatantly lied to her regarding the purpose of meetings with him.

Floating through the front door and back out onto the street, Mary decided to pay an ethereal visit to the University's Neurology department. If Parth was not pining for her at home, he would be doing what he did best – burying his sorrow in his work. She took the most direct route to the campus, straight across the park. Despite her new found abilities giving her an all access pass through walls and ceilings, habit forced her to arrive at the main entrance and follow the well-trodden corridors of her husband's department.

***

"I'm sorry sir, but I simply cannot allow you to enter." Simon, the postgraduate student, stood between Cyril Plender and the door to Zone Six. Mary's consciousness floated above the insignia, recalling the evening when she and Dan had removed the scrappy cardboard sign that read 'The Crypt'.

"Do you know who I am, boy? I am the Director of Biomedical, and as such, I have security clearance for every lab and broom cupboard this side of campus. Now let me pass." Cyril's greying whiskers looked all the more prominent as his skin flushed crimson in temper.

"With all due respect, Professor, you are the *Acting Director*, until Professor Haas returns. It is more than my life's worth to allow you to enter this zone without proper authorisation."

Mary chuckled to herself. It was a refreshing change to see someone courageous standing up to her bully of a boss. She lingered, enjoying the verbal joust.

"What utter nonsense. Your life will be worth nothing when I have finished with you, young man. I have every right to question the practices and legal implications of every study under my purview." Cyril had raised a finger, wafting it level with Simon's nose.

"Nevertheless, sir." Mary admired Simon's resistance. She watched him stare down Cyril, his features unmoved.

"I want to speak directly to Arora. Fetch him for me, now." Cyril took a step forward, jutting his chin up towards the lanky student.

"Dr Arora is unavoidably detained, sir. He is conducting a particularly delicate procedure and cannot be disturbed." Mary recognised those words. Parth had trained all his research fellows to memorise them for use in just these circumstances. Anytime Parth did not want to speak with someone, his faithful team members would regurgitate them verbatim.

"That'll be this mysterious *Project Sleepwalk*, no doubt. Now let me in, you arrogant little upstart, or I shall speak to the Dean about having your PhD funding revoked." They eyeballed each other for a painful moment, Cyril squinting at Simon demonically. "Fine! You asked for it. Don't say I didn't warn you." Professor Cyril Plender marched off, punching the double doors open with a theatrical display of anger. Simon watched him leave through the glass panes and then stepped clear when the door to The Crypt bumped into his left side.

"What's the rumpus, Simon?" Parth said, habitually arriving at the most opportune time.

"Plender. Making threats again about *Sleepwalk*. He is on his way to the Dean." Simon placed both hands on his cheeks, gulping in the air. He looked grey. Parth took note of his state and squeezed Simon's shoulder.

"Don't worry, I'll sort it. Can you go and finish the extraction? I have some calls I need to make."

Simon headed down the stairs into the bowels of Zone Six. Parth walked towards his office. Mary was torn. More than anything she wanted to be alone with her husband, to listen to his baritone intonation, to ascertain the depth of his sorrow at her loss, and perhaps find a method to send him a message that she was alive. She longed to feel that contentedness and sanctuary of physical contact with the one person who loved her as intensely as she did him.

The ache for him grew all the more desperate upon seeing him. That rigidly upright stance, those square shoulders and the way his hair grew to a cute point at the nape of his neck. Parth disappeared through more doors and around the corner. *He didn't seem very upset. Perhaps he is hiding it in front of colleagues. I really want to follow him, but I really want to see what they are up to in The Crypt. Just a quick peek.*

Mary slipped through the security doors and passed the panel of fuse switches and power connections, descending the great length of concrete stairs into Zone Six, The Crypt. A small foyer lay at the base of the steps. To the left was a service elevator. It was a large capacity type, capable of carrying hefty loads. Instead of Up and Down buttons, there was another access scanner. On the right hand side of the stairs, a set of windowless fire doors.

Curiosity drove her on, squeezing her consciousness bubble through the solid wood and into a suite of high spec labs beyond. These were not the laboratories that she was expecting to find. Each room had a series of large cubicles kitted out with top of the range medical equipment and life support machines. The first two bays that Mary passed, were empty, just a space between the equipment for a hospital bed. She edged forward to the third cubicle in the row.

There, among the beeping machines and artificial respirators, lie an unconscious man. His shaved head, raised on the special motorised bed, bore the marks of recent operation scars. Protruding from the back of his skull was a tiny transparent tube no more than a couple of millimetres in diameter, clamped at the free end. Mary gasped. *This is one of Parth's confidential studies. Is this Project Sleepwalk?*

Simon appeared wearing a surgical mask, latex gloves and goggles. A technician that Mary did not recognise followed him to the patient's side, carrying a kidney tray of sterile instruments. The similarities to the scenes she had witnessed in Lars Visser's base of operations, unnerved her. She watched as Simon inserted the needle of a tiny syringe into the tube, and signal to the technician, who, without fanfare or ceremony, switched off the man's life support equipment. Mary could feel her emotions falter as the heart monitor flat lined and Simon drew out the miniscule plunger from the syringe.

"That's a better fluid yield. The last one was barely enough to test. Can you get the concentration of DMT confirmed quickly, please? Dr Arora is in a great hurry."

Chapter Sixteen

Mary urged herself to remain unruffled and absorbed. Her previous extracorporeal travels had been of short duration. Any shock to her emotional state would destabilise her subconscious alpha wave generation and pull her back into her physical body. This added to the tension of knowing that Alexi would be checking up on her in her prison cell at any moment, made the urgency all the more critical.

Parth's team is deliberately killing patients in order to harvest chemicals from their brains. How can he do that? How can he sleep at night knowing that he is the cause of their deaths? The technician delivered the kidney tray containing the fluid sample to an adjacent lab, then began stripping the body of tubes and cables and making notes on an electronic tablet.

This is just monstrous. At least Visser's intentions is to keep the patients alive or he would not have commissioned Plender's project. There must be another explanation. Parth would never kill people just for an experiment.

Leaving Simon to his victim, Mary exited the basement, ascended the stairs and slipped through the Zone Six doors. She hurried along the corridor. Parth's office door was ajar. She could hear him on the telephone, his voice unusually clipped and laden with spite.

"Hmm, yes I know. Loathsome little prick. Why the hell did you marry him?" There was a long pause. Mary entered the office. Parth slumped over his desk, propping his head up on an elbow. Gaunt hollows appeared in his cheeks as he talked, unconcealed by stubble that almost formed a beard.

"It does suggest that, yes, but it's rather more difficult to prove. So far, it appears that the production of melatonin and possibly psi-conducive beta-carbolines in the pineal gland, is affected not only by light and stress, but also by changes in electromagnetic fields" another long pause. "The yield of naturally derived DMT seems to be highest at point of death, but we have been unable to replicate that in semi-conscious subjects." Parth swivelled around on his chair, leaned over to his lab coat hanging on a hook at the side of a bookcase and removed a black leather notebook. Flicking it open on his desk, he thumbed through the pages, checking his notes. "In Mary's absence, Dan might be our only hope."

Mary's attention piqued. She moved closer hoping he would sense her proximity. *In my absence? Is that what passes for grief, Parth? Don't you care that I have gone from your life?* Her vision fluctuated as she fought the onset of tears.

"You think I don't know that? My team are working around the clock on this. They, like myself, have practically moved into the medical facility. At least my staff are making some progress. Which is more than can be said of yours. How many times has Flynn lost him now?" Parth snarled down the telephone receiver. "Wait a second, I can hear someone in the corridor…"

Mary heard them too. A faint tap tapping, the sound of soft footfalls against industrial linoleum without landing the corresponding heavy heel. They stopped moving. Parth cocked his head sideways, listening intently. He inhaled a slow breath. When he opened his mouth to continue his conversation, new sounds flowed. Sounds that are intelligible only to those who, by happenstance of birth or by deliberate study, learned the Cyrillic script. Then built the words on which great Baltic and Slavic nations were founded. A growling intonation that could easily have been a vinyl record played backwards, for all that Mary understood. The most shocking of all, was that Mary had no idea that her husband was fluent in Russian.

She gasped her astonishment. The ramifications of this discovery sent her brainwaves into a tumult of confusion and doubt. Her body yanked the ethereal tether to her psyche with such force, the distance travelled took a mere moment, like a bungee strap snapping her back to the launch site. The subsequent re-entry into her physical self, jolted her immediately alert.

***

Back in her cell, Mary wailed her distress in a torrent of tears. In the nine years since she had first met Parth, as an undergraduate at Cambridge, she had not heard him utter a single word of Russian, nor had he ever expressed an interest in learning it. He was proud of being both Indian and British, revelling in the traditional customs of either nation. His studies had been purely scientific, predominately medical in nature. When did he find the time to read languages too?

With the cruel seesaw of fate tipped, she mourned the loss of his affections, his intimacy, and his love. He showed no ill effects of bereavement, no disruption to his daily routine just an increase in the time he could devote to his work. It was almost fortuitous that she was out from under his feet.

He had learned and knew the whole of her. Her likes and dislikes, the way that she held people at arms-length with a barrage of searching questions until she made their heads spin. He knew her irrational fear of all her teeth falling out at once, leading her dentist to chastise her for over-brushing. The way she stamped on her slippers prior to wearing them in case spiders had crawled into them during the night. He knew her body and soul, and had protected, cherished and so she had thought, loved her for their entire time together.

How much of his true personality had he concealed from her? All the care and affection he had shown for her over the years. Had he been acting all along? To what end? Was Parth really in danger from Visser's threats on his life or was he working secretly with Visser too, but refusing to collaborate with Plender? How did Yelena fit into it and where had she heard the name Flynn before? A cocktail of perturbing and unanswered questions, garnished with a sprig of treachery and a dash of bitter lament.

The bolt clanked across and the key turned in the lock of her cell door. Mary snuffled, wiped her face on the bath towel and sat upright.

"Dear Mary, whatever is wrong?" Alexi was fussing again, a brief dip back into his compassionate persona. “Is migraine very bad? You need me to give you stronger pain killer?” He sat on the edge of her bed. Mary thought for a moment. Another white lie would give her time to think. She nodded. “It is much worse Alexi, but I don’t want to take any more drugs. Please can you ask the guards to switch out the lights? They are hurting my eyes.”

“Yes, I will. Visser very pleased with you. We work again in the morning.” He patted her back. “You need anything else? Tea, ice pack?”

“No, thank you. I just need to be alone.”

Alexi bustled out of her cell. Mary heard the rod slam across and listened for the familiar click. The noise made when the guard presses the bolt handle down between steel stoppers, against the wood of the door. It did not happen. Neither did they remember to twist the key in the lock. Complacency borne from the belief that Mary was too ill to give them any trouble, or that cooperation earlier in the day provided them with evidence of her acquiescence.

All that stood between her and freedom was a metal rod and a few dozen guards. She lay very still. Alexi growled his orders to the guard monitoring her camera feed. The lights went fully out and all was quiet at last.

Fighting with the hysteria that threatened to burst forth, enveloping all rationality and common sense, she allowed her sight to acclimatise to the darkness, homing in on the tiny red flashing light of the camera. *Keep it together, Mary*. She intoned inside her head. *I cannot afford to lose the plot now. This might be my only chance to be free. Whatever Parth’s role is in all this, I have to get out of here and somehow alert the authorities about Visser's intentions.*

The quivering radiated outwards from her gut. The more she clenched her stomach muscles, the greater the muscles shook in her limbs. She concentrated on her breath, counting to four to slow each inhalation and again for each exhalation. Parth's cold and clinical words drifted back to her, "In Mary's absence." The shudder threatened to consume her once again. *I have to be more detached - deal with my shattered marriage at a later date.*

Rolling off the bed, Mary went to the bathroom and retrieved the dead guard's watch from her washbag. It was still early. The summer sun would not set for at least another three hours. The guards changed duties at ten o'clock. She decided to act before then, in case they checked the lock and bolt on her door. The guards at their post now, would also be weary towards the end of their shift, which should be another factor in her favour.

Flash, flash, flash. The little red LED was incessant and all-pervading in the darkness. It crossed her mind that they had not argued about the lights being off. Did that mean that they had infrared vision capability? She couldn't take the chance. Mary hid the watch beneath her pillow and laid back down on the bed, assessing her method for escape.

Mary could only take control of one guard's mind at a time, and that took her body out of action, rendering her incapable of physical movement. Blowing up equipment would trigger full mobilisation of all troops, and they were too many to run from. She could wait until she was alone with Alexi and put her newly acquired knife to his throat, but she was not confident that Visser or the guards valued his life worthy of saving. Besides, the dagger was so small, the guards would laugh at her and overpower her in an instant. Time ticked on. Mary had exhausted all but one plan of action, and that would entail the murder of at least one more guard.

***

The watch displayed 9.30pm. It was time to act. Mary started to sing. Her subconscious rose almost immediately, and took a direct route through the wall of the cell and into the alcove next door. She wove between the monitors. The guard was rocking back on his chair, munching on an apple, his dirty army boots resting on the desk in front of him. His mousey hair had a messy quality about it, with some sticking up in a cow's lick above his forehead, while the rest flopped down covering one eye.

Mary focused on the visible eye, tuning herself with the guard's wavelength, infiltrating his mind. She could feel his consciousness resisting her, wrestling against her will to command him. A mental tug of war, to rule over the neurons in his body, he was no match for Mary. Her strength came from desperation, the kind that has nothing left to lose. There was no delicate handling of his nerves, no consideration for his faculties in fear of damaging his nervous control. This required jack boot persistence and raw will power.

Flicking his awareness to one side, Mary grasped the reins of his neural network and lowered his legs from the desk. She raised a hand to the guard's face, sweeping back the curtain of hair. With his sight unimpaired, Mary scanned the switches on the computer screen, relieved that the software was English. Her intention had been to disable just the camera feed to her cell, but with the mouse cursor hovering over the menus, she located the command that disabled all camera feeds. An inability to track and radio through her whereabouts would improve her chances to flee. She clicked the button, and hoped that it would be some time before anyone noticed that the flashing LEDs had vanished from all cameras.

The guard's body was still clutching the half chewed apple in his left hand. She threw it down and forced the guard to stand. She walked his body out into the corridor. Another uniformed man, standing guard at Mary's door, looked in her direction.

"Where are you going? We have another thirty minutes till shift change." Thank God he spoke in English, or was it that she understood the Russian, having filtered it through a Russian brain first? It did not matter. She had to answer him, and fast.

"I need a pee. Won't be long." Mary paused, waiting for his response. Did Russian people say 'pee'? Would her word choice alert the guard? She looked at him for one agonising moment, then he laughed. Mary took the cue and marched as manly as she could down the corridor, turning out of sight as soon as possible. Her memory of the wards housing the Hive Mind was shaky. If she could just get to the room housing the solenoids, she might be able to disable the electromagnetic shielding technology, rendering them vulnerable to detection.

After a few wrong turns and almost stumbling into a staff room filled with relaxing guards, she located the room in which she had first met the Hive. Next to the ward, a guard stood in front of a chained and padlocked cupboard door. There was no hope of her accessing the mechanical equipment and she could not see any computer terminal which might control it. There were too many military personnel in this area of the hospital for comfort, so Mary made a hasty retreat.

Picking up the guard's feet, she made his body run. She ran as far and as fast as she could, until there were no more corridors or wards to run through. Mary sat him down against a wall, and extracted her consciousness from his brain. As she seeped out of his neural network, she left his eyes closed, hoping he would continue to sleep. A quick soar up and out into the dusk light, her mind glided over the rooftops of the hospital buildings and gracefully reintegrated with her awaiting body.

In total darkness, Mary felt her way around her room to the door. *I can do this. Just move the bolt with a trickle of electromagnetism. How do I trigger electromagnetism?* Running the palm of her hand against the crack between the door and its frame, she scrutinised any changes in feeling. Starting at waist height, Mary felt the sensation of the smooth paintwork and the cooler air through the gap from the corridor. As she moved her hand near to shoulder height, a brief tickle in the centre of her palm caught her attention.

That must be the metal of the bolt. Okay Mary, this is it. I can do this, I can do this... She felt for the tickle again, halting exactly where it felt most intense. Mary pressed her hand against the wood, and visualised the energy flowing from her hand, through the door to the steel bolt. At first, her skin pulled taut bearing the resistance, then she heard it move. A distinctive squeaky clatter as it shifted and ground against the door. Mary stopped, fearing the noise would alert the guard. Stock still, she listened. Only her nervous breath broke the silence. She tried again, disengaging the metal shaft from its retainer ring. As the bolt slid free, the door swung inwards a tiny fraction.

What if I cannot initiate a surge of energy to stop the guard? What if I lose focus and my power fails? Mary took a deep breath. She shoved her hand down her cleavage and retrieved the small knife, unsheathing it from the leather holster. Peering through the opening in the doorway, Mary looked at the huge man standing guard. A white wire protruded from his breast pocket and trailed over his shoulder into his ear. A faint scratchy noise told her he was listening to music. He glanced at his wrist, then stepped out, gazing down the length of the corridor, looking for his colleague.

I can do this, I have to do this. Holding the knife firmly, Mary charged through the door and thrust the dagger into the man's chest with all her might. It hit a rib and skidded sideways, slashing his skin and the fabric of his shirt open in a unified tear. He yelped, more in surprise than pain, grabbing at her shoulders and neck. Mary thrust again, ripping into the sinewy abdomen, his blood, spurting up her arms and face. Still, the guard clung on, constricting her throat and calling her every Russian curse word at his recall. He was so strong. She let the knife fall, clawing at his knuckles and fingers to release the pressure on her neck. He squeezed tighter, his fingers digging into her flesh, her attempts to breathe reduced to a feeble gurgle. An ounce more force and he would snap her spine.

With the last molecules of oxygen burning in her lungs, Mary put both hands on his chest and directed a massive burst of electromagnetism right through the guard's heart. She looked into his eyes as they radiated fear, then panic and finally cold resignation as the blood stopped pumping through his veins, depleting the life giving gases to his brain. Fatality number twelve loosened his grip on her throat and buckled to the floor.

"Hey you!" It was the man whose body Mary had taken for a walk to the furthest reaches of the building. "Stop!" He grabbed at the button on his radio and shouted for help. Mary sprinted along the corridor, through Alexi's lab and into the preparatory room. The guards were mustering their forces all around her. She heard men shouting, in Russian and English, through the single paned glass of the ward windows, their boots clomping down passageways in pursuit. Mary jumped down the concrete steps and rammed the fire door handle down, releasing the catch and allowing her into the balmy evening air of the courtyard.

Running again, Mary rounded the corner of the building and thumped directly into the night watchman, standing guard over the gate to the car park. Before he could come to his senses and make a grab for her, Mary swung her arms up, connecting her hands with his chest. With the merest hint of a thought, Mary directed an enormous surge of energy like a lightning strike through his body.

"Number thirteen, unlucky for some." She kicked his legs away from hers as he fell, unlatched the gate and ran across the car park to freedom.

Chapter Seventeen

Ducking away from the radiance of the street lights, Mary slowed and clutched the cramping muscles in her side. The less visible she could be the better. If she walked along the almost deserted streets to the Police Station, the guards would snap her up long before she could run there, especially in her unfit state.

Crossing the road, Mary pushed through some undergrowth and straddled a ditch, pulling herself up the other side of the bank by an outstretched tree branch. She made short work of the wooden fence that enclosed the boundary of the golf course. The long grass was damp, saturating her canvas shoes and the lower part of her sweat pants. Scurrying around the edges of the darkening fairways, Mary headed towards the nineteenth hole, a Georgian red brick building that was pullulating with middle class men quaffing gin. She could see them through the sash windows, gathered in groups, indulging in an hour or two of high class pretence.

Mary glanced down at her dishevelled appearance. The blood on her hands had seeped beneath her fingernails and was drying almost black - the guard's blood. The man she had stabbed, twice. There would be questions, difficult questions. Ones that would require complicated answers that would take too long to explain and would be hard to believe.

The ornamental pond in the formal gardens surrounding the club, provided an opportunity to rinse off some of the blood. Pungent smells of viscera lingered in her nostrils. It provoked an imprinted memory of the guard's face to flicker, then dazzle her thoughts like a distress flare. The deep-set vacancy in his eyes as his life ebbed away. Mary shuddered. Her reflection under the floodlights was grim. No doorman would let a soaking wet, blood splattered woman wearing jogging bottoms into golf club.

If I can just make it to the Police Station, at least I will be safe. I can deal with the questions once they have stopped Visser. Staying in the shadows, Mary walked through a bank of trees and across the putting greens, keeping parallel with the main road. The throaty roar of powerful engines emanated from somewhere behind her. They had found the body of the night watchman at the gate. Visser's crew were mobile.

Shiny black vans raced up and down the streets, stopping periodically and accosting gangs of kids regarding Mary's whereabouts. Mary crouched low, dipping beneath a small wall. She was almost past the perimeter fence of a nursing home. To her left, a line of poplar trees and a small lane, brightly lit with neatly spaced street lamps. Beyond that, a large expanse of scrubland lay between her and the police station. It was too late to go back. Visser's men would be combing their way through the Golf Club and its grounds. The nursing home had security like The Bank of England, with a view to keeping the residents in, rather than undesirables out.

Dodging from tree trunk to hedge and then to the line of poplar trees, Mary judged her best route across the road and into the pastures beyond. The noise of engines shifting through gear changes buzzed close by, punctuated by screeching brakes and the unmistakable *thunk*, of van doors slamming.

Mary used the line of poplars to edge further down the street and away from the stark lamps. Opposite her now, was a break in the treeline where a farmhouse drive met the lane. She glanced either side of the road. No black vans. Mary hurried across, crouching low as she made her way down the drive and out to the field surrounding the building.

Mary pushed on, aware that her silhouette would be visible from the roadside. The rabbit holes and divots made the going tough. Damp canvas rubbed against her feet, until blisters burst inside her shoes. A moment of wet relief before the soreness began again. With the sound of each vehicle passing, Mary threw herself to the rough ground, hugging the dew covered grass and stony earth patches, till her own blood mixed with the remnants from the guard.

The moon was still low on the horizon when she reached the last section of open scrubland. The constabulary was built next to a brand new mini roundabout, with exits that led nowhere. The car park was portentously deserted. Mary's mouth was dry. She wriggled her tongue to induce a flow of saliva but it was barely of sufficient quantity to swallow. Still panting from her exertions, she knew she had to gather her strength to make a mad dash across the strip of wasteland to the station undetected. The windows of the building were all in darkness. Only the reception foyer was lit. *Oh come on… there has got to be people here.*

Biding her time behind the last shrub boundary, she waited until she could neither see nor hear traffic noises, and then ran. Over the wasteland, jumping rubble and ditches, avoiding abandoned shopping trolleys and piles of bric-a-brac, the ultimate insult of fly-tipping on the doorstep of the police station. Finally, she made it onto the tarmac, tearing across the middle of the mini roundabout and up to the porch of the main entrance.

Pulling the door handle, then pushing it, then rattling it in temper, Mary choked back tears. The door was locked. The porch light shone on a laminated sign, Blue-tacked to the inside glass of the door.

"This station is staffed between the hours of 8.30-6.00pm. For emergencies, call 999. For non-emergencies, please call 101. Alternatively, you can reach us on www.police.uk/contact. Thank you for your cooperation."

Mary thumped the reinforced glass, then scanned about for cameras ready to capture her infraction. *Shit, shit, shit. Now what do I do? I can't stay here.* The porch light announced her presence like a theatre spot. The black vans were swarming again, making systematic searches of the housing estates opposite the pastures, their buzzing growing louder with each cleared street.

Breaking into a jog, Mary ran the length of the car park and across new lawns at the rear of the station. Another main road lay ahead. To her left, a long overpass leading into a superstore building. To her right was a busy multi-exit roundabout and a petrol station. It was getting late. There was no way of telling if the supermarket would be one of the few that stayed open all night. Mary watched the flow of traffic dancing in choreographed patterns around the island. A taxi turned into the filling station, its rectangular sign glowing on its roof.

Running at full tilt, she sprinted across the road, dodging the articulated lorries and late coaches that barrelled down the hill towards her and into the cover of the trees lining the road. Taking a zig zag route through the regimented parked cars, she made it onto the forecourt just as the taxi driver was pulling out the receipt from the pay-at-pump machine.

"Please can you help me?" She gasped, swallowing hard and bending low to force the air into her lungs. The man looked her up and down, squinting his eyes. She could feel his indecision. "I'm not on drugs. I was kidnapped."

"Jee-zus girl! You look like you need an ambulance, not a taxi." The driver pulled his phone from the back pocket of his jeans ready to dial.

"No. I'm not hurt. But the people who did this to me are trying to hunt me down. Please can you get me away from here?" She tugged on the passenger handle of his taxi. The door wouldn't budge.

"I can call the cops for you?" He looked at her crumpled face, the wet, matted hair and the look of fright embedded in her eyes.

"They will catch me before the cops could get here. Please?" She waited, projecting an imploring look, hoping his paternal instincts would kick in to rescue her.

"I am probably gonna regret this but…" His thumb clicked the button on the key fob, triggering the central locking system to unlock the taxi.

Mary jumped into the front passenger side of the car. “Please hurry.”

“You sure this ain’t some sort of prank? Am I gonna be on telly?” He smoothed his shirt down, holding in his stomach muscles and smiling his perfect teeth at the canopy above. Mary crouched in the foot well of the car, holding onto the seat and ducking her head below the doorframe. His expression changed. “Girl, you ain’t kiddin’ are you?” He hurried to the driver’s side and hopped in. “Where do you wanna go?”

“Please, just drive. I haven’t had time to think. I tried to go to the police but the station was closed.” She looked at his face, the puzzled smile waned and an anxious frown took up residence on his kind old face. The overhead lights strobed across the dash board and illuminated her bruised neck as he steered the vehicle off the forecourt and onto the main road.

“They do that to you?” He gestured towards his own neck with a wandering finger.

“Yes.”

“They hurt you…anywhere else?” He alternated glances at her and at the road ahead.

“They tried to. It’s not important now. What they are planning to do is far worse. I have to tell someone. He has to be stopped before he kills thousands more.” The words fell in a disorganised landslide from her mouth.

“He who? How can a kidnapper kill thousands?” His frown extended.

“Lars Visser. He is a terrorist, trying to bankrupt whole countries with natural disasters.” Mary heard herself and grimaced. “Look I know it sounds ludicrous, but trust me, this man means business. He faked my death just so that no one would come looking for me." She felt his attitude shift from concern to pity.

"You want me to drop you off at the General Hospital, little lady? It's not far from here. They will have people who can help you there."

"Thank you, no. I've had my fill of hospitals for a while." Mary manoeuvred herself onto the passenger seat and fastened the safety belt. "You think I am insane. I can understand that. After the things that have happened to me in the last few days, I'm beginning to think I am too."

"Can I take you home then? Do you have a husband, boyfriend sorry… significant other, family?" The driver said, trying to recall current phrases.

"I have, but I don't know if I can trust him anymore." Her voice broke. The cabbie reached into the dashboard for a pack of travel tissues, offering them to Mary on an outstretched hand. She thanked him inaudibly, trying to regain control.

"Well I have to take you somewhere. Can't drive around aimlessly all night. Do you want me to take you to the constabulary in the centre of town? That'll be open."

Mary thought for a moment. If she blurted out the same story to the Police, they would detain her for a Psychological Evaluation and have her sectioned before midnight. "Do you know of a bookshop just off West Walk? It's Dan something's place. Has a blue canopy over the shop front."

"Wildman's? Sells freaky books about weird stuff and the occult?"

"Yes, that's it. Please can you take me there?" *I'll borrow some money from Dan and get my story straight first.* The driver looked at the blood spatter on her clothes, the blackened nails and the finger marks around her neck and stayed quiet, nodding his assent. Mary sensed what conclusions the cabbie had drawn. An occultist's crazy ritual gone hopelessly wrong and she is covering up with a mad story.

Casting an eye at the buildings they passed in the street, Mary knew they were almost at Dan's place. She didn't have time to explain. "Thank you so much, for everything. You have been so kind to me. If you wouldn't mind waiting a little longer, I will get the fare from my friend."

Mary stood on the pavement, looking for signs of life. The shop front was in total darkness, but the curtains percolated blue light in the flat windows above. Dan was at home. She located a doorbell and pressed down, listening for a response. The taxi engine thrummed behind her and she glanced around to smile at the driver. As she did, a small flash of light caught her eye from the opposite side of the street.

Peering into the gloom, she thought she saw a shape of a man in a parked car, but when her vision adjusted, all she could see were the headrests against the whitewash of the building beyond. Mary rang the bell again. This time, the curtains moved in the flat windows. Dan slid the sash window open and leaned out.

"Dan, it's me, Mary. Please can I come in?" She shielded her eyes from the glare of the street lamp.

"But, you are…Mary, is that really you? You are supposed to be dead. It was on the news. I ordered flowers and everything." Dan froze, leaning on the windowsill, as if he needed the time to manually edit his assumptions.

"Dan?"

"Oh right, yes. Sorry. Be down in a tick." Tumbling down the stairs and tripping over book stacks piled in every available space on the floor, Dan hurried to unlock the shop door. "God almighty, you look positively resurrected. What happened?"

"I'll tell you everything in time, but for now, I really need your help. Can I borrow some money to pay the taxi, please?" Mary felt on edge again, a creeping coldness activating the receptors along her spine and neck, making her shiver. Were they just headrests in that car?

"Yes, of course." Dan walked towards the taxi, removing his wallet from his back pocket. He looked at the meter and handed the driver two twenty pound notes. "Keep the change."

"Cheers mate. Hey, look after her. I think she might have had a bump on the head or something. She was babbling a lot of crap about terrorists and being kidnapped earlier." The driver reset the meter, pocketed the money and saluted Dan with two jaunty fingers tipped to his forehead as he drove away.

Dan turned to Mary. "I can't believe it. I want to hug you but you look like you might break. Come inside. Let's get you cleaned up." He piloted her into the shop with the gentlest of touches to the small of her back. The fusty smell of vintage dust and old ink soothed her frayed nerves. A cocoon of aged tomes enveloped her senses, blotting out the harsh invasion of today's Wi-Fi world. Mary picked her way through counters and shelves, tables and displays to the stairs at the back of the shop.

"Turn left at the top. Can I get you something to eat or drink? A nip of Brandy perhaps?" Dan followed her up to his lounge, tidying away laundry and empty mugs as he walked. "Is that blood?"

"Yes, but not mine. I know I look a frightful mess and I'm sorry to burden you with it, but I didn't have anywhere else to go." Books filled every space. An acoustic guitar stood as the room's focal point, guarding stacks of vinyl records beneath a steel faced turntable. A bachelor pad with the tiniest hint of feminine insinuation – two floral cushions lay on the sofa and a red silk dress in drycleaner's wrap, hung from the back of the door. Dan caught Mary staring at it.

"Connie's. I picked it up from the cleaners for her." His expression dropped.

"Oh, I'm intruding. I'm so sorry. Is she here?" Mary shuffled with reluctance towards the door.

"No, it's ok. Please stay. She has vanished again. I expect that she is sniffing out another exposé, and she'll turn up in six weeks like nothing has happened." They circled the seating, choosing their distance carefully - Mary the settee, Dan in his favourite winged armchair. Mary rubbed at the bruises on her neck. They were tender to touch. "What happened to you, Mary?"

"A lot of things, terrible, unbelievable things. May I use your bathroom, then I will tell you everything." She stood up, waiting for directions.

"Where are my manners? Sorry, Mary. Plenty of hot water, towels are in the bathroom cupboard. I'll dig out some of Connie's clothes that might fit you. Shall I make you some tea? I know you are partial to it." Dan dashed about his flat, filling the kettle and checking through the laundry for stray items of women's clothing.

Mary sat on the toilet. Relieved trembling took hold of her limbs. Dan's shock in finding her alive was some comfort. She felt reasonably sure that he had no involvement in the events that had brought her to his door.

The roll neck tub looked so inviting. She wanted so much to fill it to the brim and sink under the surface for hours, scrubbing away the grime of the past few days. The bathroom clock clicked past the eleventh hour. Mary decided on a quick shower, a pair of Connie's cotton trousers and a T shirt. Dan found her a grey cashmere cardigan, but Mary declined to wear it. She remembered how Constance had put Parth in his place at the ball. Mary imagined herself receiving a savage, Parisian reprimand should she spill anything on it.

Finding a lonely teacup and saucer at the back of a cupboard, Dan used it to serve Mary a cuppa with some crumpets. With a tangle of damp, clean hair clipped high on her head, Mary relaxed into the sofa cushions to begin her story. They jumped at the sound of a heavy thud on the shop door, accompanied by the doorbell screaming continuously.

"They've found me…"

Chapter Eighteen

"Don't let them in. They will hurt us both." The bell was shrill and relentless. Fists hammering on the shop front reverberated the toughened glass in the frame.

"I'll call the Police." Dan tugged at his mobile phone stuck in a tight jeans pocket.

"No time for that. These people are ruthless. We have to get out of here." Mary gripped Dan's arm and then looked to him to take charge. "Is there another exit?"

"Wait…" He took large strides across the room to a side unit, opened a drawer and pulled out a set of keys. Grabbing a coat and the sofa blanket, he rushed Mary through to the kitchen. The key was in the kitchen door lock. Dan turned it and ushered her through and out onto the steel frame of the fire escape. Locking the door behind him, they scurried down the steps. The clanking noises echoing from the walls of the surrounding structures. They heard the glass of the shop window splinter as they scrambled through to a set of interconnecting alleyways.

"Oh Dan. They've smashed your windows in." She touched his arm, an automatic gesture.

"I'm insured. It's just glass."

Mary broke into a jog to keep up with Dan's gait down the service road leading to a row of battered grey garages. Counting out loud as they passed each faded metal door, he stopped at the eighth one in the row. "It's this one." He felt each key on the ring in turn, trying to ascertain the one that would fit the lock in the pale light of the rising moon. The clanging echoes of boots on the fire escape sounded once again. They had searched the flat and were in rapid pursuit.

"Please, hurry." There was a tone of fright in her voice. Dan handed her the blanket, and swiftly raised the garage door. Squeezing himself along the slim space between breezeblock and car, he fed his slender legs into the driver's seat.

The burgundy Gordon Keeble sports GT started first time, much to their relief. He depressed the clutch and cautiously pushed the gearstick into first. Edging forwards, Mary closed the garage door and jumped into the passenger side. As Dan switched on the headlights, Mary twisted in her seat, peering at the two figures sprinting towards them. In the crimson blaze from the glare of the tail lights, she recognised one of the men. "That's Flynn, the man with one missing finger - Yelena's lover."

"Him again. I swear that bugger has been following me around." Dan swerved to avoid a cavernous pothole in the track.

"Put your foot down, Dan."

"I'm trying but this service road is not very serviceable." He steered the vehicle along the broken concrete trails bordered either side and in the middle with lush tufts of grass.

"They are gaining on us, can't you go any faster?" Mary knelt on the seat, monitoring their progress through the back window.

"Not if I want to get out of here with the sump and rear axle intact." A break between garages revealed smooth asphalt ahead. With some caution, Dan pressed the accelerator pedal.

Flynn and his colleague ran faster. Mary watched him reach into his breast pocket. "Oh my God."

"What?" Dan turned the wheel and aimed for the void between the buildings.

"He has a gun." As she said it, a shot rang out, glancing off the far side of the car. One glowing red lamp extinguished, with a faint tinkling of fractured glass. Dan bumped down the kerb and floored the accelerator, navigating by instinct through the maze of tiny lanes. Mary watched as Flynn lowered his weapon, stopped running and concede to failure.

The car sailed along the traffic free roads and out onto the floodlit motorway. Mary wrapped the blanket around her shoulders and sighed.

"Okay Mary, start talking."

***

It was just past three o'clock when they pulled into the unkempt drive of a villa on the Norfolk coast. Dan yanked the handbrake up and left the car in gear as an added precaution from the steep slope leading off the cliff and into the sea. He nudged her shoulder to wake her from her fitful doze.

"We're here." He waited for her to shake off the exhaustion and orientate herself.

“Where’s here?” Mary stretched, then pulled the blanket closer to her, quivering with the night hours and frigid temperature.

“It belongs to Connie. She brought me here once. Said she wanted to get away from it all.” Dan got out of the car and stepped up the wooden veranda stairs, pausing to let Mary find her way to him in the darkness. The ocean swelled and receded close by, dragging the shingle with a hypnotic swish to its ebb and flow. “Wait here a sec.” He reached up to two tiles of slate bearing the house numbers and slid them apart. The key was hanging in a tiny recessed chamber. Mary smiled at the ingenuity and wondered if Dan’s Parisian girlfriend had any other household surprises in stall for them inside.

The French chic styling continued from the elegant fretwork over the front door to the open plan living space inside. Simple duck egg blue walls and white painted furniture adorned each beautifully coordinated area. Mary expected nothing less.

“No one would think to look for us here.” Dan said, throwing his coat down on one of the two sofas and wandering into the kitchen to switch on the mains utilities.

“You don’t have any other mobile devices, do you? Other than your phone? It’s just they can…”

“No, Mary. And you watched me chuck the SIM card out of the car window before we left town. There isn’t even an internet connection here. Just a landline, which I will use in the morning to get cover for my shop. You can stop worrying and relax.”

And Mary did just that. She curled her feet up on the couch and lay her head on an embroidered silk cushion. Dan closed all the curtains and blinds, locked the door and returned to the lounge area to find her gentle breaths had carried her into a safe slumber. A loose tendril of hair swayed close to her lips, brushing against them with each inhalation. Smiling, Dan swept his long fingers across her forehead with a tender touch, drawing the tress behind her ear.

For the first time since he had met her, Mary looked at peace. The haggard shadow of a woman that had appeared on his doorstep seemed to visibly regenerate under his gaze. The pinched cleft above her nose smoothed out, the blue grey channels surrounding her eyes, plumped and filled with each blessed moment of sleep.

Dan pulled the blanket over her shoulders and turned towards the stairs. Something made him look back. Her small frame occupied less than three quarters of the settee. She looked so vulnerable. The bundle of folded legs and woollen fabric pulled him back to her side. Eschewing a comfortable bed upstairs, Dan trod on the heel ledges of his shoes, prizing them from his feet and lowered himself down onto the opposite couch.

Flicking the edges of his coat outwards, he draped it over his chest and closed his eyes. Seconds later, he pushed himself up again, trying to mitigate the creaks and squeaks from the sofa springs and retrieved a number four iron from Connie's golf bag under the stairs. Propping it up against the arm of the settee, he resumed his reclined position and tried to still his unquiet mind.

***

"Morning, sleepy-head." Dan kicked the front door closed, struggling through to the kitchen with straining carrier bags of groceries.

"What time is it?" Mary said, through one open eye.

"Around ten-thirty. It is a glorious day out there. What say I cook you some brekkie while you wash and dress? There will be tonnes of Connie's clothes upstairs. The woman has more shoes than sense. Then I thought we could walk down the cliff path and figure out what to do."

"Sounds like a plan." She yawned and sauntered up the stairs, taking the blanket with her for comfort more than warmth. Nipping to the toilet first, she turned on the bath taps, leaving the tub to fill while she looked through the wardrobes for something suitable to wear.

Everything in Connie's bedroom was neat, tidy and coordinated. The hint of blushed pink on the walls, carried through onto the vintage eiderdown, the pillowslips of brilliant white Egyptian cotton contrasting against the distressed lacquered metal bedframe. French free standing wardrobes stood either side of the dormer window overlooking the sea.

It felt intrusive delving into Constance's clothes, a woman who she had barely had an introduction to at a party. Mary touched the garments with respect. Silk blouses, cashmere sweaters and coats, fine wool trousers and nestling in the base of the cupboard, handbags and shoes of all the famous names. *I can't wear these. Some of these items cost more than I earn in a month, possibly several months.*

Mary opened the second wardrobe, inside three sets of running leggings and matching crop tops, a casual linen trouser suit and a black document case resting between the running shoes on the floor. *Don't be nosy. The papers of a journalist are of no concern to you. They are private. Borrowing clothes is one thing, prying into secret files is quite another.* She scolded herself, while reaching for the case. *You have no will power at all. Grampy would be disgusted with you.* She depressed the tapered button beneath the catch and paused, listening for Dan's activities. She could hear him in the kitchen cursing to himself having dropped an egg on the floor.

Sliding the clasp through the catch, she tentatively lifted the lid, as though her cautious movements would prevent detection. The tab from the first drop file read 'Lars Visser'. Without compunction, she slid out the folio of notes and pages from the suspension file. The noise from the filling bath changed pitch. Shoving the case back into the wardrobe, Mary hurried into the bathroom with the folio and locked the door behind her.

Switching off the taps, she closed the lid of the toilet seat and perched on top, flicking through the newspaper clippings and hard copies of Connie's notes. *This must be a backup file. Why else would she tuck it away here? Surely electronic copies were what most people used in journalism.*

The first few wafer-thin sheets were of clipped newsprint, articles showing Lars Visser, Dutch philanthropist, his benefactors shaking hands with the billionaire from humble roots. She looked at a photograph of Visser wearing a lab coat and watching a scientist operate expensive new donated equipment. Mary felt the side of her mouth curl in revulsion. The second article listed all the orphanages he had sponsored in Holland and Germany.

The third sheet was a Companies House printout, showing parent companies of global conglomerates that had associations with Visser and a stock portfolio of shares in his name. *Blimey, Connie must have some lofty contacts to get hold of his shares portfolio. This woman certainly digs deep.* A stapled bundle of sheets lay at the back of the folder. Connie had typed up conversations with various interviewed sources and written her conclusions in terminal paragraphs underneath.

It read: Transcript from recordings at the Investor's Ball

Dr Parth Arora – Let me introduce you to a very big fish. Constance, meet Professor Cyril Plender, Head of Biochemistry at the University and his wife Yelena. He is conducting many fascinating studies that I am sure you will want to ask him about. Plender, this is Constance Cadot, respected freelance journalist. She has a few questions for you. If you will excuse me, I need to return to my wife.

Yelena – Nice to meet you, Constance, but I need to speak with the catering staff. Excuse me.

Professor Cyril Plender – Pleased to meet you, my dear. Say, that is a lovely dress you are wearing.

Constance – I thank you, Cyril. Kind of you to notice. Here, let me straighten your pocket square. There, you look very smart.

Mary skipped down the page, balking at Cyril's attempts to woo Connie. *Connie must have had some wireless recording device stashed somewhere. Her dress was far too revealing to have secreted it on her body.* Mary read on.

Constance – Won't you introduce me to your friend?

Plender – I'd rather keep you all to myself. Would you care to dance?

Constance – Perhaps later, Cyril. It would be trés rude, would it not? He is walking this way.

Plender – I'll hold you to that promise, young lady. Ah. Lars Visser, this is the lovely Constance Cadot. She is a freelance journalist.

Lars Visser – Mademoiselle, charmed.

Constance – You are not a doctor or professor monsieur?

Visser – Alas no. My expertise lie elsewhere.

Constance – Oh? What do you specialise in?

Visser – Investments of course. Is that not why we are here tonight?

Constance – I have read about your philanthropic efforts in Holland and Germany, Mr Visser. Do you intend to fund British orphanages too, or are you channelling your billions into something specific? Research perhaps?

Visser – Yes indeed. Cyril has many interesting projects worthy of investment, as do many of the University departments.

Constance – but perhaps your interests lie in a more pseudo-science. What is your opinion of Psi Phenomenon, Mr Visser? A little Aboriginal Dream-Time or a spot of astral projection? Do you believe in funding projects that analyse the efficacy of Amazonian hallucinogen, Ayahuasca or other DMT rich concoctions? Perhaps you prefer to fund studies into the synthetic version. Are you trying to have a spiritual revelation, Mr Visser?

Visser – So many burning questions you have, Ms Cadot. One might think you are having a personal crisis of faith.

Dan Wildman – Forgive me gentlemen, but I'd like to dance with my girlfriend.

Visser – Ms Cadot? My card. Call me. Perhaps we can arrange a more formal interview.

Plender – Jesus Christ, man. Why would you encourage her? Where did she get all that from? We've hardly begun the planning stages of the study yet.

Visser – Calm down. She's fishing. That's what reporters do. Here…take this.

Plender – How does it work?

Visser – Wear it like a ring, with the device sitting in your palm. Press the button on the side to prime it, then touch it against his back to discharge the pulse. You get caught – you're on your own.

Plender – What happens next?

Visser – Get your department organised. We will be mobilising very soon.

She's a shrewd woman. Must have slipped Plender a small bug. Her original recording would surely be enough for the Police to investigate The Walrus's heart attack as an attempted murder. I wonder if she reported it to them.

Plender – Your tall companion dumped you for his beautiful French girlfriend, I see.

Yelena Plender – Your jealously knows no bounds, husband dear.

Plender – Another new gown, dear?

Yelena – Is that hint to raise your allowance? How about you tell me what you and that perfumed ponce were talking about and I'll consider it.

Plender – It was business, and none of yours. Now if you'll kindly move out of my way, I am going to dance with my Chief Technician.

I was wrong then. Yelena can't be working with Plender and Visser, or at least, wasn't at the time of the ball. But then, why did Flynn shoot at us? Whether he genuinely is Yelena's lover or not, she admitted that they were connected.

"Brekkie is almost done." Dan shouted up the stairs. The steam was condensing on every surface. Mary cranked open a window and slid into the bath, balancing the file on the toilet seat.

"Okay, won't be long."

Ducking under the surface to rinse the shampoo from her hair, Mary squeezed the water from her nose and eyes, then reached to the rail for a towel. A quick exploration of the sink cupboard uncovered a Perspex box containing new wrapped toothbrushes and paste. She flipped to the last pages of the document while she brushed, scanning the sentences for any useful material.

Turning the page, Mary found a photocopy of a funding notification from the Ministry of Defence. The letter stated that the section for Intelligence and Countering Adversary Networks Programme was awarding a bursary of nine and a half million pounds. Constance had identified and followed Government funding trails under the Public Information Act. An accompanying application form listed the University as the site of study, but did not specify the department.

The applicant's signature was scruffy and had a jagged chaotic flourish, but the title printed beneath was clear enough. The Chief Financial Officer for the University – Yelena Plender.

Connie had made the same assumptions as Mary. Both had thought that the married couple were in league with one another over Cyril Plender's study to create DMT type hallucinogens without the need for inhibitors that cause the critical side effects. Mary stopped brushing and spat out the used foam. Tilting her head under the running water of the tap, she gulped a mouthful, swilled it around and let gravity remove the waste. She picked up the file and scrutinised the small print in the boxes. There in font size eight lettering were the words Zone Six, *Project Sleepwalk*.

Chapter Nineteen

Dan collected the plates, washed them and left them to drain dry. Mary found a beige cotton cardigan and T shirt to coordinate with the linen trousers from Connie's wardrobe when she returned the research to the box file among the running shoes. Connie's shoe size being much larger than her own, Mary laced her tatty canvas pumps back on and followed Dan out of the French windows, leading across the small lawn and down to the cliff path.

The salt breeze stung her cheeks and gave them a healthy blush of colour. Rays of delicious warmth struck her forehead and tingled for a moment, before puffball clouds blocked their intensity. Dan turned and led the way northwards along a well maintained path. The sea defences obscured the ocean view but they could hear the gulls bickering over the tourist's offerings along the seafront and the roaring waves confirmed that it was high tide.

It was refreshing to be out in the open air again. She took deep breaths, clearing her lungs of hatred and misdeed that had been her only means of survival. Dan restored in her a tranquillity and balance that she had last known sitting at her grandfather's knee playing cat's cradle. He did not pester her with demands or questions, neither did he set schedules for her to follow or medication for her to consume. They wandered along the sandy path content in their thoughts which at times, overlapped and found a voice to verbalise them.

“I haven’t thanked you – for rescuing me.” She said, scrambling down an embankment to the concrete esplanade framing the beach.

“There’s no need. I’m just glad I could help you. We need to figure out how to tell the authorities though. Particularly if, like you said last night, this Visser bloke is planning more attacks.” Dan grabbed her arm to steady her as she trod along a wall and jumped down onto the pavement.

“I’m hoping that losing me slowed them down a bit. Alexi said that Visser is not as strong with his gifts as I am.” The sun broke through the clouds and made them squint.

“Even so. If it wasn’t for those experiments that we did together, I might have found your story hard to swallow. How will we convince the police that we aren’t bat-crap crazy?” They made their way onto the shingle, scraping out seat-like depressions with their feet. Mary didn’t answer. She had no answer. They sat down in their pebbled seats and gazed at the grey horizon. Dan said, “Don’t you think we should tell Parth that you are alive, at least?”

Mary swallowed hard. Her misgivings bunched up in her mouth, paralysing her top lip. “I don’t know whose side he is on. What if he is working with Visser like Cyril Plender is? What if he takes me back to the Hive?” The roof of her mouth pinched and watered as she battled against tears.

"If he was, Plender would have been collaborating with Parth over the DMT licences and studies. You said that the Post Grad student wouldn't allow Plender into the Crypt." He squeezed her forearm in reassurance.

"But Parth is working with Yelena, and she is from the Soviet Union. She handled all his funding and has suspicious meetings with him all the time."

"That's her job, though. That is what she is supposed to do. There is no evidence to suggest that she is in league with Visser, despite her accent." He was still clutching her arm, dipping his head to look her in the eyes as they talked. "Don't you think it more likely that direct government funding for Parth's research indicates that they are working *against* Visser, rather than for him?"

"You read my mind?" She gasped. "You knew that I found Connie's notes?"

He chuckled. "Uhuh. I saw you inside my head. It distracted me enough to drop an egg on the kitchen floor."

Dan had a point. In her exhausted, flustered state she had assumed the worst of her husband and friend and had fit the evidence to suit her theory. It took Dan's clarity of mind to put things into perspective.

"If Parth is innocent, why isn't he grieving my death?" They locked stares for a moment, contemplating her question.

Dan's brow furrowed. "I don't know." They watched an empty crisp packet skitter along the beach in front of them and get sucked up into the wash. "I do know that he made it very clear that you belonged to him at the ball. He nearly crushed my hand. It's obvious that you mean the world to him."

"I used to think so. He was so sweet when we first met. Do you know… he brought me a cup of tea to the Ladies' dormitory in the hostel every morning on that field trip where we met? It drove the other students mad." Mary picked up a pebble and balanced it on top of another, smooth flat one. Dan lay back in the shingle and let her ramble. "He coached me on exam techniques and sourced the periodicals and studies I needed to read before my finals. He was so attentive…"

Another pebble, dusted and carefully placed in her growing stack. "He met my parents for the first time…and last time, on my graduation day." Mary stopped building, examining the pitted marks on a matt grey stone surface.

"What happened?" He left it there, hanging in the air, without apology or excuse. She turned the rock in her hands, trying to ascertain which of her ready-made deflections she should employ. There could be no hiding from Dan. His sense of her was too acute.

"Parth wanted me to stay with him after the ceremony. Go out for a celebratory meal with our friends. Dad had to get back for work and insisted that I return home with them to Brighton. Apparently, Grampy had organised a little do for me. I was horrible. So arrogant and pig headed." Her shoulders slackened and her jaw clenched. "I suppose I was a typical only child – expecting the world to bow to my whims." She scratched her nail under a dried blob of tar marring the rock's natural perfection. "Anyway, after an exchange of words that I am not proud of, I relented and packed a few things, throwing them into Dad's car in temper.

"The drive south was slow going and hot as fire. We kept getting stuck in traffic and the aircon was on the blink so we had the windows wide open. I could see that mum was wilting and starting to get a headache. She went ashen and very quiet. Dad was in one of his argumentative moods. Kept needling me about how much trouble Grampy had gone to on my behalf and how selfish I was. He was right of course, but I couldn't see it at the time." She placed the pebble between two others, a little castle wall. A sharp flint of tan and white caught her attention. She levered herself up, leaning on one arm to reach it, before lowering herself back into the bottom shaped depression. Its contours reminded her of a miniature axe – chiselled on one side and knuckle rounded on the other. Dan watched the clouds evaporate and reform overhead in nebulous swirls, listening to Mary intently.

"He kept listing all the things that they had done for me. The additional days that my mum had worked to pay for my accommodation and fees, the living costs that Grampy had deposited into my account to reduce my graduation debt, the summer jobs that my dad had arranged for me each year." She ran the keen edge of the flint across the print of her thumb, testing its capacity for harm. "I suppose I just flipped. We had a blazing row. I still dream about those final words we screamed at each other." There was a long protracted silence.

Dan sat up. "And then?"

Mary steadied her shivering chin. "And then, the airbags deployed. An electrical short they said, much later. We careened off the motorway, tumbling over and over down a steep embankment…" She threw the tiny axe flint at her wall of stones, smashing them down in an instant. There were no tears, she had not earned them. The knots in her stomach doubled and tightened.

"Electrical short?" Dan looked at her anew. The weight of her grief hooded her fixed eyes. "You think that you…?" She nodded, resting her chin to her chest. "Oh Mary, I am so sorry." Dan touched her shoulder, shuffling himself forward in offer of comfort. Mary sat rigidly upright, flinching from his hand. He moved it away. "But you can't have known that would happen. You aren't to blame."

"Not at the time, no. The forensic report took ages. Grampy dealt with all the authorities over it. I was too much of a basket case then. I recall him saying there was something fishy about the results and the insurance company quibbling over blame. In the end, some Big Wig from the police section investigating the crash stepped in and recommended that both the insurance and car company coughed up or face a massive legal dispute." Mary let her head shift to one side. She watched the progress of a container ship along the horizon, grateful for distraction.

"How long have you suspected that you were the cause?" Dan clasped his knees, digging his heels in the shingle.

"After the accident, Parth caught the train down to Brighton and we both stayed at Grampy's. I couldn't face being in my parent's house. I remember sitting on the guest room bed, blurting the whole thing out to Parth about the row and flashes of light and sparks flying. He was the one who assured me that I must have been mistaken in the turmoil and that the sparks had originated in the front dashboard, whereas I had been positive that they had started in the back, near me." The sun reappeared, briefly wrapping them in its eternal warmth.

"And that was when your electrical abilities began?"

"It must have been, although it was dormant for a very long time after. I was quite a mess back then. I was petrified about getting in a car and the flashbacks and sleepless nights seemed endless. It got to a point where I was practically a recluse. I think it may have been Grampy's idea, but one day Parth just announced that he was taking me travelling and he wouldn't take no for an answer."

The beach huts behind them were filling up with day trippers and their petulant children, dropping bags of chips and attracting noisy gulls in flocks. Wailing little sisters claiming older siblings were taunting them and mothers struggling with a superhuman amount of chores. Mary got to her feet, brushing the salty dust from Connie's linen trousers.

"Come on, let's walk for a bit. Get away from all this domesticity."

Dan slipped and righted himself on the pebbles till he was at Mary's side. They walked towards the town centre, stopping for the obligatory ice cream on the way. "So, you see I have a lot to thank Parth for. He took control of my life and made all my decisions for me at a time when I was unable to fend for myself. I suppose I let him go on doing it for far too long, truth be told. It was a habit he hasn't been able to break."

They wandered the lanes and streets, peering into shop windows and grinning at eccentric locals who barged past, grunting their resentment at tourists. A chilly breeze funnelled between the buildings, prompting them to retreat to a café that had just one vacant table left. Mary hurried over and secured it, while Dan ordered for them both at the counter.

"I love this little town. It was a favourite of my parents for family holidays." He placed a wooden spoon upright in the sugar sachet container. It bore their order number in marker pen on its concave surface.

"Do you have a big family?" She asked.

"No, not at all. It's just me and mum now. Dad passed away a few years back. They couldn't have kids of their own so they adopted me. I was just an infant at the time so they are all I have ever known. Mum always went overboard on making me feel like their own son. She gave me the car we came here in after Dad died." The waitress carried their drinks to the table, assuring them that their sandwiches would follow along shortly.

Stirring the prettily decorated milk foam into his coffee, Dan raised the subject again. "We still need to tell someone in authority about Visser's plans."

"I agree, but who? And what can we tell them? I don't know exactly what he will do next, or when. I know that he has the ability to take control of people in key positions, like at that Alaskan research facility, but according to the Captain of the Hive, he is also infiltrating the stock markets around the world. He could even be using politicians to further his cause." Mary was talking in hushed tones, aware of how close their table was to the tourists around them.

"At least the politicians and stock trader's lives are not at risk. We should concentrate on shutting him down for killing innocent victims of natural disasters. We need to know precisely what his next target will be and when. Mary, you have to go back into his base and find out."

"I can't just, you know," she whispered, "drift out of myself, here, now. I have to lie down and get drowsy."

They finished their sandwiches and drinks and made their way back towards the beach. The tide was on its way out and families were following it down the gradual slopes of revealed sand, staking their claims with beach towels and wind breaks. Dan and Mary scrambled over the wooden groynes and stayed close to the promenade wall at the high tide mark.

Mary spied a sheltered area between the sea defence rocks, where sand had deposited in a patch surrounded by shingle. The sun had burned off most of the clouds and the temperature was edging up, particularly in windless spots. "Let's make a nest down there. I don't want to go back to the villa just yet. It's so nice to be outside."

***

"So, how does this work then? How do you make it happen?" They were sitting in the sandy hollow, surrounded by boulders of varying shape and size. Mary was scooping her hands in the sand, making herself a mound on which to rest her head.

"I have to get myself all calm and still, bit like a meditation I suppose. Then slow my heart rate down. Don't laugh, but I might have to sing."

He laughed. He couldn't help himself. "Sing? Don't tell me, '*I'm a Fire Starter*' by the Prodigy?"

She scowled at him. "No, I've been singing a Beatles tune, just to get me to drift off." She laid down and wriggled in the sand.

Dan leaned his back up against a rock. "You are being serious. Sorry. Which Beatles number?"

"Just the first few lines of '*Let it be*'. You'll have to forgive the screeching. I have a lousy voice." She closed her eyes. The sun was tingling her skin again. It felt like a balm against the tension.

"I love that one. My godfather used to sing that to me when I couldn't sleep, which was often. Do you need me to do anything?" He folded his legs up to give her more space.

"Just make sure that my body is safe, from people, birds, whatever." She shuffled her shoulders, finding a comfy position.

"Like a bloody big Albatross dropping a deposit from on high?" A slow broad grin underlined his fine features. She giggled.

"And stop making me laugh!" Mary took a deep breath and let it out slowly. She allowed her mind to consider the man sitting by her side, guarding her body like a loyal Alsatian, knowing full well that he would be trying to tap into her subconscious as she travelled. It did not occur to her to feel self-conscious in his presence.

The melody began as a hum. Her vibrational frequency altered, her alpha waves tuned into the Earth's resonance and she flew. She soared above the beach, high into the atmosphere, watching the traffic turn into specks and then disappear entirely. The patchwork quilt of Norfolk's flat pastures swept beneath her, as she headed west over Cambridge and then north-west to the Midlands.

Charting her course by the proximity to the familiar golf course, Mary steered her mind to the half demolished hospital structure, which had served as a prison during her incarceration. A number of articulated lorries were parked close to a service entrance. Visser's soldiers were loading medical and scientific equipment into shipping containers on the back of the trucks. Mary drew closer to inspect the contents. Some of the containers had racks fitted to support Hive Operatives, still in their comatose state. Visser was relocating.

Rushing into the main building, Mary homed in on Alexi's lab. He was still there, tinkering on his computer and making rapid calculations via specialist software on his screen. Plender walked in from the corridor closely followed by Visser.

"Are you saying that we don't need to use inhibitors at all?" Visser expounded, his hand tucked beneath the lapel of his suit jacket.

"I had to go to the Dean for authorisation into classified Neuroscience studies, but Arora seems to have cracked it. You simply apply the DMT solution directly into the cranial cavity at the base of the skull. The cerebral spinal fluid bathes the brain in the drug so that it bypasses the bloodstream containing the deactivating enzyme." Plender blustered, puffing out his chest.

"So, in fact, I did not need to employ your services at all?" Visser pouted at Plender. Alexi stopped clicking his mouse and turned from his monitor to observe the scene. There was a brief pause. Visser addressed Alexi. "What do you want me to do with him, General?"

General? Alexi is Visser's superior officer? He played me. All the time he pretended to be my friend, he was softening me up. Good cop - bad cop. I should have realised.

"I don't need him anymore." Alexi muttered, returning his attention to his computer screen. Visser withdrew his hand from his jacket. He was holding a pistol. He aimed it between Professor Cyril Plender's eyes and pulled the trigger.

Chapter Twenty

I must stay calm. We need more information. She forced her consciousness to remain in situ and not return to her body in shock. Plender's inert corpse lay sprawled across the laboratory floor, his head obliterated by the force of the gunshot. Visser walked over to the computer bench and looked over Alexi's shoulder at the monitor.

Alone, Alexi and Visser reverted to a Russian dialect, making it impossible for Mary to decipher their plans. Hovering over Alexi's head, she read the numbers he had visible on the screen.

N39°45′00″ – N40°00′00″ and W111°45′00″ – W111°30′00″ Wasatch. She read them over and over, trying to memorise the digits and at the same time, listening for any recognisable sections in their speech. She caught the word 'Stoneghost', in among the guttural sounds before Visser switched back into English. "When?"

"Mobilise all troops. You must be ready for broadcast at midnight their time, before Five Eyes backup." Alexi did not take his attention from the screen. Visser moved towards the chemical cupboard door.

"Your English has markedly improved, General." He removed a key from his pocket and fed it into the keyhole.

"Yes, Mary was very useful. You fail me again and you will follow Plender." Alexi continued to type and click the mouse while he issued his threat.

Turning the key, Visser opened the cupboard door. Inside were floor to ceiling shelves of powders, hazardous liquids and opaque tubs of other materials. Nestled in the floor space, was a blonde woman, duct taped to an office chair. She neither screamed nor struggled against her bindings, but her line of sight above her taped mouth, darted all around the room, taking in the surroundings.

"And what shall we do with Ms Cadot, here? I rather enjoy her company. It would be a pity to ruin her pretty face with a bullet." Visser grabbed the back of the chair and dragged her into the room, the wheels catching on the metal threshold strip. Her ankles bound together below the cropped navy trousers of her suit. "Don't you find her attractive, General?"

"Not my type. Too…female."

Oh my god! If Dan is seeing this he will be frantic… A brief moment of indecision scrambled her thoughts, fluctuating the alpha waves into discordance. Her vision blurred just as Visser slid his hand around Connie's graceful neck. Mary's mind jerked backwards, her body pulling her subconscious by its leash to her physical form lying in the sand. Mary opened her eyes to find Dan panting, his forehead rippled in anguish.

"You saw?" Mary touched his hand, giving it a gentle squeeze. He nodded. "Come on, let's get back to the villa and call the police." They scrambled up the beach to the promenade walkway and sprinted along the sandy cliff path, Mary struggling to maintain pace with her leggy companion. They ran through the shrubs and across the lawn. Dan unlocked the patio doors of Connie's beach house and charged through to the central staircase.

The landline telephone perched on a cabinet to the side of bannisters. As Dan reached for the receiver, it rang. "But who would…?" Mary puffed. They looked at each other, puzzled. Then there was a loud knock on the door. Mary grabbed Dan's arm. He covered her hand with his, to still her fear. The knocking became hefty thuds, drowning out the shrill ringing of the telephone. Dan picked up the phone and held it to his ear.

"Tell Mary to let Flynn inside" a distinctive St Petersburg accent. It was Yelena. Dan looked up to meet Mary's eyes. She mouthed, 'Who is it?" Dan held his hand aloft to halt her insistence.

"And why would she do that?" Dan replied, with caution.

"Because he is a Government Agent." As Yelena said it, Flynn's open wallet, showing his Identification Card, slammed against the glass panels in the top of the door.

"Which Government?"

"British Government, Secret Intelligence Services – MI6." Yelena spoke calmly, but with an air of urgency. She was in control and taking great pains to convey that message.

"If he is MI6, why did he shoot at us last night?" Dan fumed. Mary's mouth hung open.

"I didn't say he was a good agent. Now let him in. There is no time to lose."

***

Jasper Flynn entered the villa and dialled up a Facetime connection with Yelena on his smartphone, handing it to Mary, who relayed the exact location of Visser's base and that Connie was in extreme danger. It felt good to have the backing and resources of the British Government. Some of the anxiety for Connie's life dissipated, knowing that they would be responsible for her survival. She had done all that she could possibly do. Abdicating responsibility for Visser's demise, would be an even greater relief.

Yelena appeared to be in a large, darkened room filled with monitors. In the background, Mary could make out dozens of people sitting at computer terminals wearing small communication headsets. Yelena glanced off camera and nodded to someone nearby.

"We will take care of that from this end." Yelena said to Mary, signing paperwork handed to her on a clipboard and returning it to the faceless person by her side. "Flynn will bring both of you in. We have a lot to discuss, Mary, and we desperately need your help."

Dan gathered the few items they had brought, switched off the villa's utilities and returned the key to its secret hiding place behind the house number slates. Flynn insisted on driving them in Dan's car. His colleague sped off in a black vehicle before they had even set off. "I just wanted to apologise for last night." Flynn said, with a hint of a stammer. "I was aiming for your tyres. I will, of course, pay for any damage." Dan just glared, swinging into the passenger seat and folding his arms across his chest. "I'm not normally in the field. More of a techie really, but you know how it is…cutbacks and all."

Mary climbed into the backseat of the Gordon Keeble Sports GT, clutching Dan's sofa blanket to her knee.

"How did you find us?" Mary kicked off her shoes and tucked her legs around on the seat.

"This is a beautiful old car, Mrs Arora, and particularly noticeable on traffic cams, especially since I had the registration plate to go by. We traced you to the outskirts of this town, then lost you. I drove here last night, then caught sight of Dan doing a bit of grocery shopping so I followed you back to the villa. I have been watching and waiting for the command from Yelena Plender since then."

They set off at a rapid pace, with Dan berating Flynn for his clumsy and ill-timed gear changes and demanding regular updates on the status of his girlfriend. Mary caught Flynn up with the information gleaned from her ethereal travels and then used the time to watch the world go by, content to let others take charge of her safety.

Reunification with Parth dominated Mary's thoughts. Her once unshakable trust in him was unravelling at an alarming rate. His conduct towards their cat behind closed doors, his insistence that she continued with the brain scans despite the pain, the cold hearted treatment of patients in The Crypt, his absence of feeling in light of her death. *I expect Yelena has told him that I am alive. I wonder if he stopped working long enough to acknowledge the fact.*

It was a traumatic journey, one way or another. Dan chewed the sides of his nails, fretted and complained bitterly about the lack of forthcoming information regarding Connie's welfare. Flynn apologised at every junction and traffic jam for the jolting clutch control which left Mary bracing her stomach muscles and taking deep lead tinged gulps of air from the wound down window, to stave off the motion sickness. The unforgiving country roads provided an endless supply of roadworks, potholes and horse boxes to delay their time of arrival. It was perilously close to rush hour, by the time Flynn revved the engine and hammered the accelerator pedal along the M1 slip road in Buckinghamshire. Dan read the road signs, twisted around to look at Mary sprawled along the backseat and then turned to face Flynn.

"I thought you were taking us into MI6? Wouldn't that be in the heart of London, or at GCHQ in Cheltenham?" Dan's stare bore into the side of Flynn's face, distracting his attention from a passing truck. The car wobbled close to the enormous wheels and then returned to the nearside lane.

"Not Cheltenham. I'm taking you to another defence site. You will have to sign the Official Secrets Act as soon as we arrive and that includes the entrance. Hold tight." Flynn slowed the vehicle as much as he dared, with cars and trucks closing in on him in the slow lane. He then swerved onto the hard shoulder, slowing almost to a halt at the top of a Highway Patrol parking ramp. Steering Dan's car sharp left, they trundled along a short track that delivered them to the foot of an enormous concrete plinth built into the embankment which supported an overpass. Shrouded by thick, evergreen trees was a vast steel door. Flynn touched his finger to his ear.

"Just at the Tathall End tunnel now, Ma'am." The steel door rose, gliding along mechanical runners, revealing a floodlit tunnel inside the bridge column. Jasper Flynn, fumbled with the car switches, turning the indicators, windscreen wipers and hazard lights on and off, before locating the switch for the headlights. “I suggest you wind up the windows. The echo can be a bit overwhelming.” As they drove inside, Mary swivelled around to watch the steel doors sinking behind them, cutting off the daylight and transporting her into another secure environment. Her chest constricted, her breathing rate increased and heat rushed to her skin.

“I don’t think I want to go to wherever you are taking us. Can you take me home please? I can tell you what you need to know over the phone.”

“Just relax, Mrs Arora. No harm will come to you, I promise.” Flynn assured her, depressing the accelerator and directing the car round a sweeping bend in the passageway.

“Hmm. I’ve heard that one before, only he was fond of the word befall. Is this base entirely underground?” She shuffled forward on her seat and adjusted her shirt.

“No, not at all - just this entrance. It takes you right into the middle of the base and it’s quicker to get through security. One final, gradual bend in the road and the tunnel inclined towards a check point and daylight. Mary sighed with relief. Flynn cranked the driver’s window down and passed his Identification to the armed officer on duty.

Surrounded by fields and spinneys, the base was the size of a small town in the lazy Buckinghamshire countryside. Flynn parked the car in a space reserved for visiting dignitaries and handed the keys back to Dan. Signs for crèche facilities, restaurants and gyms looked incongruous to the modern angular buildings and the secrets that lie therein. They walked to a large pyramidal shaped structure. A stern woman in a neat suit, with tamed hair and a measured stance greeted them. She shook their hands a little too vigorously and handed them a clutch of papers to sign. Dan took his bundle and wandered towards the blue foam chairs in the lobby.

"Sir, where are you going?" The suit said, scampering after him in her polished kitten heels.

"You don't expect me to sign before reading it, surely?" Dan said, making himself comfortable and kicking his right boot up to rest on his left knee. Mary stifled a chuckle.

"There isn't time for that. I am instructed to bring you straight through to the Tactical Room the moment you arrive." She presented her palms to Dan, beseeching his compliance.

"You can't have it both ways. Do you want me to sign this or do you want me to hurry along with you to tactical?" Dan raised the first page on its stapled hinge, scanning through the bland statements and threats of imprisonment on the next page. "Good grief. There's a lot of jargon on this paper."

"Technically," Flynn chipped in, "The Official Secrets Act is law. Breaching the law is a punishable offence whether you sign those papers or not. It's not a contract as such, just a reminder of your obligations to uphold the law." The suit sighed audibly and handed Dan a pen. He signed on the final page, with reluctance.

Mary leaned on the reception desk and scribbled her name on her wodge of A4 paper and handed them back to the suit. "This way, if you please." She glared at Dan, and teetered down a carpeted thoroughfare into the shadowy halls of the defence installation. The suit listed a catalogue of rules, regulations and criminal acts, learned by heart and delivered with an additional dose of threat, should they be accidentally or deliberately contravened. She timed her speech to terminate precisely upon arrival at the entrance to the Tactical Room.

Flynn led the way, holding the door open for Mary and Dan to enter. The suit retreated, clutching her precious paperwork to her chest. The room seemed smaller in real life than the impression Mary had formed while Facetiming Yelena on the smartphone. Computer operators squeezed between benching and equipment like tech nerds at a World of Warcraft Fayre. At the front was a large touch screen unit, showing a shaky video link of military personnel, taking positions and signalling one another with various hand gestures.

The low sunlight cast long shadows of the construction fencing surrounding a partially demolished cottage hospital site. Yelena Plender stepped out from the unlit seating area at the rear of the room, uncharacteristically dressed in a jersey hooded jacket and jeans. Behind her, scratching his overgrown stubble, sat Parth. He glanced up and saw Mary.

"Mary, honey. I have been so worried. Thank God you are safe. Did they hurt you?" Parth rushed to greet his wife, throwing his arms around her, squeezing the air from her lungs and smothering her in eager kisses. With her movements restricted, she managed an awkward back pat before he released his grip.

"You knew? The news article reported me as dead, but you knew that I was alive all the time?" Her emotions back pedalled from the cool detachment she had conjured during the journey. Transient confusion suffused with immense relief balled up in her throat.

"Of course. Did you think I would be fooled by that poor woman's disfigured body? I was upset for her certainly, but I know every inch of you. Yelena and I have been working night and day to get you back. Why did you go to Dan and not come to me when you escaped?" Parth held onto to her waist, his grip tightening.

"I heard you speaking Russian on the telephone." Mary felt her face redden, her voice tapering off as she spoke.

"Yelena has been teaching me. It comes in handy when Plender sends his postgrads in to spy on me."

"Very glad to have you back with us, Mary, but there is no time for discussion now. Please, would you all take a seat?" Yelena directed them to the chairs and nodded a command to an agent watching her every move. Dan shook Parth's free hand and joined Flynn in the front row of chairs, stretching his legs out in the limited available floor space. Parth pulled Mary to an adjacent vacant seat, periodically pecking her hand and clasping it close to his abdomen. With her arm outstretched and trapped, Mary grappled with her conflicting emotions and watched the action unfold on the screen before them.

"Go, go, go!" The commander of the unit batted the doors of the disused hospital open, allowing his troops to charge into the main corridor, taking up positions behind nurse desks and doorways, clearing the sections one stage at a time. Mary could feel the tension and anxiety building in her tall friend, who had heard no more about the fate of his girlfriend since their time on the beach. She saw him grasp the steel armrests of his chair until his skin stretched white and taut across his knuckles.

The troop reached the ward Mary recognised as one of those supporting Hive Operatives. The helmet camera panned around, stopping to view the medical waste strewn on the otherwise empty floor and a single black body bag, domed in the middle. More silent hand gestures and the unsteady video feed moved further down the corridor towards Alexi's laboratory. Evidence of their hasty departure was everywhere, broken glassware, spilled chemicals, spattered coffee mugs and loose cables dangling from electric sockets like severed umbilical cords.

The headcam view bobbed cautiously around the edge of a wall, scanning for potential threat. The scene was a little more than a blur. A second glimpse showed the back of a figure, bound and slumped in a desk chair. Dan held his breath. Connie's head bowed to the side, her hands taped at the wrists, then attached to the backrest stem. Her blonde locks, dull and matted. A single navy shoe had slipped from her foot and lay against a wheel of the chair.

Mary felt Dan's anguish as acute pain radiating from her chest. Her eyes reddened, flushed with restraining the stinging tears. She was a neural hitchhiker, watching the visions his mind scrambled through. All the hopeful dreams he had envisioned for their future together; of pushing the playground swings for their bubbly daughter, welcoming their son into the world at the maternity unit, attending the awards ceremony for Connie's Pulitzer Prize - all extinguished, along with her vibrant giggle and agile mind.

The commander signalled his men to spread out and continue clearing the building, while he paused over Plender's bloody remains. In the confines of the Tactical Room, all eyes fell on Yelena, waiting for her reaction. Mary shifted in her seat, poised to leap to her friend's side in her moment of grief, attempting to gauge the depth of despair. She reached out in pity, tapping into Yelena's brainwaves and synchronising to her frequency. She felt nothing. Yelena continued to observe events dispassionately. "Oh Yelena, I am so sorry." Mary offered, by way of solace.

Yelena shrugged. "Divorces are expensive and messy."

The headcam drew closer to Connie and rounded her side. Her porcelain skin looked almost translucent, brittle and fragile as an ancient artefact. Her exposed neck bore the red finger marks of savage strangulation. Dan faltered, his composure failing him, he broke down into noiseless weeping. Mary rushed from her seat to comfort him, but he pushed her aside to see the screen. Connie's face filled the wall in front of them. Even in her tortured state, she looked beautiful. The commander gently peeled back the duct tape from her mouth, pulled off his glove and positioned two fingers on her damaged neck.

"I have a pulse…get the medic."

Chapter Twenty-One

"Can't somebody take Dan to see Connie? She shouldn't be alone in hospital." Mary implored, but Yelena was adamant.

"We will arrange a Facetime chat when she is Out of Woods. We have the best doctors attending her. She will be back to normal in no time. For now, we need both you and Dan to stay here." Yelena was leaning over Flynn's computer monitor, watching him use sophisticated tracking software on all routes leading from the disused hospital site. "Our focus must now be on finding Visser and stopping his next attack. What were the coordinates you saw in your walking dream?"

"Oh, yes. It was um… N39°45′00″ and er…" Mary closed her eyes, trying to visualise the numbers in her head.

"I scribbled them down." Dan drew a wrinkled till receipt for two rounds of sandwiches, a pot of tea and a flat white coffee from his pocket. Scrawled across the back, were the coordinates Dan had witnessed from Mary's mind during her extra corporeal journey to Visser's hospital. Flynn took it from him and began typing the digits into his computer. "There was a word too. It said 'Wasatch'.

Flynn stopped typing and looked up at Yelena. “This is his next target?” he queried. Dan and Mary nodded in unison.

“You know this place, Flynn?” Yelena asked, a puzzled expression dominating her features.

“I do. Wasatch is the name of the mountain range and corresponding earthquake fault line in Utah. It is very close to the Data Centre at Camp Williams.” Now, Dan and Mary looked perplexed. Yelena’s stony face looked up at them both. Her eyes widened in recognition of the place. “They are targeting Stoneghost.”

“Yes. That would seem to be the case.” Yelena turned back to Flynn. Get me a secure line to GCHQ at Bude. We have to warn them to follow contingency protocols. How long have we got?”

“It’s a little under six hours to midnight.” Flynn handed his boss a headset connected to ports on the console desk.

“No wait.” Mary interrupted. “Alexi said, midnight THEIR time, before something about Five Eyes backup.” She looked to Dan for confirmation. He nodded agreement. Flynn calculated the time differences. Midnight in Utah, USA, would be seven in the morning, British Summer Time. They had twelve hours to find and stop Visser, Alexi and the Hive from actuating an earthquake along the Wasatch Fault.

A junior agent called Flynn over to their computer terminal. He replayed black and white video images of cranes hoisting shipping containers from trucks at East Midlands Airport. “I have requested the flight plans for the private charter but their system has just crashed, sir. Looks like we have lost them.”

Flynn left Yelena to deal with a heated discussion with her superiors and ushered Parth, Dan and Mary from the Tactical Room and into a nearby office. "Mary, you must tell me everything you can remember…and I mean everything."

"I don't understand. What is Stoneghost? I heard Alexi say it when I got the numbers." Mary perched on the edge of a desk, shortly followed by Parth. Dan stood towering over the stocky Jasper Flynn, who was ruffling his hair with both hands.

"It's a secure network of surveillance equipment, between collaborating nations. It encompasses many systems and bases, from satellite transmissions to internet trawls and everything in between."

"So, there really is an all pervading Big Brother then?" Dan snarled. "That was what all those Wikileaks were about wasn't it? The existence of Echelon and Tempora, the systems which harvest tonnes of data from the telephone, satellite and internet systems"

"And there really is a major terror threat that it is trying to counter. Look, I've heard all the arguments from both sides and this is not the time for debate." Flynn had not slept for twenty-four hours. His snippy tone reflected his anxious state. Arguments were a fruitless waste of energy.

"Would it be so disastrous if this Visser bloke downed a few servers or disabled a few networks?" Dan said, his less sedate side grumbling its way to the surface.

"If what Mary said about inducing earthquakes along tectonic fault lines is accurate, then yes." Flynn raised his palm to his forehead. "There are approximately one point five million people living along the Wasatch Fault."

***

Mary found herself in another windowless room. This time, her husband was attaching cables to the neural cap on her head. "Can't they just shut down that research facility in Alaska for a while? That would stop Visser activating it."

"Not really, darling. There are quite a few Ionospheric Heaters in the world. There is an enormous one in Norway and similar ones dotted all over the place. We can't be sure that they will use the Alaskan one again, especially since you know about it." He sank the jack plug into a port on a small box of electronics and clipped it to the reclining chair where Mary lay.

"I don't know what you expect me to do? You stand a far better chance of locating them with conventional methods. Track their flight paths or something." This was not what she had envisioned when she relinquished control of the situation to MI6. Parth seemed more thrilled to have her back as his patient more than as his wife.

"Yelena's people have tried that, love. They seem to be able to cover their tracks. If Visser and the Hive can infiltrate minds, they are probably instructing British air traffic controllers too." Parth patted her leg and offered her more consoling tea. She declined and removed the cap, hooking it over the end of the armrest.

"Alexi uses shielding technology, something to do with solenoids, to prevent any device from detecting the electromagnetic flux of the Hive. He only switches it off when they are broadcasting. I can't hear them when it's activated. Besides, I wouldn't have a clue where or how to start looking for them."

"Solenoids? Of course. Cancelling out the fields. Sneaky bastard." Parth stopped moving, staring into space while he considered the scientific ramifications. Mary analysed her husband. He looked weary and unkempt, lean and a good deal older than last she saw him. The scientific fervour had not dampened though. He was still driven to achieve the manifestly impossible and that seemed to depend on her cooperation.

"Are you surprised by the things I can do now?" She sat upright and looked directly at him, observing every muscle group in his face that could betray a lie.

Parth cupped his hand to her cheek as a languid smile took shape on his lips. "I had a notion that you had capabilities. I'm just saddened that you had to discover them under such unpleasant circumstances." He pushed her legs aside and sat on the edge of the chair, sliding his hands around her back. "I have missed you." He touched his forehead to hers, closing his eyes and breathing her in. He moved in to kiss her. Mary snapped her head backwards and raised her arm between his chest and hers. She would not let him worm back into his affections that easily.

Dan wandered in. "Yelena sent me to help you…oh sorry, bad timing. Didn't mean to interrupt." He backed out of the room, swinging the door closed by the handle.

"No, it's okay, Dan. Come in." Parth said, jumping up and stilling the progress of the closing door. "I wanted to thank you for being so kind to Mary. I don't know why she came to you at the bookstore last night, but she obviously trusts you." Parth extended his hand for Dan to shake. "Please, come in." He repeated, beckoning Dan towards a second reclining chair by the wall. "Yelena had me set this room up as soon as you were both sighted. You can't imagine how relieved I was to hear that Mary was safe."

Dan frowned and sat down on something resembling a padded dentist's chair, bewildered by Parth's change of attitude towards him. "Anyone would have done the same."

"But you are not just anyone, Dan. I have something I need to tell you both, but I am not sure how you will react."

Dan's forehead pinched tighter. They sat motionless, waiting for him to continue.

"You remember that we took blood samples from you both back in the Neurosciences department?" Mary and Dan did remember. "Well, after that remarkable experiment, when Dan drew Tower Bridge in London, I had your blood tested for genetic markers."

"And?" Mary growled.

"It suggested a remarkable degree of genetic congruence." Parth beamed, expecting them to have ascertained the rest.

"Which means?" Dan sighed his impatience, slowly shaking his face from side to side.

"It means that you two are closely related." Parth clapped his hands together. It was obvious that the news had delighted him and was anticipating their corresponding elation.

Mary curled her lip at both sides. "As in distant cousins?" She looked at Dan. He certainly had a similar complexion. There was a passing likeness in the contours of his nose and the dark mahogany eyes. Perhaps a fleeting resemblance was evident.

"No, closer than that. It suggests that you are siblings." Parth returned to Mary's side, resting on the seat next to her knees and touching her thigh.

"But I'm an only child. How can that be possible?" Mary's thoughts switched back to her childhood. Flashes of long summer holidays spent pottering about the garden, alone but for her stuffed animal friends. Of Grampy reading to her on Brighton beach while her father was away on research trips and her mother prepared lessons for the following term of teaching. Could it be possible that her father cheated on her mother during one of his many trips? The thought unsettled the hero status she had always assigned him, the overhead lighting strobed, snapping her thoughts back to Dan. "Are you saying that we share the same father?"

"I suppose it could be possible." Dan said, folding his arms defensively across his chest. "I have never attempted to locate my biological parentage. It always upset my adopted mother whenever the subject arose."

"No, that's not what I am saying. The genetic markers match too closely. You have the same mother and father. You are fully brother and sister." Parth looked up at the flickering lights overhead then back at Mary. "Try to stay calm, honey. I know this is a bit shocking."

"But that would mean that mum was pregnant with Dan…"

"While they were at University," Dan said, chewing again on the edge of his thumb. "It might be worth asking Flynn to trace my registered biological parents from the adoption papers when all this Visser stuff is over with."

"Does that mean that having these odd abilities is genetic? Do you think Dan and I inherited them?" Mary shuffled forwards on her seat, stood up and wandered around the room. "Is that why you were testing us in your department?"

"It would indicate that, but we could find no anomalous genes or alleles that would point to new traits. But then, it could be hidden in the redundant DNA. Honestly, I haven't been able to find the causal link." Parth's voice tailed off, the solitary passenger of a new train of thought.

The air conditioning unit switched on, whirring mechanically. It drew Mary's attention, highlighting the lack of windows and the overt security surrounding them. She felt trapped. The expectation that she would conform to their demands was a burden of increasing intensity. They had replaced Visser's threats of torturing Parth to the heavier accountability of one and a half million lives in Utah.

Feeling the heat, she peeled off her cardigan and gathered up her hair in a bunch, holding it in a ponytail and fanning her neck with her free hand. The bruises from her own brush with death, were still visible around her throat. Had Parth even noticed them? She scanned the room erratically. Were the walls closing in? Her stomach gurgled.

"So, what was the point of you killing all those people down in Zone Six?" Her tone dipped a few degrees lower than frosty. Parth visibly twitched, as realisation dawned that he too was a target for observation during her bodiless flights. A fox caught in the hen house with two powerful weapons bearing down on him.

"Those people were already clinically dead. They had donated their bodies to science so technically, I am not responsible for their deaths. I had to redirect projects to focus on the pineal gland after your scan. It seemed too much of a coincidence that DiMethylTriptamine, ingested in tribal cultures, induced anecdotal evidence of extracorporeal travel. In some instances, there have been reports of other abilities that mirror yours, Mary, and a level of introspection not seen with any other type of recreational drug. When you started having peculiar experiences and we discovered your enlarged pineal gland, a site of natural DMT production, it became the focus of study to pinpoint the triggering factor." His eyes followed his wife as she paced about the room with a dissatisfied scowl.

"To what end? Supposing you did find the trigger? Presumably that was why you were all set to augment more unsuspecting volunteers and saturate their brains with drugs. What were you supposed to do with these specially activated lab rats?" A fluorescent tube blew out above her, showering her head in fleeting sparks and glass fragments. She stepped clear, shaking the tiny shards from her hair and clothing.

"Darling…please. Don't get yourself all worked up like this." The rest of the lights continued to flash and whine around them. Dan could not refrain from grinning at Parth's unease.

"Oh right, yes. You'd prefer me to be as docile as a kitten, so that you and Yelena can use me instead of Visser." She moved closer to Dan and sat on the side of his chair. "You have no idea what I have had to do to survive. No concept of the distress and agony that they put me through. I have half a mind to walk right out of here, right now. And take Dan with me too." Her nails dug into her palms as she screwed up her fingers into tight fists resting on her knees. Parth observed the dual force of fury mounting against him. He was under no illusions as to their combined strength.

"Mary, please. Why are you getting so angry? I have done nothing to put you in jeopardy. Yelena needs your help… and Dan's. Think of all the innocent people at risk in Utah. Let's take a break while the techies are doing their thing. Why don't we all go for a bite to eat? There is no need for this to become hostile." Parth hopped up and walked with feigned confidence to the door. Standing in the open doorway, he looked back at his wife and held out his hand. "Please?"

An unregistered black Range Rover pulled up and collected them from the entrance of the pyramidal building, driven by an armed officer in a black suit. His confidence alone, conveyed his high level of security clearance. Dan sidled around the two military guards, who had escorted them from the windowless room to the roadside, and jumped into the front seat. Parth opened the rear door for Mary and slid onto the backseat beside her. He reached across for her hand, but she snatched it away. "I'm still mad at you." She barked.

I'm mad about him switching off life support to clinically dead patients, when I have killed three soldiers and caused the deaths of ten innocent New Zealand residents. I'm the monster here. Perhaps they do need to keep me caged for everyone's safety. God, I feel sick.

"When this is over, we will sit and talk about everything. No more secrets, I promise." He tried again to hold her hand. She shuffled further away and rested her forehead on the car window.

"You are right about that. There won't be any more secrets – from Dan and me at least."

Black clouds scudded overhead with stark luminescent outlines where the sun wrestled against its cumulous barriers. They passed a grassed enclosure, surrounded by barbed wire and sub machine gun toting guards. At the heart of the lawn was a concrete path leading to a staircase down to an unknown destination. *A base within a base,* Mary thought. *Wonder what they have squirrelled away down there? A bit of an over kill. Like anyone could get inside this installation, let alone into one of these buildings without authorisation.* As their Range Rover passed the eight-foot-high gated entrance, the guards changed stance abruptly, holding their guns at the ready. It made Mary shudder.

The entire area felt like something left over from the Cold War. As if years of political intimidation had ingrained an oppressive state of readiness, with hair trigger reactions to attack. She spotted an algae covered satellite dish sitting in its own square of brittle concrete. A brass plaque, mounted on a wooden board stood beneath it, a monument to the grandfathers of technology. It was too far away for her to read it, but she could guess its sentiment.

"Where are we going?" Mary said, shaking off the feeling of impending trouble. She shifted in her seat and readjusted the safety belt several times.

"The nicest food is in the Foreign and Commonwealth Office restaurant, madam. There is a cafeteria, but they only serve sandwiches and snacks. I thought you would like a hot meal before things start to kick off." The driver looked in his rear view mirror and saw Mary shiver. "It's always lovely and warm in there." Mary looked up to meet the driver's reflected gaze and smiled. He winked back. "First time at the base is always a little unnerving, madam, but you'll get used to it. We aren't all miserable hard arses."

Mary snorted. Was he reading her mind or just guessing from her body language? Parth did a double take at the exchanges between his wife and the driver, folding his arms and harrumphing his discontent.

They arrived at the restaurant moments later, parking their vehicle in a bay reserved for government gentry and important personages. The driver jumped out of the car and opened the rear door for Mary to climb out. He flashed his lustrous blue eyes at her and smiled. Her hand slipped on the doorframe. He reached out and gently held her by the elbow until she alighted. An infinitesimal spark of frisson passed between them. "I will need to accompany you while you eat, but I will try and keep my distance, as difficult as that may be for me." He guided her to the entrance, leaving Dan and a glowering Parth to trail behind them.

The driver spoke to the maître'd, handing over his identification to authorise a request that their order be charged to hospitality. While the driver sat at the bar area and ordered coffee, a waiter directed them to a table. Mary looked on the striped waistcoat of the young man walking in front of her. There was a loud guffaw, a heavy thud and the sound of clinking silverware ricocheting from plates. Something about the bellowing laugh reminded her of awkward dancing. She craned her neck over the waiter's shoulder and squinted.

A portly man with immense greying whiskers was holding court three tables ahead. Mary could not believe what she was seeing. There before her, looking the picture of ruddy health was The Walrus, Professor Florian Haas.

Chapter Twenty-Two

Mary stopped walking when she reached Haas's table. Fragments of left over dinner encrusted the stacks of crockery that leaned against two empty bottles of Merlot.

"Professor Haas. What on earth are you doing here?" She glanced at the collection of suited women in his entourage. One of them pulled at his handlebar moustache cheekily before they said their farewells and returned to their administration positions within the FCO building opposite.

"My dear Mary. How good it is to see you. Oh, look at your poor neck. We will make those animals pay for what they have done to you. Come, sit with me. Assure me that you are unharmed and forestall the indigestion that will inevitably follow." Haas signalled the waiter to remove the clutter of dead plates and wine glasses and reset the table. Dan and Parth squeezed themselves uncomfortably into the seats facing Mary and The Walrus. Dan introduced himself.

"If only you had been in my department, instead of with that twisted tosser Plender, we could have kept a closer eye on you. You must try the duck. The sauce is a little rich but it complements the Merlot very well." Haas opened the menu folder, directing Mary to his recommendations.

"Haven't you heard?" Parth leaned across the table and whispered. "Plender is dead. Shot through the face by Mary's captors."

"Plender is dead? Oops, said that a bit loud. Had a little drinkypoo too many. How is Yelena taking it?" He downed the last gulp of red wine from his glass and shook it aloft at the waiter for more.

"With her usual steely aplomb" Parth said, pointing to his choice of Sea Bass on the menu for the waiter. Dan asked for the same. Mary played safe with the grilled halloumi.

"Professor, how long have you worked for British Intelligence?" Mary asked, gathering the menu folders up and handing them back to the youth in the striped waistcoat.

"Oh, you know, forever. I had a couple of exciting overseas missions back in my day. One or two with your father, Mary. He was a good man – a bloody good man. Why don't you call me Florian?"

"You knew my father? What missions – he was a Physics lecturer?" Mary nervously shuffled the salt and pepper shakers, aligning them with the place mats and cutlery on the table.

Haas sucked at the droplets trickling down his upturned, empty glass and straightened his back to look over the heads of diners for the waiter. "Yes, bloody marvellous physicist, but approached by Six during his fresher year at Uni. Brilliant agent but a bit too engaged, if you know what I mean. There was a spell, a year or so after he was recruited when your mother and he broke up. What a stunning woman she was and you have inherited all her charms and more, Mary dear." One of his eyelids drooped involuntarily, while he attempted to focus on Mary's face.

"Please go on, Florian." The sound of his name, ignited his smile and loosened his tongue.

"I don't know all the details, my dear, but I suspect that your mother couldn't tolerate his frequent unexplained absences – assumed he was cheating on her. He wasn't of course…utterly devoted. Your mother took a year out after that."

"Parth believes that Dan could be my brother. There are five years between us, do you think she could have given birth during her year out?" She stopped fidgeting.

"That's possible. Anything is possible."

Dan sat opposite Haas engrossed in his account.

"I'll have to ask Grampy about it." Mary urged Haas to continue.

"Your dad had a bit of a silver tongue when he was young. Got back into your mum's good graces and they married shortly after graduation. At some point, your dad took a sideways step in the organisation to spend more time with your mum, especially after you came along, dearest Mary."

The waiter arrived with another bottle of red wine and plonked it down in the centre of the table. Haas scooped it up and aimed the neck at Mary's glass.

She placed her hand over the top. "No thank you, I don't."

Dan and Parth shook their heads and muttered their thanks in declining his offer.

"Oh well, more for me." He sloshed the dark red liquid in, filling the glass to the brim.

"Shouldn't you be careful with what you eat and drink, Professor? It's not long since, well you know, since the incident at the ball." Mary considered her choice of words. She had not had an opportunity to discuss Plender's involvement, and his use of the mysterious electrical device, with Parth.

"It takes more than a heart attack to put this old dog down I can tell you. Do you know, the medical team reckon that I am as fit as fiddle? Had the whole bloody lot of 'em amazed. Poking and prodding bits they had no right to prod. Shoved a nasty camera up the blood vessels in my groin and had a good gander at my heart, they did. Can't seem to find the cause of the heart failure. See Mary, you aren't the only one with peculiar abilities." He slapped the table, his raucous laugh echoing in the restaurant again.

Their driver heard the commotion over at the bar and winced. His pocket vibrated with a smartphone text from Yelena. He hurried over to their table.

"Sorry to interrupt, folks, but Yelena needs you to return immediately. I will have your meals packaged up and sent over to you." He stepped aside as Mary rose from the table.

"I'll just powder my nose first. Won't be long." Mary said, moving towards the restroom. She could hear the booming tenor of Haas as she strode away.

"I should come with you to Tactical. I could lend my voice of experience to the cause." Haas gazed up at the driver hopefully.

"Yelena says she will contact you if we get in a tricky spot." He gestured for Parth and Dan to move to the exit.

"That'd be right. Nobody needs old Florrie anymore…"

Mary took her time in the Ladies' Room, assimilating all that she had learned. Her father had been a British Intelligence Agent all along. Not just a respected scientist, but also a spy. Now his periodic absences and mutterings about conspiracies started to make sense. The lecture trips to foreign universities, even during the long summer vacation; the strained silences between her parents while he packed his cases behind closed doors and the strictly enforced rule barring her unaccompanied entry to her father's study. She splashed cold water on her face and looked at her reflection in the mirror.

Grasping a braid of hair from either side of her face, she pulled them backwards and examined her features. Mary was often told of how much she resembled her mother. The high cheekbones, the widow's peak hairline and natural wavy hair. The way her wide eyes could turn her father to mush and make him concede to any, and all requests.

Did she inherit her gifts from them? Was her father able to project himself out of his body or read minds? Was that the reason MI6 recruited him? Was he rushing back to Brighton on her graduation day for college work or for a mission? What little she knew about her parents seem to be unravelling by the hour. How could she now separate the facts from the myths?

***

On their return, Yelena called Parth into Tactical, while their driver escorted Dan and Mary back to the windowless room that served as a temporary laboratory.

They adjusted their reclining chairs to the upright position and sat opposite each other.

“It’s a lot to take in.” Dan said, looking at Mary with fresh eyes. “I always used to imagine what it would be like to have a sister. I had an active imagination as a child. I would envy friends who had little siblings, watching them bicker and argue and have their tantrums, but when the chips were down, they knew that they had each other to rely on.” He took his jacket off and draped it over the back of the seat.

Mary sat still, with her hands relaxed and folded in her lap. The muddle of new information ran laps around her brain, tangling her synaptic transmissions and overlaying thoughts. “I don’t know how to be a sister. I have two sisters-in-law, but I rarely see them. I mean, I am pleased that you and I get along so well, but other than birthday and Christmas presents, I’m not sure what a sister is supposed to do.”

“If you are willing to find out, so am I. I have been an only child – an adopted only child for so long, it would be nice to have a sense of belonging for once. And, strange though it may seem, I do feel protective towards you.” His mouth wrinkled into an embarrassed grin. There was a brief pause, allowing them to fortify their emotions.

“I should like you to meet Grampy. Other than Parth, he’s the most important person in my life. And he’s your grandfather too.” Her head tilted. Were Dan’s eyes misting up? “Perhaps we should all visit him when Connie has recovered. Maybe he can explain what happened during mum’s sabbatical from Uni.” Dan nodded, dipping his head low and clearing his throat.

An agent wheeled in a trolley of covered hotplates containing their meals, along with a selection of juices, tea and coffee. “Ah, meals on wheels.” Mary said, breaking the atmospheric seal of tender sentiments. She jumped up and began lifting the lids and exploring the compartment beneath. They ate their meals on lap trays mostly in silence, keeping Parth’s congealing sea bass on the warming plate awaiting his return.

“What is your – our – grandfather’s name? I mean, your surname is only Arora because you married Parth. What was our family’s name?” Dan kept his eyes on his dinner. He couldn’t lose control at a time like this.

“The family name is Lawrence. David and Lily Lawrence were my - our parents.” She shovelled another forkful of food into her mouth and bit down. The squeaky cheese reverberated right up to her ears.

“And grandfather?” Dan mopped the last of the buttery sauce up with a new potato and munched it hungrily.

“Phillip Lawrence, people call him…”

“Pip. It’s not Doctor Pip Lawrence, is it?” Dan slid the knife and fork together on his plate and glanced up at Mary.

“It is, yes. How do you know him?” She hesitated between sips of her tea, balancing the mug back down on the tray.

“He’s my godfather.”

***

Parth’s food had desiccated to an inedible husk of white flesh by the time he returned to them in the temporary laboratory. He looked drawn and his posture tense. Mary and Dan each inferred the same conclusion

- events were not going well in the Tactical Room. They waited for Parth to stop pacing around the lab, tidying his computer station and winding up spare cables. Their driver and armed escort tapped gently on the door, levering the handle at the same time. He was clutching a Perspex box.

Mary strained to look through the glass panel in the door. She could just make out a small black device with an attached battery. Parth rushed over and pushed the man back through the opening, pulling the door closed behind them. They conducted their discussion in hushed tones, but Dan and Mary could hear enough to realise that Parth was refusing to cooperate with a direct order from high up in the organisation. Parth returned to the lab. Beads of sweat formed on his upper lip and brow and he was panting with indignation. Resting his hands on his hips, he took deep, slow breaths to steady himself.

"What's going on?" Mary demanded, twisting around in her chair to maintain eye contact with her husband.

"It's nothing. Don't worry about it. You both need to concentrate on helping to locate Visser." He started pacing again.

"You said no more secrets. Tell us immediately, Parth, or we will have to resort to other methods to find out." Mary and Dan both slid from their seats like cheetahs homing in on their quarry with quiet, imperceptible but deliberate steps, moving in telepathic coordination.

"That's just it." Parth wailed bitterly, throwing his arms in the air. "They want to block your Other Methods. Neuter you both with untested prototypes."

"What are you talking about?" Mary peered deep into his amber flecked eyes. An exhausted, defeated shell of a being, stared back.

"They consider you a threat to national security."

Parth moved closer to Mary, resting his hands on her shoulders. Dan instinctively backed away, giving the couple their space. She locked his gaze, experiencing the medley of feelings welling up behind her husband's submissive exterior. Training her brainwaves to his rhythms and thought patterns. Fragments of an argument with Yelena replayed in his mind; *you can't do this to her, after everything she has been through... She is not a weapon, she is my wife!*

His fear and anger amalgamated into a corrosive molten malevolence, eating away at his mind. Images of interrogation rooms with Mary probing the deepest regions of a prisoner's consciousness, without them having the slightest clue as to the reason for their incarceration. Thoughts about forcing Mary into infiltrating the minds of foreign dignitaries. Directing them to take their own lives or vote in policies against their conscious wishes. Visions of her compelling security teams to turn traitor and discharge their firearms into the brains of presidents, prime ministers and members of royalty.

Her heart pounded arhythmically, punctuated with a sharp sporadic pain. Were these his pains or hers? Their synergistic sensations gave him acid reflux and her an unwelcome resurgence of grilled halloumi.

"I will not let them take you away from me." He whispered. She felt his overwhelming distress of losing her, of loneliness and despair. In this one moment in time, she understood his perpetual, unflinching driven nature and his complete dedication and intent to crack the secret behind triggering supernatural abilities in sensitive individuals.

A method by which, he could provide British Intelligence Services with an alternative candidate to using his wife. She comprehended his late nights and early mornings, working on carefully crafted reports to the Ministry of Defence regarding his progress. The extreme studies on clinically dead volunteers in The Crypt. All to spare Mary from perpetual incarceration and being used as a captive resource. To spare her the indignity of living out the rest of her days in the underground bunker surrounded by machine guns and razor wire. A living weapon stored in the base within a base, to be utilised at the command of a faceless bureaucrat in Whitehall.

"They are not going to let us leave, are they?" Mary said, her mental entrainment fluctuating in intensity. Dan and Parth both shook their heads. "What about our human rights? They cannot detain us against our will, can they? Surely we have some rights under civil liberties?"

Parth tried to wrap his arms about her but she dodged his attempt, retreating to a distance beyond his reach. "I tried that avenue. Apparently, the Civil Contingencies Act 2004, allows the Minister of Defence to make emergency regulations that can override almost all other legislation when there is a threat of terrorism. Visser has unwittingly given them full authority to do whatever they like."

Her meal was opposing gravity in her gullet. Mary tried to swallow but her mouth was as arid as the

Savannah. “I escaped the clutches of a Soviet terror cell, I can do it again.” The words caught in her throat.

“They would track us down in a heartbeat. Whatever your mental capabilities are, honey, our bodies remain vulnerable to attack. We can’t fight the system. Believe me, I have been trying for a very long time.” Mary couldn’t breathe. Fresh air – she needed fresh air. Mary held her hands to her chest, forcing the air into her lungs.

Parth failed to notice her dismay. “There are any number of ways they could dispose of us. Accidental poisoning of our food, a not so random brake failure on our car, hey, they could even dose us with polonium and point the finger of blame at Visser’s lot.”

Mary unhooked the neural activity cap from the armrest of her chair and examined the electrode nodules regularly spaced in the fabric. She thought of Alexi. In his strange way, he had been kind to her, treated her with respect. He had no intention of castrating her neural activity with electrical devices that could short circuit her brain. Now they were coercing her into a mission that could potentially result in Alexi’s death.

If only Dan had driven her to an airport instead of a coastal town in Norfolk. They could be hiding out in some exotic country without fear of extradition. She breathed deeply, then sighed. “We still have to find a way out of here, before our situation gets worse.” She muttered.

“What about the one and half million people living along the Wasatch Fault, relying on us to save them from an earthquake?” Parth said, the gravity of their plight etched upon his forehead like a memorial plaque.

"They also have Connie." Dan said, raking his face with tense fingertips. "They have my Constance, God knows where. As soon as she regains consciousness, they will interrogate her relentlessly and if she refuses to give up her sources…"

Chapter Twenty-Three

"No. I won't be manipulated like this. There has to be a solution, we just haven't figured it out yet. If we put our heads together, we are more powerful than anything they can come up with." She perched on the footrest of her reclining chair facing Dan. Parth lingered by the door, watching their driver peer at them through the glass panel.

"Darling, I have every faith in you, but I don't think it wise to discuss it openly. These walls have ears, and more besides." Parth gestured towards the nosy driver. Dan and Mary turned to look in the proffered direction. The driver winked at Mary. She scowled back at him.

"Okay, we will do it my way…" Mary fixed her stare at her brother, locking eyes and synchronising with the agitated beta waves escalating in his brain. Without arousing suspicion, she began her silent communication. "*Can you hear me Dan? Nod if you can.*" A broad grin appeared on his face. He signalled with a single, definitive, curt nod. "*We have to maintain the upper hand here at all times. They are scared of what I can do. Together, we are an unstoppable force. It's clear that we have to stay long enough to stop the deaths of all those innocent people in Utah, but we cannot allow them to detain us, or worse still, impair our abilities"* Another curt nod. *"Okay, now you try and respond to me, inside your head."*

Dan shuffled on the chair, looking down at his feet. *"No, Dan. Keep eye contact with me. To start with at least."* He looked directly into her pupils. They were almost indistinguishable from her rich cocoa irises. Parth looked on. He could guess what Mary was attempting to do. He had seen the same expression on Dan's face the night he drew Tower Bridge. Dan squinted between intense frowns, hoping she could hear him say a simple, "Hello." It wasn't working. Mary waited patiently, watching him relax and take a breath. It was then she heard him.

"I'm scared too, Mary."

Mary gasped, a smile breaking out between her lips. *"It is a scary situation, but we have each other to rely on now."* A moment of peace filled Dan's thoughts. His beta rhythms slowed to calmer alpha waves, in the knowledge that Mary was in control. *"I'm going to distract the guard and see what I can find out. You practice on Parth while I'm gone. A partial Hive Mind is better than none."* Another nod from Dan and Mary stood up, touching her husband's shoulder with affection as she passed. "Just nipping to the loo. Won't be long."

Out in the corridor the cheeky driver, sent to guard them, escorted her to the restrooms then stood equidistant between the laboratory door and the Ladies' Room. Mary shuffled slowly, taking in her surroundings and trying to catch a glimpse of those inside the Tactical Room. As she neared the toilets, an older gentleman with hooded eyes and an upper lip so stiff as to render it immobile, bumped into her. “Oh, I am sorry.” Mary trotted out, automatically.

“No, no. My fault, young lady. I was checking my flies and not looking where I was going.” He gave her a slack jawed smile and she watched him waddle down the corridor and let himself into Tactical. Mary recognised him at once, but maintained her composure. She sauntered into the powder room and used the facilities while a nebulous plan began to coalesce into tangible action.

Winky the guard was waiting for her, eager to recommence the flirtatious banter. She had no time to waste. The Secretary of State for Defence had just entered the Tactical Room and she needed to hear what they were saying. Hurrying back to the lab, she turfed Parth off her chair and made herself comfortable. *“Dan, keep Parth busy and the guard off my scent. You know what I have to do.”* More nods, then she closed her eyes. Her larynx vibrated with the Beatles number once again.

It was like the flipping of a switch, her consciousness detached from her brain and whooshed through the door, along the corridor and she was inside the Tactical Room within seconds. Yelena and the Minister were mid snarl. Flynn was directing events from his computer terminal and listening in on their debate a few feet from his station.

“Please, Minister. I cannot stress this enough. We have employed every technical and electronic means at our disposal and we cannot locate Visser’s Hive Mind. Without Mary, Fort Williams will become an expensive pile of rubble within eight hours, and the Five Eyes data stream along with it.” Yelena stole a quick glance at a sympathetic Flynn, before turning her penetrative gaze on the politician. She knew this dance well and had yet to twirl him into submission.

"She is just too dangerous. The whole thing is too unstructured to control. How do you know that they didn't brainwash her into assisting them while they held her captive? She could be a Soviet Asset by now. No, it just won't do. Get that prototype working on her head or sedate her. Hell, sedate the lot of them, to be on the safe side." His loose bottom lip was thick with saliva, which he wiped away with a nonchalant thumb, rested against his mouth.

"We could still do that, but *after* she has helped us to stop the annihilation of our secure data feeds. Just think about all the innocent lives lost if we fail. Bude GCHQ are already working with the NSA, trying to re-route the streams through Harrogate, but they just haven't the spare capacity. If Mary can find the Soviets, think of the kudos you will have earned with the Americans…" Her hand was on the upper sleeve of his arm, administering tender strokes to his body as well as his ego. "I have known Mary for a long time. She is a kind-hearted, gentle soul. Putty in my hands. Let me mould her, Minister."

Yelena dipped her voice down a seductive octave and guided him towards the viewing area at the rear of the room. She sat beside him, allowing her knee to connect with his. "Leave it to me, sir. I can have this all wrapped up in a bow with your name on it before the PM has cleaned her teeth tomorrow morning."

Yelena was the performer, dancer and actress of great cunning and notoriety. Here the seductress, all charm and promises. Once the wife, fierce businesswoman and friend, now the spy, wielding her influence and intelligence as deftly as Shakespeare brandished his quill. So many masks, so many faces. How many more guises lurked beneath those passionless eyes? "*All the World's a stage…*" The echo of Grampy's voice replayed in Mary's mind.

Mary had heard enough. It was obvious that information was far more important to this government than lives. She allowed her consciousness to drift back to her physical self, reconnecting her mind and body fully before slowly opening her eyes. Yelena was a skilled manipulator. Mary would need to dance carefully if she was going to bring about a satisfactory conclusion to this affair.

***

Their driver knocked and entered the lab. "Dr Arora, the pathologists have sent through images from the initial stages of the post-mortem on the dead Hive Operative. If you would like to follow me, I can set up a video link between you and their theatre. Perhaps you can give them some direction to speed up the process." Parth seemed momentarily dazed, then grappling with his thoughts, he wandered towards the door.

"Will you be alright here, Mary? Shall I ask them to bring some coffee to you?" He scratched at the back of his head, blinking rapidly.

"Coffee? You know I never touch the stuff. Actually," Mary said, sliding from her chair and facing the guard. "Would it be possible for Dan and I to get some fresh air? It is so stuffy in here. Can we go and sit outside for a little while?" Mary conjured her most imploring look at the driver. He raised one eyebrow and smirked.

"I'll make the arrangements. Wait here." He gave her one last hope filled flash of his sparkly blues and turned to leave with her husband.

Dan and Mary waited in silence until another agent arrived to collect them. Muscles bulged beneath the straining fabric of his charcoal twill suit and when he leaned forward through the door, his jacket hung open to reveal the gun holster strapped tightly against his ribs. "Follow me." He said, with neither introduction nor civility. They walked several paces behind him, his swagger filling the width of the corridor. Unlike their driver, Muscles trained his attention on his surroundings, glancing in all directions as though he was expecting a marauding hoard to attack.

Passing through the air conditioned foyer through the front entrance, the oppressive heat seemed to radiate from every paving slab and brick. Past the dimly lit paths was the blackness of the Buckinghamshire countryside. Just an occasional bleat from a sleepless sheep, to remind them that life extended beyond the silent confines of the base. Mary noticed a trail leading down to a grassed area.

"What's down there?" Mary asked the agent. She watched him sniff and pucker one corner of his lip up.

"A drainage pond." He swept the sides of his jacket backwards, digging his fists into his trouser pockets and pushing his chest in her face. "Look, lady. I have better things to do with my time than babysit a couple of clueless civilians. Do what you have to do quickly, then I can get back to doing them." He planted his feet stiffly on the tarmac, locking and unlocking one knee in frustration. Muscles watched his pet civilians walk down to the pond, hesitating while their sight adjusted to the darkness.

They sat on a wooden bench overlooking the water. Bull rushes grew thick and wild and there was a slick of algae coating the surface. It was a far cry from her favourite duck pond in the park near to the university. How she longed for those simpler days. It felt like months since she had ridden, carefree and happy through the muddy puddles on her push bike. And now, the fate of one and a half million people rested on her ability to find a Soviet terror cell who have access to unlimited means and technologies.

"I don't think King Kong back there can hear us if we keep our voices low." She whispered, raising her chin to the massing clouds above and clicking the joints in her spine free of tension. Mary told Dan all that she had discovered from the Tactical Room and shared her consternation over the Defence Minister's brash disregard for their civil liberties. "Unfortunately, I think Parth is right. If we mount an escape, we could be seriously injured, or worse. If we did manage to get free, there isn't a corner of the world where they could not find us eventually. Our best hope is to broker a deal through Yelena. She still believes that I am harmless." A triple flash of light lit up the sky on the horizon.

"I think I can be of help with that. Leave it to me, I have an idea." A protracted grumble of thunder made Dan raise his voice.

"Why, what are you going to do?" Mary said, snapping a small twig from a shrub and dissecting each attached leaf in turn.

"I discovered a new trick while I was practising reading Parth's mind. I think it will come in handy if the minister cuts up rough. You concentrate on stopping Visser's Hive and I will do my best to get us out of here." He leaned back on the bench, stretching his long legs to the water's edge.

"Are you going to tell me what that is?" She stopped peeling the stem and faced him.

"Hmm, not yet. Let me sort a few things out first and then I'll tell you about it." A mischievous smirk assembled beneath his nose. "Do you think the storm is heading this way?" He said, changing tack.

"The metaphorical one or literal one?" They smiled, knocking shoulders together. "It'd be good to clear the air. It's been so humid for days now."

"I love thunderstorms. A good one can be exhilarating to watch." As he said it, a streak of fork lightning stabbed the grassland in the distance. The sheep were silent.

"Me too, well any meteorological event is exciting." The shrubs and small trees surrounding the pond area began to rustle, buffeted by the strengthening breeze. It cooled and tingled Mary's skin.

"I definitely inherited that from Grampy. He is obsessed with forces of nature. He took Dad and me to Iceland once, just to see the Northern Lights. Mum wasn't interested so she stayed at home."

"It is an amazing sight, I must admit. I went with a bunch of mates from college. I think they were expecting to get crazy drunk and have some sort of spiritual experience under the Aurora Borealis. By the time we had travelled up to a latitude high enough to see it, my mates had drunk themselves into a stupor and had passed out in the truck. Daft sods."

The latency period between lightning strikes and corresponding thunderclaps had shortened noticeably. Single drops of rain splattered and rippled the tiny algal disks on the pond, forewarning them of the storms arrival. Neither of them indicated a desire to find shelter.

"You didn't get drunk with them?" Mary asked, cupping her hand out in front of her and catching the odd droplet in her palm.

"No. I was taking antibiotics for a cut that had become infected on my arm. I knew I shouldn't have waded into those Icelandic Hot Springs. They are just teeming with bacteria. It's like human stew. Hind sight is a wonderful thing. Anyway, alcohol and peer pressure plus a small wound and in I went. At least it made me lay off the booze so I was able to enjoy the lights."

The sporadic rain droplets continued to entertain them. Dan stuck out his tongue and caught one in his mouth. "A weird thing happened while I was there though."

"Oh?" The volume of thunder claps was gradually increasing. It quickened her heart beat, stirring a release of pleasant dopamine into a bloodstream that was already rich with adrenalin. The tangy smell of ozone, prickled her nostrils and dissolved into her taste buds, combining with particulate odorants from the parched vegetation opening their pores to the storm.

"We were in this convoy of trucks, being bumped and bounced around. You could see the Aurora shimmering in the gaps between the trees. We had a fancy truck with skylights as well as side windows. The higher up the mountainside we drove the easier it was to see. Then the green and pink lights, wafted and changed colour to mostly red. The cables between the telegraph poles suddenly showered us in sparks and caught fire. Then the engines cut out. We were completely stranded. No heat or light or mobile phone signals." A streak of lightning forked out in crooked fingers across the sky.

"Cor! That was a good one." Dan effused, distracted for a moment. "The guides built big fires and kept everyone as warm as they could. They said it must have been a surge of geomagnetism from an intense solar storm reaching our atmosphere." The crack of thunder was ear-splitting. The storm had arrived.

"What year was this? When did you go to Iceland?" Mary looked stern. The rainfall was steadily increasing, chilling her skin and dampening her clothes.

"Erm… it would have been… 2001. We were lucky. The tour that left a couple of hours before us had a terrible time. We found out later that some little kid had collapsed during the blackout with seizures. Poor mite." Dan stood, pulled his trousers up by the belt loops and faced his sister.

"That little kid, Dan," Mary said to her silhouetted brother. "Was me." Thousands of synapses popped and fizzled in their brains, connecting all the pieces of their histories into one inescapable conclusion. The one factor that both siblings had in common other than their shared genetic configuration. Both were present during the same explosive discharge of solar particles. Had they been genetically predisposed to their new abilities? Did the electromagnetic radiation cause a mutation in their DNA? Did Grampy know about their condition all along? They shared the collaborative thought progression telepathically.

Mary asked Dan to keep the revelation a secret, even from Parth. A part of her wanted to protect his professional integrity, after his years of searching for the trigger leading him to artificial chemical inducement. Another part of her agreed with Dan's initial thoughts, that these gifts were too dangerous to unleash on a wider population.

Mary had visions of Alexi subjecting the Hive Mind Operatives to increasingly more hazardous levels of ionising radiation in an attempt to secure Mary's limitless powers. She also feared that Parth would start a new research study funded by the British Government. One that began with Dan and Mary restrained and sedated in a medical laboratory.

"Hey, guys!" Muscles yelled. "Getting wet over here. You done?"

Chapter Twenty-Four

The storm discharged a torrent of rain just as they had made it back to the foyer of the building. Parth was pacing up and down the lab when they arrived. "Mary, darling. How's your head? Are you feeling okay?" He rushed to embrace his wife, planting an unwelcome peck on her wet forehead. "Are you in any pain at all?"

"Fine, thanks. What's the matter with you?" She disengaged herself from his arms, pushing him away.

"I got the pathologist to crack open the Hive Operatives skull and dissect the brain. It was riddled with tumours, particularly on the pineal gland. We won't know for sure if they were malignant till the tests are concluded. Same with tox screens, but it's safe to say that habitual use of high doses of the chemical concoctions poured into that man's veins, overloaded his limbic system. I suspect that his liver will show signs of strain or damage too."

The wakeful nights and heavy workload had paid a toll on Parth. The deep furrows in his face remained visible even after his expression changed to relief upon hearing that his wife felt physically well. Mary took a peek inside his mind. She couldn't help herself. Where she expected to find regimented order and constraint, she discovered a maelstrom of fright and disarray. His thoughts were a clamouring mess of chaos and anxiety. The video image of the Hive Operatives cancerous brain swam through his mind. It alternated with a vision of Mary lying on the pathologist's slab, her skull sawn open for examination and her eyes milky with the cataract of death.

Parth gestured to a side table laden with pump action thermos flasks of hot water, canisters of dried coffee, teabags and a plate of biscuits. "You should keep well hydrated, love. I got you some ginger cookies. Would you like one now?" His eternal care for her was habitual, but mildly endearing. She dialled back her recent terse manner.

"You know I hate ginger, Parth. Are *you* feeling okay?" She turned to Dan, distracted by his sniggering. Dan held an apologetic hand aloft. Mary squinted suspicion towards her brother. She projected a message telepathically. *"Did you do something to his memory?"* Dan couldn't help but laugh and nod. Parth was blinking at an unnatural rate and scratching his scalp.

The driver returned, dispensing with the formality of knocking, he barged into the lab. "Yelena wants you all in Tactical." Dan held the door for Mary, then waited for Parth to come to his senses and follow on behind.

Flynn spun around in his seat as they entered the darkened room, raising his index finger to his mouth and then pointing towards the seating area. Yelena was mid video conference with an irate U.S. military man, dressed head to toe in beige uniform. The screen definition picked out the pock marks and faded scars in his skin, each one a talisman marking the trauma he had witnessed. Attached to his blazer were tiny rectangles of coloured cloth sewn in strips. He seemed intent on making them the focal point of his impassioned speech, jabbing his thumb at them repeatedly.

"Urban myth. Never heard such nonsense in all my long distinguished career." His elongated vowel sounds pinned him to the Mississippi flag. "Begging your pardon, ma'am, but these scares come along every once in a while, and nothing ever comes of it. Every whack job and nutter west of Georgia has a conspiracy theory that threatens mankind. There ain't been a quake in Utah since before the early settlers and there ain't a goddamn shred of evidence to suggest that mankind can start one either." He adjusted his cap, the hatband sticking to his sweat greased forehead.

"With respect, general, you are wrong." Yelena's lazy eyelids were the only indicator of frustration in her perfectly composed demeanour. This latest mask of British Official, did not sit well with her. "Under specific controlled conditions, high frequency pulses are amplified by the ionosphere and reflected to precise locations across the globe. At the correct frequency, the waves can cause damaging resonance within the ground rock. We have solid intel that points to such an attack on the Wasatch fault, specifically the Salt Lake section. We believe that The Data Centre at Fort Williams is the target."

The general removed his cap altogether and blew air through his teeth. "Well, ma'am. I will take that warning under advisement and get back to you should the need occur." He swiped his thumb across his neck, his forehead dropped into a scowl. The Tactical screen went black as the feed was cut.

"Arsehole." Yelena muttered, then turned to face the audience. She gave Flynn the nod.

"We have an all ports warning out on the tail number for Visser's private charter. Without access to the flight plans, all we can do is wait till they land and scramble all tech to trace their whereabouts." Flynn shot a millisecond glance at the Defence Minister who was sitting in the back row with a sour look. "Mary, is there anything else that you can remember that could help us to locate them? Anything at all."

Dan leaned over to Mary and whispered. "They spend billions of tax payers' money on a Big Brother that snatches away personal freedom and anonymity and yet they are still reliant on a Brighton born university lab tech to solve their crisis. Bloody typical." Mary rolled her eyes, then caught Yelena staring icily at her. She needed to keep her on side. Give the illusion of humility. It felt all too reminiscent of her experience with Alexi. Project one persona but hide the reality. Make them believe that they hold all the cards. The minister shifted uneasily in his chair, straining to observe the movements and body language of those gathered.

Mary sent her rebuke straight into Dan's mind. "*Be compliant. Don't give them an excuse to confine us.*" She pretended to be in deep thought, pinching her chin between her thumb and side of her index finger and resting her elbow on her knee. "Alexi told me that Visser's gifts are relatively weak. To communicate with the Hive Mind, he has to be physically close to them and he tires easily. If he is to infiltrate the minds of those controlling Ionospheric Heaters, he might need to move the Hive closer to the research facility they plan to use. Wouldn't it be wise to monitor the incoming flights at airports close to those research facilities? I would definitely be looking at Fairbanks Airport in Alaska."

Flynn gave Yelena a 'told-you-so' look, then swivelled his chair round to face his computer terminal, tapping and clicking his way round software applications at a phenomenal speed.

Yelena ignored him. "And it was their intention for you to replace Visser in this infiltration, Mary?"

"Yes. Alexi was attempting to train me to collaborate with the Hive. They threatened to torture and kill Parth if I refused to cooperate." Mary laid her hand on her husband's wrist, tightening her grip.

"But why did they need you, if Visser can direct the Hive Operatives?" Still Yelena bore no telling expression. Her chiselled face remained motionless.

Mary choked. She had been avoiding this discussion, the one that spelled out her full capabilities and her ability to use a combination of her gifts as a unified power. To be able to send her consciousness to unlimited destinations, take control of a targeted person's mind and feel every synaptic transmission from their senses. Visser achieved this power using a cluster of minds. As far as she could tell, Mary was the only one who possessed the talent of emitting electromagnetic pulses. She saw no indication that any from the Hive could do the same. That made her uniquely valuable.

The Defence Minister cleared his throat. They were impatient for her answer. Only she and one other knew that Alexi outranked Visser. Dan had been her subconscious passenger during her out of body travels back to the disused hospital. He had witnessed the scene through Mary when Alexi ordered Visser to shoot her former boss in the head. Could she use this information to deflect attention? Mary tried her luck. “Perhaps Alexi had grown tired of Visser’s incompetence.”

Yelena drew a sharp breath, her eyes dilated. Every person present noticed the breach in her serene outer shell. For a moment, Yelena was speechless. Flynn carried her.

“Mary. Do you think you could try and uplink with Visser’s brain? Take direct control?” He rose from his seat and took centre stage in front of the viewing area.

“I’m not a computer, Flynn.” Mary said, shaking her head. “I can’t just tap in an IP Address and plug myself into a network.” Even the idea of being inside Visser’s sinister head again made her heave.

“But the Hive is a like a wireless network, is it not? It relies on convergent frequencies that are being broadcast.” He was waving a biro towards her and getting into his stride.

“In a way, I suppose. Providing Visser is travelling with them. But it is a shielded network. Unless they switch off their solenoids, I cannot detect them. And that assumes that the Hive Operatives are all together in the same place or set of vehicles. Captain Thirty-Four…” She paused, taking in the looks of disbelief, “Yes, that was his designated name. The Captain told me that there was a segregated group of operatives devoted to infiltrating the minds of city bankers and such. I got the impression that they were physically separate too.”

Flynn’s computer made a beeping noise. He returned to his terminal swiftly and was opening applications before his rear had made contact with his seat.

“What is it?” Yelena said, regaining her equilibrium. Flynn did not answer. He repositioned his monitor and opened a command prompt window. Typing in script, he launched a small application that he had designed and written for himself. It sent a message directly to the destination servers, requesting a single ping back, confirming that all was fully functional. "Flynn?" Yelena urged.

The Tactical Room fell silent, all movement ceased, barring the key strikes beneath Flynn's hands. "It's not good." He said in earnest. "Fairbanks Airport servers are offline."

"But…wha'…what, ahem." The Defence Minister rose and stomped down the steps at the side of the viewing area. "What does that mean, exactly?"

"It means that Fairbanks Airport has no air traffic control, no security barriers or cameras, no heating, no runway lighting…I could go on." Flynn looked in desperation at Yelena. She was at a loss for words.

"Well get them back online, man. What are you waiting for?" The minister huffed, gesticulating wildly at Flynn's computer.

"Sir. I cannot remote access a powered down server. Someone there will need to physically power up the machines and allow them time to reconfigure the systems check before launching software."

"English, man, English!" All but the minister had grasped the repercussions of what Flynn had announced. Mary listed all the computer controlled aspects of landing multiple aircraft on different runways in her head. Even if they had some warning of system failure, it was doubtful that they could risk attempting to sequence flights manually. The inevitability of casualties smothered their hope.

In slow, overly enunciated words, Flynn said; "There is nothing I can do, sir."

"Don't they have some kind of emergency power supply to prevent this from happening? Jeez, even hospitals have back-up generators for surgical units and life support." His limp bottom lip flapped as he blustered, sending globules of spittle into the air.

"Yes, they do. High capacity power packs ensure that servers aren't exposed to fluctuations in current. It's standard procedure. It does suggest that someone has deliberately shut them down." Flynn faced Mary.

"Visser." Mary whispered. She massaged her temples. Flynn nodded.

"Put up a satellite feed on the main screen there. I want to see what is going on." The minister made a circling motion with his finger towards the Tactical Room wall. "I should really appraise the PM on events, but she is locked in talks all night at Ditchley."

"Sir, I haven't got that level of clearance." Flynn was still looking at Mary. Her grey pallor seemed to leech the life out of her.

"Bugger clearance, man! Can you do it, yes or no?" More tapping and clicking his computer terminal and a satellite feed flickered up on the screen.

There was an image of the Alaskan brain mounted in pixels for all to see, the white permafrost, decorating the mountain ranges and forming the outer edges of the organ. The glacial ravines picking out the cerebral fissures and the peninsula forming the brain stem, Mary thought it was beautiful.

The minister huffed. "I don't think you fully understand, Flynn. If those Soviet bastards…forgive me Yelena… get their way, there won't be a need for clearance levels. There won't be a satellite feed for you to access. Cripple Stoneghost and we will not have a leg to stand on. No internet trawls, no telephone transmissions, email surveillance… nothing. We will be utterly blind."

Flynn ignored the minister's rant and zoomed the satellite imagery along a large winding river above the brain shape to the Alaskan city of Fairbanks. The twisted ribbons of muddy river courses forked and split between the sandbanks and smaller deltas beneath the airport; so much water and lush vegetation. He panned upwards, closer to the landing strip.

An odd assortment of aeroplanes taxied in a growing queue adjacent to the runway, waiting their instructions from the tower. Huge aeroplanes carrying passengers, some of cargo while other smaller jets nudged forwards as impatient as their wealthy owners. A Boeing 747 reached the front of the line, sweeping in a great ark to the foot of the runway, crawling ever forwards.

From the edge of the satellite range, the afternoon sun shone on the wings of an executive jet making its final approach just as the 747 rolled into its flightpath. Mary held her breath as the glinting jet tried to pull up, lifting the undercarriage clear of the passenger plane's fuselage. It failed.

The wheels tore into the curved roof panels of the 747, yanking the jet's nose down and crushing the cockpit into the first class cabin section. As the jet toppled, it smashed into the Boeing's wing, snapping it clean if half and rupturing the fuel tanks. An orange ball of flames erupted from the mangled shards of metal, partly shrouded in a massive plume of black smoke.

Silver and white fragments of a hot aluminium littered the asphalt along with pools of flaming aviator fuel.

“Oh, God.” The minister stood transfixed. The staggered refresh rate of satellite images delivered the devastating carnage in a juddered series, each frame engraving itself in their memories. Mary calculated the potential death toll in her head and shuddered. An inflatable slide appeared from the rear exit of the 747 like a giant party blower, just as the remaining fuel tank ignited. The explosion filled the Tactical Room wall. “Jesus wept.” Billowing smoke obscured over half the screen. Fire trucks encroaching from every direction, suddenly stopped. Nothing could be done. “I’ve seen enough. Shut it off.” The minister swallowed hard.

Flynn blocked all emotion and concentrated on his manual and intellectual dexterity, his keystrokes a continuous clatter in an otherwise hushed room. “I sent another ping. Their servers are back online. I’ll try and access their site wide security cameras, but don’t hold your breath. It’ll take time but I should be able to get into Fairbanks traffic surveillance. Their coverage is extremely limited, though.”

“I’ll get onto the HAARP Research facility in Gakoma – see if they can isolate access to the software controlling their Ionospheric Heater. Maybe they can disconnect their electrical source.” Yelena pushed an agent from his computer terminal and took over, donning a communications headset as she sat down.

The Secretary of State for Defence turned and loomed over Mary. The violence of his conviction manifested in a visible tightening of muscles in his neck and fists. He chewed at his slack lower lip and inhaled a noisy breath through his nose.

"Mary. I want you to get inside that bastard's head and make him eat a couple of bullets. Do whatever it takes. D'you hear me? I want him dead." Mary, Dan and Parth exchanged glances. There was a brief second in silent contemplation between them. Parth stepped up to the challenge.

"Wait just one minute. You cannot order my wife to kill another human being. I understand fully what is at stake here and I can see that you feel you have no other choice. Mary is not military personnel, you have no authority over her. To expect her to infiltrate and murder whomever you demand makes you no better than the terrorists she escaped from. Whatever happened to twelve good men and true in a proper trial? What makes you the supreme judge and jury? You are putting her in the exact position that you claim has made her a threat to national security. In effect, you are forcing her to tie a noose around her own neck."

Chapter Twenty-Five

The Minister's elite superiority oozed from each and every syllable. Parth was well matched in the escalating row that sent Mary and Dan slinking out of the Tactical Room, virtually unnoticed.

"You are damned if you do and damned if you don't. I certainly don't envy your position." Dan drooped his arm over her shoulders and gave her a brotherly squeeze.

"Would you mind if I had a few minutes in the lab alone, Dan? Nothing personal. It's just all the clamour. I need to think." He removed his arm and stepped away from her.

"Of course. It's a big decision. I am going to see if I can't find that uptight, lady-suit. You know, the one who greeted us with a broom shoved up her arse. *Ms Official Secrets Act*. I'm sure Mr Muscle, over there, can arrange for me to see her." They tittered in the agent's direction, who looked quite affronted by the nickname.

"Do you need her for something specific?" Mary inquired, her interest piqued. Dan was walking backwards down the corridor towards the reception area.

"I'll tell you later." He tapped the side of his forehead in exaggerated prods.

“Oh, right. Okay.” She understood.

The water in the thermos flask was tepid. It made her tea look like dishwater and taste even worse, but the caffeine was a welcome buzz in the early hours of the morning. Her tummy gurgled but the hatred for ginger deterred her from consuming one of Parth’s biscuits. Perhaps she would relent later.

Mary reclined in the dentist chair and looked up at the ceiling tiles. She listened to the whirring of the air conditioning unit and the intermittent roll of thunder, drumming overhead. It reminded her of Brighton. Night time summer storms seem to be a frequent occurrence back then. Days of relentless humidity would see panting dogs and her overwrought mother, scurrying for the shade and praying for the weather to break. When at last the wind changed, it carried away the blistering heat and with it, her mother’s genial mood.

As the storm raged, Mary would lie on her bed, listening to her parents spitting venom through clenched teeth, trying to keep their voices low so as not to wake her. Forward wind twenty-five years and the British Government were still at the heart of family rows. Did her mother know she had married a spy? Had they kept tabs on Mary all her life? Professor Haas certainly had extensive knowledge about her. Did Yelena have a dossier overflowing with reports about every peculiar event that had taken place in her life since birth? Did MI6 know that Dan and Mary were siblings before Parth tested their blood? It was a sobering thought.

The stillness felt good. The leather backrest cradled and supported her body. She resisted the urge to let her eyelids close, the ceiling tiles blurring through the thick mass of lashes in front of her pupils. If only she could project her entire body out of the pyramidal building and away from the intense security and aggressive atmosphere of the government facility. To fly like a superhero up into the air, with Dan and Parth in each arm. Mary stifled a giggle. There she was, harbouring extraordinary abilities and her extra normal husband was still fighting her battles for her back in Tactical.

Would it be so bad if she did manage to access Visser's mind and compel him to commit suicide? He was a murderer of innocent people and of his own guards, but then, so was she. The memory of the New Zealand earthquake trickled into her thoughts. The families of ten antipodean victims, wholly unaware that their deaths were by unnatural causes. All those people mourning for relatives whose lives Mary had unwittingly snuffed out.

How many more gruesome and painful fatalities would result from Alexi's latest plan? How many families shattered by the loss of loved ones living along the Wasatch Fault? Surely their survival was justification for taking one more life. If she exterminated Visser, would Alexi find another mind reader to lead the Hive in his stead? For all Mary knew, the organisation behind Alexi's terror cell was vast and fragmented. She thought it entirely feasible that he had the backing and support of a much larger political entity. She had heard both Visser and Alexi referred to with military titles. Could it be that they were acting under the orders of the highest Soviet authority?

Mr Muscle was looming outside the lab. He peeked in at Mary and leaned against the door, the thumping noise as it connected with the wooden doorframe engineered to remind her of his presence. She snapped out of her reflections and forced herself to make a decision.

Closing her eyes, Mary hummed the tune. Her body went limp. Mary's mind soared into the wild and electrified night sky, through the lashing rain and up above the condensing mists. Large swathes of England lay under a thick blanket of storm cloud but she was able to make out a faint outline of the coast. Brightly lit towns and cities edged the English Channel like the lower branches of a Christmas tree festooned with fairy lights. *I need to go north. Get to Alaska and then focus on finding Visser.*

Drifting past Cardigan Bay and then the Irish Sea, she found it slow going without the aid of the Hive to boost her energy. Which was the quickest way to travel, over the North Pole or across Northern America and Canada? *The Arctic might get confusing – all that snow and few landmarks, I might get lost.* Crossing the Atlantic Ocean, Mary kept the thought of one and a half million Utah residents at the front of her mind. They had just five hours of blissful ignorance until Visser unleashed the Hive Mind and initiated a catastrophic quake. A dose of endorphins stimulated her neurons, kicking her brainwaves into a faster beta frequency. She surged ahead, making rapid headway across oceans and landmass. Before long, Mary spotted the silted trails of the Tanana River that underlined the airport at Fairbanks.

Where do I even begin to look for them? How can I find them if Flynn, with access to all that technology, cannot? Mary paused high above the Fairbanks skyline, analysing each trunk road and thoroughfare for convoys of similar trucks, but to no avail. *Think. What can I do that technology can't? I can synchronise with other people's brainwaves. Maybe I am looking at this problem from the wrong angle. Instead of attempting to find Visser's body, perhaps I should be tuning in to Visser's mental frequency, like a radio.*

An image of Lars Visser wafted into her unconscious thoughts. Those verdant feline eyes, masking the decades of depravity they had witnessed; the jawline jowls weighing down the corners of his mouth and the dark malefic recesses of his deplorable mind. She could feel his impatience and pent up anger simmering in his hippocampus. A cauldron of smelted hatred and envy, his hunger for power was barely contained within his neural network. It lurked just beneath the surface, awaiting an opportunity for release.

Mary felt a wave of revulsion. She could almost sense his presence, but the link was tenuous. Why was this so difficult? She had infiltrated his mind so easily back in her hospital prison. A fleeting image of an air freshener in the shape of a moose head, hanging from a rear view mirror passed through her subconscious. It swung erratically to the side of a large steering wheel. Visser was in the driver's cab of a truck. She could see the tattooed knuckles of the driver clinging onto the wheel as the lorry lurched across uneven ground.

The link was failing. Her sight blurred and faded and an electronic squeal resonated through her skull. A tremulous pulse fractured her beta rhythms, sending her body into convulsions. The disharmony jerked her psyche across thousands of miles into the lab of the government facility and back into her bucking and heaving physical form.

Half conscious, Mary writhed and clashed with the dissonance in her biological circuits, her back arching away from the chair and her arms flailing in unpredictable spasms. Mr Muscle saw Mary in distress. Spurred into action, he bounded into lab and cradled Mary's thrashing skull with his enormous hands, allowing free movement of the rest of her body. A quick tap to his earpiece, and Muscles was able to inform security of the situation. Within moments, Parth was at his wife's side and shortly after, a team of medical professionals.

***

By the time Mary's fitting had ceased and synergy restored between heart and mind, she awoke to find herself surrounded by medical equipment and monitors of every distinction. Her temples itched from the electrode adhesive pads connecting her neural activity to a series of cables supplying the computer terminal. Parth was holding her hand and balancing his forehead on the arm of her chair. Whether he was resting or praying, she could not tell.

"Parth? What happened?" Mary peeled the sticky pads from her forehead, one by one. Parth sat upright on a tall lab stool, beaming with relief.

"Darling, how are you feeling? Are you in any pain?" He jumped to his feet, leaning over her and brushing loose strands of hair behind her ears. Mary swiped her tongue around her dry mouth and held the back of her throbbing head. He kissed her awkwardly on her forehead. She froze, unable to avoid him. "As far as I can tell, you had some sort of seizure."

"How long have I been out?" She shuffled forward on the chair, dangling her feet over the side, trying to reach the floor. Her scalp prickled with radiating pain. It disorientated her.

"For quite some time. It's a quarter past six." He clutched her arm, steadying her movements. Mary held a protracted blink and sighed.

"I'm not much help at all, am I?"

He didn't answer her. He moved to a side bench and switched a newly arrived kettle on to boil. Mary stayed perched on the footrest of the seat. "Have they found Visser yet?"

"No. Looks like their trucks avoided main routes from Fairbanks airport where the traffic cams were. Flynn said he's running out of options." Parth handed Mary a plastic strip containing paracetamol and codeine tablets. She accepted them with a grateful smile. Parth made two cups of tea and sat with her while she took the pain killers.

"What set off the convulsions, honey? What were you doing?" He sipped at his tea, trying to appear nonchalant, but the knotted brow conveyed his anxiety.

"I was trying to find them. I managed to link briefly with Visser's mind but then there was this God-awful deafening noise and everything shook inside me. The pain was excruciating, then it all went dark." Mary let the steam from her cup ease the tension above her nose.

"Do you think it was the affects from their screening technology? They could have rigged up portable solenoids in the trucks." Parth dipped a ginger biscuit into his tea and took a huge soggy bite.

"I don't think so. Their tech didn't cause me pain or seizures, just stopped me from detecting the Hive chatter." She traced her fingertips across her tender scalp.

Parth turned to face the computer and tapped in some commands. Sequenced images of Mary's brain activity appeared on the monitor. Her pineal gland in the heart of her limbic system was glowing, showing intense and continuous action. "I'm a bit concerned that your brain morphology is changing. You have never had seizures before, have you, love?"

"Well, just that one time. When I was fifteen."

Parth spun back around. His jaw hung open. "When was this? You didn't tell me." Mary stood up and stretched her legs, turning to face her husband.

"When Grampy and Dad took me to Iceland to see the Northern Lights. It's funny you know, because Dan told me earlier that he was in Iceland at the same time. Isn't that a remarkable coincidence?" Parth didn't answer her. He opened a new browser window on the computer and searched for meteorological sites that could confirm or refute his suspicions. Knowing full well that Parth would be impervious to any attempt at discussion during these bouts of extreme concentration, she left the lab and made use of the Ladies' Room.

On her return, Mary passed the uptight suit-lady. She bustled by gripping a stack of freshly photocopied documents. They smelled of hot, bitter toner. Suit-lady rounded the foot of a flight of stairs and scurried up the steps, her kitten heels clicking against the metal treads.

Mary loitered near to the Tactical Room. Even in the gloom, she could see the minister and Yelena arguing through the small window in the door. It was like watching an old silent movie in black and white, but without the subtitles. Behind them, the wall monitors displayed a giant digital clock. The countdown ticked away with thirty-one minutes remaining. She felt sick.

"Good to see you back on your feet, madam." It was Mr Muscle. "Is there anything you need?" He had suddenly found his manners and was using them to persuade Mary to return to the lab. A few hours ago, he would have simply ordered her to return. She thanked him for his kindness and made her way back to Parth.

"Mary, come and take a look at this." Parth beckoned her over to his side. "This website lists all the major solar storms that the earth has experienced going back thirty years. They often follow X-class flares or coronal mass ejections at the sun's surface, then the storm arrives a day or two later, depending on the strength of the flare. I am willing to bet that the date Grampy took you to Iceland is somewhere on the list. Furthermore, look at this weather watch update…it appears that we are currently under the influence of another geomagnetic storm right now." He looked up at her. It took a while for the information to seep through the grogginess.

She leaned closer and whispered. "You think that I am sensitive to geomagnetism? That's what caused my seizure and why I couldn't link easily with Visser?"

Parth reached out for her hand. She withdrew and made a point of sinking both fists into her trouser pockets. A pained expression overtook her husband with a realisation that he could not smooth over this level of hurt and betrayal with clumsy skin deep affection. "It would make sense. Not a particularly scientific hypothesis, but proving that theory would be dangerous to your health."

Mary thought about the conversation she and Dan had earlier that night at the pond. How she had begged him to keep the secret of the Icelandic storm from Parth. She felt stupid thinking that he would not piece together the clues. And now he had blurted out his suspicions in a lab that was almost certainly rigged with covert cameras and microphones. It would be all the information they needed to initiate a fresh set of studies into sensitive individuals.

The aircon pumped out a cooling stream across the side of her neck. She closed her eyes and recalled fragments of their wedding day. How his sisters had railed against a mixed religion marriage, their outright refusal to be her bridesmaids. How his mother had scoffed at the registry office ceremony and his father had argued with Grampy over finances. She scolded herself for not seeing the warning signs sooner. "How has it all come to this? This is not the life I dreamed we would have together when you proposed to me on your parent's veranda in Colaba."

Parth turned to face her. The rigid lines framing her mouth were scars of his duplicity. A glaze of saline balanced on the brims of her eyelids. "Will you give me a chance to fix us? I can make it all up to you, I swear." He implored, his shoulders slumping towards his lap.

Parth had always looked after her, provided comfort and protection whenever vulnerabilities had her beaten. He had been the voice of reason throughout many trials and tribulations. He had been her best friend and confidant. It made the stinging barb of deception all the more grievous. Lowering her voice once more, Mary pulled in close to her husband's ear. "I'm scared, Parth. I don't want to be trapped here being poked and prodded by government people. This is no way to live."

He stood up and embraced Mary for the benefit of any active cameras watching them, dipping his head to bury his nose in the side of her hair. "It wouldn't be so bad, would it? There are a few houses on this base, and unlimited funding for you to buy whatever you liked. I could set up a whole new lab with incredible equipment and we could start again together, from scratch. You could be the deciding factor on the War against Terror. Just think of that. You could save the world as we know it."

Mary pulled away, horrified. She knew Parth had always been ambitious, but to sell her freedom for his career was beyond comprehension. Hot blood rushed to the surface of her skin. Her hands tingled with static. She moved to the farthest wall and tightened her fists against the rage building inside. He followed her, backing her into the corner. "I mean, this could be a good thing. We can get clearance for Grampy to come and visit, send for that fur ball of a cat you love so much – I mean really, it wouldn't be so very different from being at home."

"Except you would be free to come and go as you please. To continue your research in your department back at the university. To see your colleagues and friends while I am locked up like a lab rat with magnets strapped to my noggin. Are you quite mad?" The tingling intensified in her arms and chest. She pressed her hands against the wall, trying to control the energy welling up inside.

"It wouldn't be like that. You would be an incredibly important person here. You would be at the heart of all their crucial operations and manoeuvres, but from a safe distance. It's a brand new career for you. I thought you'd be pleased. You always said that being a lab tech didn't stretch you enough." He reached out to touch her face. She blocked him with an unyielding arm.

"Did you know that Professor Haas offered me a research placement? A PhD in Biomedical." She examined his features. How could he be so calm at a time like this?

"Yes, he did mention it. A daft idea, if you ask me. What use is a doctorate to you? Whereas this is a chance for you to be involved in something extraordinary. It could change the course of history. Maybe I could find methods of increasing your efficiency, too. This could be great for us both."

Mary side stepped Parth and walked away, fearful that the power gathering in her limbs would seek to earth itself through her husband's body. His opinions tore at her heart, ripping the substance that had bound her love for him. The ballast of her steadfast and loyal feelings slipped away, casting him adrift.

Chapter Twenty-Six

Mr Muscle summoned them to the Tactical Room. The countdown clock now overlaid a real-time traffic camera image of Route 68, which ran between Camp Williams and the NSA Data Centre, south of Bluffdale in Utah. Flynn clicked an icon on his computer and the main wall screen sectioned into smaller monitors, showing different video feeds from the mid-west state.

Some were of urban areas, others showing military personnel at the fort. Mary sat next to Dan in the viewing area, distancing herself and her feelings from Parth. Dan laid his hand on her arm. “You had us all worried sick. Are you okay?”

She forced a smile and nodded. “Have you been plotting?” Mary whispered.

Dan reached into his inside jacket pocket and edged the corner of a folded document into view. “Uhuh.”

“No luck, sir.” Yelena pulled the communications headset away from her mouth. “The HAARP facility cannot isolate power to their equipment without taking all other systems offline. I cannot see that it would help matters anyway, since Visser could simply compel someone to power them back up. He has done it before at Fairbanks Airport." Yelena removed the headset altogether and walked towards the rear of the room.

"Mary." The Secretary of State for Defence turned from Flynn's computer to address her. "I hear that you attempted to connect with Lars Visser. I'm sorry to hear that it made you unwell. Never the less, we are still in rather a fix, vis-à-vis locating the um, Hive. Can you shed any light on their plans? Where they might be headed? Is there any possibility that you could try again?" The minister's straggly eyebrows lowered over his hooded eyelids.

Mary could feel him transferring his responsibility, and any subsequent failure, to her. She looked around the room. Every person in Tactical fixed their attention in her direction. Acid reflux returned. Mary looked at the clock. There were nineteen minutes left till Alexi's deadline.

"Even if I could get to Visser's brain and somehow…disable him, it wouldn't make any difference. By now, he would have given his orders to the Hive. They would carry them out whether Visser was connected to them or not." At least it rendered the internal conflict over remote assassination moot. They all contemplated her point, watching the seconds tick by on the countdown.

Yelena broke the silence. "If you could just tell us what you saw, during your connection, we might be able to piece the bits together." The sparkle in her eyes had dimmed and her neck had receded into the knotted muscles of her shoulders. For once, Yelena looked older than her years.

"We have drones on standby at Eielson Airforce Base, south of Moose Creek, in Alaska. We just need to provide the coordinates for the strike." Flynn chipped in. As he turned in his chair, his elbow clanged multiple empty coffee cups together on his desk. He checked each one for remaining dregs to supplement his waning buzz.

"Drones? You plan to bomb all the operatives in the Hive? They are living breathing people who are just following orders. You cannot just slaughter them." The residual headache stinging in her grey matter did little to temper Mary's animosity.

"They are complicit in killing perhaps thousands of innocents with the likelihood of killing many thousands more." The minister tucked the back of his wrists into his waist and jutted his drooping chin forward. Mary saw him transform into an elderly vulture, preparing to pick the bones of victory and collect any scraps of ministerial praise for his small but deadly input. "They cannot be allowed to go on unchecked."

"And by unchecked you mean to eradicate them from the face of the planet. Those men have wives and families. They did not volunteer to be drugged into oblivion." Her voice rose an octave.

There was nothing she could say that would convince him. This man had made up his mind long before meeting her, that none of the Hive should survive. A public trial would reveal the extent to which governments in the west monitor civilians across the globe. How they circumvent laws via covert operations between collaborating nations. There is no such thing as private and confidential in the enormous information pouring of our electronic soup. This would be vindication at last, for the whistle blowers of the last decade.

A vision of a tabloid newspaper flashed in her thoughts. The headline read, *Soviet Soldiers Can Control Minds*. She wondered how the media would receive that little bombshell. A midsummer April Fools prank? More likely the beginning of an evidence trail that could uncover the covert experimentation on gifted human beings, funded by feuding and opposing governments the world over. She was willing to bet that Parliament would be eager to quash that particular line of enquiry with something more lethal than a D-Notice.

"Never the less," the vulture continued, "they are still soldiers. They must not be allowed to destroy our secure data feeds and disable the Stoneghost network." He flapped an arm about him, gesturing towards the electronic equipment around the room.

"Well, good luck finding them." Mary stood up and flounced towards the exit.

"Young lady…if you fail to help us, we will have you indefinitely detained for collaborating with terrorists." He glowered through the whiskers of his brows at her. Mary halted, same jeopardy, different threat. What made the Secretary of State for Defence any less of a bully than Visser or Alexi? Either side was driven and determined to achieve their devious goals regardless of the causalities incurred or the violation of Human Rights. There were no depths this man would not sink to in order to keep this situation contained.

"I will help you," Mary stumbled over the due deference of calling the minister, *sir*. That implied he deserved the authority with which he held and wielded with careless force. "But, you must stand the drones down. When they switch the solenoid shields off, I should be able to talk directly to the Captain of the Hive. He is a reasonable man. I think I can talk him round." Her little frame sagged in defeat. They had co-opted her husband, leveraged her brother with the seclusion of his girlfriend and threatened to take her liberty. What more could they inflict? "Once I have their location, you can arrest them."

"What about the geomagnetic storm? We have no idea what damage that seizure had on your mental faculties. Is it wise to risk such a valuable ability at this time?" Parth said.

All Mary heard was that Parth's prized lab rat, new studies and unlimited funding were slipping away before his eyes. Mary shot him a withering stare. "Dan will help me." They all faced the lofty man, folded in the viewing area seats.

"I'll certainly try. If you think it'll make a difference." He looked surprised at Mary's suggestion, but warmed to the idea of assisting his little sister. "We can form our own mini Hive together."

"Precisely. We can combine our energies in the same way that the Hive does. That way, any information that I can glean from Captain Thirty-Four, Dan can relay immediately to you." Mary sensed that he was masking his anxiety behind a placid façade. His Adam's Apple bobbed repeatedly in his throat.

"That's all well and good…" Flynn interrupted, "but you might be too late. Look…"

The monitors of the Tactical wall flicked through different views. Main streets in Bluffdale, then feeds from the highway and night lit shopping precincts. Other screens showed Camp William's trucks and exterior views of buildings. All of them had one thing in common. The cameras were all shaking in unison. Visser had begun his attack.

“But there is still ten minutes till midnight in Utah.” Mary wailed. “I don’t understand.”

“I guess he decided that Stoneghost should be out of action well before the scheduled backup.” Flynn announced, applying his callous logic.

They watched in horror as a crack in the thoroughfare tore along a main street in the centre of Bluffdale, sending vehicles spinning in an attempt to avoid the rift. Glass from office blocks splintered and smashed to the ground, showering a funnel of patrons fleeing from night clubs and late bars. Overhead cables whipped like skipping ropes between toppling posts. Stationary Airforce vehicles bumped and jostled against concrete walls as the orderly evacuation of personnel filled the car parks and assembly points. People swayed with the camber of the rocking ground, like a pitching ferry amid a turbulent storm. The mounted cameras shook on their brackets, making it all the more difficult to witness the pandemonium developing across the Tactical Room wall.

As quickly as it began, the tremors lessened, then ceased altogether. The shaky pictures on the screens steadied. Under the Bluffdale City centre street lights, they could see that buildings had remained almost intact. Only the floodlit Wasatch inhabitants continued to move, running in circles and tending their wounds.

“Is that it?” The minister threw his arms in the air. “All that bother and a fairly minor quake is all we can expect? Get Fort Williams on the line. I want to speak with their top man.”

Flynn acknowledged the order and began placing the call. Yelena and Mary exchanged pensive looks. “That was their test run. They did the same thing in Japan. The next quake will be devastating, and soon.” Mary signalled Dan to follow her towards the door. Flynn switched the wall monitors back to full screen as the beige general flickered and pixelated before them. Mary hesitated, waiting for the man to speak and wondering whether the delay would be worthwhile.

“Well, I take ma hat off to you, ma’am. You warned me of a quake and we did experience something of that nature. It was proceeded by some very odd noises, but as you can see we’re all as right as apple pie down here in Utah.” There was a determined smugness about his smile that prompted Yelena to cringe. She had little affection for the United States and even less for their rank and file.

“General, did these noises sound like a squealing trumpet?” Mary piped up.

“Why yes, they did, ma’am. It was soon drowned out by the rumbling of the quake though.” He ran his sweaty hand through his greasy hair and replaced his cap.

“We have reason to believe that there will be a much larger aftershock. You should prepare your troops, general.” Yelena folded her arms across her chest, shifting her weight onto one hip.

Mary did not linger in Tactical. She beckoned Dan to follow her down the corridor and into the lab. Parth, bewildered by rapid events, trotted after them. Jumping into the leather chairs, Mary reclined to an almost horizontal position while Dan remained upright. “Stay with me Dan. We are in for a bumpy ride.”

"Always." The sincerity was touching. Mary smiled to herself, closed her eyes and sang.

The journey was brisk with the additional buoyancy of Dan's energy to supplement her own. It was when her consciousness reached northern latitudes that the strain was most noticeable. The continuous barrage of polarised particles in tightly packed geomagnetic fields pulsed through her psyche in waves of discordant pain. "*Stay calm, little sister. Instead of trying to block the fields, let them wash right through you*." She thought for moment, recalling the MRI scan Parth had subjected her to. The first of the scans aligned charged particles throughout her body in a head to toe direction. That procedure was bearable. It had been during the second scan, when the magnetism sliced across her brain that the intense pain caused her to react violently. She surmised that the solar storm would achieve its greatest intensity along the natural field lines, close to the magnetic pole.

Mary adjusted her route, lining up with the direction of particle flow. Almost immediately, the pain diminished, allowing her to soar towards Fairbanks. "*Okay, Dan. I'm not sure if this is going to work. I don't know if I can tune into the Hive, but if I can, your mind might combine too. That will make communication between us, without the others hearing, tricky*."

"You'll find a way. I have faith in you. Good luck."

Right then. How did I manage this before? Think about Captain Thirty-Four and his men, and the few women too. "Hello? Captain? Can you hear me?" She waited, listening intently for an answer. Her thoughts wandered to the feelings she last experienced when joined to the Hive. How their camaraderie and loyalty had effused her presence with courage. The differences in personalities put aside while they focused every ounce of strength on achieving their mission. There was no reply. *"Captain Thirty-Four, can you hear me?" Still, she heard no response.*

"Mary, what if they have been ordered to ignore you?" Dan's reassuring voice echoed inside her head. He felt closer than breathing. She considered his statement. It would make sense to disavow her authority within the Hive after she had escaped their clutches. She changed tack.

"Captain, if you can hear me, it's Mary. Colonel Visser has lied to you. Your mission is not to infiltrate a US research facility. It is to kill thousands of innocent people." She waited again. The magnetic pulsations throbbed through her subconscious like nuclear radiation in a reactor. It made her feel giddy. *"Captain..."*

"I can hear you, Mary." Captain Thirty-Four interrupted. *"We have been instructed to terminate all communication with you."*

"Please, Captain. Just hear me out." Mary listened for any signs of dissent. She could feel her energy amalgamating with the Hive energies. The boost in power was immense. "*Colonel Visser is using the Extra Low Frequency waves generated at the research facility to target plate tectonic boundaries in subterranean regions of the United States. You are triggering catastrophic earthquakes in populated areas."* She knew that the entire Hive had heard her. There were undercurrents of Russian dialects muttering in the background, louder voices telling their subordinates to be quiet.

"Wait, please." The captain said, before quizzing another numbered officer in their own distinctive language. Mary heard, but did not understand the reply to his query. He switched back into English for her sake. *"Hive member trained in geology, not sure what you say is possible. The colonel is an honourable man. He would not risk civilian lives. He said the mission is critical."*

"Ask your man who worked at the Russian Ionospheric facility at Sura. He will tell you that it is fact." She had him on a hook and was keen to maintain dialogue. A reasonable man he might be, but what would it take for him to abandon his mission and defy orders?

"Not possible, Mary. He timed out. He has gone home to his family." The Russian mumblings grew louder inside her head. The Captain had reopened a wound, a canker festering within the ranks. He shouted an order for them to be silent and the moaning and muttering abated.

"Captain. I am sorry to have to tell you this, but he did not time out. None of your former operatives have gone home to their families. They are dead." The hush was ominous and oppressive. Each entity within the Hive assimilated her news and applied it to their long-held suspicions about Visser. Belief in a person's virtue was not something that could be ordered. One of the Hive members with a deep voice, spoke to the Captain. There was a long moment of quiet before he reengaged his discussion with Mary.

"Whether what you say is true or not, Mary, we have had our orders. We must reintegrate with worker at HAARP. Colonel Visser gave us new coordinates just a short time ago." The Soviet cacophony roared again. High and low voices, harsh intonations and furious

cadences filled her head until it felt as though it might explode.

"I think your troop agree with me, Captain. They obviously have some grievances of their own." The noise died down once again.

"One of our older operatives, Twenty-Two, is a big man. I mean physically, a large man." The Captain paused, wondering how best to relay the story. *"A short while ago, Twenty-Two lost contact with us. He woke up. He told us that he could feel a tube sticking into the back of his head. Then a bright light flooded his eyes, almost blinding him. He said he was at the bottom of a stack of bunks, like in um... boat or submarine."*

Mary's mind flickered back to the vision she had seen of racks of patients inside shipping containers during Visser's evacuation from the disused hospital. The soldiers viewed the image in her mind and were getting restless again. The deep voice of Twenty-Two barked at them to pipe down. Then he addressed his captain. The Hive listened to his response and the captain translated. *"Yes, Mary. He says that is exactly what he saw. Shipping containers with us strapped inside."*

The desire for the captain to continue was all it took to prompt him. Her thoughts and his were one. *"He saw men wearing surgical clothes in the doorway. They were pulling body bag across floor. One of the men pressed button on small electronic box. It pumped liquids through tubes all around racks. Twenty-Two sleep again. Came back to us."* The Hive voices remained silent, a solemn moment of mourning for their fallen brethren.

"Captain. The volume of drugs that Visser has been pumping into each of you is seriously damaging your bodies. If you will help me to locate you, I can

arrange for medical help. I can have teams of medics transport you to a hospital to have the drugs flushed from your systems. You could be reunited with your loved ones. Your wives and children, parents, boyfriends...they could all visit you while you recover." The intonation of the voices sounded more hopeful to Mary. She heard tiny relieved chuckles interspersed between their fast words at the prospect of ending the tour of duty. Only Captain Thirty-Four remained stern.

"You seem to forget that there are often fatalities within military missions. We will honour our fellow soldier and mourn his loss, but our orders remain. If we defy them, we will all be court marshalled."

Chapter Twenty-Seven

It seemed futile. Captain Thirty-Four could see the logic in her argument but was not prepared to defy orders. More importantly, he appeared to be gearing up to infiltrate the US research facility again with revised coordinates that would more accurately target Camp Williams and the NSA Data Centre in Utah. Civilians residing near the Wasatch Fault would be merely collateral damage. She had used up all her bargaining chips and short of pleading with them, Mary had exhausted her options.

"Mary." It was Dan's voice, rich and soft in the back of her thoughts. *"The Hive are on US soil. Offer them asylum and citizenship with a promise to extract their relatives shortly after. I will negotiate the offer from this end."* She felt Dan's presence leave her. His stabilising influence was noticeable by its absence, despite the support from the Hive. Alone in her mission now, anxiety heightened her awareness. There was dissension in the ranks and a mixture of emotions that manifested as antipathy towards her.

"I'm sure you heard that, Captain, as I am sure your soldiers did too. He makes a fair point, doesn't he? You could have a new life in the United States of

America, with your family and healthcare provided until you and your men are fit and well again. What do you say?"

"You trust this man?" The captain said. She could feel his hesitation. The offer was more than he expected. The captain's thoughts strayed to betrayal and trials for war crimes, of becoming the scapegoat in what amounted to military terrorism.

"With my life." Mary replied. *"He is my brother."* She waited patiently while Russian dialogue continued all around her, voices of hope and reason outnumbering those of distrust and doubt.

"We will help you to locate us, Mary, but you must honour your word." A swell of relief engulfed the combined minds of the Hive. The sense of gratitude overpowered Mary. She felt it as a rush, like a heroin addict relieved of withdrawal. Her relief was abundant too. She had prevented further attacks on Utah, and potentially, in other countries also.

"When Twenty-Two awoke, and saw through the container door, was there anything recognisable in the background?" Again, she waited for them to confer.

"He said there were aeroplanes. Large passenger aeroplanes moving along the ground."

"He must have woken up just after the transporter plane landed at Fairbanks. They could have driven you to any number of places after that." Her level of unease was building in conjunction with the soldiers.

"No, he said that he saw a big door lowering behind the aeroplanes. The containers were inside a building."

A building large enough to house many shipping containers with shutters that open onto taxiing aircraft.

They never left Fairbanks Airport. They are in a hangar. *"I have an idea where you are, Captain, but to confirm your precise location I need to leave you and take a look outside."*

"Very well, Mary. We are counting on you."

Mary detached her presence from the security of the Hive mind and rose steadily through the darkness and into a large structure of corrugated steel. There were the shipping containers, lined up in a row with attached generators belching out diesel smoke into the air. Alone, the geomagnetic waves coursed through her cluster of energy, making her alpha waves shift and fluctuate.

Her fear of losing connection with her body and inducing another seizure crystallised her thoughts. *I can do this. Just concentrate. Why didn't I ask the Captain to come with me? That was stupid. I can do this.* Setting her attention to full power, Mary drove herself through the roof of the hangar, in search of a landmark or shape that would pinpoint their exact location.

Above the roof of the building, her thoughts clouded. The normal rhythmic waves of her synaptic transmissions quivered and her vision faded. She was losing control. In the chill of the early Alaskan night, Mary struggled against the oscillations that tore at her mind. She twisted mid-air, looking down for a moment at the building she had just passed through, before losing all focus and succumbing to the spasms racking her entire being.

***

"I've got you little sister." Dan held Mary in his arms, rocking her gently from his awkward position on the stool at her side. He had entered her mind soon after the seizure took hold, calming and restoring a peaceful rhythm to her brainwaves and alleviating her pain. She regained consciousness, in harmony once again with her physical form and peered up at her brother.

"I know where they are. Did you tell Yelena about the deal we offered them? Is it all arranged?" Mary sat upright and slid from the chair. She was still a little woozy, her gait was that of a binge drinker. Parth rushed to offer assistance. She pushed him away and made for the Tactical Room, both men following her down the corridor like bodyguards.

"Yelena said she would contact the NSA as soon as I told her about the deal." Dan said, overtaking Mary with his huge strides and holding open the Tactical Room door. And sure enough, Yelena was standing next to Flynn's desk, clutching the microphone section of the communication headset close to her mouth, in quiet conversation. Yelena glanced furtively about the room and shuffled a number of cellular phones sitting on Flynn's desk. The minister was pacing. He slung his suit jacket over a chair and loosened his tie. Mary took her seat next to Dan and Parth in the viewing area. As she sat down, she caught sight of exchanged glances between Flynn and the minister. Flynn gave the politician an almost imperceptible nod.

"Do you have their location, young lady?" The Secretary of State for Defence towered over Mary, the folds of his skin hung forward puckering his grotesque mouth.

"Do you have an assurance of asylum for those in the Hive?" She refused to allow him to intimidate her. She wondered how he wrangled his way up to the Privy Council. How many privatisation back-handers and expensive arms trade meals he had attended with the Saudis. Beneath his brash exterior, she sensed his fear. A deep-seated inadequacy rooted at the foundations of his personality.

A long-held dichotomy of clawing personal ambition marred by character flaws so heinous, the merest suggestion of them sickened Mary. She was distracted from her exploration of his inner workings when Yelena removed the headset and confirmed the United States cooperation in assisting the Hive and their families to defect.

“Well? Give us their exact location.” The minister demanded, thrusting his arm towards the satellite view of Fairbanks on the giant screen.

“They will need immediate medical attention when you send your people in. Can you arrange that, Yelena?” Mary stalled for time. Something about the minister’s attitude did not feel quite right. His impatience seemed out of place considering she had diffused the threat of further earthquakes. The precious Stoneghost servers and Data Centre were safe, at least for now. It worried her that he appeared neither relieved nor pleased. Instead, the minister resumed his pacing.

“I can arrange for medical crews.” Yelena said, the headset dangling from her hand. The minister stopped moving, Flynn swivelled around. The room hovered in suspended animation while Mary scrutinised Yelena’s impassive face for evidence of trickery. There was none. Yelena was sincere.

Mary took a deep breath, hiding crossed fingers beneath folded arms. “They are still at Fairbanks airport, in a T-shaped hangar near the cargo bays.” As soon as the words left her lips she felt the nausea rise in her throat.

"Flynn…" The minister commanded. "Do it."

"Sir." Flynn tapped a few instructions into his terminal and produced a joystick from behind a monitor. The scene on the screen changed to a jittery aerial shot that altered with every move Flynn made. The long landing strips of the airport came into view as Mary and Dan caught up with events. The T-shaped hangar was just ahead of the drone's line of sight.

"No, you can't; they trusted me." Mary wailed, but it was too late. Flynn had activated two missiles that scudded off at speed to intersect with the hangar. The explosion was colossal and definitive. Drone cameras recorded the expanding mass of flames and debris on its circle around the airfield. The fire glowed white hot and roared hundreds of feet into the air. Metal walls of the hangar buckled and splintered, then liquefied in an inferno to rival the portals of hell. Fairbanks Airport now had two smouldering sites of carnage at either end of their runways. No doubt the official press release would site computer failure for both events.

Would Captain Thirty-Four and his troop been aware of their deaths? Mary thought it unlikely given the medication streaming through their bodies. It would have been an instantaneous shutdown of all their communications as their physical presence expired in the explosion. No awareness of suffering or pain. The tender cord between mind and body severed, but what of the soul? What if by cutting the tether to their bodies, their immortal consciousness drifted into the ionosphere? Their experiences, personalities and feelings held forever by the magnetic forces high in our atmosphere as a global existential hard drive. Could she still forge a gateway to their psyches?

Yelena bowed her head and genuflected, muttering a prayer for the fallen. Flynn relinquished control of the drone to Eielson Air Force Base command and switched the screen back to satellite feeds. Tactical fell silent. The minister stopped pacing and sat down a few feet from Mary. Tears poured down her face. Her reddening eyes fixated on the image in front of her. No words could express the depth of emotion coursing through her mind and body. What lies would they tell to the loved ones of those perished? Killed in the line of duty, perhaps, but duty to whom?

The words of the Dalai Lama floated back into her mind, his analogy between our consciousness and the duplicity of thoughts to those who purport to be working for our best interests in parliament. It was almost portentous.

Mary uncrossed her fingers. They had been no protection against the minister's treachery. It was too late to trust her instincts. She knew that there was some hidden plot between Flynn and the politician, but had ignored it. Her gut was telling her not to trust them, but her mind assured her that all was well. Even with the best intentions, her honest monarch-like intentions, the Hive were at the mercy of a literal and deceitful cabinet minister. Worse still, her fate and that of her newly found brother, lay in his hands.

Exhaustion enveloped her. Mary felt herself droop in her seat. She could not handle anymore turmoil. Her scalp prickled and pain radiated through her neural pathways. And yet, there was still one more battle left to fight.

***

Dan touched Mary's knee and flicked his head to one side. "Come on." They slunk from the Tactical Room and returned to the temporary laboratory. He steered her to the refreshments table and pointed out the tiny surveillance camera nestled in the electrical socket casing behind the canister of teabags. "Wanna hear something funny?"

Mary nodded.

"Flynn's missing little finger… the big mystery?"

"Yeah?"

"Suit-lady told me he lost it during basic training. Shot it off himself, dropping a loaded gun on the firing range." They both snorted, in full knowledge that the surveillance recordings would ensure his secret would provide comic relief to all his colleagues. They continued their discussion internally. His voice rang clear inside her head. *"There are more cameras and microphones stashed all around this room. We need to act fast if we are to engineer our release from this facility. Are you well enough for another cerebral jaunt?"* Mary nodded. She would endure whatever mental exertions it took to secure their freedom.

"I think you should have a lie down, Mary. You look terrible." Dan helped her into the recliner. "I'll be in Tactical if you need anything." He disappeared from her side as she arranged her limbs in the chair and sang the tune to herself.

Despite the headache, she was able to disassociate her consciousness from her body almost immediately. Haste being the watchword, Mary left her resting body behind and rushed into Tactical. Suspended above Flynn's computer, she could see an icon depicting an antiquated telephone receiver, flashing green. Displayed beneath the image, were the words 'internal call – clinic'.

Flynn attracted Yelena's attention, pointing to the pictogram on his monitor.

"I'll take it. Put it through." Yelena listened to the information. Mary tried to hover close to the earpiece but was unable to hear the conversation. The redhead grunted her approval then gave her commands in a hushed reply. "Good. Get her to sign then sedate her. We cannot have a journalist loose in the compound." She signalled for Flynn to end the call.

A ridiculous electronic jingle emanated from the minister's jacket. He retrieved his mobile phone and hurried from the room to take the call. Mary glided through the wall after him. "No Prime Minister, everything is in hand. The threat has been neutralised and the assets acquired. No, no, I am certain that they will not present a problem. I've sequestered the bunker and R and D have been working on a prototype. I will liaise with you over the first of the covert missions, of course. Yes… I will keep you informed." There was an audible click. He moved the handset away from his ear and looked at the screen. She had hung up on him. The minister filled his lungs and exhaled slowly.

So, this was to be her new life, locked in an underground shelter at the heart of a government installation, surrounded by machine guns and razor wire. Escorted from her prison to Tactical with the prime directive of murdering people who did not fulfil the requirements of the current MoD official. Had Yelena planned this all along? Was her husband always steering her towards this eventuality?

Mary tailed the politician back into Tactical, where Parth was writing frantic lists of requirements for his next phase of studies and Flynn was adjusting the fitments on the prototype mental castration device. Dan sat in the front row of seats in the viewing area. Upon seeing the minister return, he stood up and removed a bundle of folded papers from his coat pocket. *"Mary, if you can hear me, you need to take over the minister now, then follow my lead..."*

The Secretary of State for Defence surveyed the room. Mary aligned herself with his pale and soulless eyes, merging and harmonising her brainwaves to his. She could sense the totality of his obdurate ambition, stoked by the desire to disprove his ineptitude. A blockade he had erected to shield his heart from any empathy he might feel towards Mary and her kin. The phone call with the Prime Minister had raised his heartrate and blood pressure. Sweat bled through his shirt in ugly stains and his skin flushed. Despite her abhorrence, Mary took the reins of his nervous system and tested his voice out with a throat clearing cough.

"Mister Secretary." Dan said, unfolding the papers and smoothing them out on Flynn's desk. "I have been discussing our situation with the legal team upstairs and I think you will agree that together we have found a solution to your problem."

Yelena frowned and moved closer. Flynn put the device down and picked up the documents, scanning their contents with interest. Mary made the minister cough once more. She had only spoken through another person once before. What if she got the intonation wrong? She played safe with a single word reply to test out the waters.

"Oh?" No adverse reaction – so far so good.

"The legal team have drawn up a set of promises for both sides to adhere to – a mandate of sorts." Dan had the floor and seemed determined to keep it. "Mary and I will cooperate with specific requests from the British Government and will assist in problematic missions that technology cannot resolve, providing they do not compromise or endanger ourselves or any of our family members." Dan squinted at the minister. Was Mary in control?

Flynn interrupted his assessment. "It says here that in return for your cooperation, you expect transportation to your homes unencumbered by mental inhibition devices or chemicals of any kind." They all looked at the minister. Mary panicked. She needed him to comply with the statements in as few words as possible, without raising suspicion. A tall order for such a verbose man. She stammered, his words came out as mere noises.

"Bub..ta..well, that seems perfectly reasonable to me." Then remembering the minister's former harsh stance on the issue, she added; "but Yelena is to maintain direct contact – be your handlers as it were, and we must have an assurance that your abilities will not be used to tamper with those in authority or there will be severe consequences." The speech felt disjointed. The pitch sounded wrong. Mary compensated. "We are thankful for the assistance you have given us. Yelena, I suggest that you arrange transportation home for these good people and for that very attractive reporter…what was her name? Connie, wasn't it?"

Flynn nodded, but his lowered brows conveyed his misgivings.

"Don't over play your hand, Mary." Dan sent his reproach telepathically to her wavelength. "If that is all in order, would you sign at the bottom, sir?" Dan flipped to the last page. Mary directed the minister's hand to pick up Flynn's pen and sign the directive. She had no idea what his signature would look like, but a squiggle with a flourish at the end seemed to suffice.

"What about my new research projects… the funding you promised me?" Parth held his list of requirements high and squared up to the minister. His vitriol came as no surprise to Mary. His priorities written large and in numerical order on the paper in his hand. Her freedom did not warrant a mention.

"You have a fully functional, government funded laboratory in your department at work. There is no need for you to duplicate that here. Be grateful for what you have, Doctor Arora." Mary shocked herself at the vehemence of her rebuke. It sounded all the more forceful in the minister's authoritative voice. Parth backed down, but his livid expression persisted.

Flynn's desk vibrated with a muffled buzz as one of three cellular phones pinged a notification. Only Mary was close enough to see the message flash briefly on its screen. It read: Thanks for the heads up. A

Chapter Twenty-Eight

The kettle had just boiled when Dan returned to the lab bearing copies of the documents. Mary sloshed the hot water over some coffee granules, added a splash of milk and handed the mug to her brother. He waved the papers under her nose. They were entitled: 'The Aurora Mandate'. Aware that the hidden cameras captured everything they said or did, Mary held her tongue, but the pantomime that had played out in Tactical grew heavy in her mind. They sat opposite one another, determined to keep their conversation locked inside their heads.

"As soon as the minister figures out what we have done, they will lock us up for good. Did you see the look on Flynn's face?" She balanced her cup on the arm of the chair and rubbed her forehead.

"I took care of it. Stop worrying, we are almost home free. Finish your drink and get ready to leave. Flynn is having my car brought round to the entrance." Dan stretched out his arms and twisted his neck till his spine clicked back in place.

"You know you got the spelling of Arora wrong, don't you?" She peeped over the edge of her cup at him, half smiling.

"Did I? What a shame. That makes it legally invalid then, doesn't it? Besides, without the Aurora Borealis, we may never have triggered these gifts, so it is appropriate." He beamed at her. A childlike smile of defiance spreading across his stubble covered cheeks.

"If it is not legally binding, then the caveats won't protect our rights either."

"My dear little sister. With our combined powers, no facility can hold us and you can fry the circuits of any device that they attempt to strap to your head. You said it yourself, we must maintain the illusion of compliance."

The conversation petered out, each of them preoccupied with the time they could finally relax in familiar surroundings. Dan's fluttering stomach and clenched muscles made strangulated noises. Mary was wistful and sad. What reception awaited her now that Parth had to adjust to the new limits of his research? Her former life of subjugation to his career path was over. Could their marriage survive such a paradigm shift? Did she even want it to? At least she had Grampy and now Dan, to lean on. The emotion stung her tear ducts.

"I'm just going to powder my nose." She announced, before placing her empty cup on the table and making her way down the corridor. The minister left the Tactical Room, pulling the door closed behind him. *Oh God, this is where it all comes crashing down. He has come to his senses and he'll have Mr Muscle arrest me. They will throw away the key this time, for sure.* Mary held her breath and walked slower. As she approached, the minister turned this way and that, blinking too fast and scratching at the back of his head. He saw Mary and shuffled towards her. She braced.

"Ah, do you work here, young lady? Could you direct me to the gentleman's lavatory? I seem to have lost my bearings."

A millisecond of shock swept through her. She restored her senses enough to point in the general direction of the toilets. Dan had worked his magic on him. He had burrowed into the Minister's hippocampus and tinkered with his memory. She watched the aged man amble away, the sweat stains beneath his arms spreading out across his back, his arthritic joints creaking and crunching, throwing him out of step. He seemed much smaller now. Her formidable opponent, diminished. The head of the Ministry of Defence for the British Commonwealth let the door of the Gents swing and smack him in the backside.

***

The morning after the storm smelled clean and filled with potential. Flynn provided Dan with a pass card for the secure exit and bade them farewell. Yelena informed them that she would be in touch soon. It sounded more like a threat than a promise. They met Mr Muscle pushing Constance Cadot in a wheelchair at the front entrance to the pyramid building. She wore a padded neck brace that held her chin unnaturally high, but it did not stop her from leaping out of the chair and throwing her arms about Dan. He lifted her off her feet and kissed her. Parth turned away. Mary watched them. They needed no words; their feelings were plain to all. The tension in Dan's body slipped away and relief softened his pinched brow.

Dan's burgundy classic car rounded the corner and stopped in front of them, driven by the agent who had taken them to the FCO restaurant. The perpetual smirk plastered across his face widened upon seeing Mary. He yanked the handbrake up and left it idling in neutral, then hopped out of the driver's side to greet them.

"You're off then?" He stood much too close to Mary, making her take a backward step. "I was led to believe that you'd be sticking around for a while." He shoved his hands deep into his trouser pockets and rocked forwards on his toes.

"Yes, homeward bound. Job done. Thank you for your help." Mary blushed. She fidgeted with the hem of her shirt, suddenly aware of the stale clothing she had borrowed from Connie's villa.

"Such a shame. I was all set to buy you a drink later at the bar. This place needs someone to brighten it up a little." The eye contact made her feel uncomfortable. It locked on like a heat seeking missile. Whichever direction Mary looked, his stare was right there before her.

Parth wedged his shoulder between them. "She doesn't drink and my wife and I won't be coming back here anytime soon." He hissed at the driver, then raised his forearm against the man's chest. "Come along, Mary." Opening the car door, Parth ushered her into the back seat. "Are you cold? Would you like my jacket?" She declined, a hint of a smile forming on her lips. She had no need to explore the depths of his mind to know how guarded he was of his possessions. That was all she was to him, a valuable possession. In that moment, she knew that she could not resume their life together as it was. He could not make any restitution for his disloyalty that would appease her.

With Connie safely strapped into the passenger seat, Dan took control of his classic car and followed the black Range Rover escort to the main exit of the base. Winding down the stiff window mechanism, he leaned out and handed the pass to the guard, who in turn opened the barriers. Two speedbumps and a right turn and they passed into the overgrown lanes of the Buckinghamshire countryside.

They had driven many miles in quietude before anyone dare break the silence. It was as though making a sound would break the spell and send them crashing back into custody and a life of servitude. Constance spoke first, her damaged voice box giving her a husky timbre.

"What happened to that sadistic bastard Lars Visser?" The mirror in the sun visor showed Mary and Parth conducting an unspoken dialogue of shrugs and grimaces. "It is okay. I am not permitted to report on anything that you tell me. They made me sign things."

Dan let go of the gear stick and patted her knee. "He's dead, Connie. He cannot ever harm you again."

"Of this you are sure? You see his body, yes? She reached up and angled the visor mirror to witness Mary's reaction. Mary averted her gaze.

Dan changed gear and hesitated at a crossroads, trying to recall the directions Flynn had provided. "Well it was a bloody big explosion, Con. It'd be a miracle if he did survive. Just know that you are safe now. No one can harm you."

"And what of the other one? The little man in the white coat?" Her tenacious journalistic tendencies would not allow her to let the matter drop.

"Presumed dead also." Dan leaned forward, looked both ways and turned right at the church.

"Presumed. So, you have no idea really then?" Connie twisted her shoulders round, trying to coax the support collar sideways to allow her to look at her boyfriend.

"Can't you let it go? We are all exhausted. Let's have some music." He pushed a faded plastic tape into the ancient audio player and increased the volume. Connie folded her arms across her chest. The stereo crackled into life with the thin sound of a piano as the track started. Paul McCartney's crisp voice rang out through the speakers, after a brief melodious introduction, with the first line of *Let It Be*. Dan started laughing before the second bar.

"Did you do that on purpose?" Mary cackled.

"No, I promise. It was already in the player." A moment shared between siblings. This, the first of many unexplained conspiratorial exchanges. They had thirty years of shared mischief and missed opportunities to recoup. Constance sighed and fixed her sight ahead.

Brighton and Hove, UK

Brighton Beach was crawling with students of every nationality when they arrived. Pip unfolded the blanket and anchored it in place with heavy stones at each corner, and then helped Mary unpack the picnic. Connie balanced on one leg while she removed a sandal, brushing away the grimy dust that had collected on the insole. Dan's cotton hat blew from his head, tumbling across the gradient towards an Asian family hunkered down in the pebbled ridges. One of their children caught hold of it by its rim and handed it back.

Pip helped himself to a vegetable samosa from a sandwich box. "What story are you currently working on, Connie?"

Constance folded herself on to the corner of the blanket, adjusting the silk headscarf protecting her hair from the warm breeze. He offered her an Indian pastry from the container. She shook her head.

"I am working on an exposé within the pharmaceutical industry. It is all very hush, hush, but I believe it will shake the infrastructure and its government ties to the core." She nibbled at a cheese straw, picking up small flakes that had escaped onto her linen trousers.

"I look forward to reading that." Pip stuffed his balled-up socks into his boat shoes and placed them together next to his crumpled sweater on the shingle. "Anyone up for a paddle?" He didn't wait for a reply. Rolling up his trouser legs and holding his hat on his head, Pip Lawrence navigated the sharp flints and smooth pebbles down to the shoreline.

Mary followed, catching him up with her flip-flop cushioned steps. She fed her arm through his, hugging his limb close to her body. They kicked and splashed through the shallow waves, pointed out the brave or foolhardy souls who had ventured into the English Channel to swim and shooed away the ever-vigilant gulls.

"Grampy?" Her rosy cheeked countenance dimmed. It was the voice of the little girl he had read bedtime stories to. The child he had picked apples with in his garden past dusk and soothed her wasp stings with a vinegar rinse. The frightened grandchild who saw monsters in every shadow.

"Yes, sweetie-pie?" He waited while she swallowed and cleared her throat. They faced the horizon.

"Did I cause the airbags to fail that day? Was the accident my fault?" Her grip on his arm tightened. He paused for a moment, dipping his head to the side and depositing a kiss on the top of her head.

"I don't know, my love. I don't think we will ever know." He reached his spare arm around and covered her hand with his. She looked up at him. His kind, old face radiated nothing but love. Not a hint or trace of resentment hiding within him. They walked along in quiet contemplation for a time, absorbed in their memories. "Now then, tell me all about this PhD you have landed."

"I start next month." She released his arm long enough to pull a tissue from her jeans pocket and blow her nose. "Professor Haas has arranged for me to work as a demonstrator in undergrad practicals at the same time as my research so that I can continue to earn."

"That was good of him. What area of Biomedical are you considering?" They had wandered along the shore towards the pier for some distance. Pip spun her around and they headed back the way they came.

"Epigenetics and hereditary transfer. Have you heard of it?" They waited for a body boarding youth to cross their path out of the water.

"I have indeed. It's the ability to switch dormant genes on through exposure to drastic changes in environmental or social conditions. The theory posits that those alterations can then be passed on to offspring as a viable trait."

Mary admired her grandfather. She beamed up at his undiminished acuity.

Pip looked quizzical. "What? I still find the time to read the odd medical journal every now and then."

By the time they had returned to the blanket, Dan had polished off a considerable amount of the picnic. Connie had picked at another cheese straw and was on her second Perspex flute of sparkling wine. Pip watched his grandchildren bicker over the last of the chocolate rolls. A contented smile took up residence and reanimated the old man's features. Mary snooped into his mind. A show-reel of scenes, leading to Dan and Mary's worlds colliding, played in his head.

The moment when a distraught student sought his help at the medical centre. Tired, pregnant and alone she confessed that the baby was Pip's grandson. The scene altered to an image of Mary's mother in desolate tears, handing over her first born to Pip's friend and colleague. The proud feeling Mary sensed in her grandfather, on the day of Dan's christening. A deliberate bonding of family ties to maintain a connection to his kin. Mary passed the foil covered chocolate roll to her grandfather. He thanked her and began unwrapping it.

"Grampy, why didn't you tell us about each other? I mean, you could have, after the accident."

"It was never my secret to tell. As his godfather, I could keep an eye on Dan; make sure he had what he needed in life and maintain your parents' confidence. I did think about telling you, but Dan made no attempt to discover his biological parentage and I didn't want to rock the boat." He gobbled up the gooey sponge and lay back in the sloping shingle, tipping his hat over his eyes.

"But you did encourage me to buy the bookshop close to Mary's home though, didn't you?" Dan turned to Mary. "In fact, Pip invested his own money in my business, making it almost impossible for me to back out." Dan grabbed Pip's ankle and shook it to encourage a response.

The old man poked the brim of his hat up and squinted at them. "Well you most certainly would not have met if you had stayed living around here." He propped himself up on an elbow.

Mary pointed at Pip, but addressed her brother. "Wait, don't tell me. Grampy was also the one who sparked your interest in the paranormal and strange unexplained phenomenon."

"Yep and guess who sent me the advert calling for volunteers in Parth's research study?" Dan said, chuckling. Connie sat with a bemused grin.

"It all worked out for the best, didn't it?" Pip pulled his hat back down and snoozed in the afternoon sun.

***

All the doors and windows of Pip's house were wide open in the listless evening heat. Dan made reservations at an exclusive restaurant and was off treating Connie to some five-star romance. Pip poured a glass of brandy and invited Mary to join him on the patio to view the muted stars.

"It's a beautiful night." Pip took a swig of the amber liquid.

"It is. I miss being by the sea." Mary sipped her tea and breathed in the briny Solent air. Steel wind chimes tinkled from the branches of the apple trees and the moon rose creamy and fat.

"I can't begin to imagine the trauma you have been through. I heard you cry out in your sleep last night. Have the nightmares returned?" He grasped a curl from her ponytail and coiled it around his fingers.

"Sometimes, yes. What's done is done. I can't change what happened but I still feel responsible." She kept her gaze skyward, willing her grandfather to change subject. He did.

"How are your migraines? Any more seizures?" He leaned forwards, trying to catch her eye.

"Not too bad, actually. Dan and I let Parth do a couple of tests on us in his department. Whatever else he may be, he is very good at his job. He says that we have enlarged limbic regions in our brains." She noted Pip's look of distress; his years of medical training leaping his conclusions to the worst-case scenario. "It's okay though. He says we have a remarkable level of neural plasticity. Our brains are adapting in structure to accommodate the changes."

"Promise me that you'll get checked out properly if you have another seizure. I still have a few contacts if you don't want to ask Parth." Pip pitched a solemn frown in Mary's direction.

"I promise."

"Hmm, see that you do. How are things between you two?" He rattled the ice cubes around his glass and raised a tentative hand to her shoulder.

"I have asked him to move out. With any luck, he should be signing a tenancy agreement on a flat this weekend. I can't avoid him entirely, what with my research position being in the same faculty, but I think we can make things work."

Pip nodded, patting her back gently. "Will you divorce him?"

"Maybe, I don't know. I don't think I will ever be able to trust him again." They dragged the patio chairs into a sheltered corner near to the French windows and sat looking up at the moon.

All the people in her world and more had tried to control her, influence her, confine and abuse her, even before she had developed her gifts. They had exploited her kindness, her fears, inadequacies and her physical weakness. They pitted strength in authority against the meek and innocent. They had fostered and rewarded greed and ambition. In her darkest moments, she had plunged to depths she never imagined possible and fought like with like. Mary had no intention of sinking to their twisted levels of intimidation to maintain the upper hand.

It reassured her to know that in times of crisis, there lie inside her a well of ruthlessness she could call upon in an emergency. An ability to protect herself when faced with the direst of circumstances. That gave Mary confidence. Not a swagger, but a calm knowledge that she had lived through a most heinous test and survived. Providing those barbarous tendencies remained in check, Mary was content. She convinced herself that there could be little left in life that would awaken her inner savage.

Cyril Plender had craved power and dominion within his small sphere. His reign was short lived, as was the brute who had attempted to force himself upon her during her imprisonment. Parth and Yelena had steered and cajoled her. The Defence minister simply bullied her into collaborating with the world's largest covert surveillance network. A community of nations, intent on dominating the global airwaves, which in turn had spawned terror attacks from those on the outside. It was hard to choose which side had behaved worse, Alexi and Visser or the minister and Flynn.

Yawning, Mary lay back on the lounger, listening to the rustling leaves in the orchard and the low babble of dialogue from Pip's TV in the house. The opening theme tune for the ten o'clock news travelled through the air, followed by the echoing chime for Big Ben. The presenter announced the headlines. *"Solar storm knocks out satellite transmissions…" Bong… "Canadian power grids fail …" Bong… "Spectacular Aurorae displays seen in record latitudes …" Bong… "Pharmaceutical giant in government tax dispute…" Bong…*

***

If you enjoyed this novel, and have a moment spare to express your opinion, **a review would be greatly appreciated**. Alternatively, you may wish to join the Aurora Conspiracy forum at www.samnash.org or read the free companion series, The Aurora Journals, available from the website.

Signing up to the forum or to the readers group will keep you up to date with promotions and release dates for the rest of the series.

Also by this author – **The Aurora Manifesto**, the second book in the Aurora Conspiracy series. Release date will be posted on the website.

About the Author

Sam Nash taught science and technology for twenty years in British schools, before turning her hand to writing science fiction thrillers full time. She lives in a small market town in Leicestershire, in the U.K, and dreams of one day owning a woodland on the Cornish coast.

Acknowledgements

Without my family, I am nothing. They are my courage, my inspiration, my guides. I will never be able to thank them enough. My heartfelt gratitude must also go to the people who have been kind enough to donate their time and their opinions, in the creation of my fictional world. To Nick Phillips, for his unrelenting kindness, honesty and encouragement and to Rae Else and Barbara Murphy Marder, for their invaluable advice, suggestions and support. Finally, many thanks to all at Carantoc Publishing, for having faith in me.

33345702R00195

Printed in Great Britain
by Amazon